For Matt

THE TWENTY

Having always been fascinated with the dark and macabre, **Sam Holland** studied psychology at university then spent the next few years working in HR, before quitting for a full-time career in writing. A self-confessed serial killer nerd, her debut novel, *The Echo Man*, shocked and enthralled readers and reviewers alike with its sinister depiction of a serial killer copying notorious real-life murderers of the past. *The Twenty* is her second novel.

THE

SAM HOLLAND

HarperCollins*Publishers*

HarperCollins*Publishers*
1 London Bridge Street,
London SE1 9GF

www.harpercollins.co.uk

HarperCollins*Publishers*
Macken House, 39/40 Mayor Street Upper,
Dublin 1, D01 C9W8, Ireland

First published by HarperCollins*Publishers* 2023
1

A catalogue record for this book is available from the British Library

ISBN: 978-0-00-846164-5 (HB)
ISBN: 978-0-00-846165-2 (TPB)

Typeset in Sabon LT Std by Palimpsest Book Production Ltd,
Falkirk, Stirlingshire

Printed and bound in the UK using 100% Renewable Electricity
by CPI Group (UK) Ltd

MIX
Paper | Supporting
responsible forestry
FSC™ C007454

This book is produced from independently certified FSC™ paper
to ensure responsible forest management.

For more information visit: www.harpercollins.co.uk/green

Prologue

The first thing he notices is cold concrete under his bare feet, gritty dust between his toes. It's dark. So dark.

He moves his head; everything spins. He blinks. Lines, corners, the edge of a table come into view: dim shapes in the gloom.

He's confused. He feels light-headed; he tries to take a long breath in but there's something over his mouth. Sticky, suffocating. He reaches up to touch it, body tensing as his hands don't move. Can't move. He tugs at them, breath quickening.

Legs the same. Secured tightly. He's sitting up, must be a chair. But his feet are freezing, his shoes and socks are off. The air is damp, cold fog edging under his shirt, settling on his skin, making him shiver.

There's a throb from his forehead, a *thud thud* in time with his frantic heartbeat. But nothing else. No other pain.

What happened? How did he get here? Think. *Think.* But nothing comes. Just darkness, just panic. He's feeling woozy now; not enough oxygen getting through. He forces himself to stop, focus on his breathing. How he was taught. In for six seconds. Out for six. Shuddering jerks, through his nose. Too fast. Not working. He tries again, closes his eyes, counts slowly.

His heart rate subsides, his breathing settles. If he does this, if he stays calm, he'll be okay. He will.

But then he feels it. His hand is uncomfortable, something's there. Something is *in* there. Cold, hard metal. He wriggles his fingers, trying not to think about what he's experiencing. There it is again. One in his hand, one in both hands. Oh, God. No. *No.*

And his feet. There too. There's no forgetting that feeling. The foreign body puncturing his skin, resting in his vein. He feels the familiar panic grow. The shaking. The sweats.

Don't pass out, he tells himself. Not now. Not here. Don't. Because if you do, who knows what will happen.

But his head feels light, blood draining south. What little he can see in the room blurs.

And in the moment before he loses consciousness, he hears footsteps. A handle being turned. And a door opening.

Part 1

By the pricking of my thumbs,
Something wicked this way comes.
William Shakespeare, *Macbeth*, 1606

DAY 1

SATURDAY

Chapter 1

It's late, the bar already full when he arrives. He works his way through the throng, taking a position at the back of the room, pressed against the wall. It's loud, crowded. Just as he likes it. He can be anonymous; nobody pays him any attention – he blends into the background of similarly dressed men.

He watches, bottle of beer against his lips: preening men at the bar, shouting drunks hurling abuse, a hen party wasted and raucous. The worst society has to offer, his own shortcomings rendered unimportant in the face of such debauchery.

A blonde staggers her way to the toilets. Short skirt, wedding ring – the man leering behind unlikely to be her husband. On the other side of the room, a tweaker shifts and fidgets. He's approached, a glance around, then a quick transaction – a flick of the fingers and cash is pocketed in exchange for a good night. Someone else looking to forget.

He notices the small details; this is how he makes his

5

way through life. He takes a swig from his beer. He resists the urge to intervene, that's not why he's there tonight.

His eyes scan the room. Something else catches, makes him stop. A black and white uniform, creating a void as he steps forward. The copper catches his eye, then lowers his mouth to talk into the radio on his shoulder.

He waits; finishes his beer. Another man comes into the bar. A big guy, dressed in plain clothes, shirt straining over his belly. The uniform points. He sighs, resigned to his fate. It was too good to be true. Another night ruined.

The man negotiates his way towards him through the crowd. He stops by his side.

'How many have you had?' he asks, pointing to the bottle.

'Not enough. Thought you were on your honeymoon?'

'Flight back was this morning.' The man frowns. 'I should've kept my phone off. Marsh told me to get you.'

'Couldn't you have called, Jamie?'

'No reception in here. You know that, boss.'

He nods slowly. Of course, he knows that. Saturday night, he didn't want to be disturbed. Off the clock, other detectives on call. Why do they need him?

But a churning in his gut tells him why. Something serious. Something out of the ordinary. He puts the empty bottle on a table and follows his detective sergeant out of the bar.

'DCI Adam Bishop,' he says, presenting his warrant card to the scene guard. He points to his colleague. 'DS Jamie Hoxton.'

Jamie shows his ID, and they're both waved through the cordon. The night is freezing; Adam pulls his coat tighter around him.

The two men pause, reviewing the scene. Wind blows aggressively across the wasteland; a bridge dominates the distant view and they stand below it, the blackened river flowing in front of them. It's a construction site, half-heartedly sealed off with chain metal and wooden boards, a sign at an angle showing a toothy Alsatian. But there's no security here. Nothing that works.

Adam knows the area well. Identified as a site for re-development, until the money ran out and the council discovered that gentrification only works if the rich actually invest. Nobody wants to live here. The view over the water is depressing; the only boats sailing past are container ships spewing diesel. So, the site lies empty, fly-tippers realising the opportunity, the homeless taking shelter in the rubbish.

They're handed PPE and suit up in the white overalls and gloves and masks. They walk across, towards flood-lights and bustle, foot plates sinking into the mud. He doesn't need to ask; he knows what they're there to find. Everything points towards a body.

It's surrounded by rubbish. An old fridge lies on its side to the left; a mattress, stained and sodden, to the right. Numerous other crap litters the scene – empty paint pots, plastic waste, an old front door. The body lies on its back, remnants of clothing hanging on. There is no indication of gender, nothing left to identify the person they used to be.

The face is half gone, bloody flesh flapping, stark white bone visible. The darkened holes of the eye sockets stare out. Scabbed, dirty, wet. The eyeballs were probably the first to go, easy pickings. The torso is completely eviscer-ated – Adam can see intestines, ribs, organs. And it looks like it's moving, a churn of maggots dining on the rotting meat.

'The animals got to it before we did,' Jamie comments. Adam can hear rustling in the rubble. He shines his torch out, and multiple pairs of yellow eyes glare back.

He shudders. Fucking rats. 'Who called it in?'

'Homeless guy.' Jamie points to a motley-looking crowd standing some distance away. 'Said it was stinking the place up and they wanted it gone.'

'Glad they have their priorities in order,' Adam replies dully. 'Any news on the pathologist?'

'Still waiting.'

As if on cue, they hear a bustle behind them, and a man arrives. Adam inwardly sighs. Anyone else, please, but not Dr Greg Ross.

Even in his full crime scene suit, Adam can tell Ross feels the same.

'Have you touched the body, DCI Bishop?' the doctor asks, disapproval dripping from his every word.

'Of course not.' It's not Adam's first case, not his first dead body. 'When will we know more?'

The reply from the pathologist is curt and quick. 'When I'm ready.'

He bites back a retort, then gestures to Jamie. They edge away, starting their appraisal of the scene.

His DS looks across the rubble. 'No security, no CCTV.'

'We're sure about that?' Adam points to the camera, a small black box near to where Jamie's car is parked. 'Go check it out.'

Jamie nods and heads off; Adam's attention is caught by someone picking their way towards him. A young woman. Contrary to the rest of the crew here, she walks

8

with a bounce in her step, her enthusiasm in stark contrast to the eerie surroundings. Curious, he walks towards her, ducking under the cordon, then pulling his hood and mask down, removing his gloves.

She smiles eagerly as he approaches, cheeks flushed. He hasn't seen her before.

'DC Ellie Quinn,' she says once she's next to him. She thrusts her hand out formally in front of her, and Adam shakes it, amused. Her palm is sweaty.

'What are you doing here, DC Ellie Quinn?'

'New to Major Crimes. Was due to start on Monday but I heard something was going on. Thought I could help.'

Adam has a vague memory from a few weeks ago: Jamie mentioning a new member of the team. 'Where are you from?' he asks.

'Fraud, boss. But I wanted something a little more . . . exciting.'

'Well, you got that.' He smiles at her. She's petite, with bobbed strawberry blonde hair, pale skin and a freckled nose. Wide doe eyes that make her look like a character from a Disney movie.

She couldn't seem more out of place. Here, in the dead of night, the wind whipping through her hair, turning her cheeks baby pink. An innocent fawn unsullied by the haunt of the newly departed.

He hears movement behind him and Adam glances back to the homeless guys. Most have wandered away, but one remains; he doesn't want to lose his chance of a witness.

'Report to DS Hoxton,' he says to Quinn, pointing towards the car park, where Jamie is exploring. 'He'll show you the ropes. Now, if you'll excuse me?'

'Yes, of course,' the girl hastily agrees, and Adam turns his attention to their bystanders.

The homeless man hesitates when he sees Adam approaching. Adam walks slowly, eye contact averted. The man's as skittish as a nervous dog, dressed in a long dirty overcoat, torn boots, a black beanie low over his eyes. Adam pulls out his packet of cigarettes, puts one in his mouth, then offers the box to the man.

The man snatches one with dirty fingers, still half turned away. Adam lights his own, then passes the lighter across, his arm fully outstretched before the man takes it.

'Was it you who called us?' Adam asks. He takes a long drag, blowing the smoke out into the cold night air.

'Yeah.' The man's standing at an angle to Adam, glancing over to the homeless encampment of boxes and sagging tents under the bridge. His safety. He hands the lighter back then sucks at the cigarette hungrily.

'Adam,' he says, holding his hand out to introduce himself.

The man looks at it suspiciously, then rests the cigarette in his lips and returns the gesture. He quickly takes two steps back again.

'Harry,' he replies.

'When did you notice it?' Adam asks.

'Only a few hours ago. Jim mentioned it.' The man tilts his head to the group sheltering under the bridge. 'Don't want to get him into trouble.'

'Not at all,' Adam replies, although he mentally notes the names. 'Did he see anyone? Do you guys ever see anyone hanging around?'

'Nah.' He edges further away from Adam.

'No vans? Trucks dumping rubbish.'

'Some.'

He pauses and Adam can tell he's holding something back. 'Please? Anything might help.'

Harry takes another drag, then is gripped by a bout of coughing that consumes his whole body. When he's finished, he looks at Adam from jaundiced eyes.

'Is he . . .' he starts. He looks down, scuffing his boot in the mud. 'Is he dead? Should we . . . A doctor . . .'

'No, mate. He's very dead.'

'But . . .' He points back to the dump site. 'A doctor . . .'

'Sorry. A doctor can't do anything for him now.'

The homeless man shakes his head, redirecting his gaze to the ground.

'No. I didn't see nothing,' he concludes.

Adam accepts defeat. Even if he did share something useful, the homeless guy's a lousy witness. A defence lawyer would shoot holes in his account in seconds.

The man gestures to the cigarette, now burned down to the butt. 'Can I have another?'

Adam pulls out the pack and hands it to him with the lighter. 'Here,' he says, then he digs in his pocket. He pulls out the cash he has – a few notes and coins – and passes them across. 'For your help.'

The man snatches them, then scuttles away with a nervous backward glance. Adam finishes his cigarette as Jamie heads towards him.

'Did he see anything?' Jamie asks when he's by his side.

'Nothing. I'm surprised they called it in at all. What have you done with our new recruit?'

'Ellie Quinn? Sent her off with uniforms for some house-to-house.' Jamie's gaze drifts back to the crime scene. 'She doesn't need to see that,' he finishes. 'Not on her first day.'

Adam silently agrees. He likes new blood on the team. Like Ellie, they're keen, desperate to make their mark. But she looks so innocent. Mentally he gives her three months before she requests a transfer out. Six, tops.

Adam follows Jamie's line of sight to the dead body. The rubbish throws amorphous shapes across the ground; it instinctively makes something in his body recoil, even from this distance.

No, they don't want to break Ellie Quinn today.

'Any luck with the camera?' he asks instead.

'Fake,' Jamie replies. 'And not a good one either, I could tell just by looking up at it. It's a perfect dump site. No reliable witnesses, no overlooking houses. Easy access.'

Adam nods, looking out at the wasteland. The flood-lights glance off broken glass, mirrors to the devastation in the mud. SOCOs are taking moulds from the few distinguishable tyre tracks with powdered stone, photographs already captured. He turns to Jamie. 'How was your honeymoon, anyway?'

'Wonderful. Californian sunshine, white sandy beaches, blue skies.' Jamie pauses, looking back to where Dr Ross is standing up from the body. 'A bit different to tonight.'

Dr Ross turns and gestures to them, a quick raise of his long arm. They walk back across.

'Male, thirty to forty,' he says, getting straight to the point. 'Maybe. Dead no more than a few days, although I'll know more when I get him back to the mortuary and review the entomology. Considerable damage to the soft tissues by carnivores, had a good go at his face and abdomen.'

'Suspicious death?' Jamie asks.

The doctor scoffs. 'He didn't get here by himself, DS

12

Hoxton. I'll do the PM tomorrow. Make sure you're there for ten.'

And he walks away without another word.

'Short but sweet,' Jamie mutters. Adam takes a long breath in.

The SOCOs gather around again, cameras capturing the scene before the body is taken away. It's a nasty final resting place: rats and foxes abound, left out to the elements.

'Didn't make any effort to bury it,' Adam comments.

'Perhaps the killer thought he'd be eaten and scattered before anyone found the body,' Jamie replies.

'Or perhaps he didn't care.'

But then something catches his eye. He'd not given it much thought before, but now, with the flashes from the cameras, the glare of the floodlights, it stands out among the mess and chaos. Daubed on the side of the discarded fridge in green spray paint, three symbols: XII.

He squints at it. It seems out of place: perfectly straight, on a fridge fallen to its side. Directly above the victim's head. A marker.

'What do you make of that?' he asks Jamie.

But he doesn't wait for an answer. He starts walking, searching through the wasteland, torch darting around the rubbish. He hears the scatter of rats, movement in the rubble. Jamie follows his lead as his eyes scan the mess.

'There,' Jamie says suddenly. 'Go back.'

Adam directs the torch to where Jamie is pointing. Lit up in the beam are three more letters.

He slowly lowers the shaft of light to the rubbish below. It's debris from a building site. Pallets of wood, bricks, chunks of cement. But the numerals, they're the same. Green spray paint. XIV.

'Oh, shit,' Jamie mutters next to him. 'You don't think . . .'

Adam turns to the scene, to the bustling SOCOs, the uniforms, the technicians going about their job.

'Oi!' he shouts. Heads turn. Adam waves his arms until he has everyone's attention. 'Oi!'

The scene quietens, all eyes on him.

'Here.' He points towards the spray-painted markers. 'Secure this area. Start excavating. And everyone else, scour the scene. Check all the rubbish. You're looking for more of these letters.' Nobody moves, everybody stares.

'Now!' Adam shouts again, and people burst into life. He turns back to Jamie; his eyes are wild above his mask.

'The number fourteen,' he says. Then he points back to the first body. 'And the number twelve.'

'You don't think—' Jamie begins again.

'I fucking do,' Adam replies. 'There are more of them.'

Chapter 2

The body emerges. A shape, fully entombed under bricks and gravel where the rats couldn't find her. Wrapped in a blanket. Baby blue check. The Crime Scene Manager calls Adam over once she's uncovered, slowly pulling back a corner. A face is revealed. Long black curly hair. Eyes closed, features intact.

'Quite a contrast to the last one,' the CSM comments.

Adam has worked with Maggie Clarke before. An efficient woman, smart, highly organised. In a different life she'd be the chair on a PTA, planning fundraisers and village fetes, but instead she commands her brood of SOCOs, blood and mud rather than cakes and dog shows. She's blunt in manner, but fast and accurate. Adam likes her. Not everyone does.

'She's almost peaceful,' Adam replies.

Maggie squints at the rubbish. 'If you say so.' She gives him a quick smile, then leaves, her attention diverted elsewhere.

The dog unit arrives. The black and white spaniels run around in circles, seemingly confused.

'Can't they find anything?' Jamie asks.

'It's not that,' the handler replies, grim faced. 'It's that they don't know where to start.'

Another body is found. Little more than bones: scattered, dismembered limbs. XVI daubed above. By the time the fourth turns up, Adam's boss has arrived at the scene. Detective Chief Superintendent Marsh stands outside the cordon and beckons with a long finger.

'It's a multiple?' Marsh asks as Adam ducks under the tape. In the harsh glow from the floodlights, Marsh's cheeks look more sunken than usual, his pallor grey. Adam nods as he pulls the crime scene hood from his head, the mask off his face. 'And I thought those days were over,' Marsh finishes with a sigh.

Adam pats down his pockets then curses as he realises he's given away his cigarettes, now regretting his altruistic gesture, given how long the night's going to be. Next to him Marsh pulls out his own packet and offers one to Adam.

'Ta,' Adam mumbles, cigarette in his lips, leaning forward as Marsh flicks the lighter into flame.

Both men stand for a moment, silent except for the crackle of burning tobacco and sighs as plumes of smoke are exhaled.

'Not the Saturday night I had planned,' Adam comments.

Marsh flicks cigarette ash onto the mud next to him. 'If you're going to hide when you're off duty, Bishop, you need to find somewhere else to go. You're not a shadowy man of mystery, you're as predictable as the rest of us. Why do you go there anyway?' Marsh takes another drag. 'You're not going to find the woman of your dreams at some sleazy bar full of twenty-year-olds.'

'It's not like that.'

Marsh snorts. 'Well, whatever. Good for you, Bishop. Living your best life.'

Dr Ross returns. He nods to Marsh as he passes but ignores Adam. 'Still making friends everywhere you go then,' Marsh finishes sarcastically, flicking his butt to the ground and following the pathologist.

Adam watches his boss leave as he smokes the cigarette to the filter. The two older men are almost indistinguishable as they get into the crime scene gear, Ross for the second time. Both are tall and slim – although Adam knows Marsh's figure is due to a lack of food and a surfeit of nicotine and caffeine, while Ross is the paragon of fitness, clean eating and exercise. In the distance, Adam can make out Jamie, his DS an altogether larger silhouette, happily settled with his wife of two weeks. Adam remembers what that's like: the pleasure of letting standards slip. Cosy nights on the sofa with home-cooked roast dinners and a family sized bar of Dairy Milk.

A shout from Jamie rouses Adam from his thoughts. He flicks his butt away from the cordon and goes to join him.

'That's five,' his DS says. The handlers are taking the dogs home, tails wagging on receipt of their rewards.

'And we're sure that's all?'

'Isn't that enough?' Jamie replies.

Adam nods grimly. Separate sites are being constructed now: individual crime scenes for each ugly discovery. Floodlights and figures mark each one, careful to avoid cross-contamination. Five bodies, in varying states of decay. Five people who were once someone, who loved and were loved and cared for.

But despite this, Adam feels a wave of apprehension. A small thrill of the challenge he's facing. He's dealt with more murders than he can count. Domestics gone wrong, pub fights ending badly, even one tragic infanticide. But nothing like this.

This is big.

Because written above all the bodies are the same spray-painted numerals. Adam doesn't need a pathologist to work it out. Number sixteen is almost fully decomposed, gnawed to the quick by the feasting rats, some bones disappeared, taken away to a hole somewhere for further attention. Number twelve – the body found today – still in the early stages of putrefaction.

Adam knows it, Jamie knows it. DCS Marsh knows it, or he wouldn't be here.

The killer is counting down.

This is just the beginning.

Chapter 3

Before bed, she goes through the same routine. Check each door – chain on the front, double lock the back. All the windows closed. Turn off the lights, one by one, but not until she is out of the room, still bathed in the puddle of light from the next. Ensure that the plug-in LEDs have come on. Reassuring and bright.

By the time she makes it to the bedroom, Phil is usually under the covers. She envies the simplicity of his life. Tonight, she can tell by his breathing that he's nearly asleep. Slow, secure, steady. She turns the nightlight on next to her bed; it's a kid's one but what she needs. It throws stars up at the ceiling, dousing the bedroom in a cool blue glow.

She turns the main light off and gets into bed next to her boyfriend. He rolls over and pulls her close, his arm around her middle, one leg entwined with hers. Safe.

When she wakes, she knows instantly something is wrong. She can sense the darkness, covering everything, deep and suffocating. She opens her eyes. There's nothing. Her breathing quickens. The nightlight is off; the room is pitch black. Her hands grope outwards, looking for Phil, but she only touches cold sheets.

And in a flash, she's back there. Alone, in the darkness. Sounds from outside the window: the hoot of an owl, the screech of a fox. Then something else. Something animal, but undoubtably human. A cry, a scream of pain. Anguish and fear.

She lies frozen in her bed. Her hands claw at the duvet; she blinks, trying to force her eyes to see something, anything, in the darkness. At last, she conjures up the strength to reach across to her bedside table. Her fingers come into contact with the flex of the wire from her lamp, then the plastic switch and she flicks it. But nothing. *Nothing.* She starts to whimper. Quiet at first, getting louder until she is screaming. Taking in great gulps of breath, then screaming again.

Suddenly, she feels a body next to hers. Strong hands on her arms. A torch switched on and swung around the room.

'Rom! Romilly,' the voice is saying. 'I'm here now, I'm sorry. There's a power cut. I'm sorry.'

She grabs at her boyfriend's arm and the light, her salvation, comes with him. He wraps his arms around her and holds her tight.

'I'm sorry,' Phil says again. 'I shouldn't have left you. I went to get the torch.' He pulls her closer, dragging the duvet up over them, cocooning them in the bed. 'There, is that better?' he asks, softly, and she curls up against his chest, her tears soaking his T-shirt.

She holds the torch in her hand, the strong stream of

light illuminating the bedroom. Her bedroom. Not then, but now.

And slowly, all too slowly, she feels the panic fade. She's safe. They're safe, she tells herself as she slowly drops into a restless, disturbed sleep.

DAY 2

SUNDAY

Chapter 4

The sun comes up over the wasteland, and the crime scene teams work on. Five bodies: it's a lot to process.

Marsh left hours ago, back to his warm house and comfortable bed. Dr Ross followed not long after.

Adam is sitting in Jamie's car, the coffee fetched by a kind PC drunk cold, Adam still clutching the empty cup. Next to him, Jamie's six-foot-three frame is slumped uncomfortably in the driver's seat. His double chin is crumpled into his chest; he's fast asleep, breathing heavily through his nose. Adam is tired too, but the addition of a constant stream of caffeine, plus the thought of what's to come, means he feels wired.

He's been gathering his thoughts, mentally preparing himself for the start of a multiple murder investigation.

A gentle tap on the car window makes him jump; he opens the door to the tired face of Maggie Clarke. Hood down, but still in her crime scene suit, she crouches next to him and smiles wearily.

'Sleeping Beauty still out?'

Adam glances over; Jamie hasn't moved. 'Always envied his ability to kip anywhere,' he comments. 'Have you got anything for me, Mags?'

'No, and we're not going to for hours yet. There's so much here, all this trash to rake through.'

'Can't you tell me anything?' he pushes.

She glances back to the crime scenes, then frowns. 'Unofficially?'

He grins. 'Unofficially.'

'First thoughts, but this all feels very deliberate.'

'How so?' Like Adam, Maggie is an old hand. Well-read in her field, Maggie is familiar with crime scenes, years of experience teaching her what's normal, and what's not. At least, what's normal in these sorts of circumstances.

'The bodies were placed on their backs,' Maggie continues. 'Heads next to the . . .' She draws a square shape with her finger.

'Gravestones?'

'If you want to call them that, yes. Whoever placed the bodies here was sending a message.' She places a hand on his arm, then pulls herself to a stand with a wince. 'I'll call you when I have something definite. Get some sleep.'

He watches as she returns to the crime scene, gathering her unruly curls into a ponytail and pulling the hood back up.

Sleep is an impossibility.

Now, he's ready.

He reaches across and pinches the bottom of Jamie's nose. After a moment, Jamie snorts, then jumps awake. He looks across, blurry-eyed.

'You're a dick, Bish,' he mumbles.

'We need to go.'

23

Jamie looks out to the piles of rubbish and dirt. 'Go? Go where?'

'Back to the station. We have a murder investigation to begin.'

Despite it being a weekend, detectives crowd the incident room. Adam had already made the call: get whoever you can in.

There is no grumbling about being summoned on a Sunday. Most have seen the news, the speculation from reporters is rife. *Bodies found. Unidentified. Details to follow.* No detective likes to miss out on the juicy cases, and all of them know this could be one of those.

Adam stands at the front and begins the briefing.

A hastily pulled together map of the wasteland fills the screen behind him as he updates them on everything they know. Five bodies, differing stages of decomposition, both male and female. The PMs are due to begin that morning, and Adam picks the next detective from the rota to attend the mortuary. The DC departs amid cheers and catcalls.

'So,' Adam concludes, once the noise has subsided. 'Let's crack on with the basics. There is no CCTV in that area, but locate the closest cameras, especially the ones for the roads in and out. Let's get the ANPR, if it exists. Tim' – one of his DCs nods in acknowledgement – 'catch up with Ellie Quinn and liaise with the uniforms doing the house-to-house. I want a statement from anyone who has so much as looked towards that patch of wasteland over the last few months. Log everything, even if it seems irrelevant, and report back to me if you see something of particular interest.'

He allocates a team to identify the victims, sets Jamie up to coordinate the efforts. Voices chatter, eager to get moving.

But Adam calms them with a wave of his hand. He holds their attention, all waiting for the final go.

'Scour all possible avenues,' he continues. 'You all know how crucial the first twenty-four hours of a murder case can be. People forget, evidence is washed away, files deleted from surveillance systems. Clearly, we are at a disadvantage. Some of these bodies have been buried a while. But if it's still there, I want it.' Despite the horrific nature of the crimes, Adam feels electrified as he surveys his team. 'And I want it now.'

With a final nod, they're off. Adam makes his way over to Jamie and stands next to his 2IC.

'Too much?' Adam whispers with a smile.

Jamie chuckles quietly. 'Just right,' he mutters back.

Adam pauses, watching the team swarm. The bustle, the energy, the drive. But despite enjoying the theatre of the occasion, he feels a swell of unease. A foreboding. Like he's caught up, entangled in something he can't control. He feels it drag him forward.

Into the mouth of hell.

Chapter 5

Jamie sits at his computer, his head slowly dropping, eyes closing. He's not had any proper rest for over twenty-four hours now.

He thinks about where he should be. The last day of his holiday. Lying on the sofa with Pippa, watching a box set. Or maybe they'd have gone for Sunday lunch and a walk after, strolling hand in hand through the forest.

He shakes his head, trying to focus on the job. People are dead. Murdered. He needs to find out who they are.

He flicks to the next missing person on the screen. He's put in search parameters but there are so many mispers. And with such limited information at this stage, few he can rule out.

He glances around. His DCs are hard at work. Bishop is talking on the phone in his office, no doubt trying to arrange more resource, more budget, more overtime. Jamie watches him, feeling the familiar mix of admiration and respect.

Adam's a machine. There is no trace of tiredness in his demeanour, no sign of the numb apathy that years in a murder team can bring. Jamie wishes he could be a bit more like him. That determination and resilience.

But enthusiasm fades; monotony intervenes. Jamie needs a break. He senses an opportunity and makes his escape.

He grabs his coat, walking quickly through the double doors and out to the car park. He needs some space. A bit of silence for five minutes.

The cars are well spread out, reminding him that it's Sunday. Wind rushes through the open walls of the concrete multistorey, and he takes his car keys out of his pocket, sitting inside and slamming the door shut. It smells of cigarettes; he curses Bishop. He opens a window despite the cold, then phones his wife.

Pippa answers on the first ring. 'Here you are,' she says, her voice tender. He can't help but smile.

'Here I am,' he replies.

'Are you still at work?'

'Yeah. Going to be a long one,' he adds, but doesn't say any more. She doesn't need to know the details, what he's dealing with today. The violence and blood and murder.

He loves his job. The challenge of piecing together the teeming mess at the beginning, of finding order in the chaos. Even the relentlessness of data and routine enquiries have never bothered him as it does others. He knows he is doing good, but some days he wishes it wouldn't make him feel so bad.

Pippa is the purity in his life, the shining ray of sunshine when he gets home. He imagines his wife sitting in their living room, feet tucked up, blanket over her knees, music playing in the background.

They met six and a half years ago, at a beach barbecue organised by Adam.

27

'You're a cop?' she'd said.

It was a scorching hot day; a cooling wind blew in from the Solent, ruffling her hair. She was wearing a yellow sleeveless dress. Her shoulders were bare and dusted with freckles; he could hardly keep his eyes from them.

'Most of us are,' he replied, gesturing across the gathering of people on the sandy shore. Someone Adam knew had a beach hut; the man himself was standing in front of a barbecue, waving a set of tongs as he told a story. The mouth-watering aroma of sausages and burgers drifted on the breeze.

'But you . . .' she started. 'You seem too nice.'

He hadn't known whether to be offended or pleased. By the end of the first hour, she convinced him to do a talk for careers day at her school. By the second, he was smitten. Why the fuck it had taken him so long to ask her to marry him, he didn't know. A lack of confidence? A worry that drawing attention to the further permanence of their relationship might cause her to wake up and find someone more suitable? Probably both of the above. Either way, she'd said yes, on that beautiful night, five years later, watching the sun go down, just the two of them. Proposal blurted out after three glasses of wine. She'd wrapped her arms around him, kissed him on his sweaty cheek, and said: 'I thought you'd never ask, you stupid man.'

'I'll try and be back for dinner,' he says now.

'I'll make sure it's something you can microwave later.' Jamie screws his face up. He hates letting her down, although Pippa knows it will be a miracle if he's home in time. 'You shouldn't walk out on Adam when he needs you,' Pippa continues. 'You being his devoted second-in-command, and all.'

She's saying it tongue in cheek, even though both of them know it's the truth. Jamie and Adam were friends even before Bishop's fast ascent through the ranks. Somehow, they've managed to stay that way.

'He'll cope,' Jamie replies. 'I spend too much time with him as it is.'

'Just don't turn into him, will you?' his wife replies.

Jamie laughs at the unlikely comparison between him and his boss, then says his goodbyes and leaves his wife to enjoy the rest of her day. The idea that he – this over-sized teddy bear of a man, a consummate people-pleaser – could ever be a force to be reckoned with like Bishop? It's unthinkable.

His new fledgling is calling him now. Ellie Quinn. And to Jamie, she does seem like a tiny bird. All day cheeping, fluttering around him. He answers his phone.

'Where are you, Sarge?' she asks. 'I think we have an ID for one of the victims.'

'Had to get something from my car,' he lies. He pushes the door open, climbing out, the phone still against his ear. 'Think, or know for sure?'

'Fairly certain,' she replies. 'The mortuary found a bank card in the back pocket of what was left of number twelve's shorts. A misper: Stephen Carey. Reported missing three days ago by his wife.'

'So the timeline fits,' Jamie replies. He pauses as he hears muffled discussion, then Ellie comes back on the line.

'The boss says stay where you are, he's coming to you.'

And with a sigh, Jamie slumps back into the driver's seat.

Chapter 6

The wife crumples into the doorway the moment they show their warrant cards; her hands cover her mouth, her eyes fearful.

'You're here about Stephen,' she whispers.

'Yes. Can we come inside?'

She nods slowly and shows them into the house. They walk through a brightly painted hallway into the living room. Toys are scattered across the floor; two small boys play noisily on the carpet with plastic cars. An older woman gets up from the sofa as they approach, her face solemn.

The wife makes the introductions: her mother, here to help in Stephen's absence. They all shake hands, formal and polite. Waiting.

The older woman ushers the boys out of the room. The wife offers them tea, coffee, water; Adam and Jamie turn them down. It's a standard introduction, the dance of social niceties that Adam is used to. The three of them settle on the sofas, the wife opposite Adam and Jamie.

'You've found him, haven't you?' the wife blurts out.

Adam steels himself, employing a level of detachment that has served him well over the years. 'A body was found last night, by Northbrook Bridge. Although we still need to do tests to confirm, we believe it's your husband, yes. We're sorry.'

She nods slowly, decorum maintained for a fraction of a second. Then her mouth crumples and she puts her face in her hands, shoulders shaking silently. Adam waits. Next to him he hears Jamie sniff, and he glances across to his DS. Jamie's chin looks dangerously wobbly; he catches Adam's eye and sets his jaw with determination.

The wife looks up, her eyes red. 'I saw it on the news this morning. And I knew. I knew it was Steve.'

'Can you tell us the circumstances around his disappearance, Mrs Carey?'

She sniffs and dabs at her nose with a tissue. 'There's not much to it. He went for a run, as he always did. Thursday night. But this time he didn't come home.'

She looks up and Adam nods, encouraging her to go on.

'At first I assumed he'd just gone a bit further than normal. Turned his three miles into four. But then an hour passed, and it was dark. I thought maybe he'd had an accident, so I called the neighbour, got her to watch the boys while I went out looking. But I couldn't find him on his usual route. I called the police straight away. I knew. It wasn't like Steve to go somewhere without telling me.'

Adam had read the misper report. Just disappeared. No witnesses, no idea where he'd gone. Response and Patrol had done a reasonable job trying to track him down. Spoken to friends, family, hospitals, with no luck. Now they know why.

'And his usual movements? Did Stephen have a routine?'

'Not much, not really.' She runs through her husband's life. A family man, the usual mundane stuff. Driving to work – a solicitor at a local law firm – going to the supermarket. Taking the kids to the park and swimming on the weekend.

'But he was always keen on his fitness,' she continues. 'Running every day.'

'Every day? What time did he go?'

'Around eight. Once the kids were in bed. He's gone for no longer than half an hour. That's how I knew something was wrong. When he didn't come home.'

'And had anything else been strange lately? Something out of the ordinary, that maybe you didn't give much thought to at the time?'

'No. Not at all.' But she pauses, thinking.

'Mrs Carey? Anything, however small or insignificant, could be useful for our investigation.'

'It's silly. But it was odd. I came down one morning a few weeks ago and the back door was unlocked. Steve swore blind he'd locked it, but there it was. And . . .'

'And?' Adam prompts.

'There was sand on the kitchen floor. Not much, but enough to make me wonder how it got there.'

'But that was it? Nothing had been stolen?'

'That was it. A bit of sand. Seems daft now I say it out loud.'

'No, thank you. That's helpful.' Adam glances to Jamie who's writing it all down in his notebook. 'Do you have a hairbrush of his? Or a toothbrush? We'll need something to compare for DNA analysis. So we can formally identify the body.'

'I thought you'd want me to do it,' the wife replies. 'Like they do on TV.' She lets out a long breath of air. 'I'm relieved I don't need to, to be honest. I don't want to see him . . . like that. I want to remember him the way he was,' she finishes, and starts crying again.

'No. This way will work fine,' Adam says. He's glad he doesn't have to tell her what happened to her husband. To try to make her understand about the rats and the foxes and the maggots. That he no longer had a face to identify.

The wife gets up to fetch her husband's toothbrush, still crying, and leaves them in the living room.

Adam looks to Jamie. 'Do you think someone broke into the house?' he whispers. 'Had a bit of a poke around?'

'Maybe. But why?' Jamie replies. 'And where was he murdered? If you wanted to kill the guy, it would have been easier to leave him where he fell.'

Adam nods. He's read the file: five-eleven, brown hair, brown eyes. Active. Not a small person to move.

They quieten as the wife comes back with a red toothbrush; Adam holds out a clear evidence bag and she drops it inside.

'How did he die?' she asks, her eyes pleading. Adam's seen it before. Desperate for a crumb of hope, that their loved ones hadn't suffered, they hadn't been in pain.

'It's still early days,' he replies. 'We'll know more soon. We'll appoint a family liaison officer to stay with you, and they'll be able to keep you updated on the investigation.'

'But he was murdered?'

'We believe so, yes.'

'Oh, God.' She crumples again, her head in her hands.

The older woman comes back into the room, the two small boys in tow, silenced by the sight of their mother in tears. Adam takes it as his cue to leave.

They walk out to Jamie's car and get in.

'Two kids,' Jamie says, fastening his seat belt. 'Did you see them? Two beautiful little boys who are going to grow up without a father.' Adam watches as he sniffs, then wipes his nose with the sleeve of his jacket.

'At least use a tissue,' Adam says. Jamie digs in his pocket and pulls one out: an old balled-up mess.

'I'm sorry,' Jamie mutters. 'It's so fucking sad. I don't know how you do it. Stay so calm.'

Adam smiles grimly. 'Hard as nails.'

'Well, I wish some of it would rub off on me. You'd think that after over fifteen years in the force I could deliver a death notice without wanting to cry.' Jamie looks through the windscreen to the house of the dead man. 'I just can't stop imagining how that would feel. To have cops show up on your doorstep.'

'Fucking awful,' Adam agrees. Jamie sniffs again and Adam chuckles quietly. 'Never change, mate,' he says with a pat on his arm.

'Stop taking the piss.'

'I'm not! I promise,' he repeats when Jamie looks at him disbelievingly. 'You're my conscience. You're the guy that keeps me human. If I didn't have you, where would I be?'

'Fine. Absolutely fine,' Jamie replies. 'With your confidence. And arrogance. Not a care in the world.'

'Thanks a lot,' Adam laughs, and Jamie looks at him, unabashed. 'But seriously, Jamie,' Adam continues, 'you're a good man. And a good cop as a result. If blubbing at a few death notifications is the price you have to pay for that then so be it.'

Jamie stares at him for a moment. 'You're a good bloke too, Adam,' he replies but Adam scowls, the words feeling dissonant in Adam's mind.

'Can we go?' he says instead, and Jamie starts the engine.

They drive back in silence, the radio filling the gap, Adam's thoughts full of the case.

He pulls the man's missing person's file out of his bag and looks at the photos again. He flicks through. A head shot, handsome and smiling. One of him with his boys. Two others of him at the end of running a 10k: fit and strong. Jamie was right. He wouldn't have been easy to overpower and drag away. Alive or dead.

'Do you think he was being stalked?' Adam asks. Jamie glances away from the road for a moment. 'Following him, working out his routine. Taking advantage of an open back door to have a look around.'

'Could be. That way the killer would know exactly when to abduct him without witnesses. But why? What makes him so special?'

'Well. That's exactly what we need to figure out.'

Was Stephen Carey deliberately targeted? Adam wonders in silence. He knows the most common serial murder victims are those who are most vulnerable: sex workers, gay men, children and infants, runaways, and the elderly. Stephen Carey didn't fall into any of those categories. Or maybe he did? Maybe he had secrets? He wouldn't be the first married man who was gay.

His phone rings, interrupting his musing. It's the DC from the mortuary.

'He's closing up,' he blurts out. 'Get down here now, boss, or he'll bugger off without telling you anything.'

Adam gestures wildly to Jamie and he turns the car fast, heading to the hospital.

Chapter 7

When Adam and Jamie arrive, Ross is still there, but only just: his coat is on and his briefcase is in his hand.

Ross sighs when he sees Adam.

'How lovely of you to join us, Bishop. I suppose you want me to delay the rest of my weekend further?'

'Yes. Please,' Adam asks, trying to keep the sarcasm out of his voice.

Ross gives him a condescending smile, then gestures for them all to move to the viewing gallery at the back of the room. In front of them, five bodies are laid out on stainless steel tables; some with sheets over the top, ready to be transferred into their body bags and fridges, others with the pathology technologists still sewing them back up, restoring their organs to their rightful places.

Ross points to the one closest. 'So, from left to right: number sixteen has been dead the longest.' Ross looks over his shoulder to them with a raised eyebrow. 'I'm assuming no more victim IDs, bar Stephen Carey?'

'We're working on it.'

'Take your time,' he adds, disparagingly. 'So, for the moment, we've named them according to their number. Number sixteen was found mostly buried under the rubble. Exposed areas, such as her arms and head have been completely skeletonised, some parts missing, probably taken away by scavengers. The torso was better protected but even after my skilled colleagues have done their work, she is quite a mess.'

Adam looks at the body. Black heavy stitching bisects the chest, running down the side, turning her middle to mush. Grey bones have been laid out, a jawless skull staring skywards.

Ross continues: 'Torso was completely eviscerated. Cause of death was haemorrhagic shock from multiple penetrating knife wounds.' He pauses, face grim. 'And there were quite a few, over twenty in my estimation. Her heart and lungs were little more than mush.'

'How long would she have been alive through that?' Jamie gasps.

'Not long, DS Hoxton,' Ross replies. 'Hypovolaemic shock would have rendered her unconscious fast. Moving on.'

He takes a step to the right, and gestures to the technician to remove the sheet. He pulls it back to show a man, younger this time. Black hair, larger build.

'Number fifteen had a better time of it,' Ross says. 'But not much. Three penetrating injuries to the abdomen. Straight through, into the heart.'

Adam looks. Sure enough, three bloody gashes scatter across the man's chest.

'But still a violent attack?' Adam asks.

Ross nods. 'They would have needed a huge amount of force to kill like this. Your offender is determined.'

Adam catches Jamie's glance. Eyebrows low; frown locked in place. An unspoken thought between them: nothing good here.

'Number fourteen, you know.' Ross says, pointing to the next. An altogether different body faces them. Adam remembers this one from the dump site, the woman wrapped in a blanket.

'This woman, and number thirteen here, male, were the same. Cause of death was exsanguination, from wounds inflicted here.' Ross gestures to the technician; he lifts one of the dead man's arms: it's covered in a mass of slashes and cuts. Adam winces. 'Same on both sides. Both victims.'

'They bled out from that?'

'Partly.' Ross frowns. 'But from the perfusion of blood to the cuts, I estimate that some of these were inflicted post-mortem.'

'For what aim?' Adam asks, surprised.

'Can't tell. To cover something up?'

'A tattoo? Identifying mark?' Jamie suggests.

'And that's not all,' Ross adds. 'These two were restrained. Ligature marks clear on both wrists and ankles. And for around twenty-four hours, given the lack of stomach contents and dehydration. The blood loss would have been slow. They took a while to die. Maybe a few hours. I've sent the blankets they were wrapped in to the lab.'

'So the crime scene will be obvious,' Adam says to Jamie.

'Once we find it.'

Ross ignores them. 'Finally. Number twelve. Stephen Carey. Not a lot left of this guy. You remember him?'

'How could I forget?'

'Left out to the elements. Considerable animal and insect activity. I'm waiting for the entomologist to confirm, but my educated guess is he's been dead for about three days. Does that fit with your misper report?'

'Disappeared Thursday night. Cause of death?'

'Same as the others. Exsanguination. Although it's hard to say from where. There wasn't much blood left in his body by the time the animals got to him. Not much body, full stop. And I'm sure you want to know time of death?' Adam nods. 'Moving from left to right,' Ross points, 'the victims get progressively more recent, with the oldest having been in the ground for about six months. We've sent blood samples for testing, plus swabs of all the affected areas.'

'Thank you,' Adam says, trying hard not to make his gratitude seem forced. 'And for doing all of this on a Sunday.'

The pathologist sighs. 'Hardly my decision.' He gives Adam a long look. 'This is a good case for you, right, Bishop?'

'Good? I'm not sure—'

'For your career. All eyes on you. How you like it. You missed out last time, now this is your moment.'

Adam quashes the ball of annoyance in his stomach. 'I want what everyone wants,' he says after a pause. 'To stop this guy.'

Ross snorts derisively; Adam glares.

But Ross is right. This investigation will attract attention from all sides: his superior officers, the press, other constabularies. It could make his career: his route to detective superintendent.

'So, cause of death is the same for all?' Jamie asks, desperate to pull the two men away from their shared dislike.

'Evisceration resulting in exsanguination, yes.'

'And all in the last six months,' Adam says. He looks along the row of bodies, thinking out loud. 'But apart from where they were found, there's little in common between them. Male and female. Age range, from about twenty to sixty, right?' The pathologist nods. 'And a mix of appearance, ethnicities, and body types.'

'So victimology is going to be a nightmare,' Jamie mutters to Adam's right.

This whole case is a bloody nightmare, Adam thinks as they leave. Nothing makes sense. Five victims, the numbers above the bodies. The first two, killed quickly, in a frenzy. Then the others: restrained and, Adam assumes from the cuts to their wrists, tortured. Left to die slowly. Prolonging their final moments.

The MO, it's evolving. And all bodies were moved after death, to the one patch of wasteland. Why? To what end? It's anyone's guess. But Adam assumes one thing about the killer: whatever his reason, whatever his motivation, he's not planning on stopping soon.

Chapter 8

The day starts like any normal Sunday for Romilly. Waking up, squinting at the light behind the curtains, knowing they have slept far too late. She feels the hazy blur of a disturbed night; warm legs next to hers. She's surprised her boyfriend isn't already up and out on a run.

She rolls over to her back and stretches slowly. The movement makes Phil stir; his heavy arm flops across her stomach, then slowly starts to steal under her top. She affectionately pushes it away, and plants a kiss on his forehead as she pulls herself to a sit.

He looks at her with heavy-lidded eyes.

'Put the kettle on?' he says with a slow smile. 'Please?'

'Since you asked so nicely.'

She gets up. The room is chilly, so she grabs the closest thing to her – Phil's sweatshirt – and puts it on. Again, nothing out of the ordinary.

She goes to the toilet. She washes her hands, checks her reflection in the mirror. She tries to wipe off the mascara that has transferred down to her cheek. With a flick of the elastic band on her wrist, she ties her hair back from her face.

The power is back on. Her hysteria from last night stings, the burn of embarrassment from something that now seems trivial in the hazy sunshine of a winter's day. Nothing can hurt her, not now. Why does she think it can?

She trudges down the stairs to the kitchen. She puts the kettle under the tap, fills it, then clicks it on. As it fizzes into life, she takes two mugs out of the cupboard and puts teabags in each. One spoon of sugar in hers – a habit chastised by her clean-eating boyfriend, long ignored by her.

She picks her phone up from where it has been charging on the kitchen counter. Idly, she scrolls the apps. Colleagues from the hospital have been out without inviting her. That's nothing interesting, nothing new. The rejection doesn't affect her anymore; there is no dent in her skin from their blows.

A well-known author is trending on Twitter, something contentious has been said. A long-held belief, mistakenly shared, or a deliberate ploy to sell books? She'll never know. And doesn't care. She didn't like their last novel, anyway.

Pointless, aimless reflections. Her brain hasn't yet woken up.

The kettle clicks off. She puts her phone down and makes the tea. She debates breakfast. Toast? Cereal? She puts two pieces of bread in the toaster.

She flicks to the BBC News. She tentatively sips her tea. And then she sees it. The headline demands her attention. She knows she shouldn't but she's drawn like a moth to the flame. The bright light that will scorch her wings, bring her down to the ground.

She clicks. The photos load. A derelict wasteland at night. A cobalt bridge, the deep water flowing, black as ink underneath. She's seen news reports for murders before, and each time she's searched the black and white text. She's always found nothing. Nothing out of the ordinary – for a murder.

But this one—

Something pulls. A flash of recognition. A fire of synapses that instinctively makes her stomach clench, a fist grabbing her from within.

She squints at the photo, trying to work out what has caught her eye in the tiny pixels. Nothing. She reads the text again. The man in charge, the Senior Investigating Officer, DCI Adam Bishop. She assumes that's what's got her attention and gives a rueful smile, but it feels strained.

The toast pops, she puts her phone down. She picks up the knife, the butter. The jam. Doing normal things, but the feeling remains. Ice in her bones. A sense of dread. Of fear.

She stops. Still.

Something feels different. Something deep, entrenched all these years.

It can't be possible, but intuition runs true.

He's back.

Chapter 9

The second identified body: number fourteen. The woman found wrapped in the blanket. Her next of kin is her mother and her sister; the tears were plentiful. Louise Edwards had been missing for three months and, looking at the case file in front of him, Adam can see the boyfriend was a prime suspect. But no evidence had been found against him, no charges brought.

'He was no good for her,' the mother had declared through her tears. A visit at the end of the day, Adam choosing to go alone. 'It was his fault, she . . . she . . .' She'd dissolved into sobs. The sister had showed Adam to the door, after.

'Don't believe the rumours about her,' she'd said. 'She was a good person. She deserves justice.' As if Adam would have stopped looking if the reverse were true.

He considers the boyfriend now, sitting back at his desk in his office. The rest of the incident room is deserted, the majority of detectives having left for the evening. He reads the interview transcript from the man: 'boyfriend' was stretching the truth. Reading between the lines, he was a casual liaison at best. An encounter that resulted in a baby, one now lost to social services. Unfit mother, the notes said, but to Adam she sounded like a woman who needed help. Alcohol, drugs, unsuitable men. A sad story.

Louise had lived alone: ground floor flat. Notes from the detective in charge indicated he thought she'd been abducted from there; Louise had been lax about safety, back door found unlocked when the PCs went around.

Ellie Quinn pokes her head into his office.

'Boss? PNC summary for victim thirteen,' she says. 'I've emailed it across to you.'

Ian Rhodes, the latest ID – and the death notice given far away by a different constabulary, something Adam was thankful for.

'Anything significant?' he asks.

'Multiple cautions for kerb-crawling.'

'Had he now?' Adam replies, then looks up from the file. 'How's your first day been, Ellie?'

'Good, boss. I mean, this is why I wanted to join your team. I heard . . .' She stops.

'Heard what?' he asks with a grin.

Her face flushes. 'That this was where the magic happened.'

'The magic?'

'You know. The confessions out of nowhere. The unlikely strand of evidence that solves the case. The magic.'

'It's just hard work, Quinn. And good detectives.' She's still staring at him, eyes full of adulation. 'Thank you for the report,' he says with finality. 'See you tomorrow.'

She blushes again, then nods and leaves. Adam wonders if they've made a mistake recruiting her, with her incredulous wonder and reverence. There's no magic here, especially not at the beginning of a murder investigation. Working late, overdue showers. Dinner from a vending machine. On that subject, he picks up the pasty in front of him and opens the plastic. He takes a bite and frowns.

'Not up to your usual standard of culinary delights, Bishop?'

Marsh stands in the doorway. Even though it's Sunday, Marsh is smartly dressed in his usual dark suit, white shirt, thick grey hair combed back from his permanently furrowed forehead. His one concession to the weekend is his lack of tie, shirt open at the bottom of his scrawny neck. Adam is aware he's still wearing the same clothes from Saturday night – shirt and jeans, now grubby against his skin.

'Didn't expect you to still be here, guv.' Adam puts the pasty on his desk, then reconsiders and drops it in the bin.

'Caught up in the bureaucracy of policing. The bits I save you from. The paperwork, the bullshit.' He pauses. 'Any strong leads?'

'Not yet, guv. I'll tell you when we have.'

Marsh is aware of this. Adam's worked for him long enough; he knows the ropes. Adam wonders why he's really there as his boss looks out into the empty room, at the black lettering on the whiteboard, his mouth down-turned. So uncharacteristically mute.

'You'll want to speak to DCI Elliott.'

Marsh says it quietly, still facing away.

'Sorry, guv?'

Marsh turns to Adam, his face glum. 'Call Cara Elliott.'

Adam frowns. 'I've run a murder investigation before—'

47

'Not a multiple murder—'

'I know what I'm doing.'

Marsh looks at him sternly. 'You need to be prepared. For anything this might throw at you. And Cara can do that.'

Adam scoffs. 'Because it all went so well for her?'

'Exactly because of the way it went for her,' Marsh retorts. 'Cara experienced first-hand how fucked up an investigation like this can get. I want you prepared. Because there is no way I want something like that happening on my turf again. You hear me?'

Adam nods.

'Call her,' he finishes, then walks off at pace down the office.

Adam watches him go, his boss's tone smarting. 'Fine,' he mutters under his breath. He'll call DCI Cara Elliott. But only so he knows exactly what not to do when the shit hits the fan.

I watched them all through their windows; those bright dioramas of happiness and joy. I watched as they cooked their dinners, kissed their wives, talked to their kids. I saw them.

Their crimes, their hypocrisy. The flaws they tried to hide.

I saw them.

But they didn't see me.

The night is cold. The wind cuts through my clothes, making me shiver. But I need to be here. I stop outside a window. The curtains are open a fraction, and through the gap she is there, on her sofa. She is watching television, alone, a glass of wine by her side. She seems content.

I don't want this. I feel a pang of regret. For what's going to happen. My ghost in the machine is real. It is my hate, my anger, my vitriol. My body doesn't want to kill, but I know I must. For I have a purpose. For the first time in my life, I am part of something special.

A man passes me as I stand on the pavement. He gives

a greeting, friendly as his dog sniffs my leg, but I recognise the look. I need to move. I walk a little way, waiting until he is gone, then turn into the alleyway at the back of her house. I know this area well. All the houses have gates. Gates that lead to back gardens and patios and a door that she does not lock. Windows that can be pushed open.

Her gate is not bolted. She has no security lights that flick on, discouraging me with their sudden glow. I walk slowly across her lawn.

I peer into her kitchen. Her plate from dinner is left on the side. The bottle of red waiting for a second glass. I can't see into the living room where she is sitting but I imagine what she smells like, how she will feel. The softness of her skin, the sweetness of her perfume.

How long she will take to die.

I place my fingers on the handle of her back door. I push down slowly; it moves. It's another sign. That she is right.

I pull the door open and listen: she laughs at something on the television.

I feel omnipotent. Strong. I place one foot inside the house.

I move into the kitchen and pull the door shut behind me. Soft footsteps into the darkened hallway. I pause next to the door into the living room, but then I hear a noise. A car, a man pulling up outside. I imagine her looking up with a smile. Greeting him with a kiss and a hug. An enthusiastic welcome I envy with every cell of my being.

I turn, reluctant to forgo my mission, and climb the stairs. I head towards the open door.

This is the bedroom. The bed is made, and I look at the tables either side. Two books on one, paperbacks –

historical fiction. A pair of glasses and an inhaler. On the other is a crumpled paperback, the spine broken, the cover pink. This is her.

I go around to her side of the bed and I pick up the pillow. I put it to my face and breathe in deeply. I know now for sure she is right. This life – this beautiful life she leads – makes me burn with jealousy. I want what she has. Love. Peace. Family. I want it.

And I will take it all.

Under the pillow is a vest top. Thin and lacy. Delicate. I rub the soft material between my fingers, imagining it's her skin. Perfect, unsullied.

I have my knife in my pocket. A simple penknife, but long and sharp. Easily hidden, quickly pulled out and used. I know there is blood on there from the others. From those who showed themselves to be unworthy. But I know this won't be her. When the time comes, I will make her last. Just as she needs to.

I press the tip of the blade against the light fabric of her top; it punctures the material easily. Gently, I push it further through. I feel the rip, I imagine it to be her skin, her flesh. I pull it down, the anticipation, the excitement catching in my throat. It's lust, but not the dirty carnal kind. It's more base than that. A need deep in my soul. I run the knife all the way through, thinking about the tear of her skin, the blood flowing.

I hear a call from the kitchen. The shout of a man's voice. I hurry to the bedroom door and look carefully down the stairs. The man is there, bottle of wine in his hand, offering her a new glass. She agrees; he hums under his breath as he pours one for himself, then carries the bottle into the living room.

I push her ripped vest top into my pocket and put the knife away. I dart out of the bedroom and scuttle quickly down the stairs. Their excited conversation masks the clunk of the kitchen door opening and closing.

I back out of her garden, close her gate with barely a click. I walk away, to the street. Back to watching everyone, from a distance. From the cold.

She thinks she is safe, in her house. In her bed as she sleeps. She thinks no one can touch her. I watch, and I know.

Not today. But soon.

Soon.

Forensic Post-Mortem Examination

Date: 20 November 1995

General Information

The decedent has been visually identified by next of kin as Grace Summers, female, aged 34 (DOB 04/04/61). Dental records have been requested and DNA samples taken for formal identification. The decedent was found in the outhouse of the garden of 'The Beeches', Gloucester Road, and death pronounced at the scene. Medical intervention was attempted by paramedics but unsuccessful. The circumstances of her death have been recorded as suspicious. Grace Summers, a professional ballet dancer, was reported as a missing person on 12 September 1995 by her husband. She was married with one child, 2.

Previous to her disappearance, the decedent was in good health. She had no long-term illnesses. She was taking no prescription medication. She had a broken arm at the age of 13, which had healed in a satisfactory manner. She was fitted with an IUD.

The body was found partially clothed in a red T-shirt and knickers, and covered in bedding. The clothes have been sent for further testing; initial enquiries confirm these to be the clothing worn when she disappeared.

The ambient temperature of the room was 5°C, rectal temperature was 33°C, body weight approximately 50 kg. This gives an approximate time of death of eight hours before the discovery of the body: between 11 p.m. and 2 a.m. on the early morning of Saturday, 18 November. Traces of rigor were reported still present on discovery of the body.

Description of body

The decedent is severely malnourished and dehydrated. She was of slim build, Caucasian, with no tattoos or identifying marks. Hair is blonde and medium length, dirty and matted. Fingernails are long and unkempt.

Hypostasis is evident across the back and buttocks, indicating the body lying on its back after death. No signs of petechiae present on skin or eyes.

Blunt force trauma is evident across the right-hand side of the head, resulting in a linear laceration to the scalp, approximately 7 cm long, and a depressed skull fracture. Large extradural haematoma associated with underlying damage to the meningeal artery and subsequent bleeding into the extradural space was found. Rapid onset of symptoms would have occurred, with collapse and death within approximately two to four hours.

Multiple lesions on both wrists and ankles found consistent with ligature restraints. Infected sores are present across the decedent's back and feet. Abrasions also evident on spine, knees and arms in a distinctive pattern: parallel lines both horizontal and vertical in a grid profile, two centimetres apart. Evidence of previous injury clear across the face, including a broken nose, and multiple abrasions, partially healed. Some defensive injuries present on hands and lower arms, including ripped fingernails on all, and breaks across the intermediate phalanges on both the index finger and middle finger of the right hand, as well as joint dislocations.

Extensive bruising, abrasions and tearing around the

vagina and anus indicates a strong likelihood of repeated sexual assault, including scarring and some healed wounds. High vaginal, low vaginal and endocervical swabs have been taken for analysis.

Cause of Death:

Ia) Extradural haemorrhage

Ib) Blunt force trauma to head

II) Malnutrition and dehydration

DAY 3

MONDAY

Chapter 10

Jamie groans as the alarm goes off next to him. Six a.m. Too early. Something that seemed so necessary last night feels insane this morning.

Pippa groans and flaps her hand at him, a gesture to say, turn that off. He reaches over and picks up his mobile, still buzzing loudly. A raft of texts greets him from Bishop. Jamie ignores all except the last: *Bring coffee.*

He imagines his boss: already up and going full tilt. A murder investigation of this magnitude needs the commitment and drive that someone like Adam brings.

In his seven years in Major Crimes, three of them under Bishop's command, he's never worked on something like this. With Adam at the helm, Jamie knows it'll be a tight ship. Bishop has his failings, but when it comes to his police work there's no corner unchecked, no procedure unfollowed. It's a masterclass watching him work.

Now, Jamie showers quickly. He goes down to the kitchen and puts the kettle on, making a cup of tea and bringing it back into the bedroom, placing it on the bedside table. He wakes his wife, lightly pressing his lips to her forehead. She looks up at him with blurry eyes and a smile.

'Have a good day,' she says, leaning up for a kiss. She has morning breath and her hair is messy from the pillow; he doesn't care one jot.

'I'll try,' he replies.

The streets are quiet as he drives, singing along to a song on the radio. Despite what he knows will face him when he arrives, he's in a good mood. Memories from the honeymoon are fresh in his mind; his wife curled up next to him in bed last night. The wisp of her hair at the nape of her neck as he kissed it, the softness of her inner thigh as his hand crept around to find her. Life is good, he thinks, and he pulls into the drive-thru at Costa, ordering a chocolate twist at the same time as the coffees.

As he waits, he gets out his phone, ignores his emails and scrolls to the news pages. There it is at the top. *Bodies found at Northbrook Bridge. Multiple murder suspected.* It doesn't take long for the speculation to mount; he knows Marsh is planning to make a press statement this morning. The photos are taken from a distance, something to fill the space, but Jamie frowns. Too much detail is visible. The locations, the number of crime scenes. Even one spray-painted number. They'll have to do something about that, tell PR and get it retracted. That's the last thing they need: crazies coming out of the woodwork with false confessions.

He drives quickly to the nick, parks his car, and sweeps pieces of flaky pastry from his ever-growing tummy. But as he walks up to the incident room, he realises he recognises the woman he's following, escorted by a PC. She's dressed in dark blue jeans, brown knee-high boots. Heavy coat over the top, which she pulls off, draping it over her arm. She hasn't noticed him, caught up in her own thoughts, and now she pauses outside the door. The copper opens it, then waits. She runs her hand through her shoulder-length hair, then goes in.

Jamie follows closely behind, curious to see why she's there.

She's guided through, straight to Bishop's office on the far side. Adam sees her coming and gets up from his desk, walking to the door and waiting. Detectives watch; the conversation in the room dulls.

Ellie Quinn comes up to his elbow, a piece of paper clutched in her hand. But she sees Jamie's attention is diverted and follows his gaze.

'DCI Bishop,' the woman says.

'Dr Cole,' his boss replies. Jamie can see by the look on his face that he's surprised but trying to hide it. Adam nods to the PC to thank him and he leaves. 'You want to see me?'

'Yes. It's important.'

Their tone is overly formal. Unnatural and clipped.

'I hope so. I'm kind of busy, in case you hadn't noticed.'

'Of course, I've noticed,' she snaps. 'I wouldn't be here unless it was absolutely necessary.'

Bishop sighs. 'Fine. Let's talk inside.'

He moves out of the way and she goes into the office. He shuts the door behind him and the conversation in the incident room starts up again. There'll be no more drama for the time being. At least, not anything they can hear.

'Who was that?' Ellie says next to him in a theatrical whisper.

'Dr Romilly Cole,' Jamie replies. He looks at Bishop's coffee in his hand, but decides not to interrupt and gives it to Quinn instead.

She takes it, surprised at his generosity. But her eyes stay locked on the closed door.

'Do they know each other?' she asks.

Jamie chuckles. He watches the figures on the other side of the door. Arms crossed; body language guarded.

'You could say that,' he replies. 'She's Bishop's ex-wife.'

Chapter 11

Romilly barely got any sleep last night. On waking, she knew she had to speak to him.

Phil had given her a long stare when she told him this morning. Eating breakfast, he looked up from his bowl, spoon in hand.

'And you think it's a good idea to see your ex-husband?' he asked. 'Isn't there anyone else you can talk to?'

'He's the SIO.' She tried to be casual. 'And it's been three years. I'm sure we can be civil.'

'It's a multiple murder case.' He directed it downwards, to his porridge, stirring the mixture slowly. 'Are you ready for that?'

'That's exactly why I need to go, Phil,' she replied and left the room to avoid further inquisition.

She'd been angry at his questions. But he was right. She'd spent the majority of Sunday in tears. Pacing, worrying, fretting about what to do. And her boyfriend had only been articulating her own thoughts. In better times, when she and Adam were married, they'd discussed his cases over the dinner table. In those days he'd been a DS – eager and ambitious. As a doctor she could offer a level of insight that put him at an advantage when talking to his superiors. How might an illness like that affect an offender's thinking? If the victim was injured in that way, how could they have walked, run, talked?

But soon it became too much and she'd asked him to stop.

That had been the beginning of the end. The closing of a door to parts of his life that only increased as time went on.

But this, she told herself, sitting in her car outside the familiar grey walls of the police station, this will be fine.

She'd picked up her bag, pulled her shoulders back, and climbed out.

Now she sits in front of him in his office. She's pleased for his success, he deserves it. Nobody works harder than Adam. Nobody puts in the hours or has the same astute way of thinking. But seeing his team, in this incident room, brings it home. He's achieved this level of professional recognition without her. He's thrived in his own company. Turns out he was better off single, after all.

'I heard you got promoted,' she says, trying to start the conversation on the right foot.

'Yes.'

'Congratulations.'

'Thank you.'

Another pause, a gap in the conversation that only serves to emphasise the yawning distance between them.

'You're well, Adam?'

He smiles. The first time since she's come in, but it's thin and tight. 'Picture of health,' he replies.

61

'That's good. Are you still going for your check-ups?'

'Why are you here, Romilly?'

She takes a long breath in, then pulls a few pieces of paper out of her bag and places them on the table. She's not sure where to start.

'I saw this yesterday.'

He glances at the text. It's the BBC News report, the photos fuzzy in the black and white printout.

'Okay . . .' he replies, hesitantly.

She needs to get the words out fast before she loses her nerve. 'It's him, Adam. It's him.'

'Romilly,' he begins, with a sigh. 'Please . . .'

'It is. I know it is—'

'Not everything is about him. Not every murder, every death—'

'No, Adam, listen.'

'So, tell me. What makes you so sure?'

She pauses. She spent the day searching the internet, reading every article, every report she could find. And she still doesn't know. Why she felt so scared, so unsteady. Like the world tilted.

'It's a feeling . . .' she begins.

At that, his face changes. From sympathy to barely disguised annoyance.

'A feeling? Come on. Can you hear yourself?' He pushes the printouts into a neat pile. She recognises the gesture: dismissive. Conversation over.

'But Adam—'

'How are you?' he interrupts. 'Are you still seeing Dr Jones?'

'This isn't me being crazy.'

He doesn't reply. *But isn't it?* the voice in her head asks.

Because if this isn't crazy, what is? Adam had always been the sane one in their relationship. The person who calmed her down, made her question what was real and what was in her head.

But that's not his role now. They're divorced; she's with Phil.

Phil is a much better match for her. They work in the same place – he understands the trials and tribulations of being employed by the NHS even though he's a physiotherapist and she's an oncologist. Adam drinks too much. He doesn't ever exercise, something her new boyfriend has more than covered. Phil has a much better body, she knows, even though Adam was never flabby. Sinewy and lithe, a metabolism that burned energy from sheer drive alone. And in the early days . . .

She stops. There's a slight smell. A lingering odour. And sure enough, she spots the packet of cigarettes and a lighter on Adam's desk.

She sits up straight. 'You're smoking again?' she exclaims, louder than she intends.

Guilt flashes across his face, before it's replaced by anger.

'What's that got to do with anything?'

'With your history?'

He pushes his shoulders back, a defiant gesture. 'You're in no position to tell me what to do, Milly.'

'As your doctor—'

'You're not my doctor. Not now. Not ever.'

She feels her body tense. Ashamed from his disbelief around the murders, the familiar irritation easily slots back into place. 'You do know how stupid it is, right?'

'Yeah. That's always been my problem. Stupidity. Stupid

to trust you, back then. Stupid to let you waste my time today.'

'I should go . . .'

'Yes. Please.'

She stares at him. His jaw is set, his eyes narrowed. Any goodwill towards her has vanished. He jabs wordlessly with one finger towards the door.

'Fine.'

She turns quickly, striding across the office, aware of the stares from the detectives. But she doesn't stop. Down the stairs, out of reception, and to her car. She opens the door and throws herself in, forcing back bitter tears.

He's such an arsehole. Nothing has changed. That man . . . that *fucking* man . . .

She shouldn't let him get to her. Nobody else has the ability to make her this angry. They're not married now, she tells herself. She's better off without him. He didn't take her seriously. He didn't listen.

She knows her annoyance towards his smoking was just something to deflect blame. She's furious with herself. For letting this take over – again – letting *him* dominate her life as it had for years. Adam was right to throw her out. He was right not to believe her.

She's an idiot. Irrational. Hysterical. And she'd been that way in front of Adam. She feels the red flush of embarrassment work its way from her core to her face. It's humiliating. How could she be so *stupid*?

'Fuck!' she shouts, hitting the palms of her shaking hands against the steering wheel. 'Fuck.'

Chapter 12

Adam feels the stare of his detectives as he strides to the door of his office. He slams it with so much force the glass rattles, then throws himself back into his seat, feeling his jaw clench. How can she still get to him like this? *How?*

It's been years since they split up. Years since they divorced. He thinks back to the last time he saw her. A few summers ago. He remembers a dinner party at Jamie and Pippa's, both invited, both trying to maintain they could be in the same room as each other without a problem. It ended in a row, of course. Romilly in tears, Jamie gently suggesting to Adam that maybe he should leave. But it wasn't his fucking fault they had split up.

There's a gentle tap on the door, and Jamie pokes his head around.

'All okay, boss?' he asks.

Adam sighs. 'What do you think?'

Jamie comes into the room, closing the door behind him. 'What did she want?'

'She thinks . . .' He doesn't want to entertain her paranoia today. He has enough on his plate. 'Never mind. Nothing of interest.' Adam spots the packet of cigarettes on the desk in front of him and picks them up, throwing them into his desk drawer. 'The usual judgement. Anyway.' He takes a long breath in. 'Any update?'

'The blankets the bodies were wrapped in have come back from the lab. Polyester-cotton mix, Marks and Spencer's. They sold approximately half a million of these across the country.'

'Great,' Adam replies sarcastically.

'Some old stains though, believed unrelated to the body. They're still waiting on results. Plus some fibres. Doing the analysis now.' Jamie pauses, leaning against the wall. 'CCTV has come up a blank. Too many routes in and out of the dump site. We have a few cameras in the local area, so if we know what vehicle we're looking for then maybe we could find it. But as it is . . .' He picks at a piece of Blu-tack stuck to the wall, then rolls it around in his hand. 'Too many possibles.'

'Any additional IDs?'

'We're narrowing them down.'

'Door to door?'

'Nothing yet, sorry, boss. Just a flurry of complaints regarding the fly-tipping on the site.'

Adam frowns. 'Have we looked into that? The fly-tipping? Have a dig through some of this rubble to see if we can trace it back to its source?'

Jamie nods thoughtfully. 'If they dumped there once they knew they could dump there again?'

'Exactly. Or at very least, someone might have seen something. If we apply the right pressure? Threaten them with a juicy fine and their memories might come unstuck.'

'On it,' Jamie replies. He turns, but Adam stops him.

'And go and see the boyfriend. Louise Edwards's bloke.' A possible suspect, a concrete line of enquiry they can follow. Someone they can rule out, at least.

'Now?'

'Now. Take Quinn with you. I'll call once you're on your way, brief you on what I know.'

Jamie does a mock salute with a smile, then leaves Adam to it.

He picks up the piece of paper that Romilly left on his desk. It's nothing new. She sees him in everything: every missing person, every suspicious death. He can hardly blame her. Trauma like that, so deep-rooted. It scars you for life.

But on the surface, she looked bloody good. After not seeing her for years, having her walk into his office had been a shock. Instantly the old feelings came back. The warmth towards her, care and concern. The love, but also the betrayal and the bitter sting of rejection.

He screws the piece of paper into a ball and throws it towards the bin. It misses, bouncing off the wall and coming to rest under a cupboard. He leaves it there. Out of sight. Ignored.

Where it belongs.

Chapter 13

A last-minute appointment, kept for emergencies. But this must be one.

Romilly rings the buzzer. On the large red painted door, between two white stucco pillars, next to the gold name plate. She finds the expense reassuring: these people know what they're doing.

Romilly is escorted straight through, past the patients in the hushed waiting room, receiving knowing glances from the haste.

One of *those*, their faces are saying. *I'm glad I'm not as bad as her.*

She sits down in the usual room, in her usual chair. She waits, taking in the neat bookshelves with their psychology tomes, the certificates on the wall, the geometrically ordered desk, a white Apple computer on top. There are no pinboards covered in thank you cards. No photographs. No hint of personalisation from the woman who knows everything about her.

Romilly remembers the early days here, in consultation

room two. The crying. The hysteria. Sobbing so much her face would ache for hours after. Dr Jones painstakingly unearthed years of ingrained trauma, then soothed, talked, and counselled Romilly into the functioning human she is today.

But now this. A new delusion. Romilly worries it's all coming back.

Dr Jones enters. She smiles, setting her glass of water down on the table to her right-hand side. Romilly has always envied Dr Jones. With her calm, her cool air of efficiency and contentment. She has neat hair, tied back in a bun at the nape of her neck. No tendrils escape, not a hint of frizz can be seen.

They sit opposite each other. The doctor folds her hands into her lap, waiting.

'Thank you for seeing me at such short notice,' Romilly begins.

Dr Jones nods. 'Of course. I'm glad you thought of me.' There's a long pause. The clock ticks on the wall, making Romilly aware of how much time she's wasting. But she doesn't know where to start.

'Begin with how you're feeling,' Jones says, as if reading Romilly's mind.

'Confused. Worried. Upset.'

'Okay.' The doctor pauses. 'So why am I not seeing that?'

'What do you mean?'

'Outwardly.' Jones smiles gently. 'Most people who ask for an emergency appointment exhibit an external manifestation of their feelings. They're crying, visibly troubled. If anything, you seem angry.'

Romilly has always liked the fact Jones doesn't talk

down to her. They're both doctors – smart women – and Jones treats her as such.

'I am angry,' Romilly acknowledges. 'I saw my ex-husband today.'

'Adam?'

'Yes.'

'And how did that feel? Being with him again?'

Romilly thinks back. He'd looked the same. Same haircut, maybe slightly longer, but it suits him. More grey, additional lines on his forehead, but whatever he's doing, it's working. And he called her Milly. Still. He's the only one that refers to her that way, something that now infuriates and pleases her in equal measure.

'Conflicted,' she says at last. The therapist tilts her head to one side, waiting for her to expand. 'He's just as . . .' She pauses, looking for the right word. She wants to say *attractive, handsome,* but doesn't want Dr Jones to see her as that sort of person. Superficial. There was always far more to his appeal than that.

Romilly knows Adam's single. She still meets up with Pippa, and Pippa passes all the gossip on from Jamie. Easily getting women, by all accounts. 'A bit of a slut,' Pippa said with a frown. 'Never faithful. You're well rid of him,' she added, when Romilly knows that was never Adam's problem.

She feels a flare of jealousy then, imagining Adam with other women, and she forces herself to focus on the parts of her ex-husband that were less than desirable.

'He's infuriating,' Romilly says. 'He's smart, successful. Everything that attracted me to him in the first place. But now I also notice his arrogance. How he sees me as this awful person who let him down.'

70

'He said that?'

'No, but I could tell. And he pities me. Thinks I'm this fucked-up mess.'

'Do you think you're a fucked-up mess?'

'No. Not usually.' Romilly feels the flash of shame again, knowing she embarrassed herself in front of Adam. 'Maybe today,' she adds quietly.

'So what happened today? Why did you go to see him?'

'He's in charge of that murder case. The one by the river. And I thought . . . I . . .'

'You thought it was him.'

'Yes.'

'Why?'

'I . . . I'm not sure. A feeling.'

Romilly feels ridiculous repeating that now. Of course, Adam hadn't listened to her. He's a man who deals in hard evidence. Proof.

'He didn't take you seriously?' Jones replies.

'No. And now I'm worried that he's right. That I'm doing it again.'

'Catastrophising?'

'Yes. Making it all about me, and him. Everything that happened in 1995.'

'What makes this different to when you did it in the past?'

'I feel better nowadays. But what if this is just the beginning? Of another episode?'

'What if it's not?' the doctor asks. 'What if you're right?'

Romilly stops. Ever since yesterday morning, the only thing in her head has been *calm down*. You're imagining things. It's not him. How could it be? Adam's reaction only confirmed her lunacy. But now, with Dr Jones's statement, she considers it from the other side.

The doctor carries on. 'You know that case better than anyone. You lived it. You saw it with your own eyes. Something in that news report sparked a memory – something that's made you worried, rather than upset. Resolute, rather than hysterical. Why the difference?'

'But . . . but . . .' Romilly stutters. 'How can it be?'

The therapist shrugs. 'You're a doctor. You're used to applying your intelligence, researching into symptoms. Find out. Dig a bit further. And if it's nothing, you'll know to let it go. But if it's something . . .'

She leaves the sentence unfinished. If it's something . . . If she's right.

Then the thought is too horrible to bear.

Before

His knees are pressed into his chest, his back curved, his head against his legs. He has been like this for a while, although time has no purpose here. It's pitch black.

His thin T-shirt and shorts are useless against the cold. The wind and the draughts creep under the gap in the door, through floorboards and walls. He shivers. The urine around him smells of despair and hatred and defeat. At first, a blessed release, quickly turning to dismay.

The dull ache that began in his lower back has started to spread. He shifts position, trying to alleviate the throbbing but in doing so a bolt of pain charges through his muscles. Tense knots of constriction that can't be relieved and that make his teeth clench. He's been like this too long. They're starting to cramp and he massages his calves with his fingers. It doesn't help. Only being able to stretch, escape, will make any difference.

But he knows not to resist. Not to protest or complain. Silence is his only friend. That, and the tears running down his cheeks. He awkwardly shifts position and wipes them away. He can cry later. When things get worse. Because they always get worse.

He hears a knock. Two quick taps on the front door, close to his cupboard. Then footsteps in heavy boots.

The door is opened; a new rush of cold air seeps inside, chilling his skin. He hears voices. His father, then another: a woman.

He gasps. He recognises her, his teacher from school. A nice lady, with a soft voice and clothes that smell of summer meadows and joy. She's here, at his house. But why? He strains forward, ignoring the fresh rush of pain that races through his constricting muscles. They're talking. They're talking about him. He can't hear every word but he can make out her concern – he hasn't been to school, is everything okay? Then his father, a tone he hasn't heard before. It's almost . . . kind. Considerate. His father laughs, a giggle in return. Hope turns to desolation. The front door is closing. This isn't someone coming to save them. This is confirmation: they are alone. In hell.

Footsteps again, on the floor outside. This time they pause. A shuffle. He imagines his father standing outside the tiny wooden door, thinking. Checking his watch.

He hears the scrape of furniture against the floor, signalling his release. But there is no freedom here. The real horror is about to begin.

Chapter 14

Romilly is glad Phil isn't there when she gets home. She arrives with new resolution: to do as Dr Jones said. Dig out what she has on the old case. Face her paranoia front and centre.

It's her day off from the hospital. She has nothing to do, bar this. She opens the loft hatch, pulls down the ladder, and retrieves the plastic storage container of old files. Dust and cobwebs settle in her hair. She climbs down and places it on the kitchen table. Pandora's box. Open it and who knows what memories will come flying out. But Dr Jones is right. She's a different person now. Stronger.

Two hours. She'll give it two hours. A boundary. She steels herself, clicking the kettle on, then notices the back door key left in the lock. She tries the handle, it's open, and feels the shiver of worry, quietly cursing herself for not checking when she left that morning. She locks it then makes a cup of tea and carries it to her office. The box next. She places it on the chair next to her desk.

Her office is the smallest room, right at the back of the house. No bigger than a broom cupboard, space for a bookshelf and a desk, but Rom has always liked it. The shelves are jammed with medical journals and textbooks, files and notes stacked up on the floor.

She opens the lid. A mess of paper stares back. Everything: collected and stored away. And piece by piece, she begins.

It's not until she hears the front door bang and Phil call out that she realises hours have passed. Her tea lies untouched and cold next to her. Lunch missed and forgotten.

'Are you in?' Phil calls again, and she tears herself away from the box.

She glances around. Paper is scattered across the floor and the desk. Photographs. Fusty, brittle newspaper clippings. Her diary from those blurry, confused days in the aftermath of his crimes. And she hasn't made any progress.

'Back here,' she shouts reluctantly, and she hears footsteps walk the length of the house. Her boyfriend pokes his head around the study door.

He's dressed in a grey and black tracksuit, out of his usual NHS garb. He pauses in the doorway, his mouth slightly open.

'Good day?' she asks him, trying to keep her voice normal.

'Same old,' he replies slowly. He comes into the room, leaning down and giving her a kiss. He smells of shampoo; his hair is slightly wet from the shower he has after the gym post work. She sees him look at the notes scrawled on the pad in front of her. They look like the etchings of a mad person. She closes it quickly.

'How did it go?' he asks.

'Same old Adam. He told me to leave.'

'So you are . . .?' he begins. 'What is all this?'

'I saw Dr Jones. She told me to follow my instincts.'

'She told you to . . .' But he stops. He keeps any further questions to himself. Doesn't want to know or doesn't care? Rom isn't sure. 'Curry for dinner okay?' he says instead.

Rom nods, and Phil leaves to go to the kitchen. She watches him go, appreciating the energy of his walk, the bounce in his step. Phil has the body of a personal trainer, the energy of a man half his age. 'Wouldn't be a great advert for my work,' he would say. 'A physio who can't even look after himself.'

Along with the gym, he runs. He swims in the sea on New Year's Day. He surfs, even on pathetic English waves. He cycles for hours on end. It makes Romilly feel quite exhausted.

She hears the radio turn on in the kitchen. She's not going to get any further with this now; her brain's as muddled as it was before. She tidies her files away and follows. In the kitchen Phil has already put the vegetables they need for dinner on the side; she gets out a wooden board and knife and starts to chop. It's an established routine – he the head chef, she there to assist – and one she likes. As they cook together, he talks about his day.

Phil tells her about a new client: a rangy yummy mummy fond of body pump and spin who's done her shoulder in at the gym.

'I could tell the moment I laid my hands on her,' he

says. 'Overtraining, and bad technique. Told her she needed to rest up for at least a week.'

'That wasn't the advice she was after?' Rom asks, passing across the chopped onions.

'No. She's trying to lose weight, although God knows why. I told her to stop swapping out carbs in favour of the bottle of red and she stalked off.'

'A bottle of red a week isn't so bad.'

'Not a week, Rom,' Phil says, turning to her, astonishment clear on his face. 'A night.'

Rom laughs and pushes the rest of the chopped vegetables across to him. He adds them to the pan along with the spices. She appreciates Phil's conversation. Something to distract her from the intrusive thoughts. A delicious smell of cumin and ginger fills the air and Rom's stomach rumbles in response.

Apart from the brief mention earlier, Phil doesn't ask more about her day. But now, over the creamy coconut and sweet potato curry, she can't ignore it any longer.

'Dr Jones says I might be right,' she begins.

Phil looks up. 'Mmhmm?'

'About my feeling about that case. I just need to work out exactly what's causing it.'

Phil nods, staring at his dinner, chewing slowly. After a moment, he says, 'Is that a good idea?'

Romilly knows he's only asking because he loves her, but she feels a sting of irritation just the same.

'Why not? Because it's related to my past, or because it's connected to my ex-husband?' she retorts, more sharply than she intends.

'Both, Rom,' he replies, seriously. 'I haven't met Adam, but from what you tell me you two weren't great together at the end.' He puts his knife and fork down. He tries to reach across to take her hand, but she pulls away. 'And you've worked so hard to put everything that happened behind you. So digging it up again? Well . . .'

He leaves it unfinished, but Rom knows what he's thinking. The nightmares, her terror of the dark.

'Even if I'm wrong,' she says softly, 'I need to be sure.'

Phil looks up. He studies her face for a moment then nods slowly.

'Whatever you think, Rom,' he says.

They finish their dinner in silence. She can sense his disapproval. But he knows that there's no point in getting into an argument: he's made his point and her mind is set.

Once Phil's finished eating, he picks up his plate, then pauses, standing behind her.

'One day, in time, you'll be free of him,' he says, and puts a hand on her shoulder. Rom knows he's not talking about Adam now. She covers his fingers with her own and squeezes. 'One day you won't feel that he's etched on your brain.'

'I hope so,' she replies.

Phil starts clearing up the kitchen. As she finishes her dinner she watches him, feeling a tug of affection. And then she stops. Her fork hovers above her plate for a moment, then she puts it down with a clatter.

She races back through the house and stands at her desk, flicking through the file. She picks up a report from the box, then the shot of the latest crime scene, printed yesterday morning. And then she sees it. A small corner of the photo. A tiny detail, lit up by an errant torch, probably not intended to be published.

The room blurs. Her vision narrows to those few pixels.

Her muscles turn to liquid, and with a small cry she sinks to the floor.

It can't be right. But it is.

And she needs to tell Adam.

Chapter 15

The house is warm and welcoming. Jamie feels a swell of happiness as he puts his key in the lock and pushes the door open.

He calls hello and gets an answering shout. He pulls off his coat and scarf, then walks through to the living room.

Pippa looks up from the sofa and smiles. He slumps next to her.

'What a day,' he says.

'Was it horrendous?' she asks, leaning into his chest and looking up for a kiss. He plants one on her lips.

'Fucking awful. You don't want to even imagine.'

He's just come away from the interview with Louise Edwards's . . . something. Jamie isn't sure how to describe him. While she was being abducted and killed, Jacob Nelson was denying any knowledge of her at all.

'Police told me she was murdered,' he'd said, insufficiently quickly after introductions. 'Fuck all to do with me.'

'So you're not the father of her child?' Jamie had asked, knowing full well he'd admitted as such in his original interviews.

'Maybe,' he'd conceded. 'But who knows. Bitches always saying I knocked them up.' He'd winked then, and Jamie had wanted to punch him. Tall, rangy, with a shaved head and pale bum fluff on his chin, he had a face you wanted to arrest on sight knowing it was only a matter of time before he'd do something stupid. Jamie wondered how he'd got one woman to sleep with him, let alone more.

'She spoke to you guys,' he'd said, with a cursory glance to Quinn. 'You did nothing.'

Jamie put his disgust to one side, sitting up straight with interest. 'What about?'

Nelson thought for a moment; Jamie could almost hear machinery turning. 'Someone was following her. But she couldn't describe them, she said it was more like a feeling.'

'A feeling?'

'Yeah. She even accused me, but I said nah, stalking wasn't my thing.' He'd looked at Jamie, an eyebrow rising. 'Was it sexual? You know, her murder? Did he rape her and stuff?'

Jamie had declined to answer, and they'd let him go after that, keen to get the man as far away from them as possible. But no, Jamie thinks now. There were no signs of sexual assault on any of the bodies.

He blocks the unpleasant thoughts out of his head, desperate to enjoy his evening with his wife. 'How was your day?' he asks.

Pippa laughs. 'Hyper kids. But nice to be back, for about an hour. Until I collected all this.' She points to the large pile of marking. 'Work for this evening.' Then she turns, her face excited. 'Wedding photos are here. Do you want to see?'

'Yes,' he replies. 'Yes, I do. Very much.'

Their wedding day had been wonderful. People said a winter wedding was crazy, but the weather had been bright and crisp. Blue skies, frost on the ground. The hotel was warm and cosy with log fires, flickering candles; displays of roses and ivy and flowers Jamie couldn't name, in red and white and green.

And Pippa was beautiful. He looks at the photos – long white fitted dress, hair loose around her shoulders. She'd taken his breath away when he'd first seen her.

'Oh, look at my nose from that angle!' Pippa exclaims. 'I should have said no profile shots.'

'Are you kidding?' Jamie stares at his wife in astonishment. 'You look amazing. You are amazing. What other wife wouldn't mind her new husband buggering off on the last day of their holiday to go to work?'

'To be honest, I'd had enough of you by then,' Pippa says. 'After two weeks of California? I was sick of your face.'

'Piss off,' he says with a smile and reaches under her top to tickle her. She cries out with laughter, pushing him away, trying to do the same. Her hands under his shirt, kissing him, lightly at first, then turning into a full-blown snog. So the honeymoon isn't over yet, he thinks, pulling her shirt over her head.

After, they lie on the sofa, a blanket pulled over the top of them. Pippa grabs the laptop with a grin and they go back to looking at the wedding photos. They move on to ones from the party. Their friends dancing, even their parents, hand in hand on the dance floor. One comes onto the screen: Adam, his face caught mid-laughter, pint of beer in his hand.

'He slept with Jane, did you know?' Pippa says.

'He did? He didn't mention it. I hope she doesn't expect him to call her.'

Pippa scoffs. 'No, she doesn't care. She said it was tradition that the bridesmaid should sleep with the best man. Had her eye on him from the beginning.' Pippa leans forward, studying the photo. 'He is a handsome bugger.'

'Oi!' Jamie complains and she laughs.

'I mean, objectively.' She leans back, resting her head on his chest. 'You're the only man for me,' she says softly. 'For as long as you want me.'

'Always,' he confirms, seriously. He kisses her gently on her forehead, thinking about how lucky he is. Then his thoughts turn to other people close to him. Other relationships – the broken ones.

'Rom came into the station today,' he says. 'She met with Adam. Something to do with the case.'

Pippa looks up quickly. 'Really? She didn't come to the wedding because she didn't want a scene, yet she goes to the police station to see him. Do you know why?'

'Adam wouldn't say.'

'And how did it go?'

'Badly.'

Pippa sinks into silence. 'I'll have to call her,' she says quietly. 'Now,' she adds decisively, 'are you hungry?'

He kisses her. 'Starving.'

He pulls on the bare minimum of clothing and heads upstairs to get changed properly. He throws his shirt into an already teetering washing basket, and as he does so he gets a waft of a strange smell. Not unpleasant, just . . . different. It makes him feel out of sorts, a moment of disquiet, like an unpleasant memory remembered. He sniffs again, moving around the room to try and find it, but it's gone.

Jamie opens a window, then shovels a load of washing into the basket and heads downstairs.

In the kitchen, Pippa is standing next to the open fridge, staring inside.

'I went shopping yesterday,' she mumbles to the shelves. 'But I don't seem to have actually bought anything to make a meal.' She looks over at him as he switches the washing machine on. 'Do you fancy pizza?'

For a fraction of a second, Jamie considers his ever-expanding tummy, his resolution to go on a diet after the honeymoon. Then he smiles.

'Excellent idea,' he says, logging onto Domino's.

Chapter 16

It's gone ten before Adam makes it home.

He'd stayed late at the station, sitting in his office, wading through hastily drafted reports from the day. They haven't got far – and the lack of progress bothers him. No leads. Just grumpy detectives sifting through rubbish at the wasteland, a lab with nothing to report, and uniforms turning in neighbourhood reports of sum fuck all.

He knew he couldn't stay there all night. His eyes were scratchy, body tired; he'll get nothing useful done without some rest.

He gets home, showers, then manages a microwaved ready meal in front of the TV with a few beers. He's already feeling his eyes closing when he hears the doorbell ring.

He glances at the clock – ten past eleven – then walks slowly to the door and opens it. His ex-wife is standing on the doorstep, folder in hand. She holds it out towards him.

'How do you know where I live?' he snaps.

'Divorce paperwork.'

'And what's this? More *feelings*?'

She scowls. 'Stop being a wanker, Adam. I worked it out.'

He sighs. He holds little hope that she'll be useful to the case, but he knows from previous experience she won't leave until he listens.

There was a similar episode when they were married. One of many, but a particular incident comes to mind tonight. They were walking through the centre of town, a sunny day, hand in hand. Buskers merrily entertained the shoppers; he felt happy, optimistic about life. Until she spotted him.

An old man. Grey hair, tall but slightly stooped, walking quickly through the crowds. Romilly stopped dead, so quickly the pedestrians behind them swore quietly in protest. He turned, confused; her face was deathly white.

'It's him,' she whispered, pointing. 'It's him.'

It took a moment for Adam to twig what she was talking about. He glanced towards the departing figure as he rounded the corner, out of sight, then turned back to Romilly.

'He's got out. It's him.' She was shaking, breathless.

'How?' He stood in front of her, taking her sweaty hands in his. 'Milly, look at me. How could he have got out of prison?'

'They've let him out. Early parole. Good behaviour.'

'We'd know. They would have told you.'

'What if they forgot?' She turned her eyes to him for the first time then. Wide and dark, full of fear. 'It happens. Every day. Bureaucracy fails. Things get missed.'

He tried to persuade her, but nothing could change her

mind. They went home, and only after Adam called the prison, pulled a few strings to confirm that he was, indeed, locked up tight, had Romilly accepted defeat and called Dr Jones.

So he knows she won't let it go.

'Come in then,' he agrees grumpily.

She walks through, her eyes taking in her surroundings. He's painfully aware that his current dwelling is nothing like the place they had together. She got the house in the divorce; he didn't want to live somewhere with constant reminders of their marriage. She had chosen the furniture, the décor – something he has no interest in, abundantly clear now.

She correctly guesses at the location of his kitchen and walks through. The unwashed plate is discarded on the side, along with the empty bottles of beer.

'Do you want a drink?' he asks, forcing politeness and gesturing towards his kitchen table. He pushes at the newspapers, the piles of bills, debris from everyday life, clearing some space.

'No, I'm fine.' She sits down carefully, as if touching something might get her soiled in some way. She places the file down in front of her.

He deliberately makes her wait, fetching another beer for himself then taking the chair next to her.

She gets right to the point. 'Here.' She opens the file, pulls out the page from the BBC website. 'These photos weren't up for long,' she continues quickly.

He nods. 'We got them to take them down this morning. They included details we didn't want shared with the public.'

'The Roman numerals.'

'Yes.'

'One for each body.'

He stares at her a moment too long. 'Yes,' he confirms at last.

'He did the same.'

Adam blinks. For the first time he notices the flush of her cheeks, the nervous shake of her hands.

'I've read the files, Romilly. Back then. You know I have. I don't remember anything—'

'It's not in the files. There were facts about that case that they never wanted in the press. The detective in charge was worried about copycats, about people . . .' She pauses. '. . . Continuing his legacy. They redacted everything. Everything but this. It must have been missed.'

She scrabbles in the file again, spreading papers across the table. He recognises news reports from that time. Other bits and pieces: scrawls he can't quite read. Official-looking documents. She finds what she's looking for and passes it to him.

'They couldn't risk it,' she says. 'But I knew. I saw it. I was there.'

'Saw what, Romilly?' he asks slowly. He looks at the report she's passed him: the SOCO report from 1995. The forensics found in the outhouse.

'There were the same markings, on the wall.'

'As this?' He gets up, goes to his bag left in the hallway, and carries the files of the five victims back, opening the top one and pulling out his own crime scene photos. He's annoyed. He's tired, and he knows he'll have to be up early in the morning. Back to a murder investigation with real evidence, not spurious links imagined by his ex-wife. He flicks through the photos quickly then puts one in front of her – the Roman numerals spray-painted in green next to the bodies.

She pauses, staring at the photo. 'No. Not like that,' she says, quieter now. 'They were scratches. On the wall.'

'Scratches? In a torture chamber.' He can't keep the patronising tone out of his voice. He's humouring her now. She realises, and doesn't like it.

'They were clear, Adam. Obvious.'

'And you never mentioned this before?'

'No. It hadn't been important—'

'What numbers were they?'

'XX. Twenty. Down to—'

'So just lines, then. Scratched into the wall?'

'Yes, but . . .' She looks at him, biting her lip. 'I'm not crazy,' she whispers. She looks like she's going to cry, and he feels a wave of sympathy.

'I never said you were.' His face softens, his body relaxes. 'Milly,' he says gently. 'This isn't him. This is some other sicko. He's in prison, you know that.'

She nods slowly, entwining her fingers together in her lap.

'Here,' Adam says. He holds out his bottle of beer. 'I find this helps.'

She smiles weakly, then takes it, tipping it against her mouth for a long swig. She swallows quickly, then has another.

Romilly's phone beeps in her pocket.

'That your boyfriend?'

'Probably.' She pulls it out and reads the message. She places the beer back on the table and stands up, picking up her coat. 'I should be going.'

'Sure.'

Adam follows her to the door, leaning over and opening it. 'You'll leave it be, now. Right, Milly?' he says.

'But—'

'Please. This is a police investigation. I appreciate your . . . help. But leave me to it, now. Please.'

She nods. He watches her walk to her car, her head down, shoulders slumped. He feels sorry for her, he really does. But fuck, this has nothing to do with her. What happened then.

He shuts the front door and goes back into his warm house. He looks at his kitchen table, the mess of paper, and picks up the SOCO report again.

He doesn't remember reading this one – and she's right. It talks about the scratches, the Roman numerals next to the door. Twenty, through to eighteen. There were four victims though, he remembers, so the missing seventeen would join them to the new murders: sixteen down to twelve. Maybe he should consider it. Maybe . . .

He shakes his head decisively. No. No, he shouldn't. This isn't the same. And the man is in prison. For life. There's no way.

No fucking way.

Streamlined Forensic Report (SFR)		MG 22 A	
FORENSIC INFORMATION – CRIME SCENE LOCATION REPORT			
Relates to:	**Operation Hursley**	Crime No:	**00075690/HURS**
Location:	**Blackstone, Hampshire.**	Forensic Case Ref:	**5686/DR/A**
Report provided by:	**Sarah Fox**	Organisation:	**Trenton Forensic Services**
Date of report:	**20 November 1995**		
Findings			

I attended 'The Beeches', Gloucester Road on Sunday, 19 November 1995 with my colleague Steph Stoddart. Also present were DCI Frank Langston and DS David Shepherd.

The address is a three-bedroom detached house. The house itself is generally clean and tidy with no obvious signs of a large-scale disturbance. The front door opens into a hallway with a door leading to the living room to the left, the kitchen at the end of the hallway and the stairs on the right. Upstairs, there are three bedrooms and a bathroom, all accessed from a landing area.

No obvious visible bloodstaining was noted in any of the rooms upstairs or downstairs in the property.

A back door from the kitchen leads out into a large garden, approximately two acres in size. An untended grass lawn opens out to a small overgrown wooded area. An old, broken child's Wendy house is to the left at the beginning of the garden.

The house and grounds are surrounded by woodland on all sides. The nearest residence is approximately half a mile away and cannot be seen or accessed from the property.

A large single-storey outbuilding/shed is located at the end of the garden. It is of concrete construction with a flat roof. It has two windows, but both are boarded up from the outside.

The door to the outbuilding has several locks including two bolt and one Yale key lock. On arrival at the scene, all appeared intact, but unlocked. The main door opens into a small hallway, and another door, secured with two bolt locks. This door leads to one main room, approximately 9 metres by 6 metres.

A number of scratches are engraved on the wooden frame next to the door. These appear to have been made recently and resemble the Roman numerals from eighteen to twenty (XVIII, XIX, and XX.) These are arranged vertically, with twenty at the top and eighteen at the bottom.

The room was dark and generally untidy. Debris, including plates of apparently uneaten food, plastic water bottles, food wrappers, and soiled toilet paper were evident. There was one bucket to the back left corner of the building, appearing to have been used as a toilet, containing apparent faecal material, urine and toilet paper. Another bucket was on the other side of the room, containing water, possibly from the outside water butt. This butt is fed from guttering on the outside of the building.

Two double-bed sized mattresses were on the floor with bloodstained bedding on top. One deceased female was found on one of the mattresses and was covered with bedding. I understand that another female has been seen by paramedics and taken to hospital prior to our arrival. Paramedic paraphernalia was next to the mattress where the injured parties were found.

Extensive bloodstaining was noted in this room, mainly in the form of contact bloodstaining and drips of the blood on the mattresses and bedding, indicating that an injured person or persons have been in this area for some time. Blood pooling was evident across the floor. Areas of damage were noted to the internal side of the door together with further areas of apparent bloodstaining within the damage.

Three large metal cages stood along the back wall, varying in sizes from 120 x 80 x 80 cm, to the smallest at 90 x 60 x 60 cm. Apart from a bloodstained blanket in one, all were empty. Contact bloodstaining was found on the metal bars, as well as clumps of hair together with some apparent skin and brain matter. All doors were open, with padlocks left on the latches. Bloodstaining in the form of impact spatter was found in all three of the cages, on the floors and extending up the walls to the ceiling. The pattern of bloodstaining indicates that an individual or individuals have been subject to an assault within these cages.

The ceiling has one large structural wooden beam running the length of the room. Two large metal hooks are drilled into the beam. An additional metal ring is drilled into the brick wall on the left-hand side. Signs of contact bloodstaining and some apparent skin and body tissue were present on all. One explanation for these findings is that the hooks have been pierced through an individual's skin, causing injury.

The outbuilding internal walls are a breeze-block construction. On examination, extensive insulation was found between the brick walls, and more placed over the windows.

Samples have been taken from the main areas of bloodstaining for DNA profiling tests in an attempt to ascertain from whom the blood has originated. At the time of writing, the search of the grounds is still ongoing and these findings, together with the results of any DNA profiling tests, will be reported separately.

Before

The crash comes just past midnight. The bang of a door being opened with force, slamming back against the wall. He lies in bed, his heart beating hard, his whole body on high alert.

His mother's voice next, gentle and soothing. But even from here he can hear her panic. The fizz from a can of beer, the chatter from the television. His father now, gruff and slurring.

Their talking gets louder. More frantic. He hears footsteps. His mother first, quick patters up the stairs. Then another set: loud thuds, two stairs at a time. Doors bang, shouting. Snippets of an argument that makes no sense to a seven-year-old boy . . . *go to bed . . . tomorrow . . . not now, Maurice, not now . . . please . . .*

Then the sound of a slap, the thump of something falling. He can hear his mother crying, quiet sobs. He knows she'll be trying to suppress it, his father's rage only intensifying in the face of outward emotion.

He creeps to the door of his bedroom and opens it a

crack. Through the narrow space he can see the hallway, his mother lying on the dirty carpet, her hair covering her face. His father stands over her. Still in his muddy black work boots, his heavy overalls. He would have gone straight to the pub after work, spending that month's wages before his mother had a chance to buy food.

As he watches, his father bends down and grabs a fistful of his mother's hair. She cries out, and he drags her, her bare feet trailing across the carpet, her hands scrabbling at his arms. He uses his free hand to punch her – once, twice – in the face. Blood drips to the floor.

He can't look away, although he knows he must. His father throws her roughly onto the bed. He paws at her clothes, ripping some as they're discarded. Her legs are forced open. His father is fumbling with his belt now, pushing his trousers down until they're around his knees.

He doesn't understand what's going on. But he's heard these noises many times, through the wall. The creak of the old mattress, guttural male groans. Sobbing from his mother, after.

He crouches on the carpet, transfixed. The expression on his father's face – it's anger, absorption. He's lost in what he's doing, his hairy belly wobbling in time with his hard thrusts, his eyes screwed shut, muscles tense.

His mother turns her face towards the door. Her left eye is already swollen shut; her nose crusted with blood. She sees him, and her good eye widens with fear.

She mouths a word, but he shakes his head, unable to understand.

She tries again, and this time, he knows.

'Hide,' she's saying. 'Hide.'

DAY 4

TUESDAY

Chapter 17

DCI Cara Elliott is late. Adam scans the coffee shop for the woman he knows from all number of infamous news reports last year, then scowls. He's a busy man, he thinks, people are dead. She could at least be on time. He orders a coffee and carries it across to a far table.

While he waits he reviews the reports from the lab. Details about the fibres found on the blanket have come back: dark green polyester. Man-made, synthetic, often used in insulation, soft furnishings, clothing or cordage. Rope, Adam thinks. Why can't you just say rope?

The analysis on the stain on the blanket is more forthcoming, consisting mainly of chloride, sodium, sulphate, with trace amounts of calcium, potassium, and magnesium. Sea salt.

'Adam?'

He looks up. 'Hi Cara,' he replies, shuffling the paperwork back into the file. 'How are you?'

But he doesn't need to ask, it's obvious from her face.

Black rings circle her eyes, her cheekbones are gaunt; he can tell she's thin even under the shapeless black jumper she's wearing.

'Sorry I'm late.'

'Thank you for meeting me.'

She smiles weakly as she sits down. 'I'm not sure Marsh gave me much choice.'

'Do you want a coffee? Tea?'

'No. Thank you.'

'What are you working on now?'

'Still CID, but barely. Robberies, GBH, B and E. The stuff no one else wants.'

'Right.'

Niceties done, they sit in silence, until she points at the file in front of him.

'This it?' she asks. Adam nods. 'Can I see?'

'Be my guest.'

He pushes the file across, and she opens it. He watches her face closely as she flicks through the bloody crime scene photos, the close-up shots of the victim's wounds.

'And the attacks are violent, frenzied?' she asks.

'On the first two. A complete lack of self-control.'

'And the others?'

'More planned. Kept them for a bit.'

'Wrapped the bodies in blankets. Shows remorse.' She pauses, studying the reports, and Adam sees the DCI she once was. 'And you think it's one offender?' she asks. 'Even with the mixed MOs?'

'That's our hypothesis. Same dump site. And there are other similarities. The exsanguination. The slow evolution to his method of killing.'

'To what aim?'

97

'That we don't know.' Adam pauses. He knows the question he has to ask. 'And you're sure it's not—'

She looks up sharply. 'It's not the Echo Man, no.'

'Not even if you factor in Richard Chase?'

She shakes her head. 'Shenton looked into it,' she says, referring to her DC. Adam has met him a few times: a quiet studious man, pale and unassuming – and their resident expert on serial killers. 'Chase had some of the same characteristics, if you consider the knife, the stabbing. But he consumed his victims, cutting out and keeping their organs to eat later. He was disorganised, frenzied. Always.' She pauses, deep in thought. 'This isn't him. The Echo Man was rigorous and obsessive. He never deviated from the MO of the serial killers he was copying.'

Adam reflects on her turn of phrase. She's talking about the Echo Man in abstract terms, like he was someone distant to her. Unknown.

'Plus, as you know,' she says, her eyes still fixed on the case file in front of her. 'We caught him.'

Adam nods. Eventually, he thinks.

'What's your view on our guy?' he says instead.

She sighs, and flicks through the pages again. 'The nature of the first disorganised kill, and the fact he was less careful with how he disposed of the most recent victim, would suggest an escalation. Even if you take into consideration the kidnapping, the slow torture of these two. Something's changed. Led him to just dump the latest body. He doesn't care about staying hidden anymore.'

'Why not?'

'It takes too much time? He's got an aim? Some goal he's trying to get to?'

Adam thinks about the numbers painted next to the

bodies. The counting down. Is it possible he's trying to get to zero?

But Cara's still talking: 'Serial killers normally fall into one of four categories.' She holds her hand up, ticking them off on her fingers. 'Visionary – the mental cases in the grip of psychotic breaks. Two. Mission orientated – they have a goal, usually to rid the world of a certain category of people. Hedonistic killers get pleasure from the act of killing itself, whether out of lust, material gain or just the thrill of inducing pain or terror. And finally, power and control.'

'Can't you argue all killers are driven by power and control?'

'To some extent, yes. But there's always a primary motivator. What's your guy getting from it?'

Now she's started talking her face has come to life. She's more animated; clearly her former career as a detective on murder investigations was something she had enjoyed. And despite his reluctance, it's interesting to meet her properly. Up close.

He knows her mainly by reputation, their names often spoken in the same sentence. Cara Elliott and Adam Bishop. The two DCIs from the two big HQs – and his competition for the next promotion. There's always a rumour making the rounds that they're looking for another detective superintendent, that Marsh can't run two Major Crimes Units alone forever, despite the budget restraints. And Elliott was a good cop. Solid. Maybe even Marsh's favourite.

But that was *before*.

'Bishop?' She's staring at him now, and he pulls his chain of thought back to the investigation.

'Sorry, what?'

'I said, he'll make a mistake. Someone will see him, if they haven't already. And' – she pauses, tapping her finger on the timeline Adam has hastily scrawled on a piece of A4 – 'take a look at the dates. Something triggered this guy. What was the inciting incident? Why did he start to kill *then*? You can't tell me that someone with this level of instability kept it under wraps for years then started killing at random. This level of crazy isn't something that happens overnight.'

Adam frowns. It's a good point. And he's not enjoying the lecture, Cara asking questions he should have already considered. 'How is he choosing his victims?' she continues. 'Why *these* people? If he's stalking them, chances are he's already looking for the next. You need to catch this guy. With a level of violence this high, there is no way he'll be satisfied. He'll kill again.'

'I know that, Elliott,' he says sharply, and she looks away quickly.

'Sorry,' she replies, chastened. 'I didn't intend to add to the pressure you're under.'

He smiles. 'I'm fine.' He doesn't want to betray any weakness and he pulls the case file back towards him, busying himself in the pages.

Sensing his hostility, she stands up and pulls her coat from the back of her chair, putting it on. 'Good luck with the case, DCI Bishop,' she says.

'It'll be fine,' he replies. 'We'll catch him.'

He feels her hesitate, and he looks up.

'That's what I thought,' she says quietly, 'when we started out.' She nods slowly. 'Make sure you do. Before he takes everything from you.' She pauses, her face downcast.

'Before he ruins your life. Like the Echo Man did to mine.'

Adam watches her go, her shoulders slumped. He remembers the operation last year. He was desperate to be involved, to be a part of the biggest murder case the UK had ever known. But Marsh had sidelined him, leaving him and Jamie and a few DCs picking up the rest of the cases that came in, keeping Major Crimes running from the different HQ as the Echo Man investigation devoured everything in its path.

But Cara Elliott hadn't been up to the job, had she? It had left her beaten and destroyed. This one is his.

His phone rings and he answers it.

'Boss?' It's Jamie. He sounds panicked. 'We have another body.'

'What? Where?' And so soon? he thinks, but he doesn't say it. Cara's right, the killer is escalating.

Jamie gives him the details, and Adam closes the file decisively, pushing it back into his bag.

He is nothing like DCI Cara Elliott, he thinks as he runs out to his car. He'll be fine.

Chapter 18

'This is one of ours? You're sure?'

Dr Ross turns to face him. Adam can read the disparaging look behind his mask.

'Who else is the SIO on exsanguinated corpses right now?'

They're standing in full white suits, outside the back gate of a small, terraced house. A plastic box of recycling is full to bursting, bottles spilling out onto the concrete next to fag butts and the roaches from joints.

'I'll let SOCO capture the rest of the scene, then I'll supervise the removal. Get him back to the mortuary and have a look for certain.'

Adam cranes his neck to see inside. 'What's your initial assessment?' he asks.

'Massive blood loss, compounded by a blow to the head. And he's fresh, Bishop. Dead no longer than eight hours. Body's still warm.' The doctor laughs darkly. 'But you'll see. Decide for yourself.'

Adam nods in acknowledgement, then heads into the small scrubby back garden where Jamie is standing.

'Watch out for the dog shit,' Jamie comments. Adam looks around the square of patchy lawn covered in small brown mounds. 'Neighbours called it in,' he continues. 'Said the house was strangely quiet. Dog barks all hours, day and night, and there was nothing this morning. Looked out into the garden and the back door was open. When they came down to investigate, they noticed . . . that.' Jamie points inside, where Adam can see a mass of SOCOs in white suits, photographing the mess. 'Wayne Oxford. Twenty-five. Single. In there.'

'Where's the dog?' Adam asks.

Jamie's eyes narrow above his mask. 'Haven't found it yet.' He points into the house. 'Follow me.'

Adam does as he's told, stepping over the threshold into the kitchen. He immediately stops. Inside is a massacre. Trails across the floor, a large pool in the middle, spatters up the walls.

The blood is everywhere.

The body sits in the centre of the room, slumped on a kitchen chair. His arms hang loosely by his sides, hands completely encrusted in dried crimson. His face is pale, his lips white. A gruesome puddle surrounds him.

'Well, fuck,' Adam manages after a pause.

Jamie nods grimly.

'Where has all the blood come from?'

He crouches down carefully on the footplates next to the body, squinting at the drooping arms. Large gashes run the length of his forearms, gaping wounds, wet and bloody. Tendons and veins are clearly visible against the whitened flesh.

'This is unlike the others,' Adam comments. 'Not restrained, or a frenzied killing.'

103

'Nasty bash to his head though,' Jamie says, and Adam can see it now. Hair matted, blood congealed around the wound and down the back of his neck, soaking the T-shirt.

'Enough to knock him out?'

'Possibly.'

'Bishop?' A shout from the other side of the kitchen attracts his attention, and the SOCO waves an arm. Adam heads across, then follows to where the gloved hand is pointing. On the dirty lino of the kitchen floor, half in a blood pool, is a large bottle of cheap supermarket vodka.

He raises an eyebrow. 'Murder weapon?' he asks in astonishment.

'Let's hope so. But that's not all.'

Adam crouches down, looking closer. 'Is that . . .?'

The SOCO nods. 'Could be a fingerprint.'

Adam feels a surge of excitement. 'Get that processed. And quick.'

He backs away, letting the man do his work. This could be it, he thinks. All they need is one good match, and they'll haul this fucker in. Maybe there's even DNA, and they can really nail this bastard to the wall.

He didn't abduct this victim. He didn't lose control and knife him dozens of times. He killed him here, in his own kitchen.

Bleeding out slowly. In a lake of his own blood.

104

I watch from afar as the police flood the house. I'm no more than a curious early morning commuter, parked, having a quiet coffee before I start my shift. I am used now to the horror after, the self-flagellating masochism of what I've done. How I killed him.

The man was alone. He was boring. There was nothing significant about him. He had brown hair and he was skinny; I could tell he wasn't someone who went to the gym. He was wearing shapeless tracksuit bottoms and a cheap T-shirt he bought from Tesco. A three-pack: one blue, one black, one white. I hated him for that. He should have taken more pride.

Different from you, in every way.

I watched him from my car. Parked in his road, I could see through his living-room window. All his lights were on, his curtains open; he made no effort with privacy. Ease of access, simple to work out who he was. How much of a problem he'd be.

I'd seen him a few times. It wasn't much, his life. He had few friends. He went to work, sat behind his computer. Had a fag at lunchtime with a girl he called 'babe' and who did a wanker sign behind his back. He wolf-whistled at women as he walked home. Stared a little too long at their breasts. He had a dog: a small white yappy thing that barked incessantly when he went to work. His neighbours must have hated him. I hope they appreciate what I did.

I watched him: sitting on his sofa, shovelling Doritos into his mouth as he watched a serial killer movie on TV. Oh, the irony.

I went around to the back door and tried the handle. It was unlocked from where he let the horrible dog out into the garden. I opened the door and the small scraggy thing rushed towards me, barking and nipping at my feet. I grabbed it, holding it up by its collar and it squirmed in my hand, trying to get at my fingers with its sharp teeth.

'Shut up!' I heard him shout from the living room. It was still barking, more frantic now. I carried it out into the garden and threw it across the lawn, where it landed, before angrily hurtling back to me as I closed the door in its face. It continued to bark, muted by double glazing.

I walked slowly into the kitchen. I listened, but there was nothing. Just the noise from the television, blaring at full volume. I looked around. I needed something heavy. Blunt. A large empty glass bottle of vodka waited on the side. I picked it up, weighed it in my hand. It would do the job.

I walked slowly towards him. He didn't move, eyes still locked on the murder on the screen, unaware of the violence about to be unleashed in his own living room. I lifted the bottle above my head, then brought it down, fast.

106

The glass didn't break, but I felt something give. His skull splintering, skin splitting. Blood bubbled through the gash. I prepared myself for another hit, but it wasn't required. He collapsed slowly to the side. Mouth open, unchewed crisps visible, crusting on his yellowed teeth.

I didn't waste any time. I grabbed his hands, heaving him from the sofa. He fell ungracefully to the floor, leaving a trail of blood from his head wound as I dragged him into the kitchen. He wasn't heavy. Scrawny, disgusting creature that he was. I see why he was chosen. Why he was so right.

With effort, I got him into the chair. His head slumped forward; his tongue lolled. There was no need to restrain him; this guy wasn't going to wake up soon.

The dog was still barking outside his back door. I didn't want anything to disturb me, so I opened it. The little terrier rushed back inside, then stopped. It knew something was wrong, but it wasn't fast enough: I grabbed it by the scruff then hurled it with all my strength against the wall. It fell to the ground, stunned, then came to its senses and went for me. The next time I wasn't messing around.

I reached for it, missed, and it bit my wrist, holding tight. The sudden pain, the surprise, enraged me – an influx of overwhelming hatred and anger. I felt my heart race, my head blur as I wrenched it from my arm and held it in front of my face by its collar. It quietened then, watching me with dark brown eyes. That was its saving grace.

I carried it, legs dangling, to the hallway cupboard, opened the door and threw it in. It cowered in the darkness. It knew a fellow predator; it knew when it was beaten. I closed the door, shaking. Fear and panic threatened, I needed to get this done.

I crouched in front of the man, then took one of his hands in mine. I rolled it over, so his white, clean forearm was exposed. Ready and waiting.

In life he had no purpose. He was not worthy.

In death, he would form a part of something. Something big. Something worthwhile.

It excites me. For the rest that are still to come.

I will get it right. For you.

Chapter 19

Adam watches as the bottle is photographed then carefully placed in a clean, white evidence box and rushed off for processing. Maybe they'll get lucky from the print. Maybe they won't. But every shred of evidence brings them closer to finding this guy. He feels the thrill of the chase, a burn of optimism in his stomach. *This* is why he loves the job.

He moves out of the kitchen and stands in the doorway of the deceased man's living room. He looks at the mess. Even from behind his protective mask, he can smell the old beer and fried food trodden into the carpet. An empty plastic tray that once contained a ready meal sits on the scratched coffee table, a fork inside. Two beer cans next to that. He feels a worrying churn, a jolt of connection to his own solitary life.

So, this guy had been having a night in. Dinner, beer, something on the telly. Adam looks back to the kitchen, then at the bloodstains on the sofa. Had the victim realised someone had broken in, or had he been blissfully unaware when the bottle cracked down on his skull? Was it a crime of opportunity, rather than planning? Adam recognises the bottle of vodka from similar ones in the empties outside. The offender comes to kill – needs to kill? – his normal routine disturbed by the police flooding his usual dump site. He grabs whatever's to hand, leaves the victim to bleed out on his kitchen floor, then what? Calmly walks away?

Adam hears a figure join him in the room and turns. Jamie's standing there.

'Any joy from next door?' he asks.

Jamie shakes his head. 'Fuck all useful. Heard the dog barking, then silence. No screams for help. The sort of neighbourhood that keeps to themselves.'

'Any strange cars in the road? How did he get away from here?' Adam's mind goes back to Cara's words: someone must have seen him. 'He would have blood on him. Hardly inconspicuous.'

'There's a network of alleyways down the back. We have the same at our place, it connects all the gardens. Easy to slip away, unnoticed. Especially last night.'

'Hmm.'

He pauses, and in the relative quiet he hears a noise. A soft whine, then a yelp. He stops, listens, turning his head this way and that to get a gauge on where it's coming from. Then, there it is again, from the cupboard. He walks across and opens the door; the small white dog springs instantly from the darkness, a mess of indescribable stench on his fur. He must have been in there all night, nowhere else to soil. It leaps excitedly around Adam and Jamie, until Adam bends down and gathers it, shit and all, into his arms. The dog licks his face; Adam recoils. But he notices something else in his fur. A trace of red.

'Here.' Adam gets the attention of the closest SOCO and passes him the dog. The man takes it reluctantly. 'Swab that.'

'You don't think it's from the victim?'

'Maybe. But if that was the case, the dog would be covered.' Adam's phone starts ringing, distracting him from the mess. 'And for God's sake, then someone give him a bath.'

Adam walks out of the house, back into the garden, Jamie following. Free of the cordon, Adam pulls his phone out of his pocket and redials. Romilly answers immediately.

'I saw it on the news,' she says. 'It's another one?'

'Yes.'

'Does it fit?'

'No. There's nothing here, Milly. If we're following your hypothesis, he's number eleven but it's not written anywhere. No spray paint. Not etched into the wall.' She's silent at the other end of the phone. He knows she doesn't believe him. 'Sorry, I have to go. I have a job to do.'

He says goodbye and hangs up before she has a chance to protest.

Jamie gives him a look.

'Was that Romilly?' he asks after a moment. 'About the case?'

'She has a theory. A connection.'

Jamie looks confused for a moment, then almost double-takes. 'You don't mean . . . to what happened nearly thirty years ago?'

Adam explains the numbers on the wall of the outhouse, in 1995. The numbers that somehow connect to the ones at the dump site.

'And this one could be the same?' Jamie asks.

111

'Except there's nothing here,' Adam says with a sweep of his arm.

'Right. But . . .'

'But what?'

Jamie pauses. When he starts talking again his tone is measured. 'If someone else brought this theory to you, someone without your history together. Without all those unresolved feelings—'

'They're not unresolved.'

Jamie rolls his eyes. 'Fine. Okay then: someone who knows that case as well as she does. Would you have believed them?'

'No! It's ridiculous,' he repeats. But he stops. Jamie has a point. Annoying sod that he is. A niggle of disquiet starts up in his brain.

'And how is Rom?' Jamie asks after a beat.

Adam glances at him. 'You know better than I do, mate. Your missus and her are still friends.'

'I meant, for you. How do you feel talking to her again?'

'Fine.'

'Just fine?'

Adam feels Jamie's stare. 'Weird, okay? If you must know. Like nothing has changed, yet everything has. What's her boyfriend like?'

'Nice guy. A little dull.' He pauses. 'He's not anything like you.'

'In what way?'

They move to the side as two SOCOs enter the crime scene.

'Pretty boy, takes pride in his appearance—' Jamie says.

'I'm offended.'

'—polite, nice. Has the sort of job he walks away from at the end of the day.'

'What does he do?'

'He's a physiotherapist. They met at the hospital. And he's buff as fuck. Makes me feel very inadequate.' Jamie pats his rotund belly under his protective suit.

'You seem to know him well?'

'Yeah, a bit. They've been round for dinner.'

'Once?'

A pause. 'A few times,' Jamie mutters reluctantly.

The two men stand in silence. Adam thinks about this guy. He wouldn't have pitched Romilly as the sort of woman who went for looks, but maybe he was wrong about her. He'd been wrong about so much else, after all.

Adam pulls his hood up and heads back inside. The SOCOs have finished photographing the scene; Ross has resumed his inspection. The body is now laid out on white plastic, showing the large bloody gashes up the inside of the man's forearms. He doesn't need Ross to tell him cause of death: it's obvious.

'How long would it have taken him to bleed out in that way?' Adam asks.

'A while,' Ross replies without looking up. He prods at the laceration with a gloved finger. 'Despite how it looks, the wounds weren't deep. I'd have expected clotting. I wonder . . .' His voice trails off as he starts to work his way up the man's arms, pushing his T-shirt higher. 'Yes, here it is.'

He sits back on his haunches and points; Adam leans down to where the pathologist is indicating. It's a small red mark, almost imperceptible.

'My guess is toxicology will show large amounts of an anticoagulant. Something like heparin or warfarin.'

'Rat poison?'

The pathologist chuckles. 'How do you think it kills the rats, DCI Bishop? It's a blood thinner. No chance for him then, even without the head wound.' He continues his survey of the man's arm. 'Another one here, and here.'

'Another what?'

'Needle mark,' Ross replies. 'Although these are a bigger gauge.'

Adam feels his vision swim, and stands up quickly, averting his gaze. He closes his eyes for a second, then opens them again, noticing Jamie's quizzical look.

The pathologist is still talking. '. . . more pronounced. Directly into the vein. Odd. I wonder . . .' He pauses, still prodding around in the bloody flesh. 'Why would someone insert a needle like that?' he murmurs to himself.

Adam clears his throat. 'And how severe is the head wound?' he asks, trying to divert Ross's attention from the needle marks.

'Caved his skull in. I'll take a proper look at the mortuary but I don't think there was much brain function by the time he was put in the chair.'

Adam mutters his thanks, then steps away from the body. He gestures to Jamie as he walks out of the house and back to the street; his DS follows him. He ducks under the cordon and lights a cigarette immediately.

The niggle persists. Another man is dead. He can't ignore any possible route of enquiry; however ridiculous he believes it is.

'Let's pretend Romilly is right,' he begins. He sees Jamie give a small smile, then quickly hide it. 'Yeah, yeah, you smug git. You're right. Maybe I don't give Romilly enough benefit of the doubt.'

114

'I wouldn't like to say, boss,' Jamie says, smirking.

Adam ignores him. 'So. If the murders in the outhouse in 1995 are linked, then it all began there, with number twenty. Then we had sixteen through to twelve on Saturday night, possibly one more today, although I can't see it.' He sees Jamie about to talk again. 'And I know what you're thinking. Why twenty? Why not start from fifteen, or ten, or some other random number?'

'It's significant somehow,' Jamie says slowly.

'Exactly,' Adam replies. 'I need you to go back to the station. Get the analysts started on the research. What stands out about the number twenty? What does it mean, in literature, in music?'

'Mathematically?'

'Anything. Everything. Let's have some theories.'

Jamie nods, his car keys already in his hand.

'And phone Control. Get them to send a unit over to the old house and do an address check. Have a good look around.'

'What are you going to do, boss?' Jamie asks.

'I need to make a call.'

He watches Jamie leave, then he pulls his phone out of his pocket. He searches for a number, and pauses.

If Romilly is right, if all this started with the death of four women, nearly thirty years ago, then this is worse than anyone imagined. This career-defining case, the one he felt such anticipation for barely four days ago, suddenly feels personal.

The man may be in prison, but his legacy looms. A shadow, haunting and dark. Closer than ever before.

115

Chapter 20

Elijah weighs up the heavy figure in his hand. He places the king on the board on its new square then takes his finger away, completing the move. He likes everything about chess. The feel of the solid wooden pieces. The intricate movements. That moment when the plan slots into place and you know there's only three moves until checkmate.

He hates to lose, but he's playing against himself. Quick decisions, swapping colours, not even bothering to turn the board. The room bustles around him – an argument breaks out, punches thrown, officers intervene – but he's used to it. The rhythm of the prison, like a heartbeat.

He feels a tap on his shoulder. One of the guards stands behind him.

'Who's winning, Doc?' he asks.

'Me, of course. Do you care to join me? What's our tally? Twelve-one?'

The guard smiles. He knows that Elijah had let him win. Just that once.

'Not today. We've received a visitor request. I know the guv'nor would say yes, but I wanted to run it by you first.'

Elijah raises an eyebrow, interested.

'The police are asking for an interview. DCI Adam Bishop.'

Elijah looks away again. Not unexpected. But not the person he wants. Not yet.

'Turn it down,' he replies.

The guard looks surprised but nods in agreement and leaves Elijah to his game. He moves the black queen forward.

'Check,' he whispers as he knocks another piece from the board.

Chapter 21

Rom didn't sleep well last night. Dreams of darkness and metal; screaming and cries for help. She wrenched herself awake almost hourly, staring at the stars projected at the ceiling, her body close and warm to her boyfriend.

She's already called in sick to work. Her junior doctors can handle the day; she's at the end of the phone if they need her. And now there's been another murder. She hesitates but can't resist phoning Adam. He's brusque, he still doesn't want her there.

When they first met, she was surprised when he told her what he did for a living. Detective in the CID.

'Yeah,' he said with a shrug. 'Murders and the like.'

Romilly couldn't imagine how this man – how this man who'd poured his heart out to her, whose nervous laugh she'd realised hid a mass of fragilities – could deal with the most violent crimes without flinching. There was something about Adam she was drawn to from the start. She liked the sound of his voice, the low burr rising to a raucous cackle when it was something he liked. And he listened to her, his head resting on one hand, leg tilted up, knee in front of him. She recognised that knee for what it was: a protective shield. And slowly it lowered. The physical manifestation of the mental barrier.

Their engagement was short, the wedding small but perfect. Neither of them close to their families, so a few friends seemed right. And they were so in love. Romilly remembers those first few years. The two of them against the world.

Since the divorce, she's managed to put some distance between them. Any time they tried to be friends, or even scrape together some semblance of civility, it fell apart with a resounding crash, causing chaos for the people around them. The couple closest to them, Jamie and Pippa, had often taken the brunt.

'I'm not going to take sides, but . . .' Pippa said on more than one occasion. Female solidarity eclipsed all else, it seems. Even despite what Romilly had done.

And Jamie has to be loyal to Adam. Adam is his boss, after all. They spend every day together. Adam tried to explain it once: a brotherhood. Bonds created by the environment they work in. If you're not in the police, you can't understand. *You* can't understand, was the unspoken message.

But now, here she is. On the outskirts, but her brain pulling her in to these brutal murders. A serial killer: she knows about those – but only what happened then. How can she help? She's tried to convince him. She should walk away. Especially given the nightmares.

She saw Phil's expression over breakfast: concern, with a touch of hostility. He can't understand why she doesn't let it go. Whatever Adam says, she still believes it's all linked. It is too much of a coincidence not to be true.

She knows what Phil would say – you need to get some distance. But she can't, for reasons he'll never understand.

He went to work, leaving with a chaste peck on the cheek. She wanted to chase after him, to apologise, but what was she saying sorry for? Talking to her ex-husband? Pushing her way into a case that has nothing to do with her? He should trust her, she thinks, summoning a wave of righteous anger, although she knows, deep in her heart, it's not that. He's worried about her, that's all.

But she can't stop. Won't.

Something pulls her in. Something that tastes sour at the back of her throat. Something she knows is bad for her but she consumes it anyway. Cheap white wine. A kebab late at night.

The guilt from a time long past.

Through all her musing, she hears the clatter of the letter box as the post drops through. It's a convenient distraction, and she walks to the hallway to pick it up. The usual mail: the catalogues from clothing companies she hasn't used in years, bills she needs to pay. And one other.

She turns the white envelope over in her hand, a slow sinking feeling working its way from her stomach to her fingertips. Her name and address is written on the front in black block capitals she doesn't recognise, but the franking stamp in the top right corner is unmistakable: HM Prison Belmarsh.

Her hands start to shake. She puts it down on the table, but she can't take her eyes off it and picks it up again. Even though it's just paper and glue, it feels hot. Charged with something not from this world.

Phil would tell her to wait until he got home and they'll

open it together. Adam would say to rip it into tiny pieces: ever the avoidant.

But she couldn't do that. What would Dr Jones say? *He has no power to hurt you now.*

With trembling fingers, she rips the envelope open. Inside are two small pieces of paper. The first is a newspaper clipping, and she recognises it. Front page news on *The Sun*, reporting the murders in the only way they know: sensationalist and overblown. Not that they'd had to try hard, with details like this. The first photo shows the dump site in all its mess and squalor, crime scene techs in their white suits going about their work. Distinctive from any number of crime photos by the fact there were five separate cordons, five separate blue plastic tents. But the second photo they'd used surprised her. It had clearly been taken outside the police station, and showed Adam talking to Jamie. The heading: *Senior Investigating Officer DCI Adam Bishop, and colleague.*

The newspaper article has been carefully cut out. Precise, neat edges. But the second piece of paper almost makes her heart stop.

Her chest tightens. She can't breathe. She drops to her knees on her hallway floor, the note still clutched in her hand. It's a piece of crisp white writing paper, thick and expensive. With a message, written in black fountain pen ink, in a handwriting as familiar as her own.

Six words, that blur her vision with tears. That stop her thoughts dead, leaving her gasping and weak.

You need to talk to me, the note says.

Chapter 22

Adam calls time at nine p.m. Energy has dissipated from the room – there is too much waiting. For the post-mortem results, the further analysis of the fibres. For the fingerprint that is taking too fucking long. They have no good leads to follow; they all need a break. Adam knows that if there's anything important Maggie Clarke will call him from the lab.

He shouts across the desks, 'That's it, wrap up what you're doing and go home. See your families. See your kids. And anyone that doesn't want to do that, come with me to the pub.'

A cheer rings out. Coats are thrown on. The usual suspects, the ones with kids and wives, head off fast before Adam can change his mind. Jamie stands by his desk, waiting.

'Why aren't you going back to your beautiful new wife?' Adam asks.

'She's out with the girls.'

'So you need to pretend you're still young and have a life and come out with me?'

'Exactly.'

Adam laughs. 'Let's go,' he shouts out. 'I'll get the first round.'

The first round turns into two and three. Food is ordered: pizzas, chips, burgers. Unhealthy pub grub to mop up the beer. There's a small group of them remaining by eleven including the new DC, Ellie Quinn. She's clearly drunk; Adam makes a mental note to persuade her onto soft drinks next.

And she's not the only one. Jamie's sunk a few pints and is leaning against a table next to Adam, his head at an angle, his eyes half closed.

'She talks about you to Pippa,' he's saying, his words running together. 'There's still something there.'

'If she does, it's only because she enjoys slagging me off.'

'Mabbe,' Jamie slurs. 'Or she still loves you.'

'I very much doubt it, mate,' Adam says, his gaze drifting around the pub. The other detectives are loud and boisterous, forcing cheer into their voices. Adam's seen it before, a thin veneer of normalcy to cover up the horror of the murders they're obliged to live through. 'And when are you going to give promotion to DI a go, Jamie?' he says, changing the subject. 'A little exam, a few interviews. You've got the experience, no problem.'

'And leave you?' Jamie comments. 'You couldn't cope without me.'

'That's true. But I'll manage.' He depends on his best DS more than he should, and Adam finds that worrying in itself. That reliance, trust in another person. He gives his friend a hearty clap to the back. 'There'll be more biscuits to go around if you fuck off, that's for sure.'

123

Jamie laughs.

'Now you,' Adam continues, 'need to go home. And sober up before your lovely new wife realises her mistake.'

Jamie downs the last few mouthfuls of his beer in one with a nod, plonks the glass heavily on the table, then sways out of the pub without a parting glance.

Adam takes a swig of his own pint as he watches him leave, a flicker of envy dancing in his consciousness. Jamie is lucky. The new wife, the promise of a promotion on his horizon. Maybe kids, a family. All things Jamie deserves. Because he meant what he said on Sunday. Jamie is a good bloke. Loyal, steady, solid. Descriptors Adam would never apply to himself. He glances across, then makes a beeline towards the bar. More beers, maybe a shot or two. Anything to push away the twitch of self-doubt threatening at the corner of his mind.

The clock ticks around and the pub closes. They put Quinn in a taxi home. The last few stragglers move on to a pub with a late licence; Adam senses an opportunity to slip away.

He doesn't want his colleagues with him on his next stop. He's drunk, unsteady on his feet; the alcohol has only fed his insecurities rather than soothed them. He walks down the high street, taking the well-worn path trodden so many times before. He needs a distraction; replace those thoughts of Romilly and his dead marriage. And if he wants that, the bar is as good a place as any.

He's in quickly with a nod from the bouncer and heads towards the source of alcohol, getting served straight away. He downs a shot there and then, taking the bottle of beer with him.

Few understand the draw here, but for Adam it's easy. Close proximity to alcohol, loud music to muffle his thoughts. Drinking alone at home makes him feel maudlin, pathetic, while at least here he is out, circulating around like-minded souls. People who don't pay him enough attention to judge. Company without commitment; they ask nothing from him, too concerned with problems of their own.

From a safe distance, he watches the crowd. A Tuesday night brings in a different group. Younger. Students, most of them, judging by the poster on the wall advertising cheap drinks with a valid NUS card. People with fewer responsibilities and even fewer reasons to get up in the morning.

And even Adam knows it's getting late. He checks the messages on his phone: nothing from the lab. Mobile reception slides in and out, it's patchy down here. But possible. It's okay. One more drink, and he'll leave. But as he's downing the last dregs in his bottle, a woman sidles up to him, tall glass in her hand.

'Are you here alone?' she asks with a gentle touch of his arm.

It's rare, but it happens – approaches from women unable to resist the brooding stranger in the shadows. He assesses her slowly. She's tipsy, but not drunk. She knows what she's doing. But there's a level of confidence that seems almost forced. A fragility behind the smile. But who is he to judge? Everyone has something they're searching for. Some hide it better than others.

He continues his appraisal. It might be okay. He feels a pull – a yearning for company, loneliness demanding to be appeased, however fleeting.

125

'Do you want to join me?' Adam replies.

She smiles up at him. 'For a drink? No. For something else? Maybe.'

She runs her hand up his arm. Her cheeks are pink behind the layers of make-up, her hair wild around her face. It's clear what she wants, a rarity nowadays. And an opportunity he's loath to pass up.

'Shall we take this conversation somewhere else?' she asks.

The women's toilets are nicer than the men's, he thinks as she steers him inside. There's no one by the sinks, and she pushes him towards the cubicle at the far end. She locks the door, then grabs his face and snogs him, hard.

Adam's surprised, but not disinterested. She tastes of something sweet, Red Bull maybe, with the energy to match. Her dress is short, her legs bare. He slides his fingers up her thighs: she's hot, slightly sweaty. He can feel her hands in his shirt, then fumbling with his belt.

They hear someone else come into the toilets – two women, talking. The woman giggles, her mouth still pressed against his, and now her hand is down his trousers. He presses his lips together, forcing himself to stay quiet but fuck, he's not sure how long he can stand this.

He grabs her wrist, stopping her, and she looks up, a wicked grin on her face. A flush from the toilets, conversation fading as the women leave and the door opens and closes. The woman – still nameless, to his shame – backs away from him, then, maintaining eye contact, pulls her knickers down and places them very deliberately on the closed toilet seat. She puts one hand on the wall of the cubicle, the other on the other side and pulls herself up, her dress now bunched around her waist. Christ, she's not messing around.

Adam doesn't wait. Condom out of his wallet, trousers around his knees, he pulls her legs around his waist and fucks her. Her hands in his hair, his mouth on her neck. No questions asked. A warm body, a moment of connection. A meeting of hot skin when he needs it the most.

Concentrating on one thing and one thing alone, the feeling of this random woman on his dick, pushing all thoughts of his ex-wife out of his mind. Her tongue in his mouth, his hands on her ass. The sweat, the spit, the futile fucking carelessness of it all.

He feels his mobile vibrate against his leg from the pocket of his trousers, but he ignores it. It stops, then starts again.

He knows he needs to answer it, but all other desires overtake his rational thought. Because this feels so good. Awkward, uncomfortable, but better than the awful sinking feeling he's experienced since Romilly walked back into his life. He just wants this woman here, feeling the heat build, the pressure, skin against skin—

His phone rings again.

'Shit,' he mutters under his breath. He can't ignore it any longer. 'Wait a moment,' he directs to the woman, who pulls away from him, a scowl on her face.

'Adam?' the voice at the other end shouts. It's Jamie, but something's wrong.

'What's up?'

'Adam . . .' The voice again, something like a howl. Reception cuts in and out, Adam curses again. He can't make out what he's saying.

The woman sighs and pulls away from him, her two

feet back on the ground, pulling her skirt down. Adam awkwardly uses one hand to pull his boxers and trousers up.

'Jamie? What's going on?'

He can hear a scattering of words now. A sentence cut into two. 'She's . . .' Jamie's saying, '. . . not sure . . . called you.'

Adam frowns.

'Jamie . . .' he starts, but then for one fraction of a second reception catches and Adam hears what his DS is saying. And it makes his whole world screech to a halt.

'She's disappeared, Adam,' Jamie shouts. 'Pippa. She's gone.'

Before

It begins with the belt. The sadist's tool of choice. A length of brown leather. Aged and worn to a sheen, the buckle at one end.

He doesn't know what's going on, not at first. He hears his father pacing the house. Angry, thumping beats, fading to slower measured steps. Then the count. Starting at twenty, and slowly, softly, working his way down.

He sits in his hiding place, behind the sofa. Confused. Listening. His father is closer now, in the room. Checking behind one chair, then another. He can smell him; the pervading cigarette smoke. Mud, diesel, tar. The unmistakable tang of cheap spirits sweated from pores.

'Come out, come out. Wherever you are.' The words are friendly, the tone anything but. Breath chokes his throat. Moisture disappears from his mouth.

Eleven. Ten. Nine.

He feels a rough hand on his foot, fingers grab at his hair. Pain in his scalp as he is pulled roughly to his feet.

'Nine,' his father calls, triumphantly.

He squeaks as he's dragged into the centre of the living room.

'Nine,' his father repeats. 'Nine punishments.'

Punishment for what, he doesn't know. But the how will soon become clear. A hand on his back shoves him to his knees. Made to bend, his head pushed painfully between his legs. A rush of cold air on his bare back as his T-shirt is pulled up.

'Stay there.'

He doesn't dare move. The number repeats in his head. Nine. Nine what?

He hears the jangle of the belt buckle. The swish of leather as it is pulled from his jeans.

Then the crack. The surprise. The burn, the sting as it hits his skin. He cries out. Tries to get up, but his father pushes him hard, back into place.

'Eight,' he says.

The slap of leather in the air. The next rush of agony. Hot. Wet. Blood, running. He tastes copper in his mouth. He must have bitten his tongue. Tears run down his cheeks. Disbelief in the sudden horror of what is happening.

seven

six

Numbness takes over. His hands ball into fists. He screams out for his mother but she is gone, unconscious in another room.

five

Worse now. Blows onto broken flesh. The flick of blood from the belt onto the wall. He would look at those spatters later. Wonder if they came from four or three.

He doesn't remember two or one; the agony dragging his consciousness into black.

The countdown from twenty ends. Seared into his skin. With pain and hatred and fear.

Part 2

Into whatsoever houses I enter, I will enter to help the sick, and I will abstain from all intentional wrong-doing and harm, especially from abusing the bodies of man or woman, bond or free.

The Hippocratic Oath, translated from Ancient Greek, estimated at fourth or fifth century BC

Chapter 23

Adam has been to Jamie's house on many occasions, but not like this. The normally peaceful road, with its carefully tended front gardens and brightly painted gates, is teeming with vans and police cars. Dazzling blue lights and reflective yellow. The crackling of radios, barked instructions. Adam is directed to a police van, and finds Jamie behind it, pacing a tiny patch of concrete, his hands tearing at his hair.

'He's got her, hasn't he?' he cries when he sees Adam. 'He's got her.'

'We don't know that.' The shock had sobered Adam in a second. He guides Jamie to the doorway of the van and makes him sit down. 'Tell me exactly what happened.'

'I got home, about eleven thirty, I don't know.' His eyes dart around the scene. 'I knew something was wrong the moment I stepped in the door. I should have called you then . . . I should have . . .' He goes to stand up again, but Adam places a firm hand on his arm.

'We'll find her. But you need to tell me exactly what

you saw. Please, Jamie. You know how important this is.'

Jamie pauses, Adam's words sinking in. He's a police officer, he knows the drill; he'll be aware of how much an investigation can be slowed by a hysterical witness. Jamie takes a long shuddering breath in.

'The hallway was a mess. Mud all over the floor, the table tipped over. You saw it.' Adam nods. He had, when he arrived. Poked his head around the cordon, where SOCOs were already working the scene. Definite signs of a struggle.

'Was the front door open?'

'Was it . . .? Er . . . No. No,' he says decisively. 'I had to use my key to get in.'

'Okay. Then what?'

'I called out to Pippa, and I searched the house, checking all the rooms. Then I called her mobile, but it rang out. Mags has it. I found it in the bedroom. She must have been getting ready for bed. All her clothes . . .' He tails off again and starts sobbing, his head in his hands. Adam puts his arm around his massive shoulders for a moment.

'Stay here, mate,' he says.

He gets up and walks to the edge of the cordon, signing in and suiting up quickly. He goes through the front door and finds Maggie in the hallway, talking to one of the SOCOs.

'You're running point on this?' Maggie asks from behind her mask. 'You're assuming it's connected?'

Adam nods. As much as he doesn't want to admit it to Jamie, it seems likely at this point. A victim, abducted like the others. It fits. 'What do you have?'

'Considerable disruption to belongings and property through the hallway, up the stairs and into the bedroom.

The back door was unlocked. It's likely the assailant entered the house that way and made their way upstairs.' She gestures with a tilt of her head, and Adam follows her up, being careful not to touch anything. She points into the master bedroom. The duvet and pillows are thrown across the floor, clothing scattered.

'Blood spatter across the wardrobe, including one line of cast off.'

'Pippa was hit a few times?'

'I think you can assume so, yes. But she was still conscious. Fighting as she went down the stairs and out into the hallway, causing all the mess.'

'So we might have trace from our offender?'

'Possibly. We've taken blood samples throughout. I'll head back to the lab now, get moving on some of these exhibits. We'll keep looking for prints.'

'Keep me posted.' Adam leaves Maggie and walks around to the front of the house. So they left from here, he thinks. Out of an open front door. Exposed. Risky. Confident – or stupid, he's not sure which.

Interested neighbours poke their heads out of their windows, standing at their front gates, some already being questioned by uniforms. Somebody must have seen something.

As he pulls his PPE off, he looks at the likely candidates. An old lady in a dressing gown: good for daytime nosiness but no doubt in bed by ten. Same with the older couple. But one of the houses looks different to the others. There's nobody out the front. The gate is hanging off its hinges, weeds flourishing in the front garden. And all the lights are on.

He walks over and rings the doorbell. After a moment, it's answered, and Adam knows his initial suspicion is correct. The man is young and scruffy. Tight jeans, baggy sweatshirt. Adam can hear music coming from inside and the sound of a television. The sweet smell of weed drifts into the night air.

The boy barely opens the door. Adam shows his ID.

'Police,' he confirms, and the boy risks a smile. 'Can I come in?'

The boy hesitates. Adam rolls his eyes. 'Look, I don't give a shit about some low-level marijuana possession. I just need your help.'

The boy glances behind him. 'I'll come out.' He moves, shutting the door firmly behind him. 'What do you want?'

'You're a student, right? You were home all night?'

'Yeah.' He points to the commotion. 'What's happened?'

'A young woman has been abducted. And we need to find her, fast. Did you hear anything, see anything?'

He frowns. 'Nah. Although . . .' He pauses.

'Please? You never know what might make a difference.'

'Stu mentioned something about a van. Thought it was his Amazon delivery, so he opened the front door to wait.'

'Can you get Stu?'

'Yeah, hang on.' The boy goes back into the house, and Adam waits impatiently. He returns a few minutes later with a reluctant Stu. The lad shifts from foot to foot, his head down, obviously stoned.

'Stu?' Stu nods, looking at Adam with hooded eyes. 'Tell me about this van?'

He shrugs. 'Small black one. Parked badly, over that driveway there, then they went around the back. As soon as I saw it wasn't for me, I went inside.' He waves his hand at his mate. 'It was like Chris's.' His mate looks blank. He turns back to Adam. 'Like surfers use.' He blinks

138

a few times, and a big smile appears on his face. 'VW Transporter, that's the one.'

Adam feels a ripple of progress. 'And how sure are you that it was black?'

'Definitely dark. Grey at a push.' He shrugs again, irritatingly vague. 'But black, yeah,' he finishes.

'Did you get a plate?'

'No, sorry.'

'Did you see the driver?'

'Yeah. No. Kind of.' He shrugs for the third time, and Adam suppresses his desire to slap him. 'Not that tall. Wearing a hoodie. Didn't see their face.' He frowns. 'Had baggy trousers on, and trainers.'

'What sort of trousers? Jeans?'

'Nah . . . like pyjamas. Thought it was odd, but . . .' He loses his train of thought. Adam snaps his fingers in front of his face, trying to wake him up.

Stu blinks. 'They were blue. Light blue.'

'Any other distinguishing marks about the van? Was it scratched, bumped? Any stickers in the windows?'

'Not that I noticed.'

'Age?'

'Look, I don't know, dude. It was dark. I wasn't paying much attention.'

'Fine. Fine. I'll get my colleague to take a statement. Try not to smoke anything else in the meantime, please?'

Stu nods, and Adam calls a uniform over.

They have something. A dark-coloured VW Transporter. He heads back to see Jamie. His DS is still sitting in the doorway of the van, motionless, his face blank. Adam puts a hand on his shoulder and he looks up, his eyes red-rimmed and hopeful.

139

'Have you found her?'

'No, sorry.' Jamie's face drops. 'But we have some leads. And I promise I won't rest until she's home. We need to get you away from here while SOCO finish up. Come and stay at mine.'

Jamie looks up at Adam again. 'He'll keep her alive, won't he?' Jamie says. His voice is desperate, cracking with every word. 'Like those other ones.'

Adam frowns. 'I'm sure he will,' he says, pulling his friend slowly to his feet and guiding him away from his house. He doesn't want to mention what the other victims had been through. Tied up, the cuts to their arms. The torture. Bleeding out slowly.

The thought that that could happen to Pippa, it doesn't bear thinking about. But he agrees with Jamie's theory. The killer obviously wants her alive, otherwise he would have killed Pippa there and then.

But for how long? That was anyone's guess.

Chapter 24

Throughout the ride in the patrol car back to Adam's, Jamie can't form a coherent sentence. He directs rambling thoughts towards his friend, half-formed worries, directions about lines of enquiry that he knows Adam will have covered. Bishop's already told him he can't come near the police station anymore. He's a relative now. Family. Off the case.

Adam lets him into his house and shows him towards the spare room. Together, silently, they make up the bed, putting sheets on the bare mattress, covers on the pillows. Jamie gets the impression not many people have been to stay here, if ever.

Then, at last, Adam leaves. His boss tells him to get some sleep, but how can he? He doesn't think he'll ever be able to sleep again, knowing that Pippa is out there, somewhere, with this madman. Images of the previous victims swim in his head, their bloody torn torsos, open blank eyes. Their dread, their pain, pushing to the forefront of his mind. The little detachment he normally manages as a police officer has completely deserted him now.

He mutes calls from Pippa's parents, no doubt notified by someone in the team that their only daughter has been abducted. He doesn't dare phone his mother, dreading the suffocating care. The sympathy he doesn't deserve.

They will ask him questions he can't answer. Why did he go to the pub? Why didn't he come straight home after work? Why wasn't he there to protect her, as he should have been? He was her husband. A *police officer*. He could have stopped this. His wife, gone, because he went for a pint.

His stomach churns, he is sick with fear. He scrunches his eyes tightly shut, but all he can see is his wife – confused, scared, crying out for him.

He saw the blood spatter in the bedroom. The smears down the wall in the hallway. The mess, the overturned furniture. The SOCOs were cagey, Adam reluctant to share details, but he knows what it means. She is injured. She fought. She's bleeding.

But she is alive. He took her alive, and Jamie knows he must hang on to that. This insane fucker wants her alive.

And Adam will find her.

The smartest man he knows, the hardest working detective in the nick. Adam will find Pippa.

Jamie clings onto those two thoughts, working them round and round in his head, as he lies in Adam's guest room. Cold. Alone. In the dark. And utterly terrified for his wife.

I stand in the doorway, watching her. She is blindfolded; her head twitches from side to side once she hears the door open. Trying to find me, desperately searching for a sense of where I am.

What's going to happen to her.

I take a step forward, hesitant. I don't want to do this. But I know I must.

She breathes in and out quickly behind the tape; she makes a quiet squeak. I feel like she's trying to talk to me. I reach forward and gently remove the blindfold.

Her eyes open wide with surprise. Tears brim before they run down her pale soft cheeks. She is beautiful. It is a pity everything will end for her in this way.

She strains against her bindings, but I've been careful. Cable ties extra tight. One of the others managed to get free, half out of the door before I caught him by the hair and pulled him back to the ground. He didn't fight as much once the knife was out. Once the blade was deep in his stomach.

You have a purpose, Pippa Hoxton.

She's still whining behind her gag, so I pull at one corner and remove the tape. She takes gasping breaths for a moment, then starts to scream. A long, high-pitched wail that consumes all of her energy, making her muscles taut. She takes a shuddering breath in, then starts again, her eyes darting around the room.

I watch her, impassive, my arms crossed.

After a moment her screams abate to sobs, snot and tears pouring down her face. I reach forward with one finger and I slowly wipe up her cheek. She stops, frozen, shaking, watching with those big blue eyes.

'I'm sorry,' I say. And I am. Any attempt to get away is futile, resistance pointless.

'Please let me go,' she replies. 'What do you want from me? I'll do anything. I can get money. What do you want?'

'I want you,' I reply.

She blinks. She pulls at her arms and legs again. I watch as the ties cut deep into her flesh.

'Do you want a drink?' I ask.

She nods slowly. I've learnt this time. If I am to keep her alive for longer, I need her hydrated. Plenty of water, maybe even food.

I turn and go to the end of the room, where I have a sandwich and a bottle of water. As soon as my back is turned I hear frantic movement, and I spin to see her trying to rock the chair, tip it over, get free.

I pick up the water and go back. I watch her for a moment as she struggles, then a burst of fury takes over. I reach out with my hand, grab a handful of her hair and pull.

She gasps, her neck wrenched back. She looks up at me, blinking, sobbing.

'Enough of that,' I whisper through clenched teeth, my mouth next to her ear. 'You try any of that shit and things will get worse for you very quickly.' I pause. She doesn't move. 'Do you hear me?'

'Yes,' she whispers, and I let go of her head. She sits up, and I offer the water. I see her lick her lips in anticipation.

'Do you want some?' I ask. I unscrew the lid.

'Yes,' she says. 'Yes, please.'

'That's better.' I smile and hold the bottle up to her mouth, tilting it so it pours in. She swallows. I repeat it, one, two more times, then put the bottle down.

'That's enough for now. We don't want any more accidents, do we?'

She's pissed herself already, from fear, from terror, but I don't mind. It's part of the process. The learning curve. I'll get it right. I have to.

I walk over to the table on the far side of the room; her eyes follow. I pick up the equipment.

She starts to babble again. 'No, please, please, let me go, please, please.'

She's distracting, so I break off another piece of tape and head back over. I grip her head and push down, sticking it into place. She breathes heavily through her nose, shaking.

I lay the equipment on a small stainless steel tray and carry it across. Her eyes immediately fix on the one thing I hadn't yet shown her. It's a needle. Long, shining. Flawless.

I take it out of the sterile wrapper, holding it carefully, the way I was taught. She wriggles helplessly in her chair, her fingers flexing, pulling, but it's only making my job *easier. Her blood is flowing faster around her body. Fight or flight has kicked in and her veins stand out on her inner forearm. I place one hand on her arm, holding her still.*

I am ready.

I press the needle against her pure smooth skin, and I push.

DAY 5

WEDNESDAY

Chapter 25

Adam's never felt pressure like it. It's a squeeze on his skull, a constant contraction in his stomach. He sees Marsh appear in the doorway and take in the bustle, but he doesn't ask. Adam knows he'll be back; he's grateful for the reprieve.

And he knows the question that must be going through Marsh's mind: should you be working on this? He's asked himself that too many times already. He is personally connected. Jamie is his closest mate, Pippa best friend to his ex-wife. But he's also aware that one of the only things keeping Jamie going is knowing that he is running the case. That he won't stop until they find her.

Dead or alive.

He stops for a moment and rubs his eyes. He's been awake for over twenty-four hours now, missing a night's sleep.

'You okay, boss?'

'Hmm, what?'

Ellie Quinn stands by his side, waiting for a response.

He remembers the state of her last night, and sees the ravages of the hangover on her face.

'We have CCTV of what we think is the van—' she says.

Adam doesn't wait for her to finish, but hurries to her computer and sits down at the screen.

They are overwhelmed with data. They've got feed from hundreds of traffic cameras across the city, as well as searches from the DVLA and PNC for all dark-coloured VW Transporters. But it seems they've come up trumps from the CCTV.

'We started from the residence and worked outwards, assuming an abduction time between twenty-two hundred hours, when the victim texted saying she was headed home, and twenty-three thirty when DS Hoxton returned.' Adam nods, impatient. 'And we have this van, headed south.'

Adam watches, his chin cupped in his hand, hardly blinking from the image on the screen. The dark VW van comes into shot, quickly disappearing from right to left.

'Then, again, here, on the A33.'

'And we're sure this is the same vehicle?'

Quinn points to the screen with a delicate finger. 'See here? The driver's side wing mirror is damaged at the top. No plate though.'

Adam's head flicks up. 'Nothing?'

'No. We've tried multiple angles but it's hidden. Dirty, maybe. And we lose it here, after the Clifton Roundabout.'

She looks genuinely distraught. Adam places a reassuring hand on her shoulder. He's surprised but pleased at how quickly she's got up to speed, learning the workings of the Major Crime team fast. 'This is good, Quinn,' he says. 'Keep going.'

He gets up from the desk and walks across to the whiteboard. It has a line of numbers across the top, beginning with number sixteen, the names attached to each victim below.

They have all the IDs for the first five bodies now. Number sixteen, Patricia Sullivan. Forty-six years old, worked for Children's Services. Number fifteen – Luke Heller – couldn't have been more different. A local shitbag. Multiple arrests for intent to supply and possession, but always class Bs and never enough to put him away for long.

They have information – time of death, cause of death – and the profiles of the victims are starting to take shape. But none of it connects. As a group, the victims are disparate: common criminals mixed with diligent public servants. Adam frowns and puts both hands on top of his head, staring at the black capitals.

Ross has completed the PM on Wayne Oxford, nothing differs from his initial assessment. And he was right about the blood thinner: massive quantities of heparin were found in his system. Nothing back yet from the fingerprint on the bottle, despite Adam's chasing.

Pippa is up there, her photo smiling out from the board. But there's no number assigned to her, and for that he's glad. She's not dead. She's not a victim.

Yet.

The word rotates in Adam's head.

The details have been written up alongside her. *VW Transporter, black (dark?), light blue trousers – baggy.*

Adam remembers how the stoner described them and writes it up alongside. *Pyjamas?*

Perhaps they were? It had been late at night, after all.

But who would wear pyjamas out of the house? Escaped hospital patients? He sighs. This conjecture is ridiculous.

He turns his attention to the other whiteboard, the one the analysts have been using to brainstorm the significance of the number twenty.

The sum of three Fibonacci numbers; a pronic number; a tetrahedral number. A variety of mathematical terms Adam has never heard of. The atomic number of calcium, the third magic number in physics, whatever that means. Twenty-twenty vision, sectors on a dartboard. An app – a silly game. An album by Pearl Jam. Books, shops, films.

Random scrawls, thoughts and associations. Written up, in case something connects. But nothing makes sense. Nothing helps.

Nothing, nothing, nothing.

He's knackered, eyes half closing. He feels himself sway slightly. He goes into his office and closes the door. He'll allow himself to rest his head for a moment. Just a moment. Then he'll go and get some coffee.

He wakes to the sound of voices. A woman calling his name. The door to his office opening.

He wrenches himself from the glue of sleep and looks up, eyes unfocused. Romilly stands in front of him.

'Why didn't you tell me?' she shouts. 'You left me to find out on the fucking news?' She stops, waiting for him to catch up to her fury. 'Why didn't you tell me Pippa is missing?'

He rubs his hands down his face, feeling ashamed. Shit. He should have.

'I've been kind of busy, Milly,' he replies, hastily pulling himself together and sitting up straight.

'Well . . . well . . .' The air goes out of Romilly's lungs and she slumps in the seat opposite him, resting her head in her hands. After a moment, she looks up; he can see she's fighting back tears. 'What happened? Is it the same guy?' she says, her voice thick.

'We think so, yes. We have a few leads.' He pauses. 'I'm sorry. I should have called you. But I was too focused on the investigation. On getting her home.'

She's silent for a moment, looking down at the floor. There's something else going on with her, he can tell. It's not just anger or worry for Pippa. Another emotion, one he's seen in her in the past too many times. It's fear.

'What's going on, Milly?' he asks.

He waits. And then slowly, she reaches into her pocket and pulls out an envelope. Her hands are shaking as she puts it on the table in front of him.

'I got this yesterday,' she says.

Adam has a bad feeling. He pulls out the newspaper clipping, then opens the note. He reads it. *You need to talk to me.*

He looks up at Romilly. Her face is deathly pale.

'Have you?' he asks. 'Spoken to him?'

She shakes her head. 'But should I, Adam?' Her voice is soft, her eyes tilted to the floor. He knows how hard this must be, for her to even consider this.

'No. You shouldn't.' For a second he goes to take her hand, but he pulls himself back. 'He's trying to control you. Again. He's sensed a way to get to you, and he's using it to his advantage.'

'But what if he knows something?'

'He doesn't,' Adam says firmly. Inside, he's not so sure. What if she's right, and the old man is connected? But his

151

visitation request to the prison had been denied. And they checked the house, the old crime scene. What more can he do?

'How did he even know my address?' she says. 'The restraining order prohibits it.'

'He must know someone. He must have friends.' Adam feels the anger growing. He can still get to Romilly, even from his tightly locked prison cell. Adam wants to do something, to protect her, to keep her safe. 'I'll get one of my detectives to take a statement from you now. Report it properly. Harassment.'

But she shakes her head. 'No, no, I'll go down to the front desk. Nothing should take you guys away from finding Pippa. That's the most important thing.'

She stands up quickly, taking the newspaper article and note back from Adam before he can stop her. Then she turns and walks quickly out of his office.

'Romilly?' he calls. 'Milly?' But she's gone.

He stands up, debating whether to go after her. To offer his help? His support? But that's not him anymore. She has a boyfriend for that.

He's always admired the way she faces up to her past, like she isn't afraid of it. That nothing can stop her, despite what happened all those years ago. It was one of the things that had first attracted him to her, that made him fall in love. Feelings that hadn't abated, but had been submerged, drowned by the worries and doubt that eclipsed them as the years passed.

Romilly is right. Nothing is more important than finding Pippa right now. Certainly not him and Romilly and their failed marriage. But the fact remains that those pieces of her, their life together, have lodged in his brain like shrapnel. And now, slowly, his subconscious pushes them to the surface.

Adam sighs, then goes back out into the incident room. He looks at the whiteboard; someone has added another thought to the list. Psalm 20, a psalm of David.

Adam's never put stock in God or the Bible; religion hasn't meant much to him over the years. But he looks at the words written on the board, the first two lines.

May the Lord answer you when you are in distress; may the name of the God of Jacob protect you.

And he thinks of Pippa.

Chapter 26

Romilly's still shaking when she gets back to her car. She hasn't done as she said: to report it would mean explaining everything, and what happened, and . . . and . . . She can't right now, she just can't.

Especially with what's happened to Pippa. Seeing it this morning on the local news was surreal. Taken straight from her nightmares and plonked into real life. She'd tried to phone Adam, but he hadn't answered.

Phil rings now, making her jump. To her surprise, Phil's advice last night had been to call Adam. 'He'll know what to do,' he'd said, giving credibility to her ex-husband for the first time.

'And?' Phil says now. 'What did he say?'

'He said not to contact him,' Romilly replies.

'Well, then. We're all in agreement.'

Romilly pulls the envelope out of her pocket and lays it in her lap. It's now crumpled and smudged, but has the same hold on her as the moment it came through her letter box.

'Rom?' Phil says. 'Aren't we?'

'Yes,' she mumbles.

'You're not going to contact the prison?'

'No.'

'Promise? Please, Rom? You know this won't do you any good. Phone Dr Jones again, if you need to. But don't contact him.'

She imagines her boyfriend standing in his consultation room at work, hand on hip, confident in his assertion. She remembers Pippa's assessment of him when they first met: 'He's so *together*,' she'd whispered, as if a sane, logical man was something fanciful. A unicorn among New Forest ponies. Rarely seen in the wild, and even more unusual, one willing to be caught. But rather than enjoying this stable, sensible influence, Romilly feels like his perfection highlights her flaws. Her madness magnified by comparison.

'I've got to go, Phil,' she says. 'I need to check on Jamie.'

She hangs up the phone, then takes the envelope and pushes it back into her pocket. She has an overwhelming urge to burn it, to get rid of it permanently, but she knows she'll never do that.

It has a hold on her, a tight grip. In the same way that he always had.

Chapter 27

The fingerprint is back. Adam is pulled away from conversation as Maggie Clarke enters the room. Out of her crime scene gear, her clothes are bright, gawdy, floral. Lurid colours and clashing prints, as if she's outwardly rebelling from the conformity and structure her work requires.

'Tell me something good,' Adam says. Around them the room has calmed to a whisper. Detectives still working but waiting for news, the anticipation of a firm lead.

Maggie frowns. 'No good, I'm sorry, Adam. Nothing we can work with.'

'And the Hoxton residence?'

'The same. Nothing useable. Although Ross has confirmed the bottle is most likely the murder weapon. Plus, more news on the rope fibres.' She hands Adam a single piece of paper and he scans it quickly while she continues. 'We've analysed the composition – it's Dacron.'

'And that is?' Adam asks, dispirited. He feels the frustration. That fingerprint could have taken them straight to the killer's door. To Pippa.

'That's the trade name, the people that make it.' She looks apologetic. 'But it doesn't help you much. We couldn't tell what thickness rope it was. So while you can probably theorise he used it to tie up his victim, we can't say where it might have originated from.'

Adam looks at the report again. He runs his finger down the list: 'Climbing, rigging, boating, netting, rope ladders . . .'

'Don't forget the film and theatre industry.'

'Fuck, Mags. Is there any base you haven't covered?' He sighs, putting the page down. 'Any DNA? Blood, saliva? Anything found on the dog?'

'Dog?' She looks blank. 'I'll check it out. Nothing we've found on the rest, although we're waiting for the samples to come through from the body from Dr Ross. Sorry, Bishop.'

She puts a hand on his arm, her silver bangles jangling, and he takes a moment of reassurance from her contact, albeit brief. But he doesn't want to encourage anything between them. Not again, he thinks, and he pulls away.

'Sorry it couldn't have been better news,' Maggie finishes, and she makes her escape.

Adam envies her ability to leave. To have done her job – this part at least – and be moving on to the next.

The detectives continue to work as night closes in and the lights flicker on. Pizzas are ordered, caffeine is plentiful. Cars looking like the VW Transporter pop up at the edges of CCTV, witness statements from the neighbours come in and Adam reads every one. But nothing. Time trickles away.

Jamie calls, and Adam answers. Although Jamie has a family liaison officer with him, someone trained to handle relatives in situations like this, Jamie would rather speak to Adam directly.

'No progress, I'm sorry,' Adam says. He's letting Jamie down; he'd like to be able to tell him anything but that.

'It's okay, mate. It's okay,' Jamie replies, his voice monotone.

'Maggie said they've released the . . . your house.' Adam stops himself from saying *crime scene*. 'You can go home.'

There's a long pause. 'I don't know if I want to.' Jamie's voice breaks at the end. 'It won't be home if she's not there,' he adds quietly.

There's nothing Adam can say. And, to his shame, he feels a release when Marsh stands in the doorway of the incident room.

'I need to go,' he says, 'Marsh is here.'

But as Adam hangs up he feels his mouth go dry. He recognises the look, the heavy movement as his detective chief superintendent walks across the incident room, as if every step is causing him pain. Adam gets up from behind his desk but his legs are solid blocks. He can't move.

'Guv?'

'I'm sorry, Adam,' Marsh says. His expression is grim. 'They've found a body. And it's a woman.'

Chapter 28

A woman. A woman is dead. A patrol car is summoned and they charge towards the location. Nearly an hour's drive from the nick: a playing field, to the edge of a residential area. Body found at ten past eight. But who? And how was she killed? Adam feels panic rising; he demands details and information that nobody is able to give.

Ellie Quinn sits in the back seat, DC Tim Lee next to her. They're silent, waiting for orders and confirmation and Adam misses Jamie, his second-in-command always knowing what action to take before he is told. He thinks of him waiting for news and says a silent prayer in his head. Please can it not be her. But if not Pippa, who?

Even given their delay, they're still one of the first people there. They stop at the edge of the park behind the ambulance, Adam running fast towards the group on the far side, the lights, the torches, the reflective yellow on the uniforms signalling the tragedy unfolding.

A paramedic stands to one side, bent in two, hands resting on his knees. A uniform guards a heap on the ground; another is talking to a couple, hands waving frantically, furtive glances back to the lump.

They approach the PC.

'DCI Bishop,' Adam says. 'Let me see.'

The uniform moves to the side and points to the body with his torch. It's a woman, young. Her eyes are staring, her mouth gaping in a scream that nobody heard. Adam struggles to gather any recognition from this shape: in life Pippa was so much more than this. Always animated, with a smile beaming on her face.

But then he realises: this isn't her. This woman has brown hair, Pippa's is blonde. They aren't the slightest bit similar. The flash of relief is quickly replaced by sorrow and guilt. This is not Jamie's wife, but she may have been someone else's. And she is dead.

'999 call at quarter past eight,' the uniform continues. 'Said they found a body. That couple there. Control tried to direct them to do CPR but they said there was no point. No chest to compress.'

Adam takes the torch from the PC and shines it onto the corpse. She's lying on her back, legs folded under her, head at a strange angle. He runs the beam down to the torso. Light reflects back: blood. And lots of it.

The whole chest is open. It's a mass of gore, bones, and organs. Ripped, brutally torn.

'Has anyone touched the body?' Adam asks.

'No. Ambulance turned up, but the paramedics didn't go near.' The PC points to the man in green, still bent over. 'That guy threw up, the other one's back in the ambulance. We arrived moments after them. I remembered the gossip from the station about the bodies you found Saturday night. Got Control to call the nick.'

'Good shout,' Adam confirms. He turns to Quinn. Ellie's standing, one hand over her mouth, eyes fixed on the corpse. 'Ellie, get whoever you can in. We need a bigger team. House-to-house, CCTV, usual enquiries. Call SOCO and the pathologist. Quinn?'

She looks up, her face pale. She blinks as if she hasn't heard a word Adam has said. He feels for her, he does; this might be the first violent murder she's seen. He regrets bringing her now, but he hasn't got time for her delicate sensibilities.

'DC Quinn? You okay? Do you need a minute?'

'No, boss. I'm fine.' She shakes her head, trying to rouse herself. 'Will do.'

Adam turns back to the PC. 'Can you help DC Lee with the cordon? Block off this whole area. All entrances to the park, all footpaths. I don't want anyone coming in or out of here.'

Ellie starts to leave, then looks back.

'I didn't think . . .' she starts. She shakes her head again. 'I didn't think it would feel so bizarre.'

She trudges away, pulling her phone out of her pocket as she goes. Adam knows what she means. The level of violence here doesn't feel real: that someone could do this to another human being – again – and there not be repercussions for that person's psyche. It must be taking its toll on the killer. They can't be blending into the background. Someone must know something.

Dimly he hears Quinn on the radio, calling the details back to Control. Confirming their location and the request for resource. He hears what she's saying, but the words take a moment to register.

Adam runs the torch up to the victim's face. The light

161

bounces from her open eyes, showing her gaping mouth.

Quinn repeats her request. 'Whoever you can spare. Yes, to the Common on Monk's Hill. PO10 . . .' She turns to the PC next to her. 'What's the rest of the postcode?'

PO10. Adam raises the torch higher. Considering, for the first time, what's been marked on her forehead. Deep cuts, inflicted with rage and hatred, blood glistening in the darkness.

The number ten. Two digits brutally slashed into the victim's skin.

Chapter 29

It is all so slow. All so fucking slow. Bishop barks orders at the uniforms who arrive in dribs and drabs; it's been a busy night in town, resource is sparse. The SOCOs are here but the park is too big. He squints at his phone in the darkness, looking at the map: there are five paths in, numerous places this man could hide if he's still here. And Adam doubts that very much.

The cordon is up, blue and white ribbons flapping in the freezing wind. Quinn gets off the phone, where she's been relaying Adam's orders back to the station.

'Scouring CCTV as we speak, boss,' she tells him. Her shoulders are hunched, her hands thrust deep into the pockets of her coat.

'Good. And the couple that found the body?' Adam asks.

'Fairly useless. Traumatised and tired. They've taken them back to do a formal statement but preliminary questions seem to indicate they didn't see anyone around.' Ellie looks over to where the body is still lying, now covered in a large blue plastic tent. 'This guy will be obvious, right, boss?'

Adam nods. He knows what she's saying. From the state of the body, the offender would be covered in blood. Over his clothes, his hands, his face. He'd be noticed.

And what of his state of mind? Someone couldn't do that to a human being – the stabbing, the damage, the sheer amount of violence – and walk away calmly. They'd be frantic, panicked, desperate.

Adam turns to Ellie. 'Where would you go?' he asks.

Ellie looks at him, big green eyes disbelieving. 'What? If I'd just brutally slaughtered a woman in a park?'

'Yes.'

Ellie frowns. 'I guess I would go where I feel safe. Home, somewhere familiar.'

'Right.'

'Or. If I was screwed up in the head, and this was my thing . . .' Ellie stops for a moment. 'I'd go looking for another victim.'

Adam frowns. 'Let's hope it's the former.'

Adam sends Ellie and DC Lee back to the station. He stays at the park, watching Mags with her team. A slickly oiled machine; movements so familiar it seems almost choreographed. It brings Adam little relief. His toes are numb, his fingers painful with the cold; he masochistically half-enjoys it, a penance as the bodies stack up around him.

A tent has been constructed around what's left of the body. Adam walks across to the edge of the cordon, slowly puts on the white protective suit, gloves and mask, and pushes up the flap.

The scene inside is strange. The blue polythene casts a surreal glow; Adam feels disconnected from what's in front of him, numb from having seen so much devastation over the last few days. The blood looks black, the lights turning her skin to white rubber. Dr Ross is kneeling next to the body, while a SOCO takes swabs from under the woman's fingernails.

'I don't hold out much hope for that,' Ross says in a flat tone. 'Our victim barely had time to blink.' He stands up, rolling his neck side to side and stretching before he faces Adam. 'Two penetrative injuries to the back, then however you want to describe what happened to the front.'

Adam crouches down to the body, peering closely for the first time at the victim's torso. The edges are torn and uneven, skin flaps wetly around the ragged gore.

'Do you think . . .' Adam feels his voice falter slightly and gathers himself before he speaks again. 'Do you think this is the same perp?'

Ross nods grimly. 'I hope so. You don't want two people running around inflicting this sort of violence. Knife. Or something similar. I'll see if I can narrow it down at the mortuary. We'll take swabs, same as before. Hope the guy cut himself in the process. He wasn't exactly being precise.'

But before Adam can thank him, he hears commotion from outside. Voices, shouting. People he recognises. He ducks out of the tent and heads towards the noise.

Jamie's standing at the edge of the cordon, Romilly by his side.

'Adam!' he shouts, desolate, when he sees him. 'Is it her?'

'No. No, mate, it's not.' Jamie's body sags, and Romilly puts her arms around him. Adam called him the moment he made the confirmation, but Jamie seems reluctant to believe him. Adam sees press hovering at the edges of the cordon, and he moves them away.

'I was with Jamie,' Romilly explains. 'When you phoned.'

'I told you not to come down here,' Adam replies. 'There's nothing you can do.'

'But it's the same guy?'

'We think so, yes.'

'So where is she?' Jamie pleads. 'Where's Pippa?'

There's nothing Adam can say. He doesn't know. He doesn't fucking know.

Romilly looks at him through the darkness. 'I need to go, Adam,' she says softly.

'This doesn't change anything.'

'It does, and you know it.'

Jamie glances anxiously between the two of them. Romilly sees his confusion.

'I got a letter,' she explains. 'From him. He says I need to go and talk to him.'

Jamie grabs her by the tops of her arms, and she starts. 'Then you have to go,' he shouts, pleading. 'Please.'

Adam places a hand on his arm. 'Jamie,' he says softly, 'she can't. It's exactly what he wants.'

'But what if he does know something? Surely, it's worth it? For that tiny chance?'

Jamie's voice is desperate, and Adam can see by the look on Romilly's face that it's exactly what she's thinking too.

'But Milly,' he says, 'you've worked so hard to escape this. You're so much better now.'

She shakes her head. 'I can do it, I'll be fine. And Jamie's right. What if he does know something? He's in prison with the craziest people. What if he's heard rumours? What if it's someone who's just been released?'

'I don't like this.'

'It's not up to you,' Romilly says sternly.

Adam turns to her. He knows the effect this man had on Romilly. He'd seen the panic attacks, the nightmares. Watched her crying for hours after sessions with her therapist. 'He's a dangerous man,' Adam says quietly. For the first time since they were divorced, he takes her hands in his. They feel warm, almost clammy. 'He tortured and raped five women. He killed four of them. He will manipulate you, as he did then, and has been doing ever since.'

Romilly stares down at his hands, then she pulls away. She looks at Jamie, his face drawn and pale.

'I'll go,' she says decisively. 'I'll go and see my father.'

LOCAL DOCTOR CHARGED WITH FOUR MURDERS

Hampshire Chronicle, 20 November 1995

The disappearance of four women came to a distressing end last night, as local GP, Dr Elijah Cole, was arrested at his home in Gloucester Road. On searching the property, police found the partly decomposed bodies of three of the missing women – Rebecca Sparkes, Claire Charters and Nicola Henshaw – in shallow graves in woodland on Cole's property. A further body, of Grace Summers, was discovered recently deceased in the outbuilding. An additional woman, not known to be missing, was found alive and has been taken to hospital. Her condition is described as stable. Police are still in the process of locating her next of kin, and her name will be released to the public in due course.

Police haven't issued a statement at this stage, but all five women are believed to have been held since their disappearances over the last four months, and subjected to sexual assault, rape, and torture over this time. Numerous restraint devices are rumoured to have been found at the remote property, including cages, chains, and handcuffs.

Local residents remain in a state of shock. Dr Cole was a respected member of the community, providing medical care from his surgery on Cannon Street. One local resident stated, 'He is such a charming man, a pillar of our community. I can't believe it.'

It is rumoured Dr Cole's eleven-year-old daughter raised the alarm, although further details are unknown. She has been taken into the care of Children's Services and is not believed to be connected to the crimes.

DAY 6

THURSDAY

Chapter 30

Years have passed, but Romilly feels the same as she pulls up in the car park of HMP Belmarsh. All through the two-hour drive she'd wanted to change her mind, looking at every junction of the motorway and telling herself: turn around. But she hadn't. As much as her gut shouts at her to stay away, another part is drawn to him. To see the man that destroyed her life all those years ago.

Phil offered to come with her, but she'd told him no. He hadn't understood why, choosing to take her rebuff personally. And in a way, he should. If Adam had offered, she probably would have said yes.

She sits in the car park now and wonders why. She's always had a feeling that Phil doesn't understand. He has two parents: nice people. His mum is a librarian, his dad a retired engineer. He grew up and went to college in the same town he was born. What does he know about having a serial killer for a dad? For your surname to be associated with evil. To be snatched from your own home, with no belongings or clothes, sent to live with families who look at you every day with fear and caution. Other children ushered away; words whispered behind your back.

Phil sees it in black and white. The man was bad, so she is right to cut him out of her life. But it's more nuanced than that.

Adam understands the grey. The dichotomy of loving your parents but hating them. How people you trust can betray you in ways you never thought possible. How you can be alone, in a second.

Romilly's mother died when she was six. After that, it was just her and her father. She had few friends, no other family. He brought her up alone, the sole GP in a busy surgery. She'd go along for house calls, waiting in the car with a book or a colouring pad. She'd sit behind the reception desk, the ladies in the back office her unofficial babysitters. He did the best he could. They'd go to the park, to the swimming pool, to the beach. Normal things. Dinners were sometimes burnt or inedible, but those were the best ones because they'd get fish and chips, greasy and delicious, eating them on their knees sitting on the low brick wall surrounding the park. She still can't smell salt and vinegar without thinking about him.

It was hard to detach that man – the father she loved – from the demon that killed all those women. And even when she'd seen the keys to the outbuilding left mistakenly on the kitchen table, and gone down the garden and opened the door, and smelt the excrement and death and seen the pain and horror, she had paused.

The police hadn't believed her at first. It seemed like a prank call. The uniforms came to their door, indulgent expressions as they spoke to her dad.

'We're sorry, Dr Cole. But do you mind if we search

your house? We're sure it's nothing. Yes, including your outbuilding.'

They even joked as they walked around the top floor and the kitchen and living room. They saw what everyone saw: the normality, the pleasant facade. Was it any wonder Romilly missed her father? Was it any wonder she'd loved him?

But then their smiles turned to horror as Elijah unlocked the door of the outbuilding and pushed it open. He hadn't hesitated. He'd looked at Romilly, standing watching from the middle of the garden, and he'd winked as the police officers turned, stuttering and panicked, placing handcuffs on her father and reading him his rights. Ambulances were called, sniffer dogs in the garden.

And the bodies were found.

Romilly pulls the key decisively out of her car's ignition. She's here now. She'll see her father for the first time since he was arrested. For Jamie. For Pippa.

The visit was approved surprisingly quickly when she'd put in the request.

'He expected you to come,' Adam said, his eyebrows knitted together with concern.

'I'll be fine, Adam,' she replied. 'I promise.'

But now she isn't so sure.

She makes her way through the visitor's centre, showing identification, leaving her property in a locker, signing her name. Progress is swift, fast-tracked through.

The prison guard smiles. She notices a coffee stain on his uniform, his shirt creased. 'You're here to see the doc,' he says. 'He's been looking forward to it.'

She's escorted through to a small room, one metal table bolted to the floor. There are creaky plastic chairs, one either side. She sits down facing the door. She picks up the plastic cup of water that's offered to her and takes a sip, wetting her dry mouth.

She places her palms face down on the table, trying to still their shaking, then crosses her arms and thrusts her hands into her armpits instead. She's hot, sweaty with nerves, heart hammering.

The door opens with a clang, making her jump. And she looks up into the almost-black eyes of her father.

'Romilly! I'm so glad you came!' he says with a warm smile. He has the manner of a man on a walk in the park, strolling without a care in the world. He's wearing jeans and a navy-green checked shirt. Trainers on his feet. Bright white, no contact with the outside to ever make them dirty. His hands are free, no cuffs.

He takes the seat in front of her, and the guard moves to stand on the other side of the room. He crosses his arms across his broad chest; he looks only at Cole, has no regard for her. Romilly feels more intimidated than reassured by his presence.

She faces her father. The first time in twenty-six years.

'I'm not here for you,' Romilly says. The words come out as a croak; she clears her throat. 'Tell me what you know about Pippa Hoxton. About this killer.'

He grins. 'I find it interesting you're involved with this case. And nice you kept your name. Romilly was your mother's choice.'

'I didn't keep it for you.'

Romilly has considered changing her name more times than she can count. Each year, on the anniversary of his arrest, when the papers call for a comment. Each time some true crime buff tracks her down, wanting an interview. But she doesn't want to hide. She's done nothing wrong; a thought she's clung to all her life.

She tries again. 'What do you know about Pippa Hoxton?'

He tilts his head to one side. 'Do you know her? This seems personal?'

'Stop messing around,' she says sharply. 'Either you tell me what you know, or I walk out of here now.'

He sits back in his chair, a satisfied smile on his face. 'I always knew you were strong. That you had something about you, Romilly. Confirmed when you called the police. I should have expected it. It was my fault.'

Romilly stays quiet. She doesn't know what to say.

'I forgive you,' he continues.

'You forgive me?'

'Yes. For calling the police. I thought we were a team. You and me against the world. After your mother died.'

'You killed four women!' she shouts. Then she hears Dr Jones in her head. *Don't let him take control. You can decide how you react to him. Only you.*

'I didn't mean to kill them,' he says softly. 'But I pushed them too far. They couldn't take it. In the end.' He pauses. 'And I would have had more. If you hadn't stopped me. I knew you had to stop me, Romilly.'

She stares at him. He looks up and meets her eyes; she refuses to look away.

'It was a test. One you passed with flying colours.'

'You left those keys there deliberately.' Romilly had always wondered: what would have happened if she hadn't noticed them there that day? If she'd been late home from school. If her father had spotted them and moved them. How long would it have gone on for? How many would he have killed?

And now she has her answer. He would have kidnapped

women, killed women, raped women, until someone stopped him.

He smiles. 'Of course I did. You didn't think I'd be that stupid, did you?' He reaches across the table towards her face, but she pulls back quickly. 'My poor Romilly. Have you blamed yourself all these years? For putting your father in jail.'

'You deserve to be here,' she hisses.

'Yes. I do. But I didn't know how much I could push you. How far you'd go. And it was further than I imagined.'

Romilly takes a long breath in, her hands balled into fists. She wills her heart to stop thumping, the panic to calm.

'But I had a need. A want. Something inside me I couldn't ignore. No more than you could resist coming to see me today.'

She can't listen any longer. To his voice, pulling her to the past. She pushes her chair back, a squeak of metal on tiling, and walks quickly towards the door.

'You think I'm involved,' he says. 'Don't you?'

She pauses, hand poised on the handle.

'But how could that possibly be true?'

Romilly turns. 'The numbers,' she says. 'The ones carved into the wall of the outhouse.'

'You think someone's copying me? Continuing what I started?' She goes to speak, and he waves his hand, dismissing his question. 'Why would someone do that? What would they be getting out of it?' He stops, and a faraway look comes over his face. 'Me? I knew that those women were mine. I owned them. I could do what I liked with them. In that shed I was king and they soon learnt there were consequences if they disagreed.'

Romilly screws her eyes tightly shut, trying to block

out his words. Some part of her recognises he's saying it deliberately, enjoying watching her squirm, but to hear it coming from his mouth, it's disgusting. She feels dirty, just listening to it. She knew, of course. She'd stopped reading the papers long ago, self-preservation, but she could hardly avoid the news reports of the trial. And the interview after. The *Daily Mail* paying their fifty pieces of silver for the whole truth direct from the Good Doctor's mouth.

She bashes once, twice on the door. She looks to the guard, but he hasn't moved.

'I've upset you,' Cole says. 'I'm sorry.'

'You don't give a shit,' she snarls back. 'You don't care about the victims today, same as you didn't care about the women you murdered then.'

'Oh, but I do! I care about them because you do. Because your beloved Adam Bishop does.' He shakes his head. 'I'm not sorry about the divorce. He was never good enough for you, Romilly. But I should have guessed you'd go for a cop. You always did like the police.'

Romilly pushes the handle down, but it's locked. She bashes again.

'Let me out,' she directs to the guard, but he doesn't move. 'Let me out!'

The guard looks at her father, and Cole nods. And only then does he take the keys from his belt and move towards the door.

'Do what you think is right, Romilly,' her father shouts after her. 'However crazy it might seem. Even a stopped clock is correct twice a day.'

But she's not listening anymore. She's running. Out of that room, down the corridor, out of the prison. Away from the man that's haunted her for her whole life.

175

Chapter 31

'What did he say?' Adam asks the moment he answers the phone. He can hear her gasping, struggling to catch her breath. 'Are you okay? Romilly?'

'Yes, yes, I'm fine. He . . . he . . .' He can hear her crying now and he curses himself for letting her go alone. But Pippa, the investigation. He can't let things slide, not even for a moment. He sits behind his desk watching the detectives in the incident room: reviewing CCTV, analysing reports, witness statements, the continued door to door on the streets.

'I'm so sorry.'

'No. I was right to see him. But he knows nothing. You were right, Adam. He used it to manipulate me.'

'So he didn't say anything useful at all?' He can't hide his disappointment, and she knows it.

'Not really, no.' She stops. 'But he knew we'd got divorced. How would he know that?'

Adam feels a wave of anger; he battles to keep it out of his voice. 'Prison guards know police,' he says at last.

'He might have bribed someone to find out. Or public records, access to the internet somehow. We need to keep you away from this now. It's not right how close he got.'

'It was my decision. I'm fine. He did say something interesting though. He asked what the killer would be getting out of it? Why they'd kill all those people.'

'Like what?'

'I don't know. Their motivation behind carrying on what . . .' She pauses, he hears her swallow. 'What Elijah started. Why would anyone do such a thing?'

'Misplaced adoration. Something fucked up in their brain. Who knows?' Adam sighs. More conjecture. More theories. 'But more importantly, how would they know? About the numbers? You remembered because you saw them. Are we looking for someone who was there, back then?'

'A journalist? A cop?'

'Or someone who spoke to Elijah in prison. A cellmate? Direct from the psycho's mouth.'

'He didn't deny it, Adam.'

'Of course, he didn't,' Adam retorts. He's annoyed. He doesn't like Romilly being manipulated like this. She's still susceptible to his charms, even after all this time. 'This is just what he wants. This attention. Getting to see you.'

'But it wasn't just that . . .'

Adam pauses at her hesitation. He feels a twinge of disquiet. 'Romilly. Did your father say anything else?'

'He said . . . ummm.' She hesitates. 'He was always coming out with these sayings, when I was a kid. You know, well-known phrases. He loved them. And he said one today. Something odd about a clock. It didn't feel right. Like he'd deliberately shoehorned it in.'

'What exactly did he say?'

'That even a stopped clock is correct twice a day.'

Adam frowns. Something niggles. He turns to his computer and pulls up the photographs from the crime scene yesterday morning, now uploaded to the system by the technicians. He scans the shots, looking closely at the bloody floor, the mass of spatter on the walls. The horrific panorama of psychopathic rage and impulse.

'Adam?' Romilly asks again down the phone. 'Are you still there?'

But he ignores her. He flicks to the next shot, then the next. But— Something grabs at his subconscious. He goes back.

And there it is. The clock on the wall in the kitchen. Everything else had been so horrifying, so out of the range of normal human experience, he hadn't given it any consideration at the time.

It was a boring analogue clock. Cheap. Ugly. But the hands. They'd been stopped. At precisely eleven minutes past eleven.

Wayne Oxford is victim number eleven. The link that Adam assumed was Romilly's imagination, that he dismissed as paranoia . . .

He'd known.

Adam is in a daze, the phone still clamped to his ear, but with that thought he jumps.

'I've got to go,' he says abruptly, and hangs up.

He leaps from his desk, shouting out to the incident room. Detectives turn, on high alert.

She was right. Romilly was fucking right. Elijah is connected. And if he is . . .

The address check of Cole's old house might have been

clear Tuesday morning, but Pippa was abducted after. Eight hours after.

There's only one place they need to be.

'We need to get to the house,' he bellows, already at a run. 'Get there now.'

If it wasn't for you, I would let her go. If it wasn't for you, she wouldn't be here.

She's quiet now. Still. Her chin is down against her chest, her hands and feet tied. I can't tell if she's asleep or passed out. I reach down and press two fingers against her neck; I can feel the gentle beat of her pulse, her heart working hard to pump the remainder of her blood around her body.

The needles have worked perfectly. Slower this time. She has a purpose, a reason to survive. For as long as I let her.

My anger has faded. It comes on fast, an impulse I can't control, funnelled towards that girl in the park. She enraged me – bobbing along, oblivious, headphones plugged in her ears. How could she be so stupid? So naïve?

I felt hot. Detached, as I plunged the knife into her back. I felt resistance, the scrape of metal against bone, but I carried on, even as she fell to the ground. My heart racing, sweating, screaming, as I plunged the knife over and over into her chest. No thinking, no hesitation. An explosion of red-hot fury.

And after, the shame, the humiliation. Fear and panic that I would be caught. Because there is only one goal.

You.

Pippa stirs slightly in her chair. She tries to lift her head, but she's groggy, confused. I look over to where my equipment has been left. Empty bags, ready to be filled. But the venesection has slowed. Her blood pressure is lower, her body shutting down. I worry. What if they find her before I have a chance to finish?

She's not so immaculate now. She's soiled herself again. Her clothes are crusty with dried sweat. With snot and tears and dribble and vomit. She was sick when I tried to make her eat. When I forced the food down her throat. What if she stops drinking, what then? I need her. I need to finish. I need to see if this will work. To the end.

I pause, a plan forming in my head.

I quickly walk across to the table and grab the syringe I've already prepared. I attach a needle, disperse the air, then stick it into her arm. She jerks awake and looks at me with panicked eyes.

'What was that?' she gasps.

'Heparin,' I reply.

'Don't . . . don't . . . please . . .' she says, and I flick at the tubing, encouraging the blood to move.

But two needles isn't enough. I fetch more cannulae, strip off her socks, and push them into the veins on the top of her feet. The blood fills the tubing, then stops, ready and waiting.

She's crying again, begging me to let her go. Last night she prayed to God, for what good that did her. There is

181

no God here. No God near me. He left me to my fate long ago; I fend for myself.

I look upwards. Not for God, but for a solution. I see the wooden beam, the hook drilled in. It's not high, but it'll do.

I fetch a length of rope and loop it over. I need to be careful. I lean down to her arms, and I carefully snip one of the ties. She jerks up, scrabbling with her free arm, but I grab it tight and wrap the rope around. She has an instant strength and I admire her determination, but it won't be enough. I undo her left hand and tie it tight. She struggles, her eyes frantic, her mouth open and screaming as I pull, tugging her arms above her head then dragging her out of her seat. She's knocked her cannulae loose in her arms, but that won't matter. I'll find another vein.

Her feet are still tied to the chair and in her panic she knocks it over. It falls backwards, wrenching her ankles in a way that must have been painful. But she doesn't stop her twisting, her body contorting, hanging from the rope.

I hold her there, until her energy dispels, and she grows slack. I stand the chair up again, and she rests her feet back on the floor.

'Gravity,' I say to her. 'The best way.'

Her eyes roll. She reminds me of a cow tied up for slaughter, sensing her last moments are at hand. She starts crying again, saying a name over and over, the words rolling into one.

'He won't find you. Not in time.' I reach down and connect the tubing to the cannulae in her feet. I leave the torn needles in her arm, turning my attention south and jerking her dirty pyjama bottoms down. I insert new needles into the femoral veins on her legs. She cries out

182

in pain and anguish, but I ignore her, just nodding in satisfaction. Blood, edging down the see-through tubing to the bags.

I stand back as my good work continues. Yes. This is it.

I watch her, as her blood flows. I feel the weight draining from my body. A lightness again. Relief, that everything is going as planned.

For you.

Chapter 32

Adam's seen the house in newspaper reports, on the evening news, but he's never been up close. Time has done it no favours.

The iron gates rust on their hinges, chains and padlocks cut in seconds as the police force their way inside. The search is quick and concise, shouts of 'all clear' as footsteps barrelled up and down the stairs, then across the lawn to the outbuilding.

The enforcer bashes its way through the outer entrance, the aged wooden slats no match for the bright red battering ram. But even before they breach the inner door, Adam knows the building is empty. The padlocks hang open on their latches, dust recently disturbed, and not just by his colleagues. He waits outside for the call; it doesn't take long. Downcast faces emerge back into the drizzle and cold, a final nod cast in his direction as they leave.

Adam pauses, a drag of disappointment that makes his bones ache. She isn't here. But she was.

They're too late.

He phones Control, hurls abuse at whatever patrol swung by two days ago. But the gate was locked, no sign of a disturbance. They did their job. It's Adam that's lacking.

He's handed a white crime scene suit and he puts it on slowly. Delaying the inevitable, when he'll see the product of his own failings. If he'd just listened to Romilly sooner. If he hadn't let the history between them get in the way. If they'd placed a guard outside the house, would the killer have left Pippa be? Or would he just have found another location for his crimes?

He steps slowly into the room.

His shoes crunch on mud and dirt. Adam sees the thick walls, the layers of insulation over the windows that suppressed the prisoners' screams. It's dark except for a thin line of light edging in from the doorway. He moves forward. Brick walls, a beam running the length of the room. Something hanging from it, a lamp of some sort. He steps forward, squints up at it. It's a hurricane lamp, modern. He reaches up with a gloved hand and presses the switch; it bursts into life, throwing shadows across the spider webs and neglect.

He can smell dust, wet soil, but also vomit, sweat, urine. It evokes a subconscious reaction in him: the hairs on his arms rising in goosebumps, a prickling of adrenaline as his body prepares for flight or fight.

He hears footsteps behind him and turns.

'You shouldn't be in here,' the woman says. He recognises her figure in the white suit. 'We need to get some foot plates down.'

'I know, Mags. But I needed to see—'

'I get it.'

In the centre of the room is a heavy wooden chair, lying

185

on its side. Fragments of what Adam recognises to be cable ties lie on the floor, as well as paper, wrapping, plastic. He crouches down next to one of them: the sterile packaging from a safety needle, *SOL-CARE* written on the side. A trickle of cold sweat runs down his spine. Next to it is a large dark puddle.

'Blood?' Adam says, looking back to Maggie.

The CSM nods. 'We'll confirm. But probably.'

There are scuffs in the dirt, scrapes and footwear marks. Spatters and splashes, some dark like the first, others lighter. Adam can't help but scan the wall – his gaze locking on the metal ring drilled into the brickwork. He closes his eyes for a second. The ghosts of the women intrude on his thoughts. This is where they were taken, where they were tortured, raped, where indescribable pain was inflicted. Where they died. Alone.

And Pippa was here too.

So where the hell has she gone?

'What am I missing here, Mags?' he asks. 'If she was here, why move her?'

'Perhaps he knew you were coming?'

'From who?' Adam struggles to believe it could be one of his team. But his mind clings on to something. A fragile ray of hope. If she was dead, he would have left her here. If she was dead, they would have found her.

'This is what I don't get,' he says. 'Everything about this – the kidnap, keeping Pippa here, carefully burying the bodies at the wasteland – it points to an organised offender, right?'

'If you subscribe to that psychology, yes. Someone smart, competent, holding down a normal job. Staging crime scenes. Maybe even taking trophies.'

'But the attack in the park?' Adam continues. 'That's more disorganised. Spontaneous. A loss of control.'

Maggie sighs and he turns to face her. She's staring up at the wooden beam, at the hooks. Where he knows Cole's first victims had been tied up, held captive for months.

'Perhaps they're losing their grip,' she says softly. 'It must take a huge toll on someone's psyche, even one as fucked up as this. It's inhuman.' She looks at him and her eyes are pained above her mask. 'My guess is it won't be long before he loses it altogether. The only worry is who he takes down in the process.' She pauses. 'Don't let it be you, Adam.'

'He won't—'

'I can see it already. Look at your face. How much sleep have you had in the past few days? Two, maybe three hours. It's not healthy.'

'None of this is healthy, Mags. Look at it.' He gestures angrily around the room. At the blood, the chair. The floor where the broken bodies once lay. 'None of it,' he repeats, quieter.

He walks away from Mags, out of the outbuilding. But before he does, he pauses in the doorway. The marks that Romilly mentioned are still here. Lines carved into the wood, one above another. Adam runs his gloved finger over them – XX, XIX, XVIII – imagining the monster that made them. Knife in hand, creating the notches, knowing he'd just buried another. How had he felt? Adam wonders. Triumphant, satisfied? Had there been any remorse at all?

The number for the final girl, Grace Summers, number seventeen, is missing. She'd been found dead in the outhouse; he hadn't had time to bury her. In the rush, he'd forgotten to mark his kill.

Disgust rises in Adam's throat, and he turns away quickly from the horrific prison Cole created. He needs to think. They still have time.

He walks around to the front of the house, ignoring the white vans starting to arrive, the teams of people setting up the cordon. They know what they're doing; another crime scene to preserve. They don't need him.

He scuffs his feet in the gravel. The driveway is covered with weeds; ivy trails up the side of the house; tiles are missing from the roof.

It's smaller than Adam expected. He knows from reports it was only a three bed, but somehow it had grown in his mind: an innocent house with a horrible secret in its grounds.

The place where Romilly grew up.

The front door is open, and Adam walks through. Adam has told the crime scene officers to focus on the garden and the outhouse, but a few are inside, not being able to resist having a look around; the legend, the horrific reputation preceding it. The hallway is dark, it smells of mould and mildew, and wallpaper peels slowly downwards to the stained wooden floorboards which warp and creak in the damp. The hallway opens out into a kitchen. Old style, untouched since Cole's arrest in November 1995. Ownership shifted to the bank: they'd left it to rot. Adam had heard true crime buffs had tried to buy it on multiple occasions, but they'd always been declined.

'I hope they bulldoze it to the ground,' Romilly had said, but they never had.

He leans down and opens a cupboard door with a gloved hand. A few belongings remain: pots and pans, the contents of a normal kitchen. It seems strange, the dullness at odds with the aberration that went on a few hundred metres away. He looks around, imagining a young Romilly eating her breakfast sitting at this table. The fridge is decorated with magnets: life-affirming misquotes and sunsets on each one. *Life isn't about waiting for the storm to pass: it's about learning to dance in the rain. We are all broken, that's how the light gets in.* And an eerie prescient *Silence is Golden.*

Adam frowns at the banality.

He leaves the kitchen, doubling back into the hallway, heading up the stairs. As the reports described, there are three bedrooms and a bathroom, and he stops at the doorway to the one on the far side.

There are faded marks on the door. Letters in the paint, where something was once stuck. ROM, they say. He pushes the door open.

The room is sparse, belongings removed. The bed is stripped back to the mattress. Desk, bedside table, wardrobe. All empty. Once the house became a crime scene anything personal had been seized. Whatever required as exhibits were catalogued for the trial, the rest taken to a huge aircraft hangar. Adam remembers Romilly telling him about going there. The surreal feeling, the sentiment it stirred. The conflict in her head knowing what her father had done. The embarrassment and intrusion: her most private belongings out on display. She'd been given an hour to take what she wanted; she'd walked away empty-handed.

Adam wonders now where everything had gone after that. All of Romilly's life before the age of eleven: erased.

His phone rings in his pocket and he pulls it out, looking

at the number. It's Marsh, no doubt wanting to know an update, keen to get Adam back to the station. But he ignores it, needing the time to think.

He sits down slowly on the denuded bed. Rests his hands on his knees. Stills his breathing. So she was here. Pippa was here. It's not easy to move a person, even a semi-conscious one. He would have needed a car, a van. This VW Transporter they still haven't tracked down.

And the debris from the equipment in the outbuilding, where was it coming from? A hospital? A doctor's surgery? Do they have some sort of medical background?

This must join up. With each piece of information, they are narrowing down the suspect pool: a Venn diagram of potential medical knowledge, mental insta-bility, VW ownership. They need analysts to look at the data; detectives to review CCTV. They will find this man: the intersect.

Adam hears a shout outside, and he stands up, looking out of the window. SOCOs are moving towards the back of the garden, towards the outhouse. He stares at it; he hadn't realised it was so close, and so clearly seen out of Romilly's bedroom window. How many times had she looked out in the same way he was doing now, unaware of what was going on at the end of her own garden?

Voices call out again, and he hears DC Quinn shout up the stairs.

'Boss?' she calls. 'Marsh wants you back at the nick.'

Adam sighs. Time to leave. He walks out of the bedroom, closing the door gently behind him.

Death, dying, so close at every turn. And nobody he can save.

Chapter 33

It takes a multi-ton HGV on Romilly's inside lane to jolt her back to reality. It honks loudly, making her swerve, swearing, adrenaline coursing in her veins. She carefully pulls into the slow lane.

She wants to call Adam, find out what's going on, but she knows she can't. She's had two missed calls from Phil but ignores them; she needs to keep the line clear.

She doesn't have many people in her life nowadays. Not many friends she trusts. She resolved early on to be honest about her father; people always found out anyway, so best to weed out the ones that couldn't cope as quickly as possible. It was the main reason she'd kept her name: if you love me, knowing who I am, then you love *me*.

Most people don't. Daughter of a serial killer. She knows the questions it raises. She's asked them all herself.

Is she like him? She has the same dark eyes, the same nose and mouth. She is clever, analytical, with a head for science. But she can also be stubborn, with a temper that comes on fast and loud. She'll feel her muscles tense, her teeth clench so hard she feels they will shatter, and she'll wonder, is this the side of her that's like him?

That could kill?

She's seen the looks, heard the whispers. Nature versus nurture. Did Elijah Cole kill because of something in his DNA, or had it been the way he'd been brought up? Her father had never talked about his upbringing, and she'd never met her grandparents, they all died before she was born. Had something happened when he was young? Had he been dropped on his head, abused, belittled, like so many serial killers before him?

She'd read the biographies, trying to find the truth among the speculation and lies. Therapy had gone a long way to undo the damage, working her way through counsellor after counsellor until she found Dr Jones. The woman who seems to understand her. Who taught her to trust again.

To love.

When her father was arrested, she'd spent the next week in a blur. Interviews with the police, shunted around from responsible adult to responsible adult. People supposedly there to make sure her wellbeing was respected, but just as curious and nosey as the one before. Social services put her in a group home for a few nights. A strange bed in a noisy room. Then to a foster home.

Nobody wanted to adopt the daughter of a killer. The slightest indiscretion and she was moved on. Place to place, never staying more than six months. Nobody tells you what to do; there is no guidebook for how to be the daughter of a serial killer. An underground community got in touch – relatives of murderers – but she found them strange. They were angry, shocked, confused, claiming that they'd always seen the psychopath seething under the surface. But Romilly – she'd never had a clue.

She was eager to please, to prove everyone wrong. She did her best: she finished school, A levels, applied to university. Her teenage years were dull, uneventful. She went to med school, went out with a few men, but no one she got close to. She didn't dare.

And then she met Adam.

Her phone rings, making her jump again. She answers it quickly.

'You were right,' Adam says, his voice dull. 'We went to the house.'

Her breath catches. Hope blossoms, only to be shattered quickly by Adam's words.

'She's not here,' he says. 'But she was.'

Romilly struggles to keep her car in lane and she's beeped again. 'When? How?'

'We missed them. I'm sorry, Milly. I should have listened to you.' A long pause. 'He had her in the outhouse.'

'Oh, Christ. Listen, Adam—'

'I've got to go, I wanted to let you know,' he says quickly, and hangs up.

The news sinks in slowly as she drives the rest of the way home. She knew it. She did. But . . . But . . . How can Elijah be involved? He's in prison, cut off from the world. She can't comprehend how this could be happening. How can he be talking to someone? Aren't there systems and processes to stop this sort of thing?

She manages to get back without any further incidents, parking her car in her drive, surprised to see Phil's next to it. She puts her key in the lock and he's standing there, waiting.

'Romilly! Where have you been?'

'Why aren't you at work?' She shakes off his attempts at a hug, taking off her coat and hanging it up.

'Because I was worried. You went to see your father, and then you didn't call. You didn't answer your phone.'

'I'm sorry. I . . . I was distracted. Adam—'

'You called Adam?' His face clouds.

'Yes.' His obvious disapproval annoys her. 'He's responsible for finding Pippa, of course I called Adam. And I was right. My father is involved. There's a link.'

'And?'

'And what?'

'Have they found her?'

'No. No, Phil, they fucking haven't.'

Romilly knows she's taking her anger out on her boyfriend, unfairly so, but she can't stop it. He takes a step towards her, holding out his hands to offer comfort but she turns and walks away. She goes into the kitchen and busies herself making a cup of tea. Mugs, kettle, water. She feels him standing in the doorway, watching her.

'Romilly, I know you're concerned, but you can't let it affect you like this.'

'Like what, Phil?'

'Like . . . this! This anger. Worry. It's taking over your life. You haven't been to work. You're not sleeping. Perhaps you should go and see Dr Jones.'

'I don't want to see my fucking therapist again.'

'And you shouldn't see him anymore.'

Romilly can agree with that one. 'I'm not going to visit my father again,' she replies. His face still looms in her mind's eye. His smile, too familiar, taking her back to her childhood. Digging up the old feelings, the worry, the insomnia. The guilt.

'No,' Phil says firmly. 'I meant Adam. I don't want you seeing Adam.'

Romilly turns quickly. 'Don't tell me what to do.'

'He's no good for you, Romilly. This investigation, these murders. It's destroying you. And he's your ex—'

'So?'

'So, from the beginning you were desperate to see him. And you're telling me there are no feelings there.'

'Fuck off, Phil.'

She walks away from him, into the living room, but he follows, close on her heels.

'Tell me it isn't true. You can't, can you?'

'If you don't trust me when I tell you that our marriage is over, then what good is anything I say?'

'I'm not talking about your marriage. I'm talking about your feelings for him. That you still want to be with him. That you're still in love with him.'

'That's ridiculous.'

'Is it?' He frowns, shaking his head. 'I can take the nightmares, the fear of the dark. I will look after you, Romilly. Because I know about you, and your father, and your tragic past.'

Her tragic past. Romilly stares at him as he says those words; slightly disparaging, slightly disgusted. Like she has an unpleasant social affliction that can't be cured.

'But this. Carrying on with your ex under my nose. This I can't take.'

'I'm not—' she starts, but he interrupts again.

'If you love me, then you will do as I say, and not see him again.'

Romilly feels a wave of repulsion. It starts in her stomach, radiating outwards, triggering something in her brain. She feels sick as anger takes over, and she points a hard finger in her boyfriend's face.

'You don't. Fucking. Tell me what to do,' she shouts with each jab.

She walks away, pushing past him through the house to her study. She slams the door with all her strength, the bang echoing off the walls. Then she stands, furious tears streaming down her cheeks.

How dare he? How dare he command her in that way? Somewhere deep in her mind she knows she's overreacting, that Phil isn't her father, but she feels the rage, the pain. Once she'd left – the house, her father and the dead girls far behind her – she'd resolved never to let that happen again. To be controlled.

But it isn't just that.

She knows she's not perfect. She knows she has more problems than the average woman, but somehow she thought she was still worthy of love. That someone could be with her no matter what. Despite her past. Despite the history that haunts her every turn.

She thought she could have it with Adam. But he had pushed her away.

And, with one comment, Phil has done the same. There are conditions, rules attached to his love. She must do as he says. Obey him. She'd done that once, as a child. And she'd resolved, never again.

Romilly knows, deep in her heart, that no matter what she does, no matter what she says, she will always be the daughter of a serial killer. And because of that, she will always be alone.

Chapter 34

The two men stand in silence, facing the whiteboard. Adam chances a look at his detective chief superintendent: Marsh's face is still, his expression impossible to scrutinise. Then he turns.

'What's your next move, Bishop?' he asks.

'We can assume she's still alive—'

'Can we?'

Marsh says it quietly, so the other detectives in the room can't hear.

'Yes,' Adam replies. 'Yes. Because otherwise . . .'

Adam doesn't want to say it. Because otherwise he's out there, killing again. Because otherwise Jamie will never forgive him. Because otherwise, what's the fucking point. In all of this.

'And you think Cole has something to do with it?' Marsh says. 'There are differences. For one, there are no signs of sexual assault on the new victims, where rape was a key part of Cole's MO.'

'Noted,' Adam replies. 'But how can it be anything else?'

'A calculating psychopath like Cole making the most of the situation? A new killer who somehow knows about the numbers? An obsessed acolyte of the Good Doctor? Who took advantage of a ready-made murder room, empty and waiting?' Marsh's eyebrows are lowered, the disbelief clear on his face. 'It could be any of those things. Cole didn't actually tell you where Pippa was, did he?'

'No, but—'

Marsh waves a hand, dismissing his objections. 'I'll sign the warrant, don't worry. Get the visitor logs and the CCTV from the prison. Have a look and see if there's a way Cole could be talking to someone on the outside. Just don't let it blinker you to other routes of enquiry, Adam.'

Adam nods, turning back to the board. But what is he missing? Is there another avenue he hasn't explored?

He wants to ask Marsh what he would do. Get the benefit of the older, more experienced detective; his DCS is no newcomer to murder, no desk monkey at the top for political reasons. He served his time in Major Crimes, the SIO on multiple high-profile cases. But Adam can't form the words. To ask for advice would be admitting defeat and he wants to prove himself. That he can run this investigation, and do it alone.

But before Adam can articulate any of this out loud, Quinn rushes up to their side.

'Boss,' she says, breathless and rushed. 'We have it.'

'Have what?'

'The guy. Our offender. Last night. We have him on CCTV.'

All resources are moved to CCTV, everyone scouring the film from different cameras across the city. Adam watches the footage, his hand over his mouth. It's a figure, dressed all in black. Head down, a hood over his face. He walks fast along the path, small footsteps, quick and decisive.

'Look up, look up,' Adam whispers, wishing for one glimpse of his face. An identifying mark. A logo. Something to use to find this guy.

But his face stays downward as he disappears out of shot.

Quinn anticipates Adam's next question, and swaps screens to a camera further along. The time stamp skips ten minutes, but there he is again. Streetlights this time. Shop windows. Even though Adam knows he must be covered in blood it's not obvious on the footage, absorbed into the black material of his hoodie.

'Check reflections in shop windows, anything that might give us a moment of this guy's face. There, there, those two.' Adam points to a couple walking past the offender. Their gaze locks on the man, clearly distracted by something about him, then they walk away fast. 'They saw him. Find them. I want a description, and I want it now.' He shouts to the rest of the team. 'Follow this guy. If he gets in a car, follow it. I want him.'

The room is a mass of energy; nothing gets murder detectives moving faster than the thought their suspect is in their sights.

His phone rings. It's Jamie. He steels himself, then takes the call.

'Adam, please . . . They said you were at the house.'

The bloody reporters again. 'Yes. Yes, we were. But she wasn't there, Jamie, I'm sorry.'

'Was she before?'

'Yes.'

'You were too late.' Matter of fact, his voice dull.

'Yes. But we have some good leads, Jamie. We're on his trail.'

There's a long pause at the end of the phone; Adam can hear quiet sobbing. A noise that wrenches at his heart. He stands, listening, as detectives buzz around him. Then he hears a loud sniff, a rustle of tissues and Jamie comes back on the line.

'I'm going to go home,' he says quietly.

'You don't have to do that. You can stay as long as you need.'

'No, no. I'll go over now. I thought it would be awful but actually I just want to be close to Pippa. And if I can't have the real thing then I want to be there. Waiting for her to walk back in the door. Because she will, won't she, Adam?'

Adam takes a long breath, looking out into the incident room where the CCTV plays across multiple monitors, faces inches away from the screens.

'She will, Jamie.'

He ends the call and goes back out.

'Where are we?' he directs, and a detective points.

'We lost him as he walked into Regent's Street car park, but then a VW Transporter exits soon after.'

'We've got a plate?'

'No. Completely obscured. But we're still tracking it.'

Adam takes a seat next to him and watches as they follow the footage. The Transporter goes out of shot frustratingly frequently, but a DC consults a map, CCTV camera numbers are shouted out, and they pick it up again.

It's moving fast, not sticking to the speed limits. They watch it drive through the centre of town, then leave, heading towards one of the suburbs. Adam knows the area: countryside, fields. It goes too far and they'll lose it.

Sure enough, the VW heads through an area out of range and it's gone. They scrabble desperately, swapping cameras and views, but nothing.

'Stick to this angle,' Adam says. 'People are creatures of habit, if he came in this way, chances are he'll drive back out by the same route.' He points to a second team. 'Have you found anything near the old Cole house?'

'There's no cameras around there, boss.'

'Well, check the surrounding area,' he shouts. 'Anything you have. Find me that fucking van.'

They scroll through car after car on the junction, studying each one carefully. Daylight creeps into shot, footage from this morning now, shadows growing shorter as the day progresses. But still nothing. The time stamp creeps frustratingly closer to their current time. He must have used a different route, taken another way out. But then a detective shouts from another screen. And there it is.

'Follow it,' Adam barks. He checks the map. It's one of the roads leading away from the Cole house. The timing is right: before they got there. Pippa must be inside. They missed her by a mere fifteen minutes.

Adam cranes forward on his seat, resting his elbows on his knees. The detectives not working on the CCTV come over and watch, curiosity too strong to concentrate on their own lines of enquiry.

The VW drives through streets Adam knows only too well. Roads change to a residential area, then it goes out of shot again.

'What streets are around that area?' Adam shouts.

'Brown Street, York Road, Robertson Avenue . . .'

The realisation hits Adam hard, making him reel. A punch in the face, right between the eyes. But he can't be . . . To go back there . . .

'Oh, God,' he whispers. 'Jamie.'

Chapter 35

Jamie's hand shakes as he puts his key in the lock; he pushes the front door open slowly. A part of him – a very small part – thinks Pippa will be there to greet him. Her bright smile. Her hug and kiss and 'here you are!'. Tempting smells wafting from the kitchen where she would have been cooking dinner. But there's nothing. The stale air of a house untouched.

He closes the door behind him and takes off his coat. All his limbs feel heavy, every movement an effort. He hangs it up and leaves his small overnight bag at the foot of the stairs.

He stands in the doorway to his living room. The initial relief when that woman slashed to death in the grass hadn't been Pippa has been overtaken by the grim knowledge that he still has her. What is he doing? This man who has slashed and stabbed and inflicted unimaginable pain on seven people, has his wife captive.

And Pippa had been there. At *that* house. In the same building Cole killed those women. Jamie wonders if Pippa had realised where she was, and the fates of the women who had been there before her. Had she panicked, screamed? His stomach contracts at the thought of her fear, his legs almost buckling underneath him, and he collapses down to the sofa. He puts his head into his hands. If Adam had got there sooner, if they'd broken down the door minutes, hours earlier, Pippa might be back with him now.

But Adam had been too late.

She had gone. Again.

He wipes his eyes, breathing slowly. His living room seems normal. Strangely so. The mess of the SOCOs and the police and the bustle and chaos had been more fitting than this order. How can the cushions be neat, when his whole life has been destroyed? He expected the mess from the crime scene techs and wonders who tidied up. Some thoughtful person, not wanting him to return to a messy house? He walks through to the kitchen, it's the same. The draining board clear, sides all wiped down. Tidier than if they'd been living here.

His phone rings in his pocket and he pulls it out. *Bishop,* it says. He hesitates. He's had the same feeling about Adam's calls since Pippa went missing. He could be phoning to say they'd found her – alive. Or he could be telling him the opposite. Before he answers it, both outcomes are possible, Schrödinger messing with his head.

He clicks on the green button.

'Have you found her?' he asks before Adam can speak.

'No, but—'

Jamie takes the phone away from his ear and ends the call. He doesn't want to hear it. He knows he shouldn't blame Adam, but he does. Bishop is the SIO, the man in charge. The best they have, if all the reports and accolades are anything to go by. So why can't he close the one case that matters?

The phone rings again but this time Jamie ignores it.

'Fucking find her,' he mutters, muting the ringtone.

He places it back in his pocket and slowly trudges upstairs. All the doors on the landing are closed, the tidying fairy at work again, Jamie thinks. He pushes on the handle to their bedroom and opens the door.

Even before he steps inside, Jamie feels that something is wrong. The hairs on the back of his neck stand on end, his skin prickles. The room is completely dark, the curtains closed. And there is a strange smell. Unpleasant. Something sour, gone rotten.

He takes one step inside, then stops again. His eyes adjust to the dim light and now he can make out shapes. He looks towards the bed. The duvet is neat, but there is a lump under it. A body-shaped lump. Someone sleeping on Pippa's side of the bed.

His heart jumps. He wants to leap forward, his mind racing towards the assumption that she's here, she's home. She came back and went straight to bed; she was so tired. It was all a big misunderstanding, a mistake—

But Jamie's frozen. He instinctively knows that's not the case.

He takes a step forward, closer. He can see hair now. Blonde hair, sprayed out on the pillow. Another step. Her head, partially covered by the duvet.

She's lying on her back, face up. Her eyes are closed. She looks like she's sleeping but the position is unnatural. Pippa never slept on her back. She curled up, like a kitten, her arm propped under her head.

Jamie slowly walks around to Pippa's side of the bed.

His breaths come sharp and shallow; his head is starting to spin. He knows something is desperately, horribly wrong. He is close now, and he slowly reaches out with his hand and pulls the duvet back so her whole face is revealed.

A sob erupts from his body and he falls to his knees. His wife is lying there, her head resting on the pillow, her hands folded up, crossed on her chest. Her hair is combed and neat. Her eyes are closed.

He reaches out, frantically clutching at one of her hands, then drops it from shock. Her skin is ice cold. Grey.

His wife is here, tucked up in bed. As if she'd been cared for, loved, looked after. But she is dead. And completely leached of blood.

Chapter 36

It doesn't take long for Adam to get there. Even before Jamie answered his phone, Adam was running out of the incident room, calling for a patrol car. He put out an alert, for someone to go to Jamie. Anyone. Because that VW Transporter had been heading to 9 Robertson Avenue. Jamie's home.

He waits for the answering call. For a uniform to confirm they've got there, and his friend is safe. But the reply isn't the one he's expecting.

'House all clear, no trace of suspect.' The voice is low, quiet. He pauses. 'But she's here, boss. Pippa Hoxton. She's here.'

And he knows it isn't good news.

The uniform lets him into the house and he runs up the stairs two at a time to the bedroom, all thoughts of preserving the scene completely out of his head. In the doorway, Adam stops. The bedside light is on, illuminating the room in a cosy warm glow.

Jamie is crouched by the side of the bed, his head in his

hands. Adam walks over, his gaze locked on the body, and lowers himself to his knees, placing a hand on Jamie's back.

As he waits for his friend to acknowledge him, Adam comes to terms with what he's seeing. Pippa has been laid out in their bed. Carefully tucked in, the body positioned deliberately. The van hadn't been there to lie in wait for Jamie; the killer had been taking Pippa home. He reaches across and moves the duvet to get a better view. She's wearing an old-fashioned white nightgown. It looks crisp and ironed. Her body is clean, her hair slightly damp.

But her skin. It's dove grey. Her lips are white. One hand has fallen by her side, the other crossed over her chest. Her nails are broken, one missing. And there are two red, raw puncture wounds in her arms.

Adam wrenches his gaze away and turns his attention to Jamie.

'Is she dead? Is she dead, Adam?' Jamie's eyes are desperate, pleading.

'I'm sorry, Jamie. Yes, she is.'

He starts crying, and Adam swallows down tears of his own as an ache grows in the back of his throat. Sadness mixed with guilt and anger and regret.

He hears footsteps in the doorway, muttered words.

'Ah, shit.'

Adam looks up and Ross is standing there, already dressed in the white suit of the crime scene.

'Jamie, I'm sorry. But you need to go.'

'I don't want to leave her. I can't . . .' He starts sobbing again, this huge man, curled up in a ball on the floor, his shoulders heaving. Nobody moves; the whole room waits. The SOCOs, Dr Ross, Adam. Everyone drowned in this man's grief.

Adam puts an arm around Jamie's shoulders. 'She's in good hands,' he says softly. 'We'll look after her. And you can see her again, I promise.'

Jamie nods slowly, then allows Adam to haul him to his feet. He reaches out to his dead wife, then pulls back, putting his hands over his face again. The family liaison officer comes into the room and leads Jamie out.

Adam turns to Ross, who points wordlessly to the protective suit being passed his way. Adam puts it on. Ross slowly pulls back the duvet to reveal the whole body.

Pippa is clothed only in the nightdress. Her feet are bare, clean like the rest of her.

'He washed her,' Adam says. 'And tidied the house. Creating a stage? Returning her as a . . . sort of gift?'

'Could be,' Ross agrees. 'Or just a forensic counter-measure. What do you want to know?'

Adam shakes his head. He doesn't want to be here, looking at the dead body of his friend. With every fibre of his being he wished for a different outcome.

Ross starts examining the body, pushing up the long nightdress to expose her legs. He ignores Adam and starts talking.

'Cannulae went in here, and here, and here,' he says, pointing to the marks on her arm and identical holes on her feet. Adam can't help but see the needles, long, thin and sharp, resting in her veins.

Adam looks away quickly. He feels his vision swimming and leans back against the nearest wall. He consciously tenses his muscles, pushing his hands into fists.

Ross continues his examination of the body. 'Bruises on her wrists and ankles probably from restraints. And the exsanguination looks extensive.'

Adam nods. Ross is still talking but he's not listening. He feels sick; a loud buzzing starts in his ears. His balance wobbles as the room starts to spin.

'This is what I suspected for Wayne Oxford,' the pathologist continues, 'but the wounds to the arms obliterated any definitive signs. He must have inserted needles there too, planning to bleed the body using that method, before defaulting to the anterolateral laceration.'

Adam clears his throat. 'Time of death?' he whispers. His tongue feels sticky and big in his mouth.

'Still some rigor present. But the body's stone cold. So over eight hours ago.'

Adam can't bear it anymore. He rushes out, hanging off the bannister as he runs down the stairs, feeling the eyes of everyone on him. He knows what they're thinking, feels their judgement.

He didn't find her. That bastard killed her, drained every single drop of her blood, then left her here.

He failed.

Chapter 37

Adam stands outside Jamie's house for five, ten minutes, the time ticking past without him noticing. Anyone watching would have seen a man thinking: his head bent to the floor, his hands by his sides, motionless in the darkness of the winter evening. But nothing is at rest inside his head. Emotions swirl: the guilt, his failure, the grief for Pippa. Anger for what she must have gone through.

He straightens up, takes his phone out of his pocket and barks orders at the team back at the station, then turns towards the patrol car waiting at the kerb. He gets in, gives them an address and they leave. She has to know, and he has to be the one to tell her.

Adam tells the car not to wait and rings the doorbell. When it's opened – his own old front door – a strange man is looking at him. The man is dressed in a grey tracksuit, but one of those posh ones that looks like it was tailor-made. It hugs his broad chest, shows off his narrow waist. Even though it's February, the man has a tan straight from the South of France in August.

For a brief moment the man smiles, welcoming. Then it fades.

'You're Adam,' he says. His voice is gruff.

'Yes. Is Romilly in?'

She appears behind him; her eyes are red-rimmed. She looks like she's already been crying, but one look at him and her face drops further.

'Oh, Adam,' she says. The man moves out of the way as Romilly ushers him in the house and into the living room. 'You found her.'

'Yes, I'm sorry. She's dead. She died. He killed her.'

He knows he's barely making sense, that he could have expressed it better. But seeing Romilly changes him from a police officer to a normal man. A human, who wants to be comforted and talked to with understanding and care.

Romilly starts to cry, standing in the middle of the room. Adam reaches out automatically but stops as her boyfriend pulls her close and she cries into his chest.

Adam stands awkwardly next to them. This used to be him. His house, his wife.

'I'm sorry,' he mutters. 'I should go.'

But Romilly stops him. 'No, don't,' she says. She pulls away from her boyfriend and hurriedly wipes her eyes. 'Sit down. Please?'

He does as she asks, perching on the edge of the sofa. She sits next to him; the boyfriend folds his arms across his chest and watches, his face stern.

The energy between the two of them is odd. Adam feels the tension, a divergence. Because of him being there? He's not sure.

'Where was she?' Romilly starts. 'Had she been . . .'

'Jamie found her. At home.' Romilly stares at him, not understanding. 'The killer took her back there. Posed her in their bed.'

Romilly's hands go to her mouth. 'Oh, God,' she says. 'Oh, poor Jamie. How is he?'

'How you'd expect. Devastated.'

'And how are you?'

Adam clears his throat. He looks down at his hands. 'I'm fine,' he replies. 'Just want to catch this bastard.'

Romilly looks at her boyfriend. 'Phil, could you make us a cup of tea?' The man doesn't move. 'Please?' she asks again.

He stares at Adam, then does as he's asked.

The two of them sit in silence for a moment. Not much has changed since Adam lived there with Romilly. The sofas are the same. The coffee table is the same. Furniture Adam helped pay for. Everything he left behind when he and Romilly split up.

He sees small differences. Books on the shelf that Romilly would never read. Tom Clancy, John Grisham. Autobiographies from sportsmen and women. A jumper left over the arm of a chair. A painting on the wall that Adam doesn't like.

'Adam?' she tries again. 'Talk to me.'

The differences in the room only reinforce how much everything has changed between them. 'I'm fine,' he says again. He forces a smile. 'I'm used to this.'

'But it's your friend that's died. Your best mate has lost his wife.'

'I'm more than aware of that, thank you.'

'It wasn't your fault, Adam.'

'Wasn't it?' he snaps. 'Whose was it then?'

But Romilly doesn't shy away from his tone. 'You did everything you could.'

'I didn't. I didn't listen to you. If I had . . . I might have . . . We could have got to the house in time. And I keep on thinking, what did I miss? I should have put pressure on the lab to go faster. Allocated more resource to CCTV. What is this guy leaving behind that we're not seeing? What am I doing wrong?'

Romilly's still staring at him.

'Adam,' she says gently. 'You didn't abduct Pippa. You didn't kill her. Don't blame yourself.'

He looks at her. At the face he knows so well. Romilly is the only person who he's ever been able to be honest with. She met him at his most vulnerable. When his defences were down and he had no option but to disclose what he was thinking. And he'd love to spill everything, right now in the place he used to call home. To share the sinking sensation in his gut, the nerves that won't shift. How he can't face Jamie, knowing he's let his best mate down in the worst possible way. That all he fucking wants to do is find this guy and stick a knife in his gut.

But he hears the kettle boiling in the other room. The chink of a spoon in a mug. Romilly realises what he's thinking and looks in the direction of her boyfriend.

'We could go somewhere else?' she says. 'Go for a walk? Get out of here.'

'No, no. I just wanted to let you know that she . . . that Pippa . . .' He stands up quickly. He feels as if he's going to cry. But he can't. He walks quickly towards the door; he hears Romilly behind him.

'Adam . . .' she says as he opens the lock on the front door. It sticks, as it always had, and he pulls hard.

'Thank you, Milly,' he says. He turns, looks at her. He sees her boyfriend watching from the room behind. 'I'll be in touch.'

And he walks quickly away. From the house where he lived as a married man. From the last place he was happy, with the woman he loved more than anyone else.

He can't let her back in. He can't let himself trust her again, not after what she did. Nobody can be relied on, not her, not his parents. And they come back to him now, the memory of his childhood. Sitting scared, shaking in an unfamiliar room, with strangers bustling around. His mother's words: *I will never leave you. I love you. I promise I will always be here for you, no matter what happens.*

But she had. And so had Romilly.

He walks away still, striding fast down the road. His chest so tight he almost can't breathe. Not permitting himself to cry.

Truthwarrior65@hotmail.com
24/02/1997 11:27:027 UTC

Not so innocent! Why didn't she know??

I call bullshit! So Romilly Cole knew nothing about her father's crimes, as determined today at Winchester court. Twelve-year-old Romilly testified this morning at the trial, outlining her father's movements for those last four months. How he said he was going down to the garden shed to do some 'carpentry'. How he always kept the door locked, said it was to keep her away from his dangerous tools? And she didn't suspect anything? What a crock of shit!

Yeah, okay, so the room was soundproofed. But that well? Really? She never went down the garden to see what her father was up to? Never heard the screams and the cries for help? Didn't notice as her father dragged his victims down the garden, locking them away to their doom? What was she doing all this time? Painting her nails? Listening to her Walkman?

And that's not even mentioning the strange circumstances around her calling the police. She blustered on the stand when she was asked by the defence, got confused and then broke down in tears, resulting in the prosecution demanding a break for the poor girl.

The prosecution claim she is traumatised, that she isn't the one on trial. Traumatised, my arse! She was part of it. She knew what her father was doing.

I know what you'll say - I should be more sympathetic. Chances are she was a victim herself, although she says she wasn't. She was probably raped by him. Fucked up the arse in the same way those poor women were — he was a kiddie-fiddler as well as a murderer. But that maniac tortured and killed those women right under her nose. In the grounds of the same house.

And they say she was an innocent bystander? Bullshit!

Chapter 38

Back at the station, the sergeants and constables that Adam has trained so well are still running at full tilt. They haven't hesitated: Pippa was loved by one of their own, and they are doing everything they can to find who did this to her. But Adam notices they haven't changed her photo on the board. The number nine has been written up, but the photo under *MISSING* hasn't moved.

The detectives see him arrive back and hush. He pauses, sitting on the edge of one of the desks next to the board, gathering his thoughts. He's calmer now, composed. He has to be.

One of the detectives speaks. 'How's Jamie?'

The others murmur in agreement.

'Destroyed,' Adam replies. 'In pieces. Listen.' He points up to the board. 'We've all been going at this investigation for five days straight. I'm sure you're all exhausted. Frustrated. I know I am. And we have a long way to go yet. But Marsh has been clear, sod the budget. There are more of us now. I want you all to be taking breaks, getting some rest. I can't risk any mistakes. When we catch this guy we want to make sure there is nothing that will get him off.'

He stands up and runs his finger down the list of names. When he gets to Pippa, he slowly moves the smiling photo under the number nine. The room is silent.

'Everyone,' Adam continues. 'Get a coffee, use the bathroom, have a fag. Because in fifteen minutes I want us all back here. Let's review what we have. And we'll all work out where to go next.'

Adam uses the time to go up to the roof for a cigarette. It's not allowed, but he knows many detectives have used it in the past, a characteristic of old nicks like this one. He can't be down in the smoking area with the others, laughing and joking. He needs the quiet.

He wedges the fire door open, then walks to the border of the roof. The world is muted up here. He flickers his lighter into flame and takes a long drag on his cigarette. The night is clear, a pepper of stars across the black canvas, and he stares up at them for a moment. The roof is edged with a low brick wall, no more than a few foot high; it comes up to his thigh. Four floors up; he leans over and peers down to the road below. The concrete pavement, the almost certain death if he plunged over the edge. He watches people walk on the street, the cars, the bustle of everyday activity. He feels a wobble of vertigo and steps two paces back.

'Going to give it a miss tonight?' a voice behind him says. He turns, and Marsh is standing there.

'Sorry, guv. I know this area is out of bounds,' Adam begins but Marsh waves his words away, lighting his own cigarette and coming to stand next to him.

219

'Just don't tell the troops. I do the same. Only peaceful space in the nick.' Marsh turns and sits on the low wall, his back to the drop. 'You okay, Adam?'

'Gathering my thoughts.'

'You couldn't have saved her.'

Adam turns sharply. 'I should have.'

Marsh takes a long drag on his cigarette, then blows the smoke out into the dark. 'I've been doing this job for over thirty years. Did you know that, Bishop?'

'No, guv.'

'Holding off retiring, because I thought, what would be the point? What would I do? Play golf?' He pauses, reflectively flicking ash onto the concrete. 'But you know what? Who cares if that's all I do? I can't be around this anymore. All this death, this murder. They rot your brain. The ones you couldn't save.'

Adam stares at him. In all the years he's worked for Marsh, the man has always been rock hard. Never giving an inch, driving detectives to achieve. To be better. To hear him admit defeat was sobering.

'When I was a DCI, like you, there was this one case. A woman, beaten up by her shitbag of a husband. We all knew he was doing it – the doctors that saw her in A and E, the PCs on the beat, the teachers for their kids. Even social services were involved. But we couldn't get anything on him.' Marsh stares grimly at his feet, shuffling a toe of his shoe in the gravel. 'My super said we needed to keep it by the book. He'd make a mistake. We'd get him eventually.'

'And did you?'

He frowns, scratches his ear. 'Yeah. Put him away for life. But not until he'd set fire to his house, killing his wife and their two girls.' He stands up, turning and looking over the drop as Adam had moments earlier. 'They didn't die straight away either. The burns killed them. Two days in the ICU, watching their skin crack, fingers burnt away, suffering painfully. One of the little girls, she was eight at the time. She'd been blinded, her eyes destroyed by the heat. So she couldn't see anyone. She couldn't touch anyone. I sat by her bedside for hours. Just reading. Books, magazines, anything suitable I could get my hands on. To offer some sort of human comfort as she died. I'll never forget her. And the smell . . .' He stops, looking back to Adam, his eyes dark. 'I'll retire, after this one, Bishop. You catch this guy, and then I'll go.'

Adam's gaze drops to the concrete as he extracts the last fraction of nicotine from his cigarette. 'What if I don't catch him?' he says quietly.

'You will. I know you, Bishop. You will.' Marsh brushes down his suit, replacing his packet of cigarettes in his jacket pocket. 'By whatever means possible,' he finishes, leaving Adam standing up there.

Adam looks to the doorway. He drops his butt to the concrete and stubs it out with his toe. It's good his boss has faith in him, he thinks, because right now he doesn't have a clue.

The team are all assembled and waiting when Adam gets back to the incident room. Chairs facing forward, notepads in hand, they look up as he stands at the front of the room.

'Let's start from the left, work around. What lines of enquiry are we all following? And shout up if you have any new thoughts, however ridiculous they may seem.'

221

He starts with Ellie Quinn; she runs through her progress identifying possible VW Transporters. As she talks, he notices movement to his left, and Romilly comes into the room. She's wearing her smart dark blue coat, over a black jumper, jeans and boots. She stands in the doorway. He's surprised to see her; it's rare that a civilian, especially one with connections to the case, would be allowed so close. She smiles at Adam, a quick flicker, then switches her concentration to Quinn.

Ellie continues: 'So we're working through the list, starting with vehicles registered in the area where the van was seen on CCTV. Checking alibis, comparing owners to the PNC. But it's slow work.'

'Good, keep going,' Adam says, and she blushes, staring at her notebook. He moves on to DC Lee.

'Tim. Any news from the lab?'

He shakes his head. 'Mags has confirmed that the blood in the outbuilding on Gloucester Road was definitely Pippa Hoxton's. But they're still working through the rest.'

'Did she say if the samples from the mortuary had been processed?'

'No, sorry, boss.'

'Get on it. If there was blood from the offender on those bodies, I want it. And where are we with the witnesses from Wednesday night?'

The detective sheepishly confirms their lack of progress, and Adam moves on. They're still scouring CCTV, checking ANPR, running house-to-house and interviewing fly-tippers from the first dump site, but there's nothing new, nothing of note.

'What about stalkers?' one of the detectives speaks up. 'Louise Edwards reported she was being stalked, and we believe the killer went into Stephen Carey's house. How about we run a check on the PNC for reports of similar cases?'

Adam notices Romilly staring intently at the whiteboard. She looks at him, then back again, before leaning forward slightly.

'Good shout,' Adam confirms to the detective. 'Do it.'

He turns his attention to Romilly.

'Dr Cole, thank you for joining us. Do you have anything to add?'

She frowns, and quickly looks out at the detectives, all eyes now shifted onto her.

'Just a thought,' she says slowly. 'About your witness mentioning they saw the killer wearing pyjamas. Have you considered scrubs?'

'Scrubs?'

'Yes, that doctors wear. Informally we always call them pyjamas. Could he have been wearing scrubs?'

The room bursts into conversation. Adam's thoughts are reeling. He's seen Romilly wearing them in the past at the hospital – baggy trousers, in a variety of colours.

'Hey, hey,' Adam shouts, silencing the room. 'Who would wear scrubs?' he directs to Romilly. 'And why?'

'Doctors, nurses, surgeons. Mostly people working in critical care, so the theatres and ICU. Maybe the emergency department.'

'But you never wore them home?' Adam says.

'No, you're not supposed to. We get changed at the hospital. But there's nothing to stop people taking them – I have a few pairs in my wardrobe. They're easy to dispose of. Comfortable.'

'Shit,' Adam mutters. It fits. It fits with the medical

waste found at the scene, the knowledge to drain Pippa's blood. But where to start?

'Tim, get a list of all staff from the main hospitals in the area. Quinn, start cross-checking them against the registered owners of the VW vans.'

'What about locums?' Romilly adds. 'Or admin staff. Anyone could potentially steal them.'

'They'd need the medical expertise. Stick with nurses, doctors, anyone that might have that know-how.'

The team explodes into activity. Romilly comes over and stands with Adam.

'Marsh called me,' she says. 'In case I could help. In whatever way possible. I couldn't bear to be at home,' she adds. 'Doing nothing.'

Adam's not sure whether his boss is making an exception to get Romilly's input or whether it's an excuse to provide Adam with a modicum of moral support, but he ruefully acknowledges the gesture. 'Thank you,' he says to Romilly. 'For coming.'

She smiles. She looks worn out. He hates to think how he's looking right now. His skin feels tight, his eyes dry. He knows he must smell bad; of cigarettes and layers of hastily applied deodorant.

There's a shout from the other side of the room, a detective holds out a phone. 'They want to know exactly what professions we're looking for,' he calls.

'I'll go,' Romilly says, and heads across.

Adam watches her. Seeing her has given him a boost of energy. A new line of enquiry to follow. But it's more than that.

Her being with him. It helps. As it always has.

Chapter 39

Romilly didn't know what to expect when she turned up at the police station, barely an hour after Adam had arrived at her door. But she'd recognised the expression on his face when he'd told her about Pippa: emotion bubbling, the desperation of wanting to talk but not knowing how. Old feelings pulled to the surface. She'd wanted to be with him, so when she'd received the call she'd walked away from Phil, got in her car, and driven here.

But this man in front of her? The Adam she knows has gone; he's pulled the mask back on, all previous vulnerabilities disappeared behind the brisk competence, the commanding manner. The detectives in his charge don't know the man she married. The one that admitted he had failings. The one that asked for help, that could show weakness. That cried, laughed, that wrapped his arms so tightly around her she knew she would never break. She misses that guy, oh, so much.

Romilly finishes her conversation with the detective and does the next most helpful thing she can think of: fetches coffees and teas for the team. The canteen is about to close for the night, but the woman behind the counter takes pity, switching the coffee machine back on. As she waits, she thinks about the moment their marriage imploded.

The man was the son of one of her elderly patients. Tall, single, broad-shouldered. Out of bounds from the start, but somehow it made him all the more irresistible. He showed an interest in her and he was attractive; she'd been flattered in a way that seems embarrassing now, that she could be so easily swayed with a little attention and a handsome face.

And everything had been horrible at home. She rarely saw Adam – it felt like their shifts were completely out of whack – and when they did connect all they did was argue. He had just been made DI, and with it came a new level of arrogance that made her stomach turn. He'd changed, she said, but he maintained he'd always been this way. And so she stormed out and went to work. Where *he* was.

His mother was ill but recovering. He came in to thank Romilly, presenting her with a bunch of flowers. He asked her out for a drink; she said yes. A trip to the pub that turned from one drink to a bottle, unfamiliar drunkenness that lowered her inhibitions and made her think, fuck you, Adam. For the hard shell, for the frown, the look of distrust. For making her feel insecure, needy, alone.

Except it wasn't Adam. It was this guy she fucked. In a hotel, down the road from the pub. She hadn't even had time to take her bra off: shoes kicked away, trousers down, a bit of perfunctory kissing and he was inside her. She barely considered what she was doing until he'd finished and was pulling the condom off, slumping next to her on the bed.

'I have to go,' she'd said, numbly pulling her knickers back on.

He gave her a cursory pat on her bum as she stood up. 'I'll call you,' he replied.

He didn't even have her number.

She stumbled back home; Adam was in bed when she got in and she lay beside him, desperately wanting the reassurance of his familiar body but knowing she couldn't.

He rolled over in bed, a heavy arm flopping over her waist. 'Working late?' he mumbled.

She knew she must smell of *him*. Musky, of sex and spermicide and thoughtless thrusting in the dark.

'Adam, I slept with someone,' she replied. And that was it.

No one considers the events that lead up to an affair. The factors that contribute to the moment of infidelity. You sleep with someone, that's it. You're the bad guy. Black and white. With the exception of Pippa, all of their shared friends sided with Adam. For the second time in her life, Romilly found herself feeling completely alone.

Slowly, she stacks the coffees and teas onto a tray and carries them back to the incident room. She'd pulled herself back from there – again – gone through with the divorce, allowing Adam to have anything he wanted. But he'd drifted further away. Take it all, he'd said, like nothing related to her made a dent.

She feels her phone ringing in her pocket, and pauses in the corridor, hands full, not being able to answer. It stops, a pause, then the beep as the message is recorded.

Drinks are taken with appreciation, one left for Adam, and she looks across to where he's talking on the phone in his office, door open. She puts her phone to her ear and listens: it's Phil. His voice stilted, annoyed, rhetorical questions she can't answer. *Where are you? When are you coming home?* And the one said with the most venom, spat down the line before her boyfriend hung up: *Are you with him?*

She carries the coffee into Adam's office. He looks up when she comes in, smiles and wordlessly gestures for her to sit down. She places the mug in front of him but stays standing as he wraps up his call.

'Thank you,' he says with a tired grin, cupping his hands around the coffee. 'And thank you for coming in.'

'I have to go—' she starts. She holds out her phone, as if the small block of electronics can explain the complexities of needing to go home to your current boyfriend you suddenly can't stand, while wanting the man in front of you so much your body aches.

'Of course.'

His face clouds, the shutters lowering once more as he shifts his gaze to his computer screen.

'Adam?'

He doesn't look up from his desk.

'Are you okay?'

'I'm fine. Thanks, Romilly.'

'Call me if you need anything.'

A quick flick of eye contact, an artificial smile. 'I'm fine.'

She feels the flash of dismissal and takes two steps out of the office.

'Milly?'

She turns back.

'Had Pippa mentioned anyone following her? Like she was being stalked?'

Romilly feels disappointment, but what did she expect? He isn't going to pour his heart out to her. Not here, not now. Not ever. 'No, she hadn't. But I could call—'

'No, it's fine. I'll call Jamie. Good night, Romilly.'

She nods, her face reddening. Feeling Adam's rejection as strongly as she had then, all those years ago.

Chapter 40

Jamie doesn't want to be here. So, so much. He wants to be at home, on his sofa, watching some god-awful Netflix-produced romcom. The ones that Pippa loved, that he had always complained about. He would watch nothing but those for the rest of his life, if only it brought her back.

Instead, he is standing in Adam's hallway. The family liaison officer chatters away next to him. He hates this woman and what she represents. That he is now a victim. Told only what they decide: the palatable soundbites they think he'll be able to cope with.

'Go away,' he says, under his breath. Then louder: 'Go away.'

The woman turns to look at him, paused in the middle of her sentence. 'But Jamie . . .'

'Go. Away.'

He wants to shout it, scream in her face. Take all of his anger and frustration and red-hot burning rage out on her. But she's only doing her job, and he's still a nice guy, despite all this, so he says it quietly but firmly, and she gets the message.

'You have my number,' she says as she closes the front door with a click.

Jamie stands still in the hallway. He closes his eyes for a second, feels the blood pulsing in his veins, his heart pumping it around. But he is as empty as Pippa was. As drained. As broken.

He knows he needs to go to bed, but he doesn't dare. Sleep only brings the morning, when he wakes and must remember all over again what has happened.

He needs to call Pippa's parents. There is a funeral to plan, but when? When will they release the body? He can't bear their grief, their mourning on top of his own.

For now, he drops his coat on the carpet and walks through into Adam's living room. It's minimal, few belongings and little decorative flair. None of the touches that make it a home. No photographs, no artwork on the walls, no books or records or love. He used to see Adam as lucky, a man free to come and go as he pleased. Adam's lack of distractions led to a career that was flourishing, while his was stuck. But for the first time, he sees it as it is: the home of a man with nothing in his life but work. A lonely guy, who doesn't have the energy or the inclination or the pride to put down roots.

And where has it got him, this career? Not so he could save Pippa. The one thing that mattered. She was murdered, under Adam's watch.

He feels a wave of anger, a flood of emotion that's quickly joined by the devastating sorrow that's been threatening to consume him since he found Pippa's body. The weight of it crushes him, and he crouches in the middle of Adam's living room. His hands over his face, raking at his hair. His knees up to his chest. A noise comes out of him, a wail, a howl of grief in the darkness.

He feels like it's going to kill him. That he can't breathe, can't live, can't survive without her.

And he sobs, alone, curled up in a ball on the living-room floor of his best friend. The man who'd let his wife die.

Department of Clinical Psychology – Patient Report

Name of Patient: Catherine Sutton (DOB: 05/06/77, age 18)
Consultation date: 28 November 1995

Catherine has been referred to the department of clinical psychology following admission to hospital after a recent traumatic event. There are no ongoing physical medical diagnoses; she has been receiving treatment solely for malnutrition and dehydration after initial assessment in the Accident and Emergency Department. Catherine is due to be discharged, pending psychiatric and psychological review.

History
Police investigations are ongoing, but detectives from Operation Hursley have disclosed Catherine was found as the sole survivor after a period of forced imprisonment, as well as possible sexual assault and torture. Four other women were killed, and Catherine may have been a witness to these crimes.

Current Situation
Catherine was reluctant to talk at first, avoiding eye contact and attempts at building rapport, sitting in silence for the first two sessions. In the third meeting, Catherine started to open up, talking about her past and disclosing that before her kidnapping, she was homeless, surviving through begging and prostitution. Based on notes from her medical assessment on admission, a drug addiction may have been likely, although Catherine has not confirmed this. She is not showing any signs of withdrawal.

Catherine generally talks with little emotion, with a flat affect, showing signs of psychological numbing. She discussed insomnia, and feelings of loneliness, guilt, helplessness, and isolation. She mentioned she has little to live for 'now it is over'. When I asked questions directing her to think about her future, she shook her head repeatedly, as if refusing to consider this likelihood.

Contrary to expectation, she was openly hostile towards the police and solicitors when discussing the investigation, growing agitated and angry. She asked about the suspect, but the knowledge that he was in prison only worsened her distress, culminating in a panic attack requiring pharmaceutical intervention. She maintains she will not testify at the trial and will not meet with the CPS.

Clinical Formulation

In my opinion Post-Traumatic Stress Disorder (PTSD) would be the primary diagnosis at this time, with secondary depression (including suicidal ideation) and panic disorder.

Additionally, as the sole surviving victim, Catherine is subject to 'survivor syndrome' from having endured the trauma where others have perished. This could result in strong feelings of guilt, shame, anxiety, and social withdrawal, thus compounding her depression.

Risks

Catherine has no support network or family, so nowhere to live on discharge from hospital. Without this support, there is a risk she will end up back on the streets, with a strong likelihood she will take her own life.

In addition, exposing Catherine to further trauma by forcing her to testify at the trial will only compound her anxiety and panic, and is strongly opposed.

Proposed Future Interventions

In the immediate future, Catherine should be put on suicide watch and monitored closely. Admission to a psychiatric bed is advised, where she should be assessed for counselling, cognitive therapy, and appropriate drug treatments.

Given that a social worker is not currently involved, I will also be referring the case to social services.

Dictated, not checked or signed to avoid delay.
Dr Rebecca Forrest
Consultant Clinical Psychologist

Chapter 41

By the time Adam gets home, it's past eleven. The house is silent; he hopes that Jamie is in bed. Jamie must be distraught, but he needs sleep. And, if the truth be known, Adam hasn't got the energy to face him.

There is still no news. No good leads. And how does he tell his best mate that? He's experienced it in the past. With relatives and friends of victims. Then, he could walk away. He had space. Here, he has none.

And as he walks into his living room, Jamie's there. Sitting on his sofa, glass in hand. Jamie lifts his head, directs his rolling eyes towards him. He lifts the glass in a mock toast.

'The great detective. He's home,' he slurs.

'Hi Jamie,' Adam says. He sits down on the edge of the seat across from him.

'No suspects in custody?' Jamie asks. He tries to take a sip from his glass, but it's empty and he stares at it, annoyed, then holds it out to Adam. 'Get me another, will you?'

'Don't you think you've had enough?'

'Don't you think you should have caught this guy by now?' Jamie shouts. The change is sudden, an outpouring of fury, channelled in Adam's direction. 'Before he killed Pippa?'

Adam clenches his teeth. A million responses fire in his head but there's no point in saying them. Jamie won't listen to reason. He's angry, and Adam is a convenient conduit for that rage.

'Not got anything to say, DCI Bishop?' Jamie continues. 'No well-meaning soundbite? No platitude or words of sympathy? Can't be helping your career much, this one, can it?'

'Jamie, we're doing our best,' Adam says softly.

'Well, it's not good enough. It *wasn't* good enough.' Jamie stands up, knocking the glass to the carpet where it rolls onto its side. He faces Adam, his hands bunched into fists. Jamie has the height over Adam by a long way, and he definitely has the weight. But his balance is completely off, skewed by the alcohol. Adam doesn't want to get in a fight with him. Not now. Not ever.

Adam turns quickly and strides out of the living room. He hears Jamie following, bumping against walls and doorframes in his drunkenness.

'What? The great Adam Bishop isn't up for a fight? Not man enough?'

Adam grabs his coat from the hook, opens the front door and walks out into the cold. Jamie doesn't follow him. He stands in the doorway, shouting out into the street.

'Where are you going, Adam?' he hollers. 'By yourself? Who can you turn to? When everyone who loves you has gone?'

*

Adam walks fast as Jamie's words fade into the darkness. He knows Jamie's hurting, in pain, and is taking that out on Adam, but he's right. He's damn well right. Where is he going? His legs carry him without thought. To the only place where he can be surrounded by people but be alone.

Being anonymous works well for Adam here. He stands in the shadows of the bar, bottle of beer in his hand. The first shot of vodka didn't make any impact, and the two after have barely hit the sides. He hears Jamie's words in his head. Who does he have? Who is he looking for here? A friend? A future wife? Someone to silence the nagging in his head, the self-loathing?

A woman comes wobbling towards him. She looks out of place, in jeans and a long-sleeved shirt, and as she comes closer he recognises her.

She waves awkwardly, and he frowns.

'Ellie? What are you doing here?'

'I . . .' She pauses, looking uncomfortable. 'Needed somewhere to go.'

He knows this is bad, but the alcohol numbs his thinking. 'Go home, Ellie,' he mutters.

'Don't you want some company?'

He does. But not her. She's his DC, she works for him. In the middle of a major murder investigation, when both of them should be getting some much-needed sleep.

But instead he says, 'Sure. Why not.'

'Same again?'

He waves the bottle of beer and she heads off to the bar. She's drunk already, he can tell that, and he needs a few more himself. She's sweet, Ellie Quinn. She'll do as someone to talk to. For now.

She meanders back towards him, two beers in one hand,

and four shots in the other, one finger in each glass. She plonks them all down on the table.

'Shots?' he says.

'Thought you might need to play catch up. I'm pretty pissed.'

'No shit,' he says, and she laughs.

They down the shots, the bass line thumping in Adam's chest. He feels the anxiety abate; he's aware of Quinn chattering on, barely listening.

He realises she's stopped and is waiting for him to reply. 'Sorry?' he says.

'I asked, when did you and Dr Cole get divorced?'

'Oh. About three years ago.'

'And you still get on?'

'As well as we can.' He feels her staring at him. 'She's with someone,' he adds.

'Ah. And you're single?'

'These are very personal questions to be asking your boss, DC Quinn?'

She giggles. The alcohol has overridden her usual nerves around him. 'Sorry,' she says. 'Just curious. From one singleton to another.' She wobbles slightly, and he places a hand on her upper arm to steady her. She looks up, her big green eyes beseeching and eager. Her freckles look black against her skin in the flashing lights of the bar.

'More drinks?' she says.

He should have said no at that point. Fuck, he should have walked away, from her, out of the bar, gone home. Put Jamie to bed with a pint of water and done the same for himself. But he didn't. They drank more. She laughed, flirted, pressed her body against his as they talked, her

239

hair tickling his face as he moved closer so she could hear.

Things got worse. All good sense went out of the window as she kissed him. As he let her. As they hailed a taxi. As hands went places they never should have gone on the drive back to hers.

She fumbled her key on the doorstep, slurred something about her housemates being away. She kissed him in the hallway, offering him another drink but pulling him towards her bedroom. At every stage he knew he should stop. But he didn't. He carried on. Desperate to be next to someone. Someone who actually liked him, who wanted to be with him. Who didn't intimately know his shortcomings and his problems and blame him for theirs.

He feels good, with Ellie. As she grabs his bum, pulling him closer to her. As she pulls her shirt off over her head. They lie together on her bed, kissing, groping, him on top. Her trousers are off, her bra undone, and he realises her movements have slowed. He looks down at her. Her eyes are half closed, her breathing heavy. She looks at him, blinking.

'Oh, fuck,' she says. 'I'm so pissed.'

She closes her eyes for a moment. He feels her hands loosen in his hair.

And then he sees it. His consciousness takes a step back; he watches himself from above. Another person, seeing what Adam Bishop is doing. He's on top of this woman, semi-naked, her legs apart. And she's out cold.

He jumps back, almost falling over in his haste to get away.

'Fuck,' he shouts. Fuck. What was he about to do? Shit, shit, shit. A woman who works for him, who's drunk past the point of comprehension? Oh, fuck.

He pulls his trousers up quickly. He rakes his hands through his hair in desperation, still staring at her. She's lying on her back, mouth open. Completely dead to the world. Then she stirs. She makes a retching noise, her stomach contracting, and he jumps forward before she's sick, rolling her onto her side. She throws up violently onto the floor; he grabs the first thing closest to him, her wastepaper bin, and holds it under her head as she vomits again. It goes everywhere, in her hair, on the carpet, over him.

She stops and rolls back onto the bed, groaning, her eyes still closed.

Adam sits back on the carpet, breathing heavily through his mouth. The smell is everywhere, it turns his stomach, and he gets up quickly, running to her bathroom. He vomits, once, twice, a gush of alcohol and acid and hatred. He smells it in his nose, the grit of it between his teeth, and he pukes again, retching up nothing but yellow bile this time. He crouches on the tiled floor of Ellie's rented bathroom, gasping, eyes watering. He shouldn't have drunk that much. But it's not just that making him sick. It's him. What he was about to do.

The man he's become.

DAY 7

FRIDAY

Chapter 42

Adam wakes, with a crick in his back from the sofa, a raging thirst, and a burn in the pit of his stomach that has nothing to do with the hangover. He stands in Ellie's kitchen, a pint of water in his hand, dressed in his clothes from last night. He looks at the photographs on the fridge. Three women featuring in all, Ellie smiling and laughing.

He smells vomit on his shirt, the taste in his mouth.

What happened last night, it was unforgivable. After Ellie finished puking on the floor, he cleaned her up as best he could, then rolled her gently into the recovery position, pulling the duvet over her. He fetched a bucket and cloth, whatever he could find, and cleaned the vomit from the floor.

The smell was disgusting. He retched again, once, several times, but finished the job. Then he placed the now-clean bin next to Ellie's head and left her to sleep.

He hears footsteps on the stairs, and looks over as Ellie appears in the doorway of her kitchen. Her hair is roughly tied back, matted to her head on one side. Her make-up is caked around her eyes. She's wearing light blue pyjamas with stars on them. She stops and stares at him.

'I'm sorry,' he says hastily. 'I didn't want to leave you last night. You seemed . . . ill. I was worried you'd be sick again.'

'Er . . . right.' She clears her throat, closes her eyes for a moment, then opens them again. 'Boss—'

'Adam.'

'Adam.' She shakes her head in confusion. 'What are you doing here?'

'We . . . er . . .' Adam hesitates, not sure how much to share. 'We were at the same bar last night. You invited me back here.'

'We . . . Oh, shit.' She closes her eyes tight and puts her hands over her face. 'Did we . . .? I remember us kissing.'

'Yeah. A bit. Sorry.'

'But nothing else?'

Adam shakes his head quickly. 'No. You were sick.'

'Oh, God.' She slumps down into one of the chairs next to the table and puts her head in her hands. 'Oh, God, I'm so sorry.'

'No, no, you have nothing to be sorry for. It should be me who's apologising. I'm your boss—'

'I know . . .' She lets out a long wail and starts crying.

Adam stands awkwardly in front of her. 'Do you want a cup of tea? I'll make you a cup of tea.'

He puts the kettle on, grabbing a mug from the odd array in the cupboard above. It says *Happy 25th Birthday* on the side, and he wonders, with even more shame, exactly how old Ellie Quinn is.

He makes the tea and sits down opposite her. She wipes her eyes on the sleeve of her pyjamas, sniffing loudly.

'Thank you,' she says, with a wan smile. 'Was I a mess?'

'I've seen you in better shape, yes.'

She tries to run her hands through her hair, then holds a few strands between her fingers and grimaces. 'Did I puke on you?'

'Just missed.' He returns the smile. 'But you got it all over your carpet.'

'I did?' She looks puzzled.

'I cleaned it up. Well, I tried. You might need to have another go.'

She puts her head in her hands again. 'I'm so sorry,' she says through her fingers. 'Are you going to report me?'

'Report you?' Adam sits back in the chair in surprise. 'Absolutely not. Ellie, I'm the one at fault here. I'm your superior officer. And we were drunk, very drunk together.' He doesn't mention the rest. 'But let's say I leave here, and you have a shower and breakfast, and when we meet again at work we never mention this to anyone ever again.'

She looks up, her eyes grateful. 'Yes, that would be good, thank you.'

He feels like crap. But he nods. 'Now drink your tea. It will help.'

Adam stands up, puts one hand on her arm for a second, then leaves, closing the front door behind him.

He starts to walk quickly. Down her street, away from her house, as if putting distance between them will ease the churning in his gut, the feeling in his bones. He's an utter shit. Even discounting how close he came to having sex with her, they shouldn't have been drinking together in the first place. The line of inappropriate behaviour was crossed the second she appeared by his side. He should have walked away, told her to go home. But he was so pathetically desperate for company that he allowed it to continue. And the kissing, the . . . everything else. He can't even bring himself to think it. Two shots more and what would he have done? Would he have stopped? Would he have—

He bends double, his stomach contracting as he throws up in the gutter. He rests his hands on his knees, and lets out a groan, of disgust, of pure self-hate, and pushes the heels of his hands into his eyes.

He hears footsteps pass and glances up to see a woman in a smart coat hurrying by. What must he look like to her? He sees himself for who he is. A sad, lonely, forty-year-old man who picks up women in late-night bars because he can't stand the thought of real intimacy.

He stands up again and starts walking. He knows where he is, but he's not heading in the right direction. He realises, in his daze, that he's taken the route towards his old house. His ex-marital home, where he lived with Romilly.

He was a different person when he was married to her. He was happy then; he struggles to think of a time when he's been that way since. Not alcohol-induced happy. Or laughing with the team. But the glow of contentment he felt from the inside out.

The walk takes him another half an hour. The streets are busy as the world comes to life. He glances at his watch: eight o'clock. What will Romilly be doing now? In their old life they'd eat breakfast together. Side by side in their kitchen, passing the milk, mugs of coffee in front of them. She'd smell of freshly washed hair, and as they kissed goodbye, of toothpaste and perfume. But what does she do now, with her new boyfriend?

At the end of the road, he pauses. He can see the house

245

in the distance, two cars parked in the driveway. She still has her old Ford; her boyfriend has a VW Golf.

He walks a few paces closer, then stops again. Their curtains are open, they must be up, and as Adam watches the front door unlocks. He ducks down behind a parked car, desperate to see but remain hidden.

The man steps out of the house. Phil. He looks fresh and clean, and, Christ, the man's much better looking than him, Adam realises anew. Jamie was right. They're not even in the same league. He turns back, waiting, as Romilly steps onto the doorstep. They lean forward and kiss, no more than a quick peck, but Adam feels a flash of jealousy towards this man. Living in his house, with his wife.

Adam shifts, his muscles straining in the unnatural position. He waits as Phil climbs into his car and drives off in the opposite direction.

The front door closes, Romilly going back into the house. She's alone now. He desperately wants to walk up to her door, to knock, to see her face. He wants to sit in his own living room and talk to her about how he's feeling. Share the hatred he has for himself, the self-doubt. How much he knows he's let down his best friend.

That he took advantage of poor Ellie. That *she* felt guilty. That *she* felt she needed to apologise.

How, since they split up, he's slipped out of his own skin; become a man he no longer recognises. No longer wants to be.

He wants to say all of this to the one person who would understand. Who would probably put her arms around him and give him a hug.

But he knows he won't.

Something inside him won't let him. He can't be that

person again. He trusted the people closest to him once and look what happened. He trusted Romilly, and she destroyed their life for a cheap fuck.

Look where trust got him. Look how loving someone made him feel.

Everyone leaves him. He is alone.

The wind blows hard, and he pulls his coat tightly around him. His cheeks feel cold, and he reaches up, surprised to discover he's been crying. He wipes at the tears with disgust, then turns and strides away down the road.

Before

He holds his breath as the counting stops. Seventeen. He hadn't managed to stay hidden for long. Good places are becoming harder to find.

Rough hands pinch his upper arms as he's pulled from the cupboard.

He stands in front of his father, eyes averted to the ground. He knows his father will be looking at him, thinking, deciding what to do next. He glances towards his father's belt, still fastened around his middle. His father sees him and laughs.

'Not tonight, Eli. Not tonight.'

He grabs his arm and pulls him across to the television. His father's old armchair sits in front, his usual position for the football game that Elijah knows is on now. A pint of beer waits for him on the side table, along with his packet of B&H.

'Sit there,' his father directs, pointing to a patch of carpet to the side.

Elijah glances to his mother, confused. She's standing

nervously in the doorway, picking at the skin on her split lip. Her eyes dart between her son and her husband.

The man slumps down in the chair with a grunt. He gestures to his wife; she steps forward and turns on the television. Instantly, the brightness fills the room, the sound of the commentators and the roar of the crowd. He reaches to his side, selects a cigarette from the nearly full pack and lights it, taking a long drag.

Elijah stays as quiet as he can. Small light breaths, not shifting a muscle. He thinks his father might have forgotten him. Maybe there's no punishment tonight.

'Hold out your arm.'

Elijah doesn't move. He's frozen in place.

His father shifts position, turning around to look at him. His eyes flash with anger. 'I said, hold out your arm. Here.'

He points to the arm of the chair. Elijah stares at it. At the loose orange threads, at the stains from the curries and pizzas ingrained in the material. Then he slowly pushes his arm towards him.

His mother takes a step forward, her hands fluttering.

'No, Maurice. Leave him be,' she pleads.

He looks to her, leers, then grabs Eli's wrist tightly. With the other arm, his father pushes his sleeve up, revealing pale, clear skin, before he pushes the cigarette butt hard against it.

Elijah cries out. He hears the crackle of fire, the smell of tobacco. He sees the black as his skin scorches. The burn of pain. He instinctively tries to pull away but his father holds fast, turning the cigarette until the flame is out. Then he takes it away, flicking the spent butt at the television.

Elijah collapses into a ball to the side of his father's

chair. He knows better than to try and get away but his mother leaps forward. But she's not as quick as his father. A fist catches her to the side of the face and she falls to the floor, still pleading.

'Do it to me, Maurice. I'll take it for him. Please.'

'Shut it,' his father snarls. 'Or I'll double the punishment.' He turns back to the television and takes a sip of his beer.

Elijah grips his arm with his free hand, squeezing tightly, trying to stop the burn that throbs deep into his skin. He looks to the open packet of cigarettes.

One down, he thinks, biting back the sobs. Sixteen to go.

Chapter 43

Romilly saw Adam that morning. At first she thought she was imagining things; but once she went back into the house, she properly looked out of her window. And yes, there he was. He looked like shit, shifty as hell as he scuttled away. But definitely him.

Now, she makes a cup of tea, feeling an odd mixture of concern and confusion. Why was he lurking outside? Should she have called to him, invited him in? But what would she have said?

Things with Phil are still tense. He made an effort that morning as he left for work, trying to keep things normal, maintain what was left of their relationship. But the same undercurrent remained. He didn't want her seeing Adam. He wanted her to go back to work, forget about her ex-husband. Leave Pippa's murder to the cops. All things she knew she couldn't do.

Phil's worries about Adam are warranted; he's been on her mind more than an ex-husband should be. Thinking about him as she drifted off to sleep, as she ate breakfast this morning. She thinks about Pippa too, the sadness for her murdered friend close to overwhelming, but when the tears come the comfort from Phil isn't what she needs. She wants Adam.

Her phone buzzes a reminder. She hasn't got time for Adam this morning. She needs to leave for an appointment she should never miss. Especially not now.

Romilly is early, Dr Jones on time. At precisely nine thirty, her doctor appears in the doorway of the waiting room, the usual small smile on her face. Today she's wearing navy blue trousers, a white blouse, and smart brown brogues on her feet. Flat shoes, ever practical.

The therapist escorts her through to her office. The room is unchanged. Neat. Tidy. A faint smell of something delicate and floral is in the air.

Dr Jones sits down. She crosses one leg over the other and rests her notepad in her lap, waiting.

'Twice in one week,' Romilly says, with a nervous laugh. 'You've probably had enough of me.'

'It must be a difficult time for you, Romilly. I've seen the news. How are you doing?'

'I'm fine,' she replies automatically. Jones tilts her head to one side, a gesture that says, *Really?*

Romilly tries again. 'It looks like my father is still killing. From prison, however that's possible. My best friend has been murdered. I'm arguing with my boyfriend. And my ex-husband . . .' Romilly feels her throat tighten. She stops and composes herself before she speaks again. 'So, yes. I've had better weeks.'

'But?' the therapist asks.

252

And there is a 'but', Dr Jones has sensed it. Despite all this, Romilly feels something different.

'All this time, ever since I was eleven, I've thought this would happen. That my father would kill again. My dreams, my nightmares have all been about him coming back. And now he is . . .'

'You feel like you were right all along.'

'Yes. It's a relief.' Romilly laughs, awkwardly. A sense of calm, of sanity. 'That I'm not crazy.'

'Maybe you never were,' Dr Jones says. 'And why are you arguing with Phil?'

'He thinks I shouldn't see Adam anymore.'

'And why do you think that is?'

'Jealousy. He wants to control me.'

'Or?' Romilly's used to this. Dr Jones challenging when she gives statements as fact. 'What's the alternative story?' the doctor asks.

Romilly sighs. 'That he loves me and he's worried. That he wants to keep me safe from an investigation that can only hurt me.'

The doctor nods solemnly. 'And Adam? You didn't finish your sentence.'

'It's complicated.'

'Try to explain.'

Romilly's thoughts immediately turn to Jamie. She went to the house – Adam's house – yesterday, to see him.

When she arrived, just past eight p.m., the curtains were closed, the house quiet. She locked her car and rang the bell. Nothing. She tried again; this time heavy slow foot-steps made their way towards the door and it opened.

Jamie stood in front of her. His hair was at all angles, his face unshaven. He was wearing a T-shirt, socks and boxer shorts, an old dressing gown of Adam's over the top. It was almost comically small on Jamie, the sleeves only coming halfway up his forearms.

He saw her, then turned back into the house without a word.

She followed him into the living room; Rom couldn't help but wince at the mess. The smell of cigarette smoke, the empties, the booze, male sweat. He slumped back on the sofa. He wasn't wasted, but Rom could tell he was getting that way, fast.

Misery poured off him; he was a shell of the man she knows.

Rom found herself lost for words. She wanted to say something, about what a wonderful person Pippa was, what a good friend she was, how much Rom enjoyed her company, but no words seemed sufficient. Instead, she said, 'I loved her.'

Jamie turned, offering a weak smile. 'I did too, Rom. She knew that, right?'

'Oh, yes. Oh, Jamie, and she was so in love with you too.'

Jamie turned quickly away, hiding his face, and Rom sat down next to him, reaching over and grabbing him in a tight embrace. He returned it awkwardly.

'I can't think straight, Rom,' he said, after the hug. 'It's like now she's gone, she's taken a piece of me with her, and I'll never be the same again.' He looked at her with reddened eyes, grief lining his face. 'She was my soul mate. My everything. Every moment I spent apart from her – working late, out with friends, getting pissed with Adam – that was wasted. I should have been with her.' He paused. 'Don't let that happen to you, Rom.'

She felt tears prickle behind her eyes, and nodded

quickly. She couldn't answer. She's always felt the same way about Adam. That being next to him, loving him, is as natural as breathing. That they were part of the same person, implicitly understanding each other and what they've been through. She hasn't felt that same contentment since she lost him, and now he is back in her life, she feels the wave of devotion growing again.

She tries to explain this to Dr Jones, the words coming out muddled and messy.

'I can't imagine how I'd feel if that had been Adam,' Romilly says. 'I'd be utterly destroyed. And now all I can think about is how I screwed up our marriage.'

'That was your fault, was it?'

'I slept with that man. I was unfaithful.'

'And what led you to that point?' the doctor asks.

Romilly frowns. Adam's increasing distance, his pulling away that left her confused and alone.

The doctor places her notepad to her side. She leans forward and rests her elbows on her knees, looking straight at Rom. 'It seems to me, Romilly,' the doctor says, 'that you're to blame for a lot of what's gone on lately.'

Romilly feels the doctor's words physically, like a blade through her skin.

'The end of your marriage with Adam,' the doctor continues. 'Your argument with Phil, because you insist on seeing the ex-husband you're clearly still in love with. Even Pippa's death. That was your old house, she was held at. Your father, that the killer is either in awe of, or following his orders.'

The tears that have threatened for so long, start to come, running down her cheeks. But despite this, she feels a wave of indignation.

'I didn't kill Pippa. It's not my fault these people are dying.'

'Exactly. So, I'm wondering, why do you feel that it is?'

Romilly blinks, astonished, through her tears. The therapist sits back in her seat, crossing her legs again.

'When I say it out loud, it sounds ridiculous, doesn't it?' Jones continues, smooth and calm. 'You got annoyed. Angry. So why, when your own internal voice says that, do you believe it? Romilly?'

'I . . . I don't know.'

'You need to tell yourself that. Regularly. Talk to your reflection in a mirror. Speak to yourself in the car. Whatever. But you have to make sure you repeat it and you listen. You did not kill those women, back in 1995. You are not responsible for the deaths now. Right?'

Romilly nods. Dr Jones passes her a tissue, and she blows her nose.

'And speak to Adam. It's not too late to make amends. However it turns out.'

Romilly walks away from the appointment, her mind reeling. The doctor's words repeat in her head. *You are not to blame.* Up to this point, her whole life has been lived in service. Desperately trying to atone for the sins of her father.

But it's been a Sisyphean task. As a doctor, there's always one more person to help, another life to save.

You are not to blame.

She wants to believe it. She does. How nice would it be, to release the boulder, and let it all go. But how can you? her brain spits back as she gets in the car, as she goes to drive home. How can you, when you know it's not true?

Chapter 44

'You shouldn't be here, Bishop,' Ross says the moment he walks into the mortuary. 'You have a personal relationship with the victim.'

'I promised Jamie,' Adam mutters, his eyes locking on his best friend's wife naked on the slab.

Ross raises an eyebrow. 'I'm not going to pull my punches, I'm warning you.'

'Noted.'

Adam doesn't want to be there. It's hard enough seeing a human being at a post-mortem without having known them as a living, breathing person. But a promise is a promise, so here he is.

'You know the cause of death?' Ross asks, looking back to Pippa.

'Exsanguination?'

'Almost complete blood loss. It was a feat for this guy to drain her. Heparin found in her body, same as the other victim, but even so.'

'How did he do it?'

Ross points to the red bruises circling her wrists. 'Two sets of markings here. One from the restraints. Narrow, hard. Would correspond with the cable ties you found at the scene. Same on her ankles. She struggled a fair amount, causing some nasty abrasions through the top layer of the epidermis.'

Ross is looking at him closely, waiting for a reaction. 'Go on,' Adam says.

'The second markings, here, closer to the end of the radius and the scaphoid.' He points to the knobbly bones on her wrist. 'These were made by something that chafed. A rope, or similar. My hypothesis is she was suspended by her wrists, almost fully off the ground. Straining and damage to the ligaments in her shoulders would support this.'

Adam closes his eyes for a second. 'For what aim?'

'Gravity, Bishop,' Ross says. 'Pulling her up would force all her blood downwards. Then all the killer needed to do was insert the needles.'

Adam swallows, hard. He feels his body waver. He tries to distract himself but Ross is still talking, working his way down the body. 'Cannulae were initially inserted in the backs of both her hands, and some blood was taken. But once she was in the upright position, he switched and inserted two larger needles here and here' – he points to the tops of her thighs – 'plus looking at the wound here,' he adds, referring to a thin cut on her ankle, 'he performed a saphenous cut down. A procedure normally used to get vascular access in trauma or hypovolemic shock patients when cannulation is difficult. In this case, I'm assuming he used it to drain her body of blood more efficiently.'

Adam's heart beats hard in his chest. His eyesight starts to blur.

'Who would be able to do this?' he says, blinking. 'Are we looking for a doctor?'

'Well, possibly. It's not common. It's taught on trauma courses, but it's not massively technical. Assuming your suspect wasn't too worried about getting it wrong, it could be anyone who'd been around vascular surgeons, trauma docs or emergency medicine and fancied having a go. There's even videos on YouTube. All you've got to do is find the vein then stick the cannula inside.'

Adam feels a trickle of sweat run down his back. He wobbles slightly; he gulps a long deep breath but the room starts to spin. The world leaches of colour. It's too late.

His legs give way, and everything goes dark.

31 Years Ago

The boy sits alone in the hospital bed. He can see his parents on the other side of the glass, faces cast down, hands over their mouths. In front of them a doctor is talking. One of many, but the man the others listen to. The important doctor stops and his parents nod. They all look through the glass at the boy, their faces stern.

They're coming back into the ward now. His mother stands next to his bed, her hand resting in his hair. He can tell she's going to cry; she cries a lot nowadays. Ever since the nosebleeds, the bruising that wouldn't go away.

The doctor's talking to him, but he's not listening. He doesn't comprehend what's happening, why he feels so ill.

'Do you understand?' the doctor says, looking at him.

'Can I go home?' the boy asks. The doctor glances to his parents.

'No, darling. That's what the doctor is saying. You need to stay here for a while. So they can make you feel better.'

He nods. But he's thinking, *They don't. They just make me feel worse.* The aching in his bones, the tiredness. The

260

pain that takes over his whole body, as if it's growing from the inside. None of it has gone away.

The doctor has turned and is talking to a nurse. She leaves, then comes back with a tray covered in equipment. He's seen this before. Last time, he trusted them. They said it wouldn't hurt, but it did. So much. He cried, clutching his worn-out stuffed dinosaur, as they put needles into his arms, into his hands. Then they connected tubes and wires and pumped him full of drugs that made him puke.

He shakes his head. 'Please don't,' he says quietly. He grabs at his mother's hand, holding her tight. 'Please don't let them hurt me. Please,' he begs.

His mother starts crying. His father moves closer to his bedside.

'Now, Adam,' he says, his face hard. 'You need to be a brave boy so the doctors can treat you.'

He shakes his head, over and over. He grips harder on his mother's arm. He knows he's hurting her but he can't let go. He starts to cry, tears blurring his vision. 'Please don't, please don't, please don't,' he gabbles.

'Maybe it would be best if we do this alone,' he hears the doctor say.

He feels his mother pull away but he hangs on tight. Strong fingers prise him off; he starts to scream as he loses his grasp.

He feels hard hands clamp onto his arms. He struggles, his hysteria growing louder. The sheets get caught around his legs as he kicks; he feels the pinch of fingers on his skin as they hold him down.

His parents have gone now. They've left him. His muscles contract, his whole body is tense. His gaze shifts from doctor to doctor, men talking frantically, nurses struggling

261

to hold him still. People he doesn't know, faces ugly with anger.

And then he feels it. The pain, the sting in his arm as the needle goes in.

'I've missed it. Shit, hold him still, hold him still.'

The agony intensifies within his flesh as the needle is moved around, his muscle contorting as he continues to scream. Scraping against bone, pain from deep inside him. He feels the grip releasing, and he opens his eyes. One of the doctors has stepped back and is looking at him sternly.

'There. See, that wasn't so bad, was it?' the doctor says. 'It wouldn't have hurt if you'd relaxed.'

The boy looks down. The needle is embedded in his skin. He flexes his fingers; the foreign object next to tendons, blood, bone. It's wrong, alien. It shouldn't be there. He thinks he's going to be sick, his heart racing.

The nurse on the other side lets go of his arm and without thinking he reaches over and grabs. The plastic tubing, the tape, the needle, it all comes away as he pulls it free. He feels the tear down his arm, the shred of skin as it breaks. The rush of warm blood as the vein gapes, ripped apart by his action.

Then the hands again, forcing him down. The sting of pain. He thrashes to and fro, a hand on his forehead, pushing him roughly onto the bed. Another over his mouth to silence him. He struggles to breathe. He panics. He hears shouting, feels their alarm.

And all he's aware of as his body contracts with pain as more needles are pressed into his pale delicate skin is the loneliness. The fear.

He trusted them, and they left him.

Alone.

Chapter 45

Adam wakes slowly. A horrible thought: something has gone wrong. Where is he? How did he get here? He hears odd-sounding voices in the distance. A slight panic. He is lying on a cold floor, his legs raised on a chair.

'Bishop?' A voice pushes through the darkness. He opens his eyes; Ross is looming over him.

'You're awake. Good.'

He feels someone lifting his arm, taking his pulse. He pulls it away, annoyed. He has a vague awareness of having been unconscious. He puts his hands behind him to push himself up; his head swims, forcing him to lie back down.

'Take it easy, Adam. You passed out.'

He feels foolish lying here on the cold tiled floor, in the—? Where is he? Oh, fuck, it's the mortuary. He tries to sit up again, and this time succeeds.

He's handed a glass of water; he sips it slowly.

'Has anything like this happened before?' Ross asks.

'A few times,' he mutters. 'Bad reaction to needles.'

Ross nods knowingly. 'Standard vasovagal response. A

bad one too.' He chuckles. 'This is so not the murder case for you.'

Adam scowls at him. 'I am aware of that fact, thank you.' He pulls himself to his feet, wobbles slightly, then takes the chair offered to him by the technician. 'I can normally control it. Stay away from the triggers, using applied tension.'

'And what are your triggers?'

Adam's sure Ross is asking more from professional curiosity than genuine concern, the pathologist enjoying his discomfort. He answers anyway. 'Having injections, seeing needles, touching needles, watching someone else have an injection, hearing someone talk about it.'

'Most things?'

'Yeah.' He sighs. 'I tried sorting it a few years back. CBT, trigger ladders, graded self-exposure to cure. Nothing worked.'

'So when was the last time you had an injection?'

'A few years ago. The usual boosters for hepatitis and TB. I tried to punch the nurse, then passed out.'

'I hope she gave you the jab?'

'Yeah. Mags was there, next in line. She grabbed the needle and shoved it in while I was unconscious on the floor.'

Ross laughs. 'Good for Mags. Well, take it easy for a few hours, won't you?' Adam gives him a look. 'At least try. I'll write up the findings in a report and give it to someone else.' He pauses. 'I'm sorry, Adam.' Adam looks at him. The pathologist's normally disapproving gaze has softened. 'About Pippa. Please pass on my condolences to DS Hoxton.'

'I will.'

* * *

Adam walks slowly out of the hospital to the car park. He opens his car door and gets into the driving seat, putting the key in the ignition. But as he does so his sleeve pulls back and for the first time in a while, he looks at the long scar running the length of his forearm. He runs a finger down it, remembering how his vein ripped as he pulled the needle out, how it felt – the pain, but also the triumph. The thrill that it was up to him and him alone what went into his skin.

But of course, it wasn't. He was only nine, his parents were in charge. He cried, begged them not to do it, but there was no other way. Take the medicine, the needles, the poison in his veins, or die. And they left him. They couldn't watch as the doctors restrained him, as he was drugged, sedated so they could pump the chemicals into his body. It cured him. It saved his life, but to what cost?

His parents abandoned him when he needed them the most. Months in isolation for the stem cell transplant; feeling sick, tired, unable to eat or drink as the remainder of his hair fell out. Cuts that took forever to heal. Infections that wouldn't go away. The nurses did the best they could, but he needed his mum. At night, in his darkest moments, he would call out for her, receiving only silence in return as he cried himself to sleep.

Whatever the doctors did, it worked. But as he left the hospital, the needles, the fear behind, something had changed. A distance, between him and his parents. His father had tried to talk to him about it. Once, on the way home from a check-up.

'Your mother,' his father had said, eyes locked on the road as he drove. 'She couldn't cope seeing you that way.'

Adam turned towards him, frowning, as his father continued.

'She's a delicate woman. She needed looking after.'

Adam opened his mouth and closed it a few times before he was able to speak. 'I needed looking after,' he said quietly.

His father glanced away from the road for a second. 'You had the best doctors in the country,' he'd replied, his voice sharp. 'Wonderful nurses. You were being looked after.'

Adam had felt tears well in his eyes; he'd run his hands through his still-patchy hair and in that moment, known what he'd suspected since those days in the hospital. That the only person he could rely on was himself.

He went to university. He pulled away. He constructed a shell, a thicker outer skin to protect himself. He barely speaks to his parents now. A call – birthdays and Christmas, their conversations awkward and brief.

He let nobody in. Until Romilly.

He picks up his phone now, and searches for her number. He wants to talk to her, tell her how he passed out in the mortuary. Hear her soft, sympathetic laugh at his dismay, making the embarrassment feel not quite so bad, somehow. His finger hovers over the green call symbol, but instead he clicks the side button, closing down the phone.

He starts the engine and drives to the police station.

Faces look up expectantly as he walks into the incident room, the chatter subsides. He stands up at the front, waiting for their attention.

'I've just come from the mortuary. From Pippa Hoxton.' Everyone is silent, waiting for the latest bleak update. 'It

266

looks like we're definitely looking for someone with medical experience. Where have we got to with the NHS staff?'

One of the analysts speaks: 'The report has come back from the NHS trust with all the potential people with access to scrubs. Quinn is cross-checking it against the owners of VW Transporters.'

'Quinn?' Adam asks, turning to Ellie. It's the first time he's seen her since her vomit-encrusted state that morning. She's tidy now, hair washed and clean. Eyes tired, her face colours, but she maintains her composure.

'No, nothing, sorry. No matches. Boss,' she adds.

'Tim?' Adam says, moving on quickly. 'Anything back on the fly-tippers?'

The detective checks his notes. 'One interview with a construction company called Bob's Builders.' Adam gives him a disbelieving look. 'I know, I know. I didn't name them.' Lee continues: 'Debris checked back there, but it's been taken over in the last six months and the new owners deny all knowledge. Nothing useful.'

'Great,' Adam mutters sarcastically.

The whole room is silent; Adam stares unhappily at the whiteboard, at the progress they're not making. And he has one dominant thought. He needs to go. To see him.

'Boss?' Quinn says tentatively. Adam turns. Quinn takes a long breath in before she speaks again. 'We don't honestly think that this guy is trying to kill twenty people, do we? I mean . . .' She glances to the other detectives in the room. 'He couldn't possibly . . .'

Adam presses his lips together. His mouth feels dry. 'I don't know,' he replies. 'But he seems clear on his goal. I don't think he'll stop of his own accord.'

He looks around the room. Takes in his detectives, the dark rings under their eyes, their skin sallow from not enough sunlight. Too many long days under the harsh fluorescent lights of the incident room. He's aware of his own lack of cleanliness, his need for a shower and clean clothes after yesterday. But there's no time to waste.

The detectives are all quiet. They wait.

'And one thing I'll put money on?' Adam finishes grimly. 'He knows who his next victim is. He knows that already.'

Extract from *The Good Doctor:*
The True Story of Dr Elijah Cole,
by Lucas Richards, 1998

Elijah Cole's childhood was far from idyllic. Like many serial killers before him, his early years were dominated by abuse and violence. His father was a wife-beater and a drunk; his mother a quiet, unassuming housewife. Perhaps it should have been possible to predict what happened next, but nobody intervened when, on Thursday, 20 June 1968, Lucy Cole stabbed Maurice Cole to death with a kitchen knife. She had been beaten and strangled, left for dead when she took her revenge. Elijah Cole watched the whole thing. He was 11.

But, contrary to so many of these stories, Elijah Cole didn't go on to be a wife-beater himself. Exactly the opposite. Elijah says, of that day: 'Knowing what he had put my mother through, I resolved to be the best husband and father I could possibly be. To never lay a hand on my wife. To be gentle and kind with my children.'

Some speculate his wife's death drove him mad with grief. Others claim the murderous instincts were always there, but pushed under when nourished by his wife's adoration.

Whatever the reason, reports at this time agree with Elijah's resolve. Despite what he did to the bodies found in his outhouse. To the women he raped and tortured and murdered, he never laid a hand on his wife. Neighbours describe Elijah and Joanna Cole as a devoted couple, deeply in love. Their daughter, Romilly, was cherished and cared for. While some describe Elijah Cole as a sadistic psychopath, one thing seems true: he was a good husband and father.

Chapter 46

Adam stands motionless in front of the man he knows only from news reports, from breathless gossip around the police station, from legend and lore. He is not what Adam expected.

Elijah Cole is clean-shaven, smelling of soap and laundry powder. Hair neatly combed away from his forehead, thinning on top, but holding up better than most men his age. He looks just how he was described, all those years ago: the man next door. The friendly GP nobody suspected.

'DCI Bishop,' he begins. 'How nice to meet you for the first time. Although the basic courtesy of a shower and a shave wouldn't have gone amiss.'

He holds out his hand, friendly and polite. Adam stares at it, then sits down opposite, his arms folded across his chest.

'Now, now,' Cole says in a mocking tone. 'No need to be like that. I didn't have to see you.'

A visitation request agreed at short notice. Second time lucky. Adam had been surprised.

'No, you didn't. So why did you agree?'

The doctor tilts his head to one side. 'Curiosity,' he replies. Adam feels his appraisal run across his face, down his chest to his hands then back up. He has impossibly dark eyes, a smile playing on his thin lips. 'The man my daughter married. Seems a strange decision, seeing you here now. But still,' he finishes with a chuckle, 'you haven't had your best week, have you, detective?'

Adam refuses to rise to the bait. 'And what do you know about that?' he replies calmly.

'About poor old Pippa Hoxton? Dead and drained? Nothing.' He gestures around the room with a smile. 'I've been here all week. The perfect alibi.'

Adam glances towards the one guard, standing, bored, at the side of the room. Shaved head, a once muscled torso grown soft from lack of care. His face betrays nothing, certainly no allegiance to the fellow law enforcement officer sitting in the room with him.

Adam turns back to Cole. 'Who have you spoken to? Who's visited you?'

'Isn't that your job to find out?'

'Information has been slow. Deliberately obstructed, one might say.'

Cole shrugs. 'Nothing to do with me. Not my fault if bureaucracy gets in the way of good old police work.' He pauses. 'How is Romilly? I got the feeling she was upset when she left yesterday.'

'I'm not here to talk about Romilly.'

'No? Then why are you here?'

He pauses. He has to get this right; he knows Cole isn't going to tell him outright, but maybe he'll give something away. A flicker of an expression. A word, a moment of revelation. Anything.

'Do you know who's behind this, Dr Cole?' he says slowly.

The man stares at him; Adam makes eye contact. Neither of them blinks. Then Cole speaks.

'All my life, I've known that I have a special gift. A way about me, if you like.' He sighs, a slow intake of breath, then out. 'At school, my teacher – the only one who saw through me – called me sly. Others said I was sweet, charming, misunderstood. I was never the one to get into trouble. Never the one caught.' His eyes slide back, meeting Adam's. 'But always getting your own way makes you spoilt, DCI Bishop. Have you found that?'

Adam waits, knowing Cole isn't expecting an answer. Sure enough, he continues.

'A man like you. With good looks, and the personality to match. I've heard the screws talk about you around here, and the men you've put away. Quite the bloodhound, aren't you, Adam? Tenacity. Ambition. You like it when things work in your favour. So how did you cope when Romilly cheated on you? When she didn't want you?'

Adam feels his body grow rigid, but he holds on tight to his temper.

'I'm not here to talk about Romilly, Dr Cole,' he repeats. 'I want to talk about Pippa.'

Cole waves his hand in the air, dismissing Adam's request. 'Don't rush things, detective. Take the time, enjoy yourself. You're here now, aren't you?'

Adam glares. 'So what would you like to discuss, Elijah?'

'You, DCI Bishop.' The dark eyes again, on his.

'That's not up for conversation.'

'That seems unfair. You want me to talk, yet you're not prepared to share. How did you feel, detective, when your best friend came home to find his wife dead?'

'I'm not talking about that.'

'Does DS Hoxton blame you? For your failure to find Pippa? Or is he forgiving in the face of your incompetence?' Adam stays silent, his teeth clenched so hard it's painful. 'Is Romilly upset her friend is dead? Or maybe you don't know. Maybe she doesn't turn to you anymore, now she has her lovely new boyfriend to cry on at night?'

'I know what you're doing, Elijah, but it won't work,' Adam growls. 'I won't give you the satisfaction.'

'The satisfaction of what, Adam? You sharing your feelings? Letting down that facade you do so well to cultivate?' Elijah sighs and sits back in his seat. Then he turns and gestures to the guard. 'Get us both a cup of coffee, will you?'

To Adam's surprise, the guard nods, pushes himself off the wall, and leaves. The room is silent; the two of them alone.

Elijah looks back to Adam, a big grin on his face. 'Scared?' he says, mocking. 'Scared to be alone with a serial killer?'

'You're an old man, Elijah,' Adam replies, forcing confidence into his voice. But what if he has a weapon: a shank or razor blade? He feels his muscles tense. 'Bring it on,' he says.

But Elijah laughs. 'Like I can be bothered. No. No, I just want to talk.'

'So talk.'

Elijah leans forward in his seat, so close Adam can see

the small nick next to his ear where he's caught himself shaving. 'You want to know about Pippa?' he whispers.

'Yes.'

'You want to know why I chose her, why she was perfect? You know how much I like a vulnerable woman, don't you? How much I enjoy them.'

Adam feels his hands start to shake. Could Cole be telling the truth? Could he have someone on the outside, like they've assumed. But how? How is he communicating with them, telling them what to do?

He clears his throat. 'Who is killing for you, Dr Cole?'

Cole laughs. 'And ruin the fun so early? Before we're done?'

'You'll never get to twenty, Elijah. We'll stop you way before then.'

He shakes his head. 'The arrogance. The confidence. I envy you, DCI Bishop. I was like you, once. I thought I could do anything. And to some extent, I could. But I couldn't control her, could I? In the end, my overconfidence in my daughter was why I ended up in here. Coward that she is.'

'Romilly is one of the bravest people I know.'

Cole scoffs. 'You think it takes bravery to call the police? To do the *right thing*?' His tone is mocking and scornful. 'The real bravery is demanding to live your life how you want it, against all laws of the land and humanity and morality. I knew keeping those women was wrong. But I wanted it, so I did it. How many people do you know are able to live their life exactly how they please?'

'And now look at you,' Adam replies. 'Stuck in jail.'

'But they're in here.' Cole taps on his forehead with one finger. 'My girls. Exactly what they did. What I did to them. I'll never be alone again. They're mine, forever.'

Cole closes his eyes for a second and smiles, as if

demonstrating to Adam. Adam swallows down the disgust, the hatred. If he has to listen to this filth to get to Pippa's killer, then so be it.

Cole opens his eyes again slowly. 'Did the police ever work out what I was doing with the cages?' he asks.

'You locked them in there.'

Cole laughs. 'Yes, but why? It was more than simple imprisonment.' He pauses, looking at Adam. 'Tell me, what would you do? If you could do anything in the world to a woman. What would you choose?'

Adam remembers Ellie last night and instantly feels sick. He shakes his head. 'I'm not like you.'

Elijah raises his eyebrows. 'Are you sure? A young hot-blooded man like yourself.' He leans forward again, his voice low and whispered. 'If no one would find out? What are your deepest darkest desires, Adam Bishop?'

Adam turns away, pushing his seat back to put distance between them.

Elijah scowls. 'That's the problem with the younger generation. You lack the imagination.' He folds his arms across his chest, half closing his eyes. 'I'll share one from me, just for you. The cages.' He opens his eyes again, ensuring he has Adam's attention. Adam pushes his hands into fists, holding himself back. 'Three different sizes. If they were good, if they satisfied me properly – let me fuck them the way I wanted, didn't fight, didn't misbehave – then they could have a bigger cage. And I'd let them out sooner. Maybe only keep them in for four hours, five. But if they didn't . . .' He laughs and Adam feels bile churn in his stomach. 'Each rebellion, added an hour. Grace, she was a fighter. Swore, shouted, screamed. Tied her up, but I don't like it when I have to force them. I like them to agree, to nod their pretty heads and lie still while I fuck them. And Grace? I had to work hard to break her. Put her in the smallest cage once for a whole twenty hours. Day and night. She couldn't move, all scrunched up in a ball, naked. Do you know what that does to the human body?'

Adam looks towards the door. Where the fuck is the guard? Why are they still alone in here? But Cole is hardly noticing Adam now, his gaze fixed in the middle distance. 'Muscles cramping, metal chafing through her skin. No sleep. No food, no water. Except for the bucket I dumped over her head, left her shivering, crying, begging. I asked her then: "Will you let me now, Grace?" And even when she nodded I left her for another twenty hours. To really make sure.'

Elijah looks up now at Adam; Adam can't keep the look of disgust from his face. But Elijah doesn't seem to care. 'When I let her out she couldn't stand,' he continues. 'Could only crawl across the floor. Her joints screaming with pain, bleeding, desperate.' He laughs. 'She sucked my dick then, I'll tell you. I had no more crap from her. Not that day, not ever. Not until she died. That control, it's better than anything else in the world. Especially when you've been so starved of it as I was as a child. Wouldn't you like that, DCI Bishop?' he asks. 'That control. For a woman to be that compliant?'

'No. No, I wouldn't,' Adam says. He's heard enough. This man's a void, functioning on his own best guesses of emotion. The self-serving charm, the mimicry of warmth and intimacy. An arrogant narcissism he can't help but feel lurking in his own psyche.

He'll find this killer himself. He'll go back to the station, and they'll find him and they'll arrest him, without this mad man's input. He stands up, moving away from the table, desperate to put distance between them.

But before he leaves, he turns.

'We know what you did, Elijah,' Adam says, spitting the words out with anger. 'You killed four women, kidnapped and tortured a fifth. You're fucked up, ill, mentally deranged, yes. But you're not special. You're not even exceptional when it comes to serial killers – there's been far worse than you. And you're locked up for life. You'll never see the light of day again.'

Adam tries the handle, but it's locked. He bangs on the door: once, twice. He hears the scrape of the chair on the floor as Elijah stands.

'What are we at now, Adam?' he says, his voice intimidating. 'Pippa was number nine, right?'

Cole takes a step towards him. Adam can hear footsteps marching down the corridor outside.

'That leaves us, what? Eight to go?'

'Fuck you, Elijah,' Adam whispers. 'You'll never get that far.'

He takes a step away, his back now pressed against the hard door. He hears metal being inserted, locks being pulled back, and he turns, pulling at the handle. But at the same time he hears soft footsteps. He has an awareness of Elijah standing behind him. He tries the handle again, but he's out of time. It's too late. Elijah's too close, there's nothing he can do. He freezes, bracing himself for pain, for something sharp being shoved into his back. For blood to flow. But instead, a body presses against his, gentle hands caress his arms.

Hot breath on the side of his face.

'You're wrong, Adam,' Cole whispers into his ear. 'So wrong.' He pauses; Adam can feel the warmth of his body, the scratch of the man's chin against his cheek.

'DCI Bishop,' Cole continues, his voice low and quiet. 'Did you honestly think that those women were my first?'

Chapter 47

The words unfreeze Adam in a second. He turns, two hands on Cole's chest, pushing him away. The man stumbles backwards onto the floor, and in two quick strides Adam is bending over him, a knee on his chest, pushing him down.

'What the fuck do you mean?' he shouts, all restraint gone. 'Who are you talking about?'

Cole laughs. 'There are three others. Three more, you'll never find.'

'Who? Who are they?'

He raises a fist. To punch him, to threaten him, he doesn't know. But the guards grab his arms, pulling Adam off Cole and forcing him out the door.

'I need to know, I need to talk to him,' Adam shouts as he's bundled away. 'We're not finished!'

'You've done enough,' the guard replies in a strong Scottish accent. 'Leave the doc alone.'

'Why are you protecting him? Don't you know what he did, the sick fucker, he killed—'

But before Adam can say any more the guard is on him. He's pushed up against the wall, his skull banging against brick, a hard forearm against his neck. Adam gasps, pulling at the man's arm but the guard stands firm.

'Don't say another word about the doc, you hear me?' the guard says, his face barely inches away from Adam's. Adam struggles for breath, his eyes watering. He can see another officer watching them from across the corridor, his eyes wide, but he does nothing to stop his colleague.

'Do you hear me?' the guard repeats.

'Yes,' Adam wheezes, and the pressure is released. He falls against the wall on the other side, coughing, lungs heaving.

'Now fuck off,' the guard barks. And with a final hard shove, he grabs Adam by the scruff of his shirt and pushes him, leaving Adam stumbling backwards down the corridor.

He can't believe it; he turns in astonishment at the audacity of the guard. He should report it, seize the footage, but he's stunned, in shock, and starts walking towards the exit. His mind is reeling as he collects his mobile phone and belongings. How are they so under his spell? It's no wonder they still haven't received the visitor logs from the prison, if this is what's going on. And how could there be more? More bodies, more victims, that they haven't found?

He leaves and walks across to his car, but as he does so he notices another man behind him. The other officer from the altercation in the corridor. The one who did nothing. Anger swirls, and he turns to confront him.

The guard sees him coming, and drops his gaze to the concrete, walking fast in the opposite direction. But Adam is close, and quickly makes up the ground between them.

'Why didn't you stop him?' Adam shouts. The guard tries to ignore him but Adam reaches out and grabs his arm. 'Why didn't you intervene when that bastard assaulted me?'

'Get off me,' the guard growls, but Adam holds tight. The man glares. 'You don't have a fucking clue, you cops. No idea how a prison operates.'

'So tell me.'

The guard glances around. The car park is deserted, no one is watching them.

'There are rules. Not the ones you think you know about, but others. Unwritten. That you obey whether you're a screw or a con.'

'What's that got to do with Cole?'

The guard's short and tubby, Adam guesses early-thirties. Shoulders hunched, back stooped. He certainly doesn't look like the sort of man who'd be high in the pecking order.

'It's got everything to do with Cole.' He pulls, annoyed, at the grip Adam's still got on his arm. 'He's smart. The governor loves him because he doesn't cause trouble. If anything he keeps the peace, knows what to say to keep the prisoners in line. They respect him.' He glances around again. 'He knows stuff.'

'Like what?'

'Like . . .' He thinks for a moment. 'There was this prison officer. A woman. She was shagging one of the inmates.' He shrugs. 'It happens. But Cole, he found out, don't ask me how, and blackmailed her. Gossip says she was doing all sorts of stuff for him before it came out. Smuggling contraband, drugs, fags. The lot. Passing messages and letters. God knows how much shit went down on the outside as a result.'

'What happened to her?'

'She quit. Had a breakdown, I heard. So you don't mess, *DCI Bishop*.' He says his name distastefully. 'In there, you leave well alone. Unless you want something nasty to happen.' He shakes his arm clear of Adam's grasp, then takes a few steps back. 'Which I personally don't. Now fuck off. Before someone sees us talking.'

With that, he walks quickly away, head down. What he's told Adam, it's not surprising, but doesn't bode well for getting that information out of the prison any time soon. He watches until the guard goes out of sight, then pulls his phone out of his pocket, dialling Marsh. His boss answers immediately.

'Bishop, where the hell are you?'

'Sorry, guv. I've . . .' Adam catches his breath, opening his car door and throwing himself inside. 'I went to see Elijah Cole.'

'You . . .' The detective chief superintendent's voice trails off as he realises what Adam's saying. 'We talked about this. I gave permission to get the visitor logs, but I didn't say you could fuck off in the middle of a murder investigation to go and see the one person we know couldn't have done it.'

'But he's linked, guv. To it all. We know he is.'

'Because he knows a few details about the case he shouldn't?'

'Yes, but—'

'But what?'

Adam tells him everything Cole said. His description of what had happened to Pippa, his intimate knowledge of the case. His conversation with the guard and the altercation with the other one inside, and – last of all – Cole's final confession that there are three more victims.

At the other end of the line, Marsh is silent.

'So, Bishop, you're telling me that you've been expertly controlled by one of the most infamously manipulative serial killers this country has ever known?'

'It's not that, boss, I know—'

'One who also happens to be the father of your ex-wife?'

'Guv—'

'Stop it, Adam!' Marsh shouts. Adam feels the full weight of his boss's disapproval. 'We searched that house, ran dogs over the entire garden. We found all the victims. You want Cole to be linked, you want Romilly Cole to be involved, so . . . So you can hang out with your ex-wife in a misguided attempt to get her back? Fuck it, I knew I shouldn't have invited her yesterday. But that's enough, Bishop. Get back to the nick. To the current investigation. To the murder of Hoxton's wife.'

Adam is silent.

'Do you hear me, Bishop?'

'Yes, guv.'

Marsh hangs up the phone, and Adam puts his hand on the ignition of his car. But he doesn't start the engine. Instead, he makes another call. To a retired detective. DS David Shepherd.

Chapter 48

All morning, Jamie wanders the house, alone, thinking about Adam. Adam's still not been home. He walks to the kitchen, head thumping, legs wobbly. He pours a pint of water, then carries it to the sofa.

He looks at the debris in the room: at the empty bottles, the glasses with a few centimetres of liquid at the bottom, the ashtray. He feels his sore throat and picks up the nearly empty packet of Adam's Marlboro lying on the table. He remembers smoking a few, half enjoying the rebellious act, accepting the stinging lungs as some sort of penance. He coughs now and winces. He takes a long pull from the pint of water.

In the light of day, sober, his words from last night haunt him. He'd meant them then, but now, he knows he was expecting something superhuman from his friend. Nobody could have found Pippa sooner; nobody could have worked harder, pushed themselves to the limit more than Adam. And all he'd done was thrown his efforts back in his face.

Where had he gone? Where had he spent the night? That thought is worse, that he had been wandering the streets. Alone. That he is out there, still, somewhere. In the same way that Pippa had been.

But before his thoughts can turn to panic, he hears a key in the door and footsteps in the hallway. Jamie pushes himself up from the sofa and stops as Adam walks into the room.

His friend looks awful. Three days' worth of stubble, skin grey, dark rings under his half-closed eyes. Adam stops, his gaze pushed down, away from Jamie.

'Adam, I'm sorry,' Jamie blurts out before Adam can walk away from him. 'I didn't mean what I said.'

Adam doesn't move, eyes cast to the floor. 'I need a shower,' he mutters. 'I have work to do.'

Jamie reaches out and grabs his arm; Adam stares at it numbly.

'Where have you been?' Jamie asks softly. 'I was worried.'

His gaze shifts up at the hint of concern. Then he sighs, his mouth downturned.

'I've been to Belmarsh.'

'Jail? To see who?' Then Jamie realises. 'Cole? You went to see Cole.'

Adam nods.

'And?'

Adam slumps wearily on the sofa. 'He knows something. He's behind all this. He is. But I can't prove it.'

'But how?'

'Fuck, I don't know. The guards are all under his thumb, perhaps he's using them to get messages in and out.' He runs his hands down his face. 'I need coffee.'

'I'll make you one. Stay there.'

Jamie goes into the kitchen, putting the kettle on and spooning instant coffee into two mugs. He glances back into the living room: Adam is still sitting there, head in his hands. He can't believe what Adam is saying, but something about it all fits.

Jamie carries the coffees back and puts them both on the table. Adam reaches forward to the box of cigarettes, taking one out and lighting it. He takes a long drag, then holds the packet out to Jamie.

'You want one? Since this is your thing now?'

Jamie returns his tired smile. 'Didn't like it. I'm sorry, mate.'

Adam waves with the cigarette, dismissing him. 'It's done. You were right—'

'I wasn't—'

'I should have found her.' He taps the cigarette on the ashtray.

'Adam, you did nothing wrong in that investigation. Nothing. Concentrate on catching this fucker. That's all that's important.'

Adam nods slowly. After a moment he says, 'That's not all.'

And Adam updates Jamie on everything to do with the case – the heparin, the needles, the medical expertise – and everything Cole told him. Jamie's mouth drops open in surprise.

'There are more? Three more victims?' Jamie replies, astonished. 'But where?'

'Marsh says I'm being manipulated. That it's all bollocks.'

'What do you think?'

Adam shrugs, staring thoughtfully into the smoke curling up from his cigarette. 'Who cares what I think?'

Jamie's seen Adam like this before: after he split up with Romilly. Apathy, distance. His emotions shutting down. Adam's accepted his apology on the surface but underneath their relationship has changed. There are things he's not telling him – how he's feeling, thoughts he would have imparted before the argument last night.

But before Jamie can say any more, Adam's phone beeps. He looks at it, then stubs his butt out in the ashtray and stands up.

'I have to go.'

'Adam—'

'I need to have a shower. I'll be back later.' He surveys the mess. Then he shakes his head and walks out of the room.

Jamie watches him go. What has he done? When he needs his friend the most, when Adam needs him, he's destroyed everything. He'll make it up to him, he resolves. He will. He picks up the ashtray, and two of the empty wine bottles. He can at least start by tidying up the mess.

Chapter 49

It's dark by the time Adam makes it to the house. He follows directions through a normal-looking suburb, past a school, a church. A nice village, somewhere Adam might like to live one day. He dismisses the thought. In a different world. For a different person. Not him.

He pulls into the neatly tarmacked driveway and shuts off his engine. Wellington boots are racked up on sticks outside the front door, a dog bowl alongside. He rings the bell and a man answers.

'DCI Bishop?'

'Detective Shepherd?'

He holds out his hand, smiling warmly. 'Call me David. Come in, come in. You don't mind dogs, do you?'

A large black Labrador comes bowling towards him, tongue lolling, tail wagging enthusiastically. He immediately deposits a line of silver drool on Adam's trousers.

'Ah, sorry about that,' Shepherd says, pulling the dog away. 'Disgusting beast, but we love him.'

Adam smiles. He appreciates the moment of levity and bends down to rub the dog's ears. 'It's fine.'

He's shown into a cosy living room. A fire burns in the hearth and the dog slumps down next to it with a sigh. Shepherd offers him a drink; Adam asks for coffee. The man leaves and Adam settles back into the comfortable chair.

In the warmth of the fire, the comfort of the room, Adam feels his eyes closing. He can't remember the last time he had a good night's sleep. Before this all started. A week ago. Before they found the bodies.

Helplessness, worry, claw at his insides.

'I've been following the coverage on the news. I wondered if you'd call.' Shepherd puts the cup of coffee on the table next to Adam, pulling him out of his disquiet. 'I saw you went to the house.' He sits down across from him and rests his slippered feet on a small stool.

'I'm sorry to bother you.'

'Not at all. Retirement is, well . . .' He shrugs. 'The old detective instinct never leaves. You're thinking Elijah Cole's involved?'

Adam's surprised, they hadn't shared the details with the press. But the older man has clearly been paying attention.

Back then, DS David Shepherd was one of the first detectives on the scene. He wasn't SIO; that dubious privilege had fallen to a DCI called Frank Langston, but he was long dead. Shepherd was the man on the ground, conducting the interviews, at the time only mid-thirties. Now, twenty-six years later, he's retired to a nice house in the country. Slippers, Labrador, log fire. And still fascinated by the case. Leaning forward, keen to hear Adam's answer.

'We believe so, yes,' Adam replies. 'He knows things about the investigation that he could only be privy to if he was involved.'

'Or he has someone on the inside?'

'Maybe, yes. But I can't think who. I trust my team.' Adam pauses. How much should he share? But it's good to talk about it all with someone who understands. 'He's behind it. Or it's someone doing it to impress him. Either way, Cole's enjoying himself.'

Shepherd nods. 'It wouldn't surprise me. Devious bastard. He always hated losing, caused many fights in the early days in jail by cheating at poker and blackjack. He knew the ins and outs of that place – kept everyone on their toes, staff and prisoners alike. Charmed his favourites, blackmailed the others.'

Adam shares what the guard told him, and Shepherd nods. 'That sounds like him. Selectively releasing rumour and innuendo to suit his own needs. He played games with the psychiatrists sent to assess him. They refused to see him in the end. He was smarter than they were, that was for sure.'

'They said that?'

'Course not,' Shepherd snorts. 'But Cole certainly thought he was and I'm inclined to agree. He got away with all sorts of shit in his first few years in that jail. Found out he was running some sort of free clinic, even diagnosed one of the screws' daughters with cancer. Probably saved her life.' Adam thinks of the guard that morning, his arm across his throat. 'You're familiar with the original case?' Shepherd asks.

'Yes. I've been through all your files. But it's the stuff that isn't in there I'd like to know about.' He knows the scratches on the wall were left out. What else might there have been? 'Your thoughts at the time. Your suspicions.'

Shepherd pauses. 'In relation to what?'

'Did you think there were more victims?'

The man nods slowly. 'I certainly think there would have been, if the daughter hadn't called us. We didn't have a clue, until we turned up that day. Not a single suspicion it was Cole.' He picks up the mug next to him and cradles it in his hands. 'I'd been assigned to look into the mispers – four of them. All women, same ages, same body types, so we thought there was something dodgy going on. But Cole was nowhere near our suspect list.'

'I thought there were five women?'

'Yes, there were. But at the time we didn't know Catherine Sutton was missing. She was homeless, no one had noticed her absence. Our only survivor.'

'What happened to her?'

Shepherd tips his head down, a sad gesture. 'Dead. She disappeared, ten days after we got her out. We couldn't find her. Until later. I guess it was her forte – living on the streets – so she blended back in. Vanished. But every now and again I'd have a look. Search for her name, check for any Jane Does that had been arrested.' He pauses and wipes his eyes for a second. 'Unidentified female. Found in the river, and she'd been there a while so there wasn't much to go on. I always hoped she changed her name, made a new start. Got married, had kids.' He laughs to himself. 'No more than misplaced optimism. Looking for the happy ending. We never found out what happened. My guess is she overdosed. Or killed by her pimp and dumped. That's how it usually goes for these girls.' He looks at Adam. 'And Romilly Cole? How is she? I assume you've interviewed her again?'

292

Adam smiles. 'Yes, she's been helping us with the investigation. She's good. She's a doctor now. Oncology.'

'Yes, I heard. Strange how she followed in her father's footsteps. You'd think she'd want nothing to do with him. I always wondered.'

'Wondered what?' Adam says.

'We could never shake the feeling she was lying.'

The Labrador lets out a long groan, then hauls himself up from in front of the fire and slumps down again to Shepherd's side. The detective reaches down to rub his ears. Adam stays quiet. Half of him is desperate to know what he means, the other half dreading what he'll say.

Shepherd sighs. 'I shouldn't bring it up. It's unfair. There was nothing we could ever prove. But something about her story didn't stack up. The timings, the house, how long it had gone on. She must have seen *something*.'

Adam remembers the location of her bedroom, overlooking the garden. 'But she said she'd been completely unaware?'

'Right. And what use would it have been, even if we could show she'd known? She was eleven. Her life was completely destroyed. And we had him locked up. More than enough evidence to put him away for life, so why put the girl through more?'

'What was she like, in the days just after?'

'Shocked. Muddled. Crying. How you'd expect if your beloved father had been arrested for the kidnap, torture, rape, and murder of five women. But she was so under his thumb. You could see it. She would have done anything for him. Makes you wonder whether she had.'

'Whether she had, what?'

But the man shakes his head, reluctant to continue. 'She

293

wasn't the only one. Everyone was like that around him, even some of our detectives were charmed. He was so polite, and funny, and smart. You met him.'

'This morning. He wasn't so pleasant.'

Shepherd nods. 'We saw that side of him too. Turning nasty on the flip of a coin. The two faces of a serial killer. But he ran that GP practice for thirteen years before he was caught. We even got letters from some of his patients, saying how we were wrong, how Dr Cole had helped them. Placards outside the courthouse proclaiming his innocence. I would have liked to show them the photos, take them down to that outhouse. I'll never forget it. That smell.'

His eyes drift, lost in the memory. 'The girls had gone by the time I got there but even empty it was horrific. You could almost taste their fear, it was visceral. Thick, claggy, something in the air.

'When I got home I had a shower, then got straight back in and had another. It clung to you. The death. How much those poor women . . . how much they suffered.'

He looks at Adam, eyes narrowed. 'If you think these latest deaths have something to do with him – however improbable, however ridiculous – then they probably do.' He leans forward in his chair, resolute, his face hard. 'He is the devil, that man,' Shepherd says. 'The devil incarnate.'

Chapter 50

Adam thanks the detective and leaves. But before he goes Shepherd stops him.

'I didn't answer your question, the reason you came here.'

For a moment, Adam can't think what he's referring to. Then he remembers.

'The other victims.'

'Yes. And no, I don't think there is anyone else there.'

'But the house—'

'No. We checked it. The Roman numerals on the door-frame made us wonder whether there were more, so when we found the three bodies in the garden we went over the whole place a thousand times. Dogs, ground-penetrating radar, the lot. We ripped up the floorboards, drilled through concrete. There's nothing else, I assure you.'

Adam nods. 'Thank you,' he says again and Shepherd shakes his hand.

'I'm happy to answer your questions,' he says. 'Any time. But if anyone knows anything about what happened at that house, it's her. If there was anyone else involved, she'd have known. The daughter. Speak to Romilly Cole.'

Adam drives without thinking. She'd told him about her father almost as soon as they had met. She'd wanted to be honest, she said. If you can't deal, that's fine, but I need you to know. And he'd nodded and let her talk.

About growing up with him in that house, how she'd felt when his brutal crimes had come to life. She told him to read the newspaper coverage, the reports at the time detailing what he'd done, then come back to her if he had any questions. But he'd done more than that. Adam found the original case files, read what DS Shepherd and DCI Langston had found. Transcripts from the trial. Subsequent confessions on tape. After the verdict, Cole admitted his crimes, detailing them, carefully, over weeks in an interview room. Everything seemed in order. Except for one thing. How could she not have known?

He gets to her house, rings the bell; he hears footsteps. Romilly opens the door. She's wearing a blue denim shirt, open at the neck, a low white vest underneath. Her hair is wavy and loose around her shoulders. For a moment, she smiles, and he is frozen. He doesn't want to destroy this beautiful image in front of him. But she senses something is wrong and her expression changes.

'Adam, what is it?' She ushers him into the house, offering him tea, coffee, but he declines them all and tells her to sit down. She lowers herself slowly into her kitchen chair, her eyes locked on him.

He sits opposite her.

'Romilly, I need you to be honest with me.' She stares, her forehead creases into a frown. 'Did you know?'

Silence engulfs the room. Adam can hear her breathing, steady, in and out.

'Please,' he says. And silently, he thinks, *please*. Just tell me.

'Why are you bringing this up now?' she asks slowly.

'I saw your father this morning.'

He sees her blink, then swallow hard. 'And?'

'He says there are more victims.'

'And you believe him?'

'Listen, Romilly. I went there, to your house. Yesterday. I never realised it before but your bedroom overlooked the garden. How didn't you notice him out there? He must have carried the women in almost directly below you.' He reaches out to take her hand but she pulls away. 'Please, Romilly. For them. For those women.'

She shakes her head. 'Don't you think I don't know that? That I don't think about those women every day. No, Adam. As I told the police at the time. I saw nothing. I knew nothing.' Her face flushes; she starts to cry, tears rolling down her cheeks. 'You know this, Adam. You of all people. I've told you everything I know.'

He stares at her. He believes her, he has to. The alternative is unthinkable.

'I'm sorry,' he says. 'I shouldn't have asked. But this case, that man. It's making me crazy. It's nothing, forget it.' He glances up at the clock. It's nine p.m. Late. 'Is . . . Is your boyfriend around?'

'No, he's gone to stay with a friend for a few days.'

'Now?' Adam asks, disbelieving that the guy would leave his girlfriend alone when things were like this.

'Yes. We . . .' She sighs. 'We had a fight. He needs some space.'

297

'What did you fight about?'

She laughs, short and sharp. 'You, Adam. It's always about you.'

'Me?'

She smiles and shakes her head sadly. 'He can't understand why I don't leave this case alone. Why I can't leave you alone.' She pauses, bites her lip. 'He says I'm still in love with you.'

Adam swallows. He clears his throat. 'And are you?'

'Do you even need to ask?'

She looks at him. Her eyes meet his, dark hazel brown, almost desperate. She's looking for a response from him, something, and he wants to. So, so much. But—

'I have to go, Milly.' He stands up quickly; he hears her make a noise. Soft – a mixture of regret and frustration.

'Fine, go,' she says. 'Walk away, like you always do.'

'I'm not . . . I have a case to run, Romilly. I can't—'

'Can't, what? Say how you feel?'

He turns quickly. 'Trust you. Trust you again. After what you did.'

'Christ!' Romilly's jaw juts out. She's angry, her face red. 'Yes, I made a mistake. Yes, it was my fault we split up. But before—'

'Before you fucked someone else?'

'Yes, before that! See, at least I can admit what I did. While you . . . You pretend that everything was fine. That we were happy and in love, when you'd been pulling away from me for months.'

He stares. 'That's not—'

'Yes, it is, Adam. The man I married was kind and open and . . . and . . . he told me things. Shared how he was feeling. When he was upset, or worried, or . . . or in pain.

298

But you—' She points an accusatory finger at him. 'You're not him. This man here is arrogant, and stupid, and shags around, and . . .' She stops, the fury blown out. 'And is wasting his life,' she continues quietly. 'You've put up a wall, and you think you're fine, but you're only living half a life, Adam. Please. I want my husband back. I want you.'

Adam shakes his head. He can't do this. Not now.

He turns and walks quickly out of her house, slamming the door behind him. She's wrong. She's wrong, he thinks as he gets into his car. He's fine. Yes, he doesn't share his *feelings* all the time, as some people do, but that doesn't mean he has problems. He let his guard down for her, and look what happened. He ended up alone. Same as his parents, all those years ago.

No. He is fine. He can live without her. He doesn't love her. That's over, he tells himself. He takes a cigarette out and lights it with shaking fingers. But still the pain in his chest won't go away. An ache, from deep within his bones.

You have spoken to him. The time is right.

I must act fast.

I walk quickly; it's cold out, there aren't many people. Especially not here. Where the streetlight doesn't reach the path, where shadows lurk in the trees. Nobody notices me. Like you, I am alone.

I reach the house; I walk around the side. The back gate is unlocked, the catch old and rusty. It opens without complaint. I push past the bins, the piles of glass recycling, neatly stacked. They are young, the people who live here, I can tell by their choices of wine. Cheap. Nasty. A taste that sticks in the mouth.

I stand to the side in the back garden. I can see someone in the kitchen, a woman, singing loudly to a song. She shouts out to the living room, voices call back. There are three people here, but I know I won't be seen. I am never seen.

The woman pours large glasses of wine and carries them through. Laughing. Oblivious. She's not beautiful, but lovely in her own way. I move forward out of the shadows, place one hand on the back door. It's unlocked. Another sign. Safety in numbers, they probably think. How wrong they are.

I push the handle down and walk into the kitchen. Pots and plates lie on the side, daubs of sauce left on the cooker. The music is louder here, happy and bright. It jars.

I pause in the hallway, listening. The chatter of three young women having the time of their lives. Laughter, joy. How I hate them. It makes me love you all the more. For your diffidence, for your maturity.

I leave the bright happy scene and walk carefully up the stairs. Floorboards creak but I won't be heard. I know which bedroom is hers – from the light yesterday – and I head towards it.

I open the door. I let my eyes adjust to the dim. The bed is unmade, cheap gawdy clothes litter the floor. The smell of perfume hangs in the air. This is where I need to be. I have a look at the room, for the best place to hide. There is no space below the bed, and the wardrobe is stuffed full. I stand behind the door and wait. Still. Patient.

As I always was.

Fragments of memory cut in and out: from then. The smell of chipboard, new furniture, as I sit under the desk. Coming, ready or not – the shout loud and joyful. I hold my breath, excitement almost making me giggle as I hear heavy footsteps. Then, your dark eyes, creased at the corners, laughing. Those were the happy times, the ones I miss.

Dreams remind me when I sleep: nightmares of being alone, discarded. Lost and abandoned, I walk on empty

301

roads, frantically looking. I feel the grasping loneliness, the fear, the tension in my stomach – and when I wake my face is wet from tears.

I try not to think about them. The people I've killed. I know they deserved it, that they are the stooges of a system that fails to protect the innocent. That they were destined to die. But still. I hear their screams, their begging for mercy.

But now, it's time.

Music turns off. Footsteps and laughter on the stairs. Exclamations of 'good night' and 'sleep well'. The door opens, the light switches on, dazzling me. But I wait, hidden behind the open door. She is humming under her breath; I watch as she flits in and out of view. She gets undressed and I see her: young and taut, unmarked. My breathing gets faster. With my right hand I touch the knife in my pocket, the blade sharp, stinging as I run my fingertip along the edge. I pull it out and sure enough, bright red blood is blooming from a narrow cut. I put my finger in my mouth, still watching.

She takes her bra off, puts on a T-shirt for bed, then goes into the bathroom. The confidence, the ease of youth; I hate her with a fury that makes my teeth grind. I walk out of my hiding place, pushing the door closed with a click. There is a key in the lock and I turn it, pulling it out and putting it in my pocket.

We are alone now.

Coming, ready or not.

She is cleaning her teeth, looking at herself in the mirror. She sees me in the reflection and freezes. She drops the toothbrush.

'What are you . . .' she starts, but the sight of the knife makes her stop.

She takes a breath in to scream and that's when I strike. I step forward, jabbing the knife towards her middle. She sees it coming and deflects with her hand, but she's not quick enough. I'm too close. The knife hits her forearm, cutting into the flesh, sharp and efficient. She cries out, blood splashes across the sink, across the mirror as she flails with her injured arm, panicking.

'Please . . .' she begs. But there's no point in her pleading. She's seen the files, the previous victims. She knows how she'll end up. It's just a matter of time.

She backs away from me, but there's nowhere for her to go except into the white tiled cubicle of the shower. She's crying now, her hands outstretched in front of her. Sobbing harder as I push the bathroom door shut. She sinks down into a crouch on the floor of the shower.

'I'm sorry,' she says, but I don't know what for. The blood from her arm streaks her skin, running down to the drain. Her position, curled into a ball below me, makes this difficult.

'I don't want to hurt you more than I have to,' I say, and she looks up at me with those big green eyes, disbelieving. 'You know this is coming. You don't need to suffer.'

She blinks, tears rolling down her cheeks. 'Please,' she whispers. 'I don't want to die.'

'We all die,' I reply. Her eyes dart to the door; I know what she is thinking.

'I only want you,' I say. 'But shout and scream – make them come running – and I will kill them too. Do you want that?'

She closes her eyes, tight. 'No,' she says softly.

I gesture with the knife. 'Then stand up.'

She starts wailing now; I can see her body shaking. I smell her urine as it spills onto the shower floor. 'Please,' she says again.

'Stand up,' I repeat. 'And I'll make it quick.'

But she doesn't move. She stays, knees up to her chest, crying, burbling platitudes.

I am getting angry. 'Do you want me to take you apart, piece by piece?' I say. I feel the familiar tensing, my hair trigger about to explode. 'Because I will. Carve the flesh from your arms. Slice the fingers from your hands, one by one. Cut off your ears, your nose. Take your eyes while you're still alive?'

She shakes her head, over and over. 'No,' she says.

'Can you imagine how those other victims suffered? How much they screamed as I cut them open?'

She doesn't say anything, just continues to cry, big wracking sobs of snot and tears.

'Do you want that to be you?'

'No,' she wails.

'Then stand up.'

She lets out a long cry – of anguish, of fear and sadness – then slowly puts her hands out to the walls. They slip at first, blood streaking the tiles, but she pulls herself to her feet. Her teeth chatter, her whole body shakes; her eyes dart from the knife to my face and back again.

But I am true to my word. When the knife goes in, it is quick and sharp. It punctures her soft stomach like butter, blood coating my hands, my arms, and I pull up hard. But it could never be painless. I see the agony in her eyes, feel the tension in her muscles. But it doesn't last for long. She didn't have a chance.

She crumples slowly back down to the floor, her legs

slipping out underneath her in the wet. I pull the knife away and the rich blood flows.

I reach down and grab her by her upper arms, pulling her out of the shower and onto the bathroom floor. She resists slightly, moaning, so I push the knife in one more time, hard, through her chest into her heart. The resistance of muscle, the bubble of air as I catch her lungs.

Blood is coming fast, a slip-sticky lake on the floor. She is motionless now. Gone. My job here is complete.

I am ready. I am ready for you.

Chapter 51

It's quiet in the station when Adam arrives back; he takes solace in the peace.

He sits down at his desk, then looks out into the incident room where only two detectives remain, the others having gone home for the night.

They haven't made much headway in his absence. Adam knows he has reports waiting in his inbox, updates from his detectives on lines of enquiry they've been following, but he also knows that nothing important has been found. If it had, someone would have called him.

His phone beeps, a message from Jamie: *Going to bed. There's dinner for you in the fridge.* It says nothing and everything at the same time. That Jamie – who is grieving, who shouldn't be alone, who is vulnerable – is looking after him. He knows he's trying, but he still hears his words in his head. The betrayal. That Jamie had thought all those awful things about him all along.

He sits quietly and opens his inbox. His body feels empty – of food, of thought, of motivation – but he reads one report at a time, not taking in the information.

He frowns at the reports, then clicks through them again. He looks out into the incident room where DC Lee is still working.

'Tim?' he shouts through the open door.

'Boss?'

'Have we had the DNA results back from the lab?'

A pause. 'No.'

'For fuck's sake.' Adam feels a flush of annoyance and picks up his phone. 'Maggie,' he says, jumping down her throat as soon as she answers. 'Where are my DNA results?'

'Nice to hear from you too, Bishop,' Maggie replies. A gap, while he hears talking; murmured voices on the other side of the receiver. Maggie comes back on: 'We haven't received them from the mortuary. You're shouting at the wrong person.'

Adam swears loudly, then redials. The pathology technician who answers gets the full extent of his anger, and he shouts at her for a full minute before she calls out to Ross.

'DCI Bishop,' Dr Ross says, his voice dripping with disdain. 'Why are you yelling at my staff?'

'The samples from Wayne Oxford. The ones the lab are supposed to check for possible DNA from the killer? Where the fuck are they?'

'We sent them Tuesday. Straight after the PM.'

'The lab don't have them.'

'Well, if someone's fucked up, it's not us. Shout at someone else.'

'So you're saying they're lost?' Adam feels his muscles tense, barely managing to sit still. 'Valuable samples that mean we could potentially find the guy who's killing all these people, and between you and Maggie Clarke they've disappeared?'

He hears Ross breathing loudly at the other end of the phone. 'Fuck off, Bishop,' he says at last. He's furious, his words clipped, his voice low. Adam can tell, but he doesn't give a shit.

'If I find out you've done this deliberately—'

'You arrogant prick!' Ross bellows the words so loudly down the phone it makes the receiver buzz. 'You fucking arsehole. You never stop to think, do you? That maybe these shitty things happen to you because of your actions. Your divorce. The death of Hoxton's wife. The way this investigation is going down the pan. Who's the common factor in this, Bishop?' Ross spits. 'Perhaps you aren't the nice guy you think you are.'

'I didn't lose the samples—'

'No. But I bet Maggie Clarke isn't going out of her way to find them.'

And with that, the line goes dead. Adam's frozen, the receiver paused in his hand, then slowly he lowers it back to the phone. His initial anger has been replaced by something else. Dread. Fear. And bitter self-hate.

He knows his professional relationship with Maggie Clarke never quite recovered after their brief encounter. Last September, a work night out, too much to drink. Another woman in his long line of conquests. And nothing he was proud of.

But Mags hadn't wanted more, she'd said so. Her life was full and busy, with work and the lab, weekends spent in the great outdoors on her time off. She is a hearty woman. Sturdy arms and legs from walking coastal paths; a deep tan from hours on the beach and in the sea; common sense and a no-nonsense attitude. She'd had no time for him, of that he was sure. And how did Ross know? Police station gossip has a lot to answer for.

Quick footsteps distract him; DC Tim Lee stands in the doorway.

'Boss,' he says. Adam looks up, still half in shock. He watches Lee swallow, then take a quick breath in. 'You need to come now.'

Adam barely blinks. 'There's another victim,' he says dully.

'Yes,' Lee replies, blinking back tears. 'It's Ellie.'

Adam doesn't remember much after that. Flickering images barely digested as he numbly goes through the motions. Cops on the door, a cordon already secured. Blue lights bouncing off windows. A familiar house, hysterical flat-mates, crying and hugging. The crinkle of a white crime scene suit, the feeling of his breath behind the mask. Sweat on his palms under the gloves.

He takes the stairs slowly, his legs heavy and tired. He's so exhausted he feels drunk. He remembers this place. Kissing Ellie, fumbling under her clothes. Her body, young, warm. Alive.

Eyes watch him as he goes inside, fingers point to the bathroom. She lies on the floor; blood is everywhere. He doesn't go in.

A lake of red covers every inch of the tiled floor, circling the toilet, the sink. The shower is peppered with streaks, smudges, spatter. Fingerprints, lines working downwards as she fell.

He backs away. He doesn't want to see her body anymore – the deep gashes, wounds, much like the other victims. He doesn't want to imagine her last moments. Adam's empty stomach is hollow; he presses his fingers to his lips, over the mask, remembering her kiss, her vulnerability, her beauty.

Two more SOCOs enter, evidence kits in hand, and in a stark moment of clarity Adam realises: *my DNA will be all over this room*. His fingerprints, his saliva, his skin cells, hair, present on her bed. He pulls the hood from his head, the mask from his mouth. He needs a reason why they might find it. A fuck up now, an explanation for later. But a SOCO stops him.

'Boss, what are you doing? You'll contaminate the crime scene.'

'Yes, sorry, right.' He pulls them back on, then quickly leaves the room. He won't wait, he can't.

He walks away, out of the house and to his car. He pulls off the PPE, and sits and watches, breathing hard.

He thinks of the killer. Audacious enough to walk through a house, unseen, and kill without anyone raising the alarm. In and out without a single witness. The flatmates had gone to see if Ellie wanted a hot chocolate and found the body. She'd been alone maybe ten minutes, fifteen? Was that luck, confidence, or something else?

As he watches he sees a car pull up in the road. He recognises it, a posh Jag E-type, belonging to Marsh.

Without thinking he gets out of his car and walks across; Marsh is still sitting in the driver's seat. Adam taps on the passenger side window. Locks click open and Adam gets in.

'It's DC Quinn?' Marsh asks. Adam nods. His mouth is dry.

Marsh looks towards the house, muttering profanities under his breath.

'Guv?' Adam says.

Marsh looks back at him.

'There's something I need to tell you. Something about last night.'

Chapter 52

'Fuck, Bishop.'

Marsh utters it in a frustrated sigh.

Adam tells him about the trip to the bar. Bumping into Ellie. Going back to her house. He stops short of the full details, but it is enough. A relationship with a subordinate is strictly out of bounds. Especially now she's dead.

'Fuck,' Marsh says again. 'We'll have to get a proper statement. To rule you out as a murder suspect, if nothing else, but you know Professional Standards will get involved. They'll need to investigate properly, and who knows what other shit will come out.' He stares at Adam. 'What other shit do I need to be aware of, DCI Bishop?'

Adam shakes his head miserably. 'Nothing else, guv. Nothing, I swear.'

Marsh sighs. 'Go home. I'll deal with this crime scene and we'll talk again in the morning.'

'Am I suspended?'

'No. But . . . Christ, I don't know. It was bad enough you working the case when Pippa was murdered, but this.

312

It's a step too far, Adam. There's no way I can keep you on as SIO.'

'I understand, guv.'

Without another word, Adam opens the car door and steps out into the night. He walks ten steps, maybe twenty, away from the crime scene. Far enough to be out of sight. And when he's sure he is, he falls apart.

Chapter 53

Romilly didn't expect to see Adam on her doorstep, especially not with that look on his face. He looks like the first day she met him, alone in that hospital corridor. Mouth turned down, face downcast, shoulders hunched. She knows that something is very wrong.

'Adam?' Romilly says.

He stops, his jaw tightens. 'There's another victim,' he murmurs. 'Someone from my team. I'm off the case.'

'Oh, God. I'm so sorry,' she says as she reaches for him.

She doesn't hesitate, just grabs him and holds him close. She feels him tense for a moment, then collapse into her arms, his face buried in her shoulder, his body shaking. They stand there, the front door still open; Romilly doesn't dare move.

After a while, she feels him stopping. His body resists and he pulls away. She guides him into the living room. They sit on the sofa, side by side.

'What happened, Adam?' Romilly says.

He wipes his eyes, clears his throat. 'I don't know. But he got her. I was just there. Blood everywhere.'

'But why have you been removed as SIO?'

He shrugs, but the gesture seems strained. There's more he's not telling her, but she doesn't push it now.

'Are you okay?' she asks softly.

He shakes his head. 'All the death. All these people.' He looks up and meets her gaze for a fraction of a second. 'I'm sorry. For everything that happened between us. I'm sorry I don't have you in my life anymore.'

'You still have me,' Romilly replies.

'I don't. You and I . . . I ruined that, long ago.' He twists his hands together in his lap, still staring at the floor. 'I know our break-up was my fault.'

'It wasn't, Adam. I—'

'No, Milly,' he says, his voice catching. 'You sleeping with that guy, that was my fault. I was awful to you, for so long. I pushed you away. Our marriage was dead even before . . . that. It was a convenient excuse. To blame you.' He stands up quickly, shaking his head. 'I shouldn't have come. I'm sorry.'

He walks to the door, but she grabs his arm and he turns. 'No, Adam. You should have. I'm always going to be here for you. Always. I meant what I said, before.'

He meets her gaze. They stop, frozen, her hand still on his arm. And then he takes a step towards her, takes her face in his hands and kisses her.

She remembers his smell, his taste. Nothing has changed. She doesn't even try to resist. Being with Adam feels so completely natural, so right, she gives in, her legs almost too weak to support her. Her hands are on his back, his fingers in her hair and on her neck. Everything is heightened:

315

the feeling of his stubble on her mouth, his lips, his tongue touching hers.

She leads him back into the living room. He pulls her down onto the sofa. Every now and again, as they kiss, she opens her eyes: sometimes his are shut, but then they are open and looking at her. He smiles, their lips still together, and she smiles back.

He pulls away from her for a moment. 'Are you sure this is what you want?' he asks, his voice hoarse.

She nods. 'Yes.'

Yes, she wants this more than anything else. She wants him. She wants him naked. She wants him inside her. And her hands pull his shirt over his head.

Romilly remembers the exact time she met Adam, the memory as clear as if it were yesterday. She was a junior doctor, exhausted at the end of ward rounds, dressed in a pair of worn light blue scrubs and trainers that were once white and now grey. She was paused at a vending machine, coins in her hand, debating a Twirl or a KitKat, when she spotted a man sitting on one of the plastic chairs in the corridor. His posture was the same as any number of people in the hospital: shoulders slumped forward, elbows resting on his knees, head in his hands. But then he sat back, rubbed his eyes, and looked at her.

It was only a fraction of a second, but enough to catch Romilly's attention. He had the bluest eyes, the most perfect nose. She smiled.

'Are you okay?' she asked.

He nodded, a glimpse of a smile touching his lips. 'Yes. No. I don't know.'

She turned towards him. 'Which is it?' she asked softly.

He shrugged. 'I . . .' he started, but his voice cracked and he stopped, looking at the ceiling for a second, his jaw tight.

'Can I help?' she asked. 'I'm a junior doctor here. May I?' She pointed to the seat next to him and he nodded. She noticed a hospital bracelet on his wrist. 'Are you a patient?'

'Was,' he replied. 'Just discharged.'

'And you're still here? Most people can't wait to get out of this place.'

Romilly wasn't sure why she was making conversation. She knew she needed to get home, grab some sleep before the next inevitable twelve-hour shift, but something about him made her pause. He seemed such an unlikely person to be there. He looked strong, full of health, but his manner and posture was different. Afraid.

She'd seen people like him before. Out of place, unable to talk. That sadness, the desperation. Then they go home and down a litre of vodka and a bottle of pills.

He looked at her, then away again quickly.

'Let me help,' she said.

He swallowed. 'They, the doctors, say there's nothing wrong with me.' He was still staring at the floor, pulling his jumper up over his hands. It was a childish gesture, strangely vulnerable on a man like him. 'But I can't shift the feeling. That something's up, and they're not finding it.'

'Okay. What are your symptoms?'

'Tiredness. Worn out. Nosebleeds. Same as they were before.'

'Before?'

'When I was a kid. When I was nine. I had cancer. Acute lymphoblastic leukaemia.'

317

'And you think it's back.'

'I know it's back.'

Romilly thinks for a second. 'I'll tell you what. How about I get your chart, and I'll have a look and talk you through it. I'm a junior doctor in oncology. Cancer is literally my thing.'

He turned quickly towards her. 'You can do that?'

'Of course.' She pointed down the corridor towards the coffee shop. 'Meet me there, half an hour. And we can talk.'

He smiled, more naturally this time. 'Thank you. That would be good.' He held out his hand.

'Adam Bishop.'

She shook it, his grip firm, his skin soft. 'Romilly Cole,' she replied.

She left him and went through the double doors into oncology. She stopped at the reception desk and asked for his chart.

The doctor behind the desk heard her. 'Didn't we just discharge him?' he asked. 'Why do you need it, Rom?'

'Professional interest,' she lied. 'Might fit one of the studies I'm working on.'

'I doubt it. Nothing wrong with him, except for a bit of hypochondria.'

She opened the chart and ran her finger down the numbers. 'What's his history?'

'Childhood ALL, aged nine. Managed with chemo-therapy, bone marrow transplant, the lot. Aggressive sort, they threw everything at it. But he came out the other side. Complete remission. Regular check-ups all clear, until he came in a few days ago. Temperature, sweating, nausea.

All the signs, but as you can see,' he pointed to the notes, 'all clear.'

Romilly thanked her colleague. 'Can I keep this?' she asked of the chart, and he nodded. She went to leave but he stopped her.

'Dr Cole,' he said, 'don't go near him with a needle. Don't even talk about it. Complete trypanophobia.'

She frowned. This guy just got more interesting. From a purely professional viewpoint, of course.

She half expected the coffee shop to be empty when she arrived. But there he was, at a seat on the far side. He stood up as she approached.

'What do you want?' he asked. 'I'll get you a coffee.'

'No, I'm fine—'

'Please? Least I can do. I'm sure you're a busy woman.'

She smiled. 'Thank you. Americano, hot milk.'

She took a seat at the table and watched him as he ordered. He'd taken his coat off; he was wearing jeans, brown boots, and a navy jumper. Broad shoulders, nice smile. The assistant thought so too, Romilly noted, hearing the tinkle of laughter as she passed over his change.

He placed the two coffees down and sat opposite her.

'So, am I going to die?' His words were light, but his smile was forced.

'In a word, Mr Bishop, no.'

'No?' He still didn't believe her, she could tell. He reached for his coffee, and Romilly saw his hands were shaking.

She put the paperwork down on the table and pulled his test results to the top.

'See here?' She leaned forward, her finger pointing to

the page. 'This is your white cell count. A normal result would be between four and eleven, which yours is. And here, the result from your bone marrow aspiration shows an entirely normal number and morphology of cells.'

'So the cancer hasn't come back?'

'Definitely not, no. I would guess that your symptoms were no more than a bout of the flu, coupled with some pretty nasty anxiety.'

He sat back in his seat, then ran his hands down his face. 'You must think I'm an idiot.'

'I don't, no. It's understandable, you'd panic. To experience what you went through at such a young age, it must have been traumatic.'

He nodded slowly. 'It was nearly twenty years ago, but I still remember it as if it was yesterday. Especially coming back here. I don't think I've been in a hospital since. Except when work brings me here.'

'What do you do?'

'I'm a detective. In the Major Crimes team.'

Romilly looked at him, surprised. 'That's a full-on job. Why did you choose it?'

He smiled. 'It sounds like a cliché, but I wanted to help people. To be there at the worst times of their lives and make it better.'

'So why not be a doctor?'

He laughed. 'Not clever enough. And . . .' His voice trailed off. 'Other things.'

The fear of needles, she thought, but didn't say it.

'So why did you become a doctor?'

'I didn't plan to be. Wanted to be anything but, in fact. But medicine makes sense. The science, how the body works. Nothing fascinates me more than human biology.

Still does. And, like you, I wanted to make a difference to people. Make things better, rather than worse.'

He smiled. It was a broad grin and changed his whole face. 'Well, you made a difference to me today, Dr Cole,' he said. 'Do you want another?' he asked, pointing to their now-empty coffee mugs.

She returned the smile. 'Yes,' she said. 'But let me get them, it's my turn.'

She found herself staying with him for hours. Drinking coffees until her hands shook, but she couldn't tear herself away from this guy. No one had caught her attention like Adam. She'd had boyfriends, interest from men around the hospital, but doctors were a particular breed. Smart, and they knew it. The upmanship was tiring, the entitlement exhausting. But here was this man, sharing his deepest worries with her, and they'd only met minutes before. It wasn't just the medical stuff. He talked about his childhood, how being ill so young had affected him, and how his relationship with his parents hadn't been the same since.

She knew about dysfunctional relationships with parents. But she didn't tell him *that*. Not then. But she had later. And he'd taken it in his stride. He knew the case, everyone did, so she didn't have to explain.

Eventually, in that coffee shop, in the hospital, she had to tear herself away.

'I can't possibly drink another coffee,' she laughed.

'Can I see you again?' he said. Then he looked worried. 'It's not against the rules, is it? I mean, you're not my doctor, or anything?'

She shook her head. 'No, I'm not your doctor. And I'd love to.'

321

And that was it. They went out, and he was exactly the same. They talked, laughed, shared stuff about each other that she wouldn't have thought possible on a first date. They kissed, and how she loved kissing him – and the rest.

She had hints, of course. When she went out with him and his work mates for the first time, she'd stood back for a moment, watching. Around them he was more brash. He swore more, laughed louder.

'Who was that guy?' she asked later in the car. 'Where did my Adam go?'

'It's still me,' he said. 'But what do you expect me to say around these guys? It's not the sort of place where you pour your heart out every five seconds.' He reached for her, then. 'I can be myself with you,' he said. 'Only you.'

But slowly that Adam took over. He shared less; it was as if a wall went up. Slowly, brick by brick, until she hardly recognised the man she shared a house with. She felt him pull away, until . . . Well. Romilly knew the rest. A brief moment of weakness, and it was over.

Thinking about it now, it seems ridiculous. Adam is the same man he was then, just one with problems, issues she'd made no effort to help with. She rests her head on his chest; she can hear a faint thud of his heartbeat, and she resolves never to let that happen again. He traces a line over her hip then across the curve of her stomach. For a moment she imagines him doing the same with a pregnant belly, a body bulging with life. In a normal world.

'I should have never left you,' he murmurs.

'Hmm?' She lifts her head and looks up at him.

'I shouldn't have walked out. I should have fought harder for us.'

He lies back and absentmindedly wraps a strand of her hair around his finger.

'But who knows what might have happened then,' she replies. 'Maybe we needed some space, and you would always come back to me.'

'Maybe.' He pauses. 'So what happens now?' he asks quietly.

'I want to be with you, Adam.'

'But what about your boyfriend?'

She takes a long breath in. But the answer is easy. 'It's over. He knows it, or he wouldn't have left already. But I'll need to . . . talk to him. I don't know. It'll take some time. But it'll be okay.' She stops. 'What about you?'

He doesn't answer, and she looks up. He's smiling. 'What about me?' he says.

She hits him gently on his chest. 'Don't fuck around, Bishop. Are you staying?'

This time he doesn't hesitate. 'Yes. Forever. I'll never leave.'

'But what happens now, with your work?'

'I have to see Marsh tomorrow.' His face darkens. 'But I reckon they'll suspend me.'

'What?' She's angry for him. 'That's ridiculous.'

'It's not,' he says. And as she listens he tells her about last night, the drinking, and Ellie Quinn.

'Oh, Adam,' is all she can think to say. But she doesn't move from the sofa, from his embrace. If she can help it, she'll never move again.

'You're not angry with me? You don't think I'm . . .'

'What?'

323

'A piece of shit.'

She pulls him close. 'Listen, whatever's happened. Whatever you do from here, I'll be with you. I'll help you. Whatever you need.'

He bends his head down to hers and kisses her forehead slowly, resting his lips on her skin.

'I'll never leave you,' she says, repeating his words.

'Never?' He grins. 'What about your work? Your patients?'

'I'll coordinate their treatment from here. In my pants.'

'What about the supermarket? We'll need to eat.'

'Tesco can deliver. We'll be fine. I have beer in the fridge. What more could we want?'

She pulls herself up and kisses him. Unlike before it is slow and simple and Romilly knows that everything will be all right.

She doesn't want anything more.

Chapter 54

In the dead of night, Adam wakes. He rolls over to his back and stares at the glow of the nightlight on the ceiling. He realises he's missed the stars. When he couldn't sleep, when a case got stuck or an offender too tricky, he'd lie looking upwards at the gently rotating solar system, listening to Romilly's light breathing.

Because without her, what's been the point? After their break-up, nothing changed for the better. He stopped looking after himself, didn't care about his health. Why did it matter? The fear of the cancer was nothing when compared to his more ethereal and sinister foes: self-loathing and loneliness.

Yet Adam knows he is lying in a bed where another man slept just one night before. He rolls over and looks at her. Romilly is sleeping on her side, facing away from him, and with a finger he gently traces the line of her shoulder. He wonders if she was telling the truth, whether she will leave Phil, come back to him. Whether she'll take the risk and trust him again.

Would he trust her? The infidelity, that was nothing, not really. It was the excuse, the self-righteous reason for him to walk away. Because he'd been pulling away for months.

He'd had the same concerns as Shepherd. He'd felt the same niggle: that she wasn't telling the truth. And if she was lying about that, what else might she be hiding? It wasn't conscious, but gradually he felt himself retreating, putting up a barrier, to protect himself from the hurt. The same way he had from his parents all those years ago.

The newspapers had talked about genetics, whether evil could be inherent, passed down between generations. Adam never believed the fairy tales, putting faith in hard proof, actions, and consequences. But the fact still remained. Her father was a serial killer.

Romilly always said she didn't want children. That her career was too important; she didn't feel maternal, capable even, of being a mother. And that had been okay with Adam. He'd never imagined himself with a family. Not even a wife, until he met Romilly.

Now, lying next to her, feeling so warm and safe and secure, he wonders how honest she had been. Was it that she didn't want kids, or had she known there was something deep inside of her, in her blood, in her DNA? Something rotten she didn't want passed down.

Last night he said that he would never leave her, that he would stay forever. And, caught up in the moment, her naked body against his, he'd meant it. But now, in the darkness, the endorphins fade. The doubts resurface.

He realises that nothing has changed. He still doesn't believe her; he still needs to know what happened. What she knew. All those years ago.

Chapter 55

Elijah Cole lies in his prison cell, hands behind his head, staring into the black. Around him he hears the snores of his fellow prisoners, mutterings behind walls, heavy foot-steps and the clatter of keys in metal doors; sounds that have become as familiar to him over the last twenty years as bird song and laughter once were.

His bed is comfortable, his pillow soft. He is alone in a cell built for two – luxuries he has earned. They turned his cell over today. Went through his belongings, checking his mattress, his books. But the governor left in disgust, muttering under his breath. He smiles at the memory now; he knew they were coming, of course they would find nothing. Who do they think he is?

He is a man forged in the fires of hell. A man who remembers the exact moment he learnt from his mother that control could be taken back at any time. With a knife, and a cry of rage.

That day, that final day, he'd felt triumphant. Two. He'd made it to two, shifting hiding places, using stealth to deceive his father as heavy footsteps patrolled the tiny house, counting down. But he found himself pinned in, and his father grabbed him by the hair, hauling him out and into the kitchen.

But two. Two he could take. Two of anything. Two strikes with the belt. Two cigarettes. Even two punches in the stomach would be okay, when he's had five before. But he underestimated his father. The cruelty. The psychopathy that now flows in his own veins.

His father slowly pulled a knife from the block, then walked to where his mother was lying, beaten and gasping on the floor.

'Choose,' he said.

Her eyes were scared and wide. 'Choose what?' she burbled through her bloody mouth, her missing tooth.

'Anything. Two of anything. An ear and a finger. An eye and his thumb. What should I remove?'

Elijah couldn't breathe. His hands balled into fists.

His father continued. 'Choose,' he said again. 'Or I take them all.'

And he'd grabbed Elijah, his eleven-year-old son, roughly forcing him down to the kitchen table. Fist around his neck; cheek against wood. With the other, his father grabbed his hand and Elijah screamed with absolute terror as his fingers were prised from his palm. Pushed down, joints cracking in protest.

And the knife came down hard.

Elijah hears footsteps now, becoming louder as they head towards him. He sits up, placing his bare feet on the floor. He waits. The boots stop outside his door. He hears the slow turning of the handle and the flap opens.

328

'Doc,' a voice whispers. A Glaswegian burr, and he smiles as he gets up. He knew he'd come through. Tit for tat. Easily recognisable symptoms, worries shared by the guard late at night. Followed up with a doctor – a proper doctor – the cancer quickly diagnosed; his daughter saved.

And now the guard does as he's asked; something is pushed through the flap. Cole takes it, feeling the soft aged paper between his fingers. A debt willingly repaid, time and time again.

'That book you wanted,' the voice says, and is gone.

Elijah sits back on the bed, resting it in his lap. Weighty, solid. *War and Peace*, by Tolstoy. He opens it to the centre, and in the darkness he just makes out a shape, a hole carved out of the pages. Something in the middle. He picks it up. It's older than he's used to; he flips open the lid and presses the on button. It bursts into life, casting his cell in a blue glow.

Yes, this will do fine.

The mobile phone loads, and he types in the number he knows off by heart. He sends a quick text, instructions that will be followed to the letter. The next piece of the plan is slotting into place, and if he's as knowledgeable of human behaviour as he thinks he is, he knows what will happen next.

Job done, he hides the phone in the book and lies back on the bed. Time for sleep: for thought, for reflection. His mind goes to his girls. His favourite, Grace Summers. She's the one he's partial to now, more often than not, as he lies here, in the dark. He's an old man but he still has urges.

The others, they gave up. He saw the light in their eyes fade as they submitted to whatever he wanted. As they lay there, limp, beneath him. They cried quietly; curled into a ball in the corner of the filthy mattress. They stopped eating, drinking. He didn't kill them, they wanted to go and that was the only way they knew how. But Grace? Oh, how she fought, how she screamed. He'd tie her up, suspend her from the ceiling for days, and she would still spit in his face. Even when she was bleeding, ripped, he'd have her over the others. Feel her blood mixing with his cum as he fucked her, watching her tears streak lines in the dirt on her face, beating her unconscious after.

He kept her alive the longest. Grace was the last to die. He took the credit, but it wasn't him. That was someone else's rage, someone else's doing.

A secret he's kept quiet. For twenty-six years.

DAY 8

SATURDAY

Chapter 56

Adam wakes to the smell of coffee; he opens his eyes as Romilly climbs back into bed. Her hair is rumpled and messy, she is wearing a T-shirt and knickers; to him, she has never looked better. He runs a hand through his hair, scratching at the several days of stubble on his jaw, then pulls himself up to a half-sit on the pillow next to her.

She cradles the mug of coffee in two hands and looks at him.

'What are you doing today?'

He reaches for his own mug and takes a sip; it's exactly how he likes it. He sighs. 'I need to go and see Marsh. See how much trouble I'm in.'

Her face clouds. 'How many women have you slept with?' she asks. She shakes her head. 'I know I'm in no position to ask, but I want to know. What you've been up to since we've been apart.'

'A few.'

'A few?'

'Some.' He frowns. 'Look, I don't know. Not exactly. The last few years have been a bit of a blur.' He glances at her to see how she's taking it but her face is impassive. 'It's not something I'm proud of, but I was a single man, trying to sort some things out in my head.'

'And did you?'

'Probably not, no.'

They drink their coffee in silence, the loving moment gone. He wonders if she's reconsidering what they did last night. Their future.

Then she speaks: 'We weren't together. That doesn't matter. What does matter is you're here now, and I'm hoping you'll stay.'

She holds her hand out to him. He smiles, and presses his palm against hers, their fingers winding together. In the light of day, his concerns from the early hours of the morning feel insignificant. It doesn't matter what happened back then. What matters is her, here. Now. He squeezes her hand tight, then puts his coffee down, reaching across the bed, pulling her to him. 'As long as you want me to?'

She leans up and kisses him. 'Yes. But—'

'When does Phil get back?'

'Tomorrow. I'll tell him then.'

Adam nods. 'I'm sorry.'

'What for?'

'For you having to do that. For us splitting up. For . . . all of it.'

'I'm sorry too.'

He's not sure what she's apologising for. For the affair, for getting on with her life? But he doesn't ask any more, just gets up from the bed and walks naked to the door of the bathroom. He turns, she's watching him.

'Are you joining me?' he asks.

They shower together; him on his knees as the hot water pummels his back, her hands splayed on the tiles as she comes. He stands up, turns her around, entering her quickly from behind, holding her hips firm as he kisses her neck, her back, her skin slippery and hot.

After, they dress, eat breakfast together. Adam tries to ignore the porridge oats, the breakfast of choice of another man. He cleans his teeth with her toothbrush, then they stand together at the open front door.

Outside, the day is cold. Wind whips furiously into the house, making Romilly wrap her arms around herself. It reminds Adam of the wasteland a week ago, the dead bodies discarded like rubbish, starting this whole case off.

'Milly,' he starts. He wants to ask her about what she saw, about what her father was doing. Demand the truth, the honesty. Instead, he says, 'Where would your father's patient records be?'

He's been thinking about Cole's words, the other three victims. If the women at the house weren't his first, who else might they have been?

'Don't the police already have them?' She frowns. 'Why do you want to know?'

'No, we don't. Just a line of enquiry. They'd be useful to the investigation.'

'At his old surgery then. I know they were packed up. Probably never went anywhere after that.' She pauses. 'I still have a key.'

He nods. 'Thank you.' She goes back into the house to

333

fetch it and passes it to him: an innocuous piece of metal in his palm. He leans forward and they kiss, long and gentle, a promise of more to come.

'I'll call you,' he says, and he walks out to his car.

He knows where the surgery is; everyone does. It's entrenched in local folklore; the place people point at when they drive past. From the outside, it looks normal. A boarded-up, anonymous frontage, a nail bar on one side and a charity shop on the other. Car parking spaces line up outside, and Adam pulls into one, then sits, looking at the door.

He's officially off the case; he shouldn't be here. But maybe, just maybe, if he finds something useful in all this mess then he could be redeemed slightly in Marsh's eyes.

He gets out of the car, glances around, then puts the key in the lock. It resists at first, then turns. He pushes it open.

He's greeted by a rush of cold air. A gust of wind picks up dust from the floor and swirls it around, highlighted by the unwelcome daylight. Adam steps in and closes the door behind him.

It's dim inside, the only light coming from the gaps around the boards over the windows. He walks through to the reception area – a few metal chairs stacked in one corner, a large high wooden barrier marking off where reception-ists would have checked in patients. A few old posters flutter on a notice board. It's indistinguishable from any other GP's waiting room in England.

Adam walks through into a corridor. Doors line either side; he opens one and it's a consultation room, empty bar for a rusted examination couch. The next is the same.

He doubles back and opens the one marked *Private*: it's the main office, and he lets out a relieved sigh. Stacked high in the middle are filing boxes. Confidentiality ignored, here are the records for all of Cole's patients. He opens the lid of the closest and pulls one out: a tan envelope, top open, scribbled handwritten cards inside. If they want to know if Cole had been doing a Shipman, here are the answers.

He's preparing to make a call, to sort arrangements for these to be transported to somewhere safe, when he hears a noise. A banging, repetitive and loud.

He frowns and makes his way towards it. Down the long corridor, wind whistling through, air moving where previously everything had been still.

'Hello?' he calls. No one else should be here. Someone homeless maybe, taking refuge from the cold.

He walks further. And then he sees it, the back door swinging on its hinges. Blown by the wind, it slams, then opens again, hitting the wall on the opposite side. He frowns, and pulls it shut. The lock is broken, it won't stay that way for long.

He stops, listens again. Everything is quiet. Had this been open all along, waiting for someone to close it, or is somebody here?

And then he hears it. A shuffle of footsteps, a sniff. He's definitely not alone. He fingers his phone in his pocket. He should call it in. Get a few uniforms to back him up. But he's being ridiculous. It's nothing. He's a grown man, a DCI. How much fun would Response and Patrol have, mocking him for being too scared to check it out himself.

He hears the noise again. And, mind made up, he walks decisively towards the intruder.

Chapter 57

Even as the front door clicks closed, Romilly can tell some of the old Adam has returned. A slowness to smile, a hesitation when he kissed her goodbye: the bricks being pushed back into place.

She goes to work, tries to ignore all thoughts of Adam. She buries herself in clinic, following up on results, procedures, patients. Updates from her junior doctors. But still, she thinks of him. His laughter, his wide smile. Memories of what they did last night, this morning, that make her cheeks flush and her body ache to do them all over again. She loved Phil but he's never had this effect on her. Adam changes her at a cellular level, as if her body and brain react before she's had time to think.

She knows she needs to sort things out with Phil – Adam, or no Adam – and messages him quickly. *We need to talk.* She hasn't even put her phone down before it starts to ring. She steels herself and answers it.

'So talk.' His tone is snippy and distant.

'Phil, I—'

336

'You're back with Adam.'

'This isn't about Adam.' She feels herself go on the defensive and tries to calm down. 'But you and I . . . I'm sorry.'

There's a long pause. 'Yeah. So am I,' he says bitterly. 'I'll collect my stuff when I have a moment.' Phil pauses. Romilly hears him breathe loudly down the phone. Then he talks again, a hard edge to his voice: 'He's welcome to you,' he growls. 'Fucking crazy woman.'

He hangs up, leaving Rom blinking in surprise. Maybe I am, she thinks, staring at the phone, but at least I'm not an arsehole.

At lunchtime, she goes down to the hospital canteen. As she waits in the queue, she pulls up the message she sent earlier to Adam. Bland and dull: *Thinking of you x* But she hasn't received a reply.

She looks at it and realises he hasn't even read it: there are no small blue ticks next to the message. She frowns, then calls him.

It rings – three, four, five times – and cuts to voicemail.

'Honey? Do you want to pay for those?'

The woman at the cash desk points to her sandwich and packet of crisps.

'Yes, yes, sorry,' Rom says, quickly waving her card over the reader.

'Man trouble?'

'Something like that,' she replies.

She walks away from the canteen, then pauses in the corridor. She dials a different number. Jamie answers immediately.

'Rom? Is everything okay? I heard about Ellie.'

'Yes, but . . . Jamie, have you seen Adam today?'

337

'Today? No. And he didn't come home last night.'

'He was with me.'

A pause at the other end. Then: 'Okay . . . Does this mean . . .?'

'Yes. Maybe. Oh, I don't know. But listen, I'm worried. He's not answering his phone.'

'He's probably at the nick. Caught up in something.'

'He's been suspended, Jamie.'

'What? What for?'

'I don't have time to explain now.' She thinks about the meeting first thing with Marsh. Maybe that had run on. But that question at her front door.

'When he left this morning, he asked where Cole's patient files were kept. And I said at the surgery.'

'You think he's gone there?'

'Maybe. But he might be with Marsh. Jamie, could you check? Please?'

'Course. Don't worry, Rom. I'm sure he's fine.'

Jamie hangs up and Romilly waits, the phone clutched in her hand. She curses herself for worrying. She's sure Jamie's right. That Adam's got stuck in this meeting, being bollocked by his boss, his phone on mute.

She starts walking back to her office, but her phone rings.

'Jamie?'

'He's not there.'

'He's not with Marsh?'

'No. Tim said that Marsh was in the room with him as we were speaking.' He pauses. 'I'm coming to you.'

'We have to go to the surgery.'

'Don't go there without me, Romilly. Please.' He's begging, his voice scared. 'Promise me?'

'I won't. I'm at the hospital. Come quick, please, Jamie.'

She hangs up the phone, then runs to fetch her bag from her office. With each footstep she's thinking, *Please be okay. Please be okay.*

I can't lose you, Adam.

Not now.

Chapter 58

Jamie curses the speed of his shitty Vauxhall Corsa. He should have got a patrol car, he mutters as he negotiates the streets towards the hospital.

To his relief, Romilly is waiting for him at the main entrance; she climbs into the passenger seat before he's even had a chance to put the handbrake on.

'What if something's happened to him, Jamie?' she says.

'He's fine. I'm sure he's fine.' But his words sound hollow, even to him.

They drive in silence, Romilly craning forward in her seat, swearing every time they face a red light or a slow driver. And as they pull into the car park outside the surgery, Romilly points.

'There. That's his car.'

Jamie pulls up alongside, and they both get out. Adam's BMW sits alone. He tries a handle: locked. They look towards the boarded-up surgery.

'And you think he's in there?'

Before Jamie can stop her, Romilly walks fast towards

the building and tries the main door. It opens. She glances back at him, then goes inside. Jamie follows.

He can tell someone's been through here. Footprints scuffed in the dirt, a barely perceptible feeling in the air. Like a long-abandoned fug has been disturbed. He knows they need to be more careful – put on shoe covers and gloves at least – but his priority lies with Adam right now.

He follows Rom into a room with *Private* on the door; she seems to know where she's going and Jamie wonders how she must be feeling. The place her father had worked, where she'd played as a little girl. But she doesn't pause, now standing in front of a pile of boxes. The dust has been scuffed on one of the lids, lying askew, but apart from that, there's no sign of Adam.

Romilly looks at him, wordlessly, then leaves, continuing through the building. She starts calling his name, and he silently pleads for a replying voice to shout back. But there's nothing. He pushes at doors as he goes, each room as empty as the last.

Romilly has reached the end of the corridor now; the fire door is open, banging in the wind. She's stopped, staring at the ground. As he walks up next to her, she points.

It's a patch of something dark. Jamie bends down to it, putting out a tentative hand. Still wet. He lifts it up, staring at the red stain at the end of his finger.

'But why?' Jamie says, almost to himself. 'Why would he take Adam?'

Romilly's face is pale. 'Adam has an acute fear of needles, Jamie. Almost pathological. He's terrified of them.'

Jamie takes a quick breath in. At the same time his hand reaches for his phone.

'Fuck,' he mutters. 'Fuck.'

341

Chapter 59

The first thing Adam notices is cold concrete under his bare feet, gritty dust between his toes. It's dark. So dark.

He's cold, the room's freezing. He moves his head; everything spins. The dizziness overwhelms him for a second and he stops, screwing his eyes shut. Then he opens them again. Slowly his eyes adjust to the gloom. He sees the outline of furniture: a table, a wooden chair.

There's a strange smell in the air: damp, salt, seaweed. He tries to remember where he was – the surgery, Cole's surgery – and instinctively knows he's no longer there. Where is he? How did he get here? He's confused, so confused.

He tries to open his mouth, but it feels glued, something sticky over his lips. He tries to reach up but his hands don't move. He feels the first wave of panic take hold.

He moves his legs, it's the same. Secured tightly, to what? A chair? He can still move his head and he looks down, squinting in the darkness. He's fully dressed – in the shirt and trousers he put on that morning, at Romilly's – but his feet feel cold, his shoes and socks are off.

Is it still the same day? He has no idea. There's a pain in his head, pulsing in time with his frantically beating heart. Someone must have knocked him out. But who? Not—

Oh, God.

And then he feels it. Them. The hard metal under his skin, intruding, parasitic, ready and waiting to draw his blood. He feels his head grow woozy. The familiar panic takes over, making him sweat, shake, close to passing out.

He pulls hard at his bindings, to no avail. He tenses his muscles, willing himself to stay awake, stay conscious. But the panic has him in its grasp. All he can think about are the needles. In his arms, in his feet. He feels sick, he needs to get away, he has to, he has to. Before . . . Before . . .

The blood drains south, everything fades. Adam's head drops to his chest, unconscious.

He wakes slowly. The feeling of a hand lightly tapping his cheek. A voice saying his name, over and over.

'Wake up, Adam,' it says. 'It's time.'

He opens his eyes. The room is brighter now and he blinks: a light is hung from the centre of the room, a hurricane lamp, similar to one they found in the outbuilding. Where Pippa died.

His head snaps up with a jolt. He looks around, panicking, vision blurred, pulling at his hands and feet, still securely tied. But his mouth is free now, and he takes deep gulps of air, willing his sight to clear.

Then he stops.

Someone is standing in front of him, holding a needle and syringe in one hand, a plastic bag, medical equipment in the other. They smile.

'Welcome back.'

Adam makes a croaking sound, his throat dry and sore. He tries again, this time he manages to speak.

'You,' he says. 'It can't be you.'

Part 3

My devil had been long caged,
he came out roaring.
Robert Louis Stevenson, *Dr Jekyll and Mr Hyde*,1886

Chapter 60

The incident room is silent; nobody moves, all eyes locked on Detective Chief Superintendent Marsh. Jamie is standing to the side, the ball of fear slowly eating away in his stomach. He glances across to Romilly. Her face is pale, her eyes worried: he knows he must look the same.

'Listen, and listen hard,' Marsh begins. Jamie feels the years of experience pour from this man, taking solace in his confidence and unflinching stare. 'Here's what we know. At approximately nine this morning, Adam Bishop went to the old surgery of Dr Cole, we believe to look for his patient records. His car is there, but he has not been seen since.' Marsh turns to the whiteboard, scribbling in a barely legible hand as he talks. 'If we're following this guy's MO – and the fate of his other victims – we don't have long to find him. Let's assume less than twenty-four hours. That takes us to tomorrow morning.'

What happens then, Jamie has no idea. Would Adam end up like Pippa? Dead and drained. Or does it lead to something else? Something worse?

'The lab has been working fast,' Marsh continues. 'Trace found at the scene has been confirmed as Bishop's blood. Tyre tracks out the back of the premises match the ones found at the wasteland last week, so we know he has been taken by the same offender.'

'But why?' a voice asks from the team, echoing Jamie's own thoughts from earlier that day.

Now, Marsh repeats the message to the room. 'Bishop has a phobia of needles. A fear we believe the killer has targeted throughout the investigation. Exploiting it for his own gain.'

Murmurs of surprise ripple around the room.

Marsh wasn't happy when Jamie had told him.

'And he didn't think to mention this important fact earlier?' he'd shouted down the phone.

Jamie had no reply. He'd felt the same way. There had been rumours in the past. He'd heard something happened when Adam had last gone for his routine jabs, but when Jamie had asked he'd laughed it off. It was nothing, he'd said. Allergic reaction, that's all. Stupid proud bastard, Adam Bishop. And it might be the end of him, if they don't move fast.

Back in the room, Marsh turns and points to the board.

'So, we are going to work this in two ways. First, following up the evidence from the other murders. Something will point to who this fucker is. Tim, chase up the lab for any outstanding evidence. Rich, go back to the owners of the VW vans. Something must line up. And secondly . . .'

He pauses. Jamie knows why he's stopped: Marsh never had faith in Adam's theory, the connection to Cole.

He clears his throat. 'Bishop believed that the offender

was under the influence of Cole, working under his control, somehow. Because of what we now know' – he glances to Jamie – 'that Pippa Hoxton was being held at his house, that Adam was taken from his surgery, I'm inclined to agree. Any thoughts?'

Quiet from the room.

'Then good. For some reason, we still haven't had the fucking visitor logs from Belmarsh, so I'll get the chief constable to apply his considerable influence there. The patient records have been shipped to our storeroom. I want someone to go through them today, look at staff lists, anyone that might have passed through that surgery.'

'Do you want me to go and see Cole?'

All eyes turn to Romilly. She's said it quietly, but it was what everyone was thinking.

'No,' Marsh says resolutely. 'Everyone needs to stay far away from that fucker. He's not going to tell us where Adam is, and I'm not giving him the satisfaction of jumping to his side, begging for scraps.' Romilly doesn't reply. 'Do you hear me?' he repeats, and she nods slowly.

'DS Hoxton will coordinate, working as my second-in-command. And if anything comes in – however small – tell us straight away.'

Marsh pauses. He holds the tension in the room. Everyone is poised, keen to get to work.

'This is your top – no, your only job,' he says. 'Nobody sleeps, nobody shits, nobody goes home until I say so.' Marsh looks out into the room, then locks eyes with Romilly before turning back to the detectives waiting. 'There is no bigger priority right now than finding DCI Adam Bishop.

And finding him alive.'

He's here. At last.

So handsome, so brave. So fucking angry. He stares at me with those beautiful blue eyes, glaring, breathing heavily, his nostrils flaring with the force of every breath.

The tape is back on his mouth. Once he realised who I was, he started shouting the place down, and I couldn't have that. He wasn't happy. He frantically twisted his head from side to side as I tried to stick it across. Shouting, cursing. I grabbed a handful of hair and pulled his head back hard. He didn't shut up, even then, and it took all my strength to hold him still as I wrapped the tape around his head, over his mouth, around and around until there was no chance of him getting free.

I let him go and he struggles, but the chair stays upright. It's big, heavy, there's no chance of him tipping it over. He realises that quickly and stops, saving his energy.

He makes a noise, a grunt behind his tape. He's trying to talk to me, and I smile.

'I think you've said enough, don't you, Adam?' I reply. 'You've had your turn. Now it's mine.'

I look at the cut on his forehead where I hit him. The blood has congealed now, a wet sticky mess, and I reach forward with one finger, pressing it into the scab. He groans quietly, his eyes rolling upwards, then back to me.

I turn my attention to the tubing in his arms, the cannulae I carefully inserted while he was unconscious. I know he's been trying hard not to look at them, but now I move behind him and grab his head again. I push it forward, forcing it down.

He makes a little noise, a groan of dissent, and he screws his eyes shut. His face is pale, his skin clammy.

'Look at it, Adam,' I say. He breathes hard again, the tape going in and out on his mouth. 'Look at it,' I shout.

He moves his head as much as he can, a little movement left and right, saying no. He's making me angry, his refusal to comply. I try again, and a clump of his hair comes out in my hand.

I let go of his head and it snaps back upright. I go to the table on the far side, and pick up a knife, a small scalpel, still in its sterile wrapping. I open it, light flashing on the sharp stainless steel. His eyes are open now, fixed. I carry it over.

'You see this, Adam?' I say. He doesn't move. 'Do you see this?' I shout.

He nods, a quick up and down.

'You do as I say, and we'll get on just fine.' I glance up at the clock. It's just past midday. 'I connect these cannulae, get your blood flowing, and everything will be okay for you. Simple and painless. Like Pippa Hoxton.' I know it's

351

a lie, that she died in fear, in pain, suspended from the ceiling like a pig waiting for its throat to be slit, but he doesn't need to know that. He stares at my face, unblinking. 'I doubt there will be enough time for your team to find you, but at least you won't suffer. But if you don't. If you make trouble . . .' I put the blade in front of his nose, so close he looks at it almost cross-eyed. Then I move it down to his arm.

His hand has been secured palm upwards, making sure the soft pale surface of his forearm and inner elbow is exposed for the needle. I move the blade down.

I can see the blue lines easily, protruding from his arm. Nice big male veins, ready and waiting. And he must be stressed, his heart beating hard, making them prominent.

I press the blade to his skin. For a moment it resists, then the pressure breaks, the sharp scalpel puncturing the surface.

He makes a noise, a strangulated cry of pain. I push harder and I see the muscles in his forearm tense. A small cut widens, deep, but about an inch long. I take the scalpel away so he can see.

He's looking at it now. His eyes are frightened, blinking quickly as the blood starts to flow. It covers the arm of the chair, then drips to the floor.

'Resist, and I'll do it like this. Cut by cut, slitting you open through your veins. Peeling back your skin, not caring how much you scream.'

His eyes flick to the cannula in his arm, then back up to my face.

'You'll bleed out quicker this way. Your team won't have a hope at finding you.'

He's groaning again, quick intermittent noises. I look

at him, at the tears welling in his eyes, at his frantic breathing, and I know I've won. He makes another noise, trying to say something, so I reach forward, the scalpel cutting into the tape, slowly, carefully, pulling it away from his mouth.

He takes a few gasping breaths, then looks up into my eyes.

'Do you understand me?' I ask quietly.

'Fuck you,' he replies.

Chapter 61

Jamie has jitters in his stomach that don't abate; he clasps his hands together to assuage the shaking but it doesn't help. Every moment they're here he's aware that Adam's out there. With *him*. As time ticks by. Being tortured, dying slowly. In pain.

Marsh hasn't challenged his return to work, even though it's against protocol, breaking every rule. Besides, it's personal to everyone here. They need every hand on deck – including Romilly. With her connection to the case, normally they'd keep her as far away as possible but there's a chance she might spot something – however small – as she did before with the Roman numerals on the wall.

They need everyone and everything right now.

Even though Ellie Quinn hadn't been there long, Jamie only working with her for two days, the gap left by her death – her murder – is palpable. Everywhere he looks, he sees her. Her wide-eyed fascination as she learnt about the workings of a murder case. Her handwriting on the board. Her initials against a line of enquiry she'd been pursuing.

And it's a hundred times worse when it comes to Adam.

Jamie's gaze keeps on shifting to his empty office, expecting him to walk out any moment, shouting words of encouragement to the team. Jamie is a poor substitute in comparison.

He feels useless. He tries to focus, but each time he looks at his computer the words dance on the screen. He can't concentrate.

DC Lee comes up to his side.

'We have them,' he says. 'The witnesses from the park. We have them.'

A man and a woman. The couple that saw the killer as he left the park after murdering that girl, the ones that must have seen his face. They sit in separate interview rooms; the woman looks up nervously as Jamie enters. They're both mid-sixties; the woman has short ash-blonde hair, small wireframed glasses; silver rings on her left hand which she fiddles with constantly.

He smiles and sits down in front of her.

'I'm sorry to be brief, but as DC Lee has already told you, time is of the essence. And apologies for separating you, but we've found that in circumstances like this, one person's witness testimony can distort the other. By comparing your statements we can find commonalities, things that are true.'

She nods, her face stern.

'Anything I can do,' the woman says.

'Tell me what you saw?'

The woman pauses, thinking.

'It was dark. And we only saw him for a second. He had a hood pulled up. And a scarf over his chin and mouth.'

'But you saw his face?'

'Yes. But only a bit. And we noticed him because . . . what was on it.' She stops again. 'It looked like blood. Across his cheeks. I said to Graham, it couldn't possibly be. But then we saw the news, and the reports of that girl's murder. So we called you.'

'Could you describe him?' Jamie knows next door the man is already with a photofit artist, trying to construct a picture of the guy.

'A bit. Maybe. Not that tall. Shorter than Graham. Five foot nine, or less. And he was walking quickly, but not striding. Short steps, like this.'

She pats on the table, one hand after another, quick taps of her rings against the Formica.

'Thank you.' It seems insignificant, but you never know. Jamie continues: 'White, black? Beard? Clean-shaven?'

'White. Couldn't tell you anything else. As I said, most of his face was covered with the hood. And he didn't look at us. Staring at the pavement.'

'What sort of hood? From a coat, or a hoodie?'

'A hoodie, yes. Black, I think.'

'Did it have a logo? Anything distinctive?'

She frowns, then her eyes widen. 'Yes,' she says. She thinks again. 'It was two triangles. Here.'

She points to the top right of her chest; Jamie pushes a piece of paper across and she draws it. Two flat, wide isosceles triangles. One with the tip pointing downwards; the other, on top, facing up. A diamond, split with a horizontal line.

'That's helpful.' But it's so generic, Jamie's not sure how. 'Did he have a bag, or anything else on him?' he asks.

'Bag? No. Nothing. Not that I remember. And he was making a noise.'

'A noise? Like what?'

She turns one of her rings around with the fingers from her other hand. 'It's hard to describe. Like he was crying.' The ring comes off; it falls on the tabletop, and the metallic clink jars in Jamie's brain.

There's a knock on the door, and Jamie looks up, nods, then turns back to the woman. 'The photofit artist has finished with your husband. If you don't mind taking a look?'

'Yes, of course.'

The artist is shown in. The laptop is placed down on the table, and the woman studies it carefully.

'Yes. Yes, that's him. As much as we could tell.'

Jamie looks at the picture. A hood pulled low on the eyes, the shape of a nose, the scarf covering the rest. There's little to go on. But to him it looks like . . .

He frowns. Everything is happening so fast. He can't think straight. 'Get this out to the media. You never know, it might jog someone's memory.'

'Jamie?'

It's Rom. She stands in the doorway, a piece of paper clutched in her hand. 'We've been going through my father's files. And we think we might have someone who can help.'

Chapter 62

They take an unmarked pool car, driving fast, using the siren to cut through the busy weekend traffic. Next to him, Romilly is filling him in on the details. Sandra Poole. Remarried, so they struggled to find her at first. The nurse from the surgery.

'She knew everyone.' She chews on her nail for a second. 'She didn't just work there. She had shifts all over the place: the hospital, with other GPs. She knew all the gossip. Who was cheating on their wives. Whose kids were skiving off school. If anyone can tell us who was close to Cole back then, it would be her.'

They stop outside an insignificant-looking terraced house. Jamie leads the way and rings the doorbell. Lee has phoned ahead; they know she's in and eventually hear footsteps, then a shadow behind the frosted glass. The door opens.

'Well. I never thought I'd hear from you again. Romilly Cole!' The woman is compact and stout, with glowing red cheeks and thinning grey hair. 'Let me look at you! What a beautiful woman you've become. Come in, come in.'

Jamie introduces himself as he steps over the threshold, but the woman ushers them through, keen to chat to Romilly. The wallpaper is tired, the carpet worn in the centre. The smell is of bacon, fried eggs – and one of those plug-in air fresheners turned up to max. Jamie sees it on the sideboard, white plastic. It lets out an enthusiastic puff as they walk in the room; it makes Jamie want to sneeze.

They both sit down where they're told: on an overly soft sofa, Romilly leaning gently into Jamie as his weight pulls down the cushion.

'Tea? Coffee?' the woman asks.

'No. Please,' Jamie says more abruptly than he intends. 'Sit down.'

She does as she's told, cheeks flushing at Jamie's tone. He gets a look from Romilly, and she sits forward, ready to talk.

'Mrs Poole . . .' Romilly begins.

'Sandra, please.'

'Sandra. You worked for my father from the beginning, is that right?' Romilly gives her an encouraging smile. Jamie's thankful she's there, there's no way he's got the emotional stability to interview this woman properly.

'Yes, 1983, 1984, I think it was. I remember you being born just after I started.'

'So you knew everything about the surgery. What went on, all the gossip?'

'I didn't know that,' she says quickly. Her eyes dart to Jamie. 'Is that what this is about? Because I didn't know anything about what he did. I told the police—'

'No, no. Don't worry about that, Sandra.' Romilly gives

her another smile and a reassuring pat on the arm. 'But we're curious about who Dr Cole was close to at the time. Who he might still be in contact with? Would you have any idea?'

Sandra frowns. 'Not a clue, no,' she says, and Jamie feels his stomach sink. 'He didn't have many friends. There was Joanna, and you. And he seemed happy with that. We all said at the time, what a wonderful family man he was.' Her face clouds. 'Of course, then, we didn't know,' she adds quickly. 'About . . . About the girls.'

She stops and her cheeks go red. Romilly gives her a sympathetic look.

'None of us knew, Sandra,' she says, reassuringly, and the woman returns her smile.

Jamie rolls the dates around in his head. Dr Cole was arrested in 1995; he is in his sixties now. He thinks about the victims, how the killer needed to move the bodies, transport the unconscious around. Overpower and abduct Pippa. Same with Adam.

Jamie leans forward on the sofa, resting his hands on his knees. 'Was there anyone else who hung around the surgery, someone younger. Who Dr Cole met with on a regular basis? Could have been a teenage boy?'

Sandra looks blank; Jamie's shoulders sag.

His phone rings in his pocket and he quickly pulls it out: *Lee*. He gives a tight smile to Sandra. 'Sorry. I need to answer this.'

He's pressed the key even before he's out of the room. 'Tim, give me something we can use. Anything.'

'The lab called—'

'They found the samples?'

360

'No.' Jamie's optimism fades fast. Tim is still talking: 'But they tested a different one. A swab taken from the dog.'

Jamie remembers the poor animal. The white fluffy terrier, locked in the cupboard.

'And?' Jamie snaps impatiently.

'It was a bit of a shot in the dark, but one of the samples from its mouth came back as human. And not the victim. It must have bitten its attacker.'

Jamie takes a quick breath in, apprehensive.

'No direct matches—'

'Fuck—'

'No, Sarge, listen. They did some extra tests, and they found something.' Tim pauses. Jamie feels a glimmer of hope as Tim continues. 'A paternal match. To someone on the system.'

The air is suddenly sucked out of the room. He's suffocating; can't take a breath. 'You mean . . .?'

'Our killer – they're related to Cole. Elijah Cole has another child.'

Jamie leans against the wall in the corridor, mind reeling. He hears Romilly and Sandra still talking in the room next door.

'And you're sure?' Jamie says slowly. 'That it's not . . .'

'They checked that. It's not Romilly Cole.' Jamie breathes a sigh of relief. His gaze shifts to a bowl on the chest of drawers next to him. Spare coins, keys. And a few crumpled, white business cards.

'And, Sarge—'

'Tim?' Jamie interrupts. He looks at the card, picks it up. His thoughts return to a marginally better time, day three of this investigation. 'Did we finish looking into the fly-tippers at the wasteland?'

'Yes. A hit to one company, but no witnesses.'

Jamie turns the card around in his fingers thoughtfully. 'What were they called?'

'Bob's Builders. But Sarge—'

Jamie stands up straight. His eyes lock on the card in his hand. 'You're sure?'

'You don't forget a name like that. But Jamie, about the blood results. They got something else. I don't know . . . it's not consistent . . . They're doing some confirmatory tests . . .'

Jamie's head lifts again. 'What, Tim?'

Lee pauses. Then he says quietly, 'The chromosomes in the sample. They're XX.'

Jamie doesn't understand. 'What are you saying? That the lab muddled the sample with Pippa's blood or another one of the victims'?'

'No, Sarge, you're not understanding me. I asked that. The lab was clear: there is no chance of contamination.' Tim talks slowly now, his words coming through clear over the phone. 'What I'm saying is, contrary to our assumptions . . . The person we're looking for is a woman. Elijah Cole had another daughter.'

Chapter 63

Jamie comes back into the room, his phone clutched in one hand, a small white card in the other. His face is white, and Romilly feels a fresh surge of panic. They've found him. Adam. He's dead. But he meets her eyes and shakes his head. For a moment she can breathe again.

Jamie sits back next to Romilly. So many old memories have come flooding back. First being in the old surgery, remembering how it was, back then. Sitting quietly at one of the desks in the office, pencil in hand, doing her homework. Listening to the adult conversation as the women talked, fascinated by the gossip being relayed in muted whispers. And now Mrs Poole.

Next to her, Jamie takes a deep breath. Romilly glances his way, he's clearly wrestling with something. New information he's struggling to assimilate.

'Mrs Poole—'

'Sandra, please.'

'Sandra.' Jamie flashes a quick smile. 'Where did this come from?'

He holds up a white business card, *Bob's Builders* written in simple font across the front.

Sandra stares at it. 'It belonged to my husband. He owned the company.' She looks from the card to Jamie, then down. 'He died. Six months ago. Heart attack – out of nowhere. I should throw it out, but . . .' Her face drops. 'Is this . . . Is this to do with those bodies that were found? Someone called me about that. I told them he was dead. I knew he was dumping stuff there, but he stopped. Ages ago. I'll pay the fine . . .'

Sandra keeps talking, garbled excuses and defence. Romilly stares at Jamie. His face is turned to the floor, deep in thought.

'What is it, Jamie?' she asks.

He turns his attention back to Mrs Poole. 'What happened between you and Elijah Cole?' he asks softly.

Sandra abruptly stops talking. Romilly's confused. Sandra and Elijah? Why is he asking—?

But Sandra's face has gone white. 'Wh-What do you mean?' she stutters. 'There was nothing—'

'This is important, Sandra. This is a murder investigation. We need the truth, and we need it now. What happened?'

The woman is shaking, her body collapsed in on itself, her hands over her face. The helpful, obliging mood has gone. Only a sick feeling remains in its place.

Romilly reaches out and gently touches her quivering arm. 'Sandra, please. Tell us.'

'Elijah . . . he . . .' she burbles through her fingers. 'Joanna, your mother. She was ill.' But then her head lifts. 'I loved him. I respected him. I believed your father was a good man.' Her face is bitter as she looks Romilly right in the eye.

'But he raped me,' she spits. 'Your father raped me.'

Chapter 64

Romilly can feel Jamie's impatience radiating off him. This is clearly important, but the woman is traumatised, now shaking uncontrollably.

Romilly moves to sit next to Sandra and puts her arm around her. A thousand thoughts are pummelling Romilly's brain, but she knows she needs to focus on the here and now. Finding out more. To find Adam.

Push too hard, too soon, and they'll get nothing.

'What happened, Sandra?' she asks gently.

Sandra takes a long shuddering breath in, and when she speaks her voice is unsteady. 'I was working late one night at the surgery.' She sniffs and Romilly hands her a tissue from a crochet-covered box. Sandra dabs at her eyes. 'Elijah came back. He'd been at the pub. He was . . . He was very drunk. Slurring. He said that your mum had just been diagnosed with cancer, and . . .' She lets out a quick jerking cry. 'I went to comfort him. But not like that. Not like . . . I said no. But he . . .'

She puts her head in her hands and starts weeping again.

365

Romilly can only just make out her words under the wet sobs. 'I tried to stop him but he was too strong. He held me down. There was nobody there, nobody to help. I just remember . . . That look in his eyes. He knew he was hurting me and he didn't care.'

In her head, Romilly is doing the maths. If her mum had just been diagnosed, it must have been about 1988. Before her mother died. Before Cole started killing.

Sandra could have stopped this.

'Why didn't you report him?' Romilly says. It takes her utmost effort to keep her voice level.

Sandra looks up again, her eyes pleading. 'He said he was sorry. He begged my forgiveness. He had a young daughter. You.' She squeezes Romilly's hand tightly; Romilly suppresses the urge to recoil. 'Your mother was dying. What was I supposed to do?'

'You should have gone to the police.'

'Nobody would have believed me. An upstanding man of the community like Elijah, versus me? A single woman? No chance. I wanted to move on with my life. Forget it happened. But then I found out I was pregnant.'

Romilly knows blaming Sandra is irrational. Sandra couldn't have known what Cole had planned, what other evil thoughts were lurking in his corrupted mind. And Sandra is right: no one believed Cole could kill, even when the bodies were being dug up from his garden. Sandra had no chance about the rape.

Romilly frowns. 'Mrs Poole,' she asks carefully, 'why don't I remember you being pregnant? Or even there being a baby around?'

Sandra shakes her head mournfully. 'I couldn't do it,' she whispers. 'Not at first. I went away for a while, and then, when the baby arrived, I had her adopted. A little girl. She was perfect but all I could see when I looked at her face was Elijah. Holding me down . . . Forcing me . . . I hated him. Hated the baby. So I gave her up. And things got better.' She smiles now. 'I met Robert. A good man. We got married. I forgot about . . . about him.'

'But you were still working at the surgery?'

'I worked all over the place. A and E, the hospital. Other clinics around the area. We needed the money. We wanted to have kids of our own, but Robert, he . . .' She swallows a sob. 'It wasn't meant to be. And then I started to wonder. What had happened to the baby. So I enquired.'

'What had happened to her?'

'She'd been fostered. At first. But the placement hadn't worked out.' Sandra fixes her gaze to the floor; she turns the ball of tissue around in her withered hands. 'She'd been neglected. And . . . Oh, Christ. They'd abused her. That poor little girl. No more than three years old and they'd done such horrible things to her. My daughter.'

Sandra is sobbing now, her head lowered almost completely. Romilly battles with her emotions. This poor woman. That girl. No more than victims themselves.

Romilly remembers her now. Dark curls, shy. Blushing when Elijah spoke to her. Younger than her, maybe five or six when Elijah was arrested. They used to play together, when Romilly got back from school. Under the reception desk, all around the empty consultation rooms. Romilly sometimes worried it would make her father angry – the giggling, children shouting – but he'd grin, sometimes join in. *Coming, ready or not.*

'I had to have her back,' Sandra continues. 'I told Robert everything, and he agreed. She came to live with us. She

367

always said she didn't remember, but somewhere, deep down, she knew.'

Romilly stays silent, the news sinking in. This girl, this woman – she's her half-sister. Her own flesh and blood. And she's the killer. All those times she's worried and wondered – would those genes make it more likely she could kill? Might she turn into him? And all along the answer had been here.

Yes.

She has the same make-up, the same DNA. But for her loving mother, Romilly might have turned out like her.

'We knew something was wrong.' Sandra is still talking. Her secret, now exposed, can't be withheld any longer. 'That something was wrong with her. It started when she was a teenager. She didn't have any friends. She was depressed, anxious. And she'd have these explosive bursts of rage. Utter fury, she couldn't control, directed at whoever or what was nearby. She'd smash up our house, attack Robert. She even put him in hospital once, but we got help. Intermittent Explosive Disorder, they called it. She saw doctors, the right sort of doctors. The right drugs.' Sandra looks at Romilly, realising the enormity of the situation for the first time. 'Everything that's been happening, that can't be her,' she pleads. 'She's better. She has a proper job. A career.' She points to Jamie. 'She's one of you.'

Romilly pauses, slow dread creeping across her skin. 'What do you mean "one of you"?'

Jamie's mouth drops open, his eyes widen.

'What do you mean, Sandra?' he pushes.

'Not a cop. But she would never . . . she isn't . . . You'll know when you meet her. Although maybe you have already.' Her gaze shifts to Jamie. 'She works in the crime lab. Helps the police.'

Rom's stomach drops through the floor.

'No, there's no way she did this. You'll see. Find her.' Romilly looks at Jamie. His face has gone white. Sandra continues, her voice desperate. 'She goes by my maiden name. Clarke. Maggie Clarke.'

Chapter 65

Nobody's messing around; they have a name.

Blues and twos stream to Maggie Clarke's address, the armed response team primed and ready. Back at the station, Jamie stands with Marsh and Romilly, one hand clutching his radio as though it's a talisman. The tactics are clear: go in fast and go in heavy. This woman's not afraid to kill.

Jamie still struggles to equate their Crime Scene Manager – their efficient, bustling colleague – with the person committing all these murders. It must be a mistake.

As they had driven at speed back to the nick, Romilly had filled Jamie in on everything she knew about Maggie from her childhood.

'She was a sweet kid. A little too adoring of Elijah. And Sandra couldn't always get sitters, so Maggie was often there . . .' Her voice had trailed off as they both realised the catastrophic error. Their killer hadn't been a man. They'd made the assumption – that the person committing these crimes would need to be strong, tall, violent – but hadn't stopped to consider that a woman could be these things too.

A crackle reverberates down the radio. The rumble of footsteps, heavy boots on concrete. Banging, shouting. Calls of 'all clear' echo from the small house.

Jamie sees Marsh's shoulders sag. Romilly puts her hands over her mouth and lets out a small cry.

There's no one there.

Jamie takes over the radio. 'The van,' he says. Control have already confirmed that a black VW Transporter belonging to Maggie Clarke is registered at this address. He repeats the number plate, twice. 'Is it on the premises?'

A short pause. 'Negative, Sarge.'

Jamie turns to the team, faces eager to get going. 'Get every camera, every ANPR across the city searching for that van. Plaster her face over every nick in a fifty-mile radius, so every single cop out there knows what she looks like.'

'What about the prison?' Romilly asks, reading Jamie's mind. 'Surely she'll try to make contact with Cole somehow?'

'Belmarsh is on high alert?' He looks to Marsh, who nods.

'If she goes there, we have her,' his boss confirms. 'Same with Gloucester Road, and the surgery. We'll keep teams at her own house. Everywhere is staked out.'

'But surely she'll just go to ground?' Romilly says, and Jamie hears the desperation in her voice. 'Hide Adam somewhere unknown?'

'There are only so many places you can take an unconscious body,' Jamie says. 'She won't stop. Not until it's done.' All eyes turn to him. 'Adam had a theory, and he was right.'

Marsh nods, agreeing with Jamie. 'Visitor logs came in twenty minutes ago from the prison. They didn't have a clue Cole was her father. The governor is appalled. Multiple visits to Cole spanning a period of five years. They've been in contact a while. And calls out the other way. Texts to Maggie Clarke's mobile from a number of burner cells. All cryptic, but he was communicating with her, that's for sure.' While he's been talking, Marsh has taken the packet of cigarettes out of his pocket, and now turns them around in his hands. 'Why nobody at Belmarsh was checking this shit, I'll never know,' he mutters. 'We'll make sure there's an inquiry. Shut it down so it never happens again.'

'So can we assume she has the same goal as Cole – to get to twenty? What number are we at?'

Marsh looks to the ceiling, counting. 'Are we including Cole's original victims?' Jamie nods. 'So, four. Five at the dumpsite. Wayne Oxford, our Jane Doe at the park. And—' A quick glance Jamie's way. 'Pippa. Ellie. Plus the three he claims to have killed before. So, sixteen. Not . . .'

Including Adam, is what he doesn't say.

'So she'll need to kill again,' Marsh continues. He opens the top of the cigarette packet, then closes it again. 'And fast, now she knows we're on her trail.'

'Guv? Do you want a cigarette?' Jamie asks with a smile, despite himself.

Marsh laughs. 'Fuck, yes. I swear this case has aged my lungs twenty years in this last day alone. Can we continue this discussion on the roof?'

Jamie glances towards the window. The sun is setting, and he has a sudden urge to take it all in. To soak up something beautiful, in the face of such horror.

Sometimes getting space helps. To reflect. Alleviate the pressure. Even despite the minutes ebbing away, Jamie needs a moment to think.

He nods. 'Lead the way.'

Chapter 66

Romilly follows the two senior police officers up the stairs to the fourth floor, leaving the team furiously working away on CCTV, ANPR – anything that might give them a lead.

Marsh pushes the fire door open at the top. When they were married, Adam would talk about coming up here for a smoke. She imagined it dirty, filthy fag butts covering the gravel, rain falling whatever the season, so she's surprised when she's confronted with the reality. Fresh, clear air. An uninterrupted view over the crowded city, the place she calls home. It's comforting, and she takes a long breath in.

Next to her, Marsh selects a cigarette out of the packet and lights it.

There's silence on the roof. Marsh enjoys a drag in and blows out the smoke. Romilly closes her eyes and inhales it from the air, remembering later days in her marriage with Adam; her disapproval only making him double down on his self-destructive habit.

The smell, the memory, makes her miss him all the more. She's gripped by a helpless desperation. She looks at her watch: he's been out there for eight hours. They have to get him home. They have to.

Noise from the road below drifts up: straggling commuters on their way home from work. Voices, laughter. Normal lives, and Romilly feels an irrational wave of anger at the mundane nature of it all. How dare they continue their existence, when hers is being destroyed. When Adam is out there, alone, dying, and they're failing in their every attempt to find him.

'What did you know about her, Romilly?' Marsh asks.

Romilly sighs. 'Not a lot. We weren't close then, and we didn't keep in touch after Elijah was arrested.'

Romilly squints at the sky, desperate to pull any memory from her addled brain. 'I do remember her mother mentioning that she'd not been well. That she'd been off school for a bit. But she didn't elaborate, and he didn't ask. We should get her medical records—?'

'Already requested, Dr Cole. On their way.'

'And the adoptive father's dead.' Jamie pulls himself away from where he's been staring at the sunset; he faces them both. 'So no help there.'

Marsh nods in agreement. 'He probably discussed where he was dumping his waste over the dinner table. Not knowing that Maggie would use it for a disposal of her own, months later.' He takes another long drag, then drops the butt onto the floor. 'Fuck this,' he mutters. 'We need to find Adam. I need to go home. Kiss my husband, call my kids.'

Romilly notices Jamie look at Marsh in surprise.

'I didn't know you had kids,' Jamie says.

Marsh nods. 'Two. Adults really. James is at uni, studying

374

photography. Andy's an engineer. Neither of them wanted to be cops.'

'Sensible,' Jamie replies.

'Exactly.' Then, quieter, Marsh adds: 'She can't possibly kill four more. She can't.'

The three of them digest his words. Jamie's standing close to the edge of the roof; Romilly to the side. Marsh had been pacing while he smoked and has come to a stop close to the exit, his back to the doorway.

It all happens quickly, before any of them has a chance to react. Romilly hears a noise from Marsh. It's not a cry, but a quiet moan, a rush of air escaping from his lungs. She turns, looking at him. His face has changed from weary despair to surprise, his eyes wide, his mouth open. His gaze meets Romilly's; his body seems to weaken. His legs collapse as he drops to his knees.

And she's there. Behind him.

She's wearing a blue polo shirt and black trousers. Heavy boots. It looks like a cop's uniform, but Romilly assumes it's the one worn by civilians, crime scene techs off-duty. She meets Romilly's gaze, and a smile appears on her dry, cracking lips.

'I knew you'd be up here,' Maggie says. 'Adam used to talk about smoking on the roof.'

Her face is pale and gaunt; the mere sight of her makes Romilly's heart jump, a ball of panic forming in her chest.

She's alone. So where's Adam? *And is he still alive?* the voice in her head screams.

What's she doing here? To have the gall to turn up. To the middle of a police station. She's insane, crazy. *She's your half-sister.* The words spin and blur in Romilly's head, feeling surreal. And then she sees the knife.

Gripped tightly in Maggie's right hand, the blade is covered in blood. Marsh's blood. Romilly's gaze flicks quickly to the concrete, where Marsh is now lying, motionless. As a doctor, she wants to go to him, but she doesn't dare move. She puts one hand in front of her, the other grips her phone.

'Maggie, there's no way out from here,' she says slowly. 'You're in a police station. Put the knife down, before it all gets ugly.'

'I don't want a way out.' Maggie laughs, and Romilly sees the girl from over twenty years ago. 'I need to do what he asks.'

'Who? Cole?'

'He told me all about you. You don't remember me, do you?'

'We used to play together,' Romilly replies. 'At the surgery, after school.'

'We did. I was so jealous of you, did you know that? That you were his daughter, that you got to spend time with him. I didn't even know, then, that I was his child too. And you betrayed him!' she shouts. 'How could you?'

'He was a killer. He murdered those women.'

She smiles again. 'Don't pretend you're so innocent, Romilly Cole. That you weren't involved—'

'I wasn't—'

Maggie laughs loudly, cutting her off. Romilly looks from her to the exit. She needs to get help. But she's still waving the knife; there's no way she can overpower her.

'Where's Adam, Maggie?' Romilly asks. She's forcing her voice to stay calm, but she needs to know. *Has* to know. 'Is he still alive?'

'Maybe. Perhaps. How much blood is left in his body

by now, Romilly?' Romilly doesn't reply. Doesn't know what to say that will mean this woman will tell her where he is. Maggie's face turns to anger. 'You should know! You're a doctor! How much?'

'I-I don't know,' Romilly stutters. She makes herself think, to remember her medical training. 'The average male has seventy-five millilitres per kilo, so . . . I don't know. I don't know, Maggie!' she pleads, desperately. 'Please just tell us where he is.'

But Maggie just laughs. 'You can't have him back. He's mine, forever. You took Elijah away from me. I'm taking your precious Adam.'

'That's all this is?' Romilly spits out the words, disbelieving. 'Petty revenge?'

'Petty? Petty? You took my father away from me! You put him in jail! I lived my whole life not realising who he was. And now I know, I need to make him proud. But I'll never be allowed back. I'll never see him again. And if I can't have Elijah, then you can't have Adam. You had everything. You grew up with him – cosy dinners round the table, goodnight kisses before bed. Do you know what I had?'

'You had your mother! And an adopted father who loved you.'

'My mother? The woman who discarded me at birth? I grew up feeling out of place, that something was wrong with me. But it was because of them. Dad – Robert,' she spits, 'claimed to love me but they were never honest. Elijah wrote to me. Five years ago. He told me.'

'That he was your father?'

'And the rest. What they did to me. My foster parents. That they . . . That they had . . .' She screws her eyes shut for a moment, her face a mask of pain. Romilly takes a step forward, but then she opens them again. Brandishes the knife. 'Once I knew, everything made sense,' she continues, her voice breaking. 'Elijah understands. I'd always known we had a special bond, but I didn't know why until then. My purpose. Elijah's the only person who's ever loved me. And you took him away.'

'So kill me, Maggie! If I'm the one you hate. Kill *me*.'

Maggie laughs. 'Dad would never forgive me if I touched a hair on his darling daughter's head. But his son-in-law? That's fair game.'

'So why did you kill Pippa?' A voice from the other side of the roof: Jamie's spoken.

All this time Jamie's been standing, frozen. Romilly's barely considered him, so focused on Maggie and that knife. But now she looks across.

Jamie has a strange expression on his face. Eyes locked on Maggie, his eyebrows low, forehead furrowed.

'Why Pippa?' he growls again. 'Why the other victims?'

Maggie stares at him, a small smile on her face. 'Because that's what Elijah wants. The twenty.'

Romilly blinks. She still doesn't understand. Her father wants twenty people dead? But why? And why *those* people?

'Arrest me.' Maggie holds her wrists out in front of her, the knife still in her hand. Romilly hesitates; she sees Jamie do the same, expecting a trick. 'Put me in cuffs. Throw me in jail,' Maggie continues. 'And they'll say I was insane. That I wasn't in my right mind. I'll get off. A few years in a nice mental hospital, probably released early after budget cuts.' She pauses, and her attention turns to Jamie. 'But I knew exactly what I was doing.'

Romilly sees Jamie's nostrils flare, the tension in his jaw.

'I knew what I was doing when I went to your house,' she says to Jamie. 'When I beat your wife over the head. When I dragged her to Elijah's shed, tied her up.' Jamie's shoulders are heaving; he's breathing fast, shallow breaths. 'When I suspended her from the ceiling, cut her open, drained her blood.' She smiles. 'Why do you think they string animal carcasses up at the abattoir, DS Hoxton?'

It's the final straw. With a roar, Jamie leaps forward. He goes for Maggie, arms outstretched, one hand closing on her neck, the other tight on her arm. And he swings her like a dog with a ragdoll towards the edge of the roof.

The knife clatters to the concrete. Her feet are lifted off the ground, her body dangles over the side. Jamie's legs are braced against the low wall; he leans out. One slip, one wrong move and they'll both go over. He lets go and Maggie will fall.

Maggie makes a strange noise, a half-laugh.

'She knew she was going to die,' she says, her voice coming out strangled in Jamie's grip. 'She screamed, she begged.'

'You . . . you . . .' Jamie's not making any sense, half-formed words coming out of his mouth in a tortured shout.

Romilly pulls her phone out of her pocket. She dials 999, then shouts to the operator: 'Dr Romilly Cole. I'm with DS Hoxton, Detective Superintendent Marsh. At the central police station, on the roof. Send backup, send an ambulance.' Control struggles to make sense of what she's saying. 'Yes, on the roof. Marsh has been stabbed. She's here. She's here.'

She doesn't take her gaze off Jamie and Maggie.

Maggie's still hanging over the drop, looking up into Jamie's eyes.

Romilly can see Jamie's hand shaking. They're close, too close.

One wrong move, and they'll both be dead.

One wrong move, and they'll never find Adam.

Chapter 67

He has her. His wife's killer, in his hands. Jamie tightens his grip on her neck; he sees her eyes bulging, her face turning puce. Jamie can barely think; the red-hot burning rage fills him, pushing out from his core.

Maggie's eyes are fixed on his. Her hands dangle limply at her sides; she's making no effort to get away.

'She was beautiful, your wife,' Maggie says, her voice thin, constricted by his grip. A flash in Jamie's mind: Pippa, lying sleepily in bed next to him. Her slow smile as she kissed him goodbye, the gentle touch of her hands. *Here you are.* Why hadn't he saved her? Why hadn't he got there in time?

'Her perfect pale skin. So full of life, of energy.'

Jamie wants to stop her talking. She has to stop talking. He leans another few inches over the edge.

'It's what she wants!'

A voice shouts next to him. He doesn't turn, but Romilly calls again. 'Please, Jamie. She wants to be one of them.'

Jamie looks down. A drop of four floors. To the ashen-grey concrete. To her certain death. He sees a few people below, looking up, pointing. Shouts of alarm. Of fear.

'She said your name,' Maggie whispers. His face is so close he can smell her breath. The sourness, a stink of death that makes him gag. 'She cried out for you, over and over again. As she died.'

He feels sick; his stomach contracts, but he forces it down. What this woman did. To Pippa. To all those other people. The pain she must have inflicted. Marsh, lying dying less than ten feet away from them. Adam, who knows where.

'She said she loved you. She was calling out for you, but you never came.'

He almost lets go then. His muscles turn to water; he feels weak, Pippa knew he wasn't enough. As she died, that he hadn't been able to save her.

'Put her down, Jamie, please,' Romilly shouts again. 'This is what she wants. You, her, Marsh, Adam. That's the twenty. The final four.'

He feels the hard brickwork against his legs. The only thing stopping him from falling over the edge. And he looks down again. This life, his existence without Pippa, it's too much. He deserves to go down with Maggie. Punishment for his failure.

'She died in pain, DS Hoxton. In fear. Covered in her own puke, and piss and shit. I killed her, and you did nothing.'

His hand is cramping now. He's starting to shake. To let go, to jump. How hard could it be? He starts to cry, tears rolling down his face, falling, falling. One simple movement. To get his revenge. Maybe even see Pippa again. Hear her laughter, her voice.

'She needed you and you couldn't save her.'

'Jamie, don't do it. What would Pippa tell you?'

Romilly is next to him now. He knows Romilly can't physically stop him, he's much stronger, much bigger than her. And all he has to do is let go, lift his leg from the ground a few inches.

He feels a hand on his arm. And that one touch, the warmth, makes him stop.

He hears Pippa in his head. *Here you are.* The thought of her makes him ache, a pain eating at his broken heart. *Don't,* she's saying. *Don't.*

With a strangled cry, he throws himself backwards. He pulls Maggie with him, to the roof, throwing her hard onto the concrete. She lets out a cry of anger; Jamie watches as people arrive. Men in black, forcing her face into the asphalt. Handcuffs go on. She screams in frustration, knowing she's beaten.

Jamie falls back onto the ground. He starts to sob; he feels Romilly crying as she holds him close.

Next to them, Marsh is surrounded by paramedics, working frantically to save him. Shouted instructions, medical equipment being passed to and fro. The officers carry Maggie away. She's still twisting, screaming in frustration, as they drag her down the stairs towards the cells.

'Wait!' Romilly shouts. They pause and Jamie watches as she rushes over, standing, determined, in front of the killer.

'It's all over now, Maggie,' she says. 'Tell us where Adam is.'

Jamie lifts his head, watching them through blurry eyes. He feels completely drained; all adrenaline vanished the moment he pulled back from the edge. In front of him the woman that killed Pippa lifts her head, then smiles.

383

'Nothing's over,' she says. 'Nothing's finished.'

'You're four away, Maggie. You'll never—'

'Less than that now,' she says, indicating towards Marsh with a tilt of her head. Marsh is still surrounded by paramedics but Jamie can see his eyes are closed. He's still and the sight makes terror race in Jamie's veins.

'And what about Adam Bishop?' she says. 'Hide and seek, DS Hoxton.'

All the police officers pause. Maggie's voice is singsong and eerie in the quiet of the night. 'Coming, ready or not,' she says.

Chapter 68

In the darkness, Adam stirs. He's been drifting for a while now, in and out of consciousness. The pain comes in slow waves, his limbs aching, his head heavy. He forces himself to open his eyes.

Alone.

Cold.

So very very cold.

Around him, blood dries. Black and sticky, like tar. At first it poured from his arms, his racing heart rate intensifying the bleeding, but now it's slow. A drip drip, to the floor. Steady. Constant.

How much longer does he have? Time is meaningless; hidden in the black. He'd watched the light fade behind the boards, disappearing into night.

Nobody knows where he is.

Nobody will find him.

He doesn't have long left. He can sense it. By the quick, frantic beat of his heart. The confusion. The sweat cooling on his skin.

Drip. Drip.

So very very cold.

He is tired. He closes his eyes again.

Darkness consumes him.

Chapter 69

Adam is still missing.

The thought rotates around Jamie's head, a mantra that won't abate. He is utterly numb.

Maggie has been taken away. Jamie knows she is being interrogated by detectives downstairs but she is refusing to say a word. There is no news from the hospital about Marsh.

He stands in the incident room, in front of the detectives who wait, silent and tense. Then he tells them the news in short, sharp sentences.

He wants to send them all home. To their families, their loved ones. For comfort and support. But Adam is still missing.

Adam is still missing.

'Where are we with the house?' he asks DC Lee.

'SOCOs are still there,' he replies. 'Nothing to note yet.'

And Jamie knows he has to go. To see where she lived. To get into her mind. And then, perhaps, he'll find Adam.

*

The house is a mess of chaos and disorder; now he's here, Jamie doubts what help it'll be. But still. He has to try.

He puts a crime scene suit on and steps over the threshold; the smell hits him like a sucker punch to the face. A mixture of something rotting, death, sweat, and human waste. He's glad of the mask, the gloves on his hands; he holds his arms close to his chest as he walks through.

Belongings scatter the floor and every surface. A SOCO has pushed the door open to the front room: again, this one is a mess, but he can't see anything significant. Just evidence of a troubled woman, falling apart.

He picks up a black boot, lying on its side in the hallway and turns it over in his hand. Stones, broken glass, mud, sand, stuck in the heavy tread. And there's something tacky down the side. He takes his hand away and looks at the transfer on his gloved fingers – dark red, viscous. He closes his eyes for a moment, swallowing down a swell of horror. Don't think about it, not now, he tells himself as he hands it to a SOCO to bag.

Not now. He has a job to do.

He backs away, into the kitchen. This – this is different. It's where the smell is coming from. The room is filthy. Thick, layered dirt coats the floor and the surfaces. Even the ceiling is spattered.

And it looks like the fridge is rotting. Black blood oozes around the door, leaking out of the appliance and on to the lino around it, as if it had once been a living thing and was decomposing in front of them. Jamie takes a tentative step towards it, opens the door, then retches behind his mask. Bladders of blood rest on the shelves; souvenirs taken, he assumes, from the victims. Some leak, rivers of indescribable, thick gunk running from the shelves to the floor. And there it congeals, a marble of black and scarlet and brown.

He gags again, barely able to suppress the vomit this time, and shuts the door quickly.

Cutlery and plates lie on the side, coated in mould and dried food. Pieces of paper sit in rough piles on the dining table, scrappy handwriting in biro on all. Jamie leans down to look at one; there's nothing that makes sense. Jumbles of words, delusions and ramblings. The tableau of a broken mind.

He can't take any more. The thought of what this woman was doing, it's horrific. He walks quickly out of the house.

Rom is waiting for him outside the cordon. He stands on the other side of the blue and white tape.

'Anything?' she asks.

'I don't know. Nothing obvious. And you don't want to go in there. She's . . . It's . . . fucked up,' he manages.

She looks towards the house; her face is pale with worry. Jamie knows exactly what she's thinking.

Adam is still missing.

'I'll go back in,' he says. 'Keep looking.'

'I'm coming with you.'

He hesitates, going to stop her, then lets it go. So many protocols have been broken already, what's one more? And two heads are better than one.

'Suit up,' he says.

He can't bear to go back in the house, so he makes a turn around the side and through the wooden back gate. Romilly follows him, hesitantly, Jamie's torch lighting their way. The garden is neglected, and he walks across the tiny lawn to the shed at the end. No more than a small wooden box, with a window on one side. He tries the door, it's padlocked, so he puts his gloved hands against the glass and peers through, shining the beam of the torch inside. He can't see much. A set of metal shelving, boxes and tools jumbled across. A black wetsuit, hanging at the back. A surfboard. What looks like a lifejacket, next to loops of dark green rope. He looks at it for a second, then turns to Romilly. She's doing the same, squinting through the window.

'How do we make sense of all of this, Rom?' he asks. He can feel himself shaking. Panic threatens. There's too much evidence, not enough time.

He feels suffocated in the crime scene suit, his breath hot. He pulls the mask off, gasping for air, then slumps on the grass in the darkness, putting his head between his knees.

He feels Romilly sit down next to him, then place a steadying hand on his shoulder.

'Do you remember when I met you? For the first time?' she says quietly. He shakes his head, then pulls his hood down, raking his hands through his hair in exasperation. 'At that barbecue, the one for my birthday. I must have been . . . what? Thirty-one, thirty-two? Adam and I had been married for a few years, and he was talking about this new DC that had just joined Major Crimes.' She laughs softly. 'If you'd been a woman I would have been seriously worried, Jamie. The way he talked about you. Like he'd just met his soul mate.'

Jamie stays quiet, unsure why she's telling him this. It only adds to his failure, that Adam had such high hopes in him and he was letting him down.

'He invited you, along with half his team from the nick, and you weren't at all what I expected.'

He looks up now, into Romilly's eyes. 'What did you expect?'

'I don't know. That you'd be like him – the confidence, the charm – but you couldn't have been more different.'

'This isn't helping, Rom—'

'No, no. That's not what I mean. You were exactly what Adam needed. He was a loose cannon in those days, and you kept him in check, made sure he focused.' She places a gentle hand on his arm, and smiles. 'Adam is a great cop because of you.'

'That's bullshit—'

'No, it's not. You're just as smart, just as hard-working. But you're calmer, more controlled. And you can do this. You can find him.'

Jamie sighs. His mind still feels fractured, broken by the loss of his wife. 'That was the first time I met Pippa, that day.'

'It was?'

'Yeah, at that barbecue. On that awful beach. Don't you remember? Those bloody seagulls trying to steal all the bread rolls, the wind throwing the sand into . . .' He pauses. A thought catches. He glances back to the shed, and the lifejacket hanging inside. He remembers the evidence from the first crime scene: the traces of salt on the blanket. The nylon cording. 'The victims were being held near the sea,' he says slowly.

Romilly gapes at him. 'But where?'

'Think about it logically. She would need a large shed or a storage unit. And Maggie got here fast. It needs to be reasonably close. But remote. Somewhere where she wouldn't be disturbed.'

He pulls his phone out of his pocket and dials Lee, back at the nick.

'Tim,' he says the moment he answers. 'I need you to

run an ANPR check. Look for the VW Transporter heading to the coast.' Next to him, Romilly has pulled the maps up on her phone. He looks over her shoulder and reads off the names of the roads. 'A27 towards Swanwick. A326 towards Calshot. M27 towards Hamble.'

'This is going to take hours, Sarge,' Lee comments.

'Just do it,' Jamie snaps, but he's right. They don't have hours. They need something else to narrow it down.

He stands up, walking back into the house, the phone still clamped to his ear. The boot from the hallway has been taken away but its twin lies on the carpet, and Jamie picks it up. He pulls at a stone wedged in the tread, looking closely at it. It's a piece of flint, broken in half but well worn. Edges smooth, like it's spent an eternity being buffeted by waves.

'Look for a rocky beach,' he barks to Lee. Then the logo jumps into his mind. The two triangles, one on top of the other. Could it be a boat? 'And a sailing club,' he adds.

There's a pause, nothing but the crackle of static on the line before Lee speaks again. One word.

'Calshot,' he says.

Jamie turns, breaking into a run to his car, keen to get on the radio. It fits. The traces of sea salt on the blanket, the rope. Quiet and deserted in winter.

He glances at his watch. Nearly ten p.m. Over twelve hours have passed since Adam was abducted.

They need to get to Calshot. And fast.

Chapter 70

The call comes back: CCTV shows a black VW van visiting a boathouse on the far side of the spit. It's isolated, alone. Perfect, for whatever Maggie had in mind.

They arrive in the darkness with a screech of brakes and a howl of sirens. The place seems deserted. Black water laps gently at the edge of the jetty; the boathouse is quiet, the air still. Men in black vests and helmets are ready to go, but Jamie can't hold back. Fuck procedure, fuck the risk assessments – his friend is in there.

He sprints towards the property, feet pounding the boards. Shouts of 'Armed Police' echo behind him; gulls take off into the sky in alarm.

The first door is locked; the armed response officer to his side smashes through it with ease. There is a large opening, leading out via a ramp to the water. The next door is open. He steps through into the second room then stops, stunned.

The room isn't big. He reaches up to the lamp strung up in the centre and turns it on, lighting all four corners.

Grey concrete floor, bare brick walls. One window on the far side, boarded up; an ARO ignores protocol and tugs at the timbers, letting the meagre moonlight inside.

Adam sits in the centre, arms and legs bound to a wooden chair. His head is slumped forward, he isn't moving.

And there is blood.

Everywhere.

His shirt and jeans are soaked in it, stained almost black. Red pools surround him, splashes, speckles all across the floor. Jamie can see a nasty gash on the left-hand side of his forehead, dried blood running down his face, down his neck. And his arms, fuck. *Fuck.* Jamie's hands go to his mouth in shock. His skin is a mass of red, narrow cuts and gashes, all across his forearms, some still oozing blood. His feet are bare, with what look like two needles sticking out of the flesh.

Behind him he hears the crackle of the radio. 'Victim present, conscious and breathing, multiple wounds. Ambulance to scene on the hurry up, please.'

The paramedics encircle Adam, a bustle of movement, shouting instructions. He hears mutters about cannulation, conversations whether they should use the ones already in situ. A decision is made, and tubes and bags of clear fluids are rigged up next to him.

Adam's still unconscious. Numb, Jamie waits with Romilly, his arm around her shoulders, pulling her closely to him. Barely contained panic rolls off her; he can feel her breathing heavily, her body tense.

Jamie hears a helicopter, then moments later more paramedics rush in, clutching bladders of bright red liquid. Again, they're hooked up to Adam, hands squeezing the vital blood into him.

Please. 'Please,' he begs.

'He's going to wake up, isn't he?' Rom whispers.

'Yes,' Jamie replies, but he's not so sure. *Please be alive.* Then slowly, he sees Adam's head start to stir, move side to side. He squeezes Romilly close. 'Yes,' he repeats. 'He's going to be fine. He is.'

The paramedics talk to Adam, trying to get his attention. The bag of blood is changed for a new one; other paramedics try to clean up some of the mess, bandage his wounds.

Adam's head is up now; a paramedic looks into his eyes with a bright light. He looks dazed, struggling to focus.

One of the medics comes over to talk to them.

'Nasty contusion to the head, although on first check it looks superficial. Main problem is the lack of blood and the lacerations to his forearms. That's where it's all coming from. You were good to find him when you did. Who knows what might have happened.'

They hear noise, and the paramedic turns. Adam's fully awake now, cut free from the chair, but writhing under the grip of the men in green. Romilly hurries over.

'Adam! Adam, stop.'

Jamie can see him struggling, looking down at the needles still in his arms. He has never seen that look on his boss's face before. Desperation. And pure fear.

'Please, please,' Adam cries weakly. 'Take them out.'

Romilly kneels in front of him. She takes both his hands and he calms slightly, his eyes locked on her. Jamie can see the horror on his face. People say they're scared of heights, of spiders, of snakes, but this is something else. A deep-rooted phobia, terrifying him to his core.

'Please,' he whispers.

'I will,' she replies. 'Just stay still. And I will.'

Adam stops moving, but Jamie can see him shaking, tears now tracking clean lines in the dirt on his face. Romilly takes the dressings offered to her, and slowly she removes the needles as Adam squeezes his eyes tightly shut.

'There. Done. All gone.'

Adam opens his eyes and looks. Despite all the blood, the cuts on his arms, he visibly relaxes, and leans forward into Romilly's outstretched embrace. She holds him. His face rests on her shoulder, eyes closed, completely still, and all around them the paramedics continue their work. Placing dressings on his arms, cleaning up his wounds.

Jamie watches.

The sense of relief is all-consuming. Adam has been found. He'll be okay. But at the same time he feels the discontent. Why hadn't they been so lucky with Pippa? Why did she have to die when Adam lives?

He turns away from the scene and walks out of the boathouse to the waterfront. It's a pebble beach, scattered with rocks and seaweed. Quiet, but for the wash of the tide on the shore. Seagulls squawk, their cries loud in the air, like children fighting over the last sweet in a box.

There are a few paths leading away from the boathouse; he picks one and walks fast along it, channelling his anger downward, feet thumping to the ground. Headlights guide his way. His first thought when they found Adam: I must phone her, tell Pippa he's okay. And the feeling that came after – remembering anew that she had gone, that she would always be gone – crushed him almost as strongly as it had the first time. He knows that it will be like this now. First thing in the morning, reaching out for her.

Making a cup of tea, getting one mug out of the cupboard rather than two. Every sunset, every friend's baby being born: every fucking cliched happy memory would be his and his alone.

Knowing who killed Pippa and all those other people doesn't provide the relief he was hoping for. It hasn't brought his wife back; it only adds fuel to the anger burning in the pit of his stomach.

He tilts his head, staring upwards into the night sky. It's clear and the stars shine bright, easily seen away from the normal glare of civilisation. The sight calms him. Pippa believed in God. Not enough to go to church, but she'd say a quiet prayer when times were hard. She thought something, someone, was up there. He hopes so too. So she can be at peace.

Something had been looking out for Adam. Or maybe it had just been him, and good police work.

He turns and looks back to the boathouse where the blue lights of the patrol cars still flash. Torches dance in the night sky. He pulls his shoulders straight, for the first time thinking about his future.

He found Adam. He's a good detective. A fucking great one. He'll finish this murder investigation. They'll put Maggie Clarke away and justice will be served.

Then he'll apply for that promotion.

He'll make his wife proud.

Chapter 71

Romilly kneels next to Adam, his hand in hers. He's still slumped in the same bloody wooden chair, his eyes closed. He holds an oxygen mask to his face. The paramedics mill around; Romilly can tell they're keen to get him to a hospital. She echoes their thoughts to him.

But he shakes his head.

She looks up at Jamie as he walks back into the boat-house.

'Tell him, Jamie,' she says. 'He needs to be seen by a doctor.'

'You're a doctor,' Adam mutters.

'The appropriate doctor. In a hospital.'

'She's right, mate,' Jamie says.

'Adam, please get looked at properly,' Romilly pleads. 'Look at yourself. You—'

But she can't bring herself to finish as tears threaten. She came so close to losing him; she couldn't bear it if anything happened to him now. His head is still bowed, his eyes heavy-lidded. It's taking all his effort to breathe.

398

Probably from the lack of blood in his system, most of which is drying around them, tacky on his skin, his clothes.

'We need to catch her.'

Romilly glances to Jamie. One of the first things Adam said when he was conscious was Maggie's name, directing them to go and find her. But that's as far as they got; there's so much Adam doesn't know.

'She's in custody, Adam,' Jamie says slowly.

Adam looks at him, almost disbelieving. He pulls the oxygen mask off again. 'You have her?' he repeats.

Jamie nods. The relief is clear on Adam's face.

'I'm still not going to hospital,' he says. He gestures to a paramedic who's holding a bottle of water. They pass it to him and he takes a long gulp, then another. 'No fucking way.'

'Adam, you need fluids, you need blood—'

'No one is sticking fucking needles in me!' He shouts it suddenly, his hand pulling away from hers, his body rigid.

'Fine, okay,' she says softly. She can only imagine the trauma – to be faced with his greatest fear and be trapped, not knowing if anyone was on their way. She glances around. 'But let's get out of here. Please?'

The paramedics look uneasy as Jamie takes one arm, Romilly the other and they help Adam up. He seems unsteady at first but gains strength as he shuffles towards the exit.

He still has bare feet, but he doesn't flinch as they walk down the path to Jamie's car.

Once in the back seat, he takes another swig of water. He leans back and closes his eyes. He's pale, his skin almost translucent against the stark white bandage on his forehead. She knows he should be getting medical attention. Some sleep, at least.

Jamie starts the engine of his car. 'So where to, boss?' he says.

Adam opens his eyes slowly. 'Home,' he mumbles. He reaches for Romilly. 'You're coming too,' he says.

She grips his hand, enclosing it tightly in both of hers. 'Too fucking right, I am,' she replies with a smile.

Chapter 72

Adam feels awful. His head is pounding; he feels dizzy, every muscle weak. He rests his head back in the seat as Jamie drives, willing his body calm, his mind quiet.

But still the panic comes. In waves, starting in his stomach, as he remembers the cold under his feet, the bindings on his wrists and ankles. The complete helplessness as she inserted the blade into his skin, feeling the sharp pain, intensifying as she drew it along his vein. The nausea, the dizziness, the disgust, as the blood poured. The horrifying knowledge that he could do nothing to stop it. If his team hadn't found him he would have died there. Alone.

Maggie was true to her word. Angry, she had gagged him again, both hands wrapping the tape so hard around his head his neck jarred. Then she turned her attention to the selection of medical instruments on the table next to her.

'My mother taught me the essentials,' she said. 'How to administer injections, insert a cannula. Basic first aid – plus a bit more. She thought I'd be saving lives.' She picked up another needle, removing it from the sterile wrapping and holding it up to Adam's face. His heart raced in response; he couldn't help but imagine the tip entering his vein, the metal inside him. He closed his eyes again. *Get a fucking grip,* he told himself, to no avail.

'I've worked it out,' she continued. 'Practised on the others. It depends on the situation, the metabolic requirements of the tissues being underperfused, but I reckon you'll stay alive just less than a day. Do you think they can find you in that time?'

They can. They can. But you had a week, the voice in his head said. Look how far you got. You couldn't even find the killer right under your nose.

'But a bit of this—' she added, and he opened his eyes then. The scalpel, barely inches from his face. '—and it'll probably be a lot less.'

He couldn't take his eyes off that blade. The light from the overhead lamp reflected off the metal, shining, sharp and dangerous. He followed its path as she lowered it towards his arm. She stopped then, watching his response. He tried to speak, shook his head to and fro, but there was nothing he could do.

The pain came on hot and fast. Every muscle in his body tensed, his breath stopped dead in his chest, as a gush of blood flowed from the wound. And he screamed, his agony, his fury and pain, muffled behind the tape.

He screws his eyes shut, willing the images away. He can't think about that now. She's gone. The needles, they're gone. He lifts a hand and runs it gently down his arm to reassure himself. The cuts throb and sting, but there are only bandages there now, the hastily applied steri-strips holding him together.

He glances forwards to Jamie. His face is set, almost expressionless as he drives. He can't imagine how he must be feeling. Adam's failure to find Pippa, and how Jamie had managed to save *him*, weighs heavy on his mind.

His head spins again, and he raises the bottle up to his lips and takes another swallow. He's had water, sugar in the form of a hastily found Mars bar, any way to get vital nutrients in him without . . . Without . . .

He feels a hand in his, Romilly next to him. He looks over and she smiles. 'I thought I'd lost you,' she whispers.

'It would take more than a psychotic serial killer to do that,' he replies, and she leans across and kisses him.

He sits back, then winds the window down so the winter's air blows on his face. The weather is cool and crisp, the cold breathing life into his bones. He even enjoys the glare of the streetlights as they drive, blurred smudges against the night sky.

He's here. He's alive. And the killer, she's gone.

DAY 9

SUNDAY

Chapter 73

Adam lies in his old bedroom, in Romilly's house. Jamie's snoring is reassuringly loud from the spare room next door; a dim morning light trickles in between the gap in the curtains. A new day beginning. He likes the feeling it brings: the promise of something good. Hope.

He hears Romilly's footsteps on the stairs, then the door opens and she comes in, a tray balanced in her hands.

'I don't want to hear any shit from you,' she says as she sets it down on the mattress. 'You need decent food and water.'

He pushes himself up slowly. He feels the cuts on his arm stretch and throb with every movement. Last night, after a much-needed bath and clean clothes, Romilly had re-stuck and dressed them, doing the best she could without the involvement of any sort of needle. Painkillers and Super Glue. Gritted teeth. White sterile bandages and steri-strips holding the perfectly straight edges of the cuts together.

After, with the help of a few pills, he had fallen asleep in seconds. A dark dreamless slumber, twelve hours of nothingness and for that he is glad. But this morning, everything aches. Muscles that had been tensed slowly relaxing.

He leans against the pillow and she passes him the warm bowl of porridge. The bland mush is the only thing he can stomach; the events of the day before have left him weak and nauseous.

He eats it slowly, feeling her eyes on him. He remembers the evening just gone. Jamie's haunted eyes. Adam trying to block out the events of the day before. Romilly trying to persuade both of them to get medical attention. Physically there wasn't anything wrong with Jamie, and Adam persisted in his refusal to let anyone near him. Mentally, he knows they both have a long way to go.

Jamie told him what happened to Marsh. Quietly, they waited for news. And soon, it arrived: he had died. Massive blood loss; the knife had gone in from behind, nicking his heart. There was nothing they could do on site, and even less by the time they got to the hospital. Everyone had been notified, including his family: Detective Chief Superintendent John Marsh was dead. Killed in the line of duty.

Adam had stared for a long time at the official notice sent to his phone. Despite everything his boss had done for him – his unwavering support, his mentorship, and in the end, his friendship – he didn't think he'd ever known Marsh's first name.

And Adam knows there is still more to be done. Maggie has been charged with multiple murders, detained in police custody until her appearance at the magistrate's court on Monday. But the case against her has to be carefully constructed: exhibits collated, mental health assessment, interviews. But not by him; he's a victim now. His own statement needs to be recorded, entered into evidence.

'Will you go?' Romilly asks quietly, interrupting his thoughts.

He looks at her, then puts the bowl to the side, appetite gone. The request came in last night: Dr Elijah Cole wants to see him. Only him. Alone.

Heated debates had flown up and down the chain of command. Should they bow to a murderer's wishes? Was it safe? Was it worth the risk, even if he had information vital to the case? In the end the decision had come back: it was up to Adam. He is a senior detective, as well as a victim. He would have the final say.

But he hadn't had to think for long.

'Yes,' he replies to Romilly. 'For my own sanity. I need to confront him, see what he wants to talk about. Otherwise, I'll always wonder.' He sees her face, lost in thought. 'Is that okay?' he asks slowly.

She sighs deeply, then presses her lips together, looking down at her hands. He notices she's shaking.

'Yes,' she says at last. She looks as if she's going to cry. 'But first, we have to talk. And someone else needs to be involved.'

Chapter 74

There were four of them in the end. The dead girls. Grace, Rebecca, Claire, and Nicola. She hadn't known their names until their happy faces shone out of the front pages of every national newspaper. At the time, she could only identify them by their screams, their begging. The drag marks they left on the lawn. Their hands clawing the mud as he pulled them into the shed.

Romilly sits in the warm sitting room, the fire burning in the hearth, the Labrador snoring. She has a cup of tea in her hands, but she doesn't sip from it.

A detective sits in front of her, his eyes intent, listening. He's older than she remembers, but it was nearly thirty years ago. He must be in his early-sixties now. On the other side of her, is Adam. He waits, silent. She can still see the ravages of the previous day: his face pale, the cut red and raw, black and green bruises on his forehead.

In the night, while he slept, she heard him murmur, his head thrashing from side to side, in the grip of a horrific scene playing out in his dreams. In the morning he said he didn't remember, but he will, she knows. He will.

But right now, it is about her.

'I knew, Detective Shepherd,' she says. Neither man speaks, waiting for her to continue. 'But you were aware of that, weren't you?'

He nods.

'It must have been the second girl to be abducted. Rebecca? Was that her name?' Another slow nod. 'I heard his car coming back, and the garden gate being opened.'

Romilly remembers, all too clearly. The shine of the moon, lighting up the garden as if caught in floodlights. Her father coming around the back, something over his shoulder. Something heavy, unwieldy. And then she'd realised: it had a head. And a long flow of hair. It moved, struggled, but her father held tight. He carried it to his outhouse, and then they were gone. She waited, but he didn't emerge. Confused, she went back to bed.

In the morning she thought she must have dreamt it. Her father sat at the breakfast table, his coffee and bran flakes in front of him as usual.

'Did you go out last night?' she asked.

He stared at her. 'What makes you think that?'

No denial.

'I thought . . .' She shook her head. 'Nothing.'

But it played on her mind all day. And when she got home from school she went out to the outhouse and pulled at the door. It was locked. She'd never known it locked before. She tried to look through the windows, but they were covered. She listened: nothing. She frowned and went back to the house.

After that, she kept a lookout at night. He would go

to the shed, but always by himself. He'd stay there for a few hours, then walk back. Slowly. Relaxed.

'What are you doing out there?' she asked.

'Carpentry.'

'Why is the door locked?'

He turned to her and grabbed her hands in his, so hard it hurt. 'You keep away, you hear me?' he said. Then, calmer: 'There are tools in there. Things you could hurt yourself with.'

But it wasn't her being hurt.

The second girl she saw screamed as he carried her across the lawn. She fought and bit and got away. She made it halfway back before he caught up with her: his hands grabbing her hair, pulling her to the ground. Romilly watched as he punched her in the head, over and over, then carried her, unconscious, to the shed. She stood, her hands gripping her windowsill, her feet numb, waiting. Waiting for him to come back out.

And an hour later, he did. He walked halfway across the lawn, and then, as if sensing her, he stopped. He looked up to her window, straight into her eyes.

She gasped and ran to her bed, pulling her duvet up over her head. She lay, shivering, as she heard the back door close, his footsteps on the stairs, then her door creak open. She felt his weight on her mattress, sitting down slowly next to her.

'Romilly,' he said.

She didn't move.

'Romilly.' The duvet was slowly pulled away. She looked at him with wide, frightened eyes.

The curtains were still open, and the moonlight cast a dim glow across his face. His cheeks were streaked with mud, and dirt, and something else she didn't like to think about.

'Romilly. What did you see?'

She shook her head quickly. 'Nothing.'

'You saw me with that girl, didn't you?' He didn't wait for her to answer. 'Well, okay then,' he said calmly. 'What happens next is up to you.'

'Up to me?' she gasped.

Cole nodded. 'You're old enough now to make your own decisions. You know what you saw. So call the police. Have them look, arrest me. That's what you should do, isn't it?'

It felt like a test; she stayed silent.

He shrugged. Nonchalantly. 'But what would happen to you, Romilly? Where would you go?'

She knew the answer to this one. She'd listened to him talk at the dinner table; about poor children, with nowhere else to live. They ended up in places where they were beaten, abused. Made to sleep in cold dormitories. Even at the age of eleven, he'd told her the horror stories: of the 'parties' where men who like little girls paid to fuck, finger, and destroy young delicate bodies.

'Into care,' she murmured.

'And you don't want that, do you?' he asked. She shook her head.

'So what are you going to do?'

'Keep quiet.'

'Pretend it didn't happen,' he said with finality. He stood up, watched her for a moment, lying silent in her bed. Then he leaned down and gave her a kiss on her forehead.

So, at night, from then on, she kept her eyes closed. She

didn't look when she heard the slam of his car door, the noise of a shovel in soil at the dead of night. But in her dreams, she heard their cries. Her subconscious at work, imagining them there, tied up. Dead, unconscious. The rest she didn't know. She was eleven. She hadn't heard about anal rape, about fisting and foreign objects and forced oral sex. About wrists and ankles so damaged by their shackles they grew infected and maggot-ridden. Women so traumatised by their pain and torture they slipped into catatonic states.

He would tease her. On the mornings after he was out there.

'Did you sleep well last night, Romilly?' he would say. And she'd nod.

'Yes, Dad.'

'Nothing woke you?'

'No. Nothing.'

The detective sits silent as Romilly talks. The cup of tea is cold in her hand. The Labrador stirs from his position by the fire and goes over to her chair, resting his heavy head on her lap, looking up at her with brown, baleful eyes. She places a hand in his soft fur and realises she's crying.

She looks over to Adam. His mouth is turned down, his eyes fixed on hers. She can't tell what he's thinking. Just after they got married, she thought about telling him. But what would he have said? How would he have reacted to the knowledge his new wife had been complicit in her father's murders? She'd have lost him then, as she might do now. But she can't hold it anymore. Locked up inside her.

'What happened?' Adam's voice comes out hoarse, and he clears his throat. 'That day?'

She knew the keys were a test. Left there on the kitchen table when she got back from school. Her father wasn't careless; he wasn't stupid. She picked them up, held them in her hand. Five keys in all, different sizes. She put them down again, then paused, looking over to the shed.

A week ago, there'd been another burial. Another patch of disturbed ground in the garden.

And here were the keys.

Without thinking, she picked them up and walked quickly down the garden. With shaking hands she put them into the locks, one by one. The outer door first, three locks, click click click. Then inside.

She ran her finger over the notches carved in the door-frame. XX, XIX, and XVIII. Three dead, but she didn't know that then.

Here, she could hear noises. Rustling, quiet taps on the floor. Voices, frantic whispering. It chilled her body, making her shiver. But still she pressed on. She had to know. The last few locks, and she pulled open the door.

At first, she couldn't make anything out. It was dark inside, and her eyes took a moment to adjust to the black. But she could smell it. Sour sweat, shit, piss. And something else.

Death.

Then, a voice.

'Please.' Whispered softly, through the dark. Romilly blinked. There was a figure there, a body. No, two. Entwined together on the mattress.

'She's sick. She needs to get out of here.'

412

A woman looked at her, then slowly pulled herself to her feet. White shining eyes in a blackened face. Clothes, no more than rags. Skinny limbs, lank greasy hair. She took a step towards Romilly, and with that, the fear tore through her.

The woman looked inhuman; her face was little more than a skull with skin, jutting cheekbones, teeth missing. Dried blood, dirt, who knows what, coating her body. Metal circled her wrists, limiting her movement as she held her hands out, pleading, towards Romilly.

She leapt backwards, through the door. She pushed her full weight into it, closing it and pulling the locks shut again.

'Please!' the woman begged through the wood. 'Please!' then a thud. Two more. Banging, screaming, frantic cries, pleading for Romilly to open the door, to call the police to get help.

But Romilly did nothing. She turned and closed the outer door, locking it tight. She ran back down the garden, placing the keys where she found them on the table. And when her father came home, he picked them up.

'Did you go in?' he asked.

'No,' she replied.

'What made you call the police?' the detective asks.

'I saw her in my dreams,' Romilly replies. 'Begging. Covered in blood. I woke up crying. The same way I have every day since.'

The detective nods solemnly.

'But I was confused. When you interviewed me. I knew I'd fucked up.' Romilly talks faster now, her brain desperate to expel the information after all this time. 'I said that I

413

saw the keys when I came home from school and I knew you'd realise I waited before calling the police. So I lied. Over and over again. I said I had no idea what he was doing.'

'But you did.'

'Yes. All of it. And I did nothing.'

The room is still. The fire is starting to burn out, needing another log, but nobody moves.

'Those women are dead because of me.'

'No.'

She looks up. Adam's spoken: firm and loud.

'No, Romilly,' he repeats. 'You were eleven. A child. You were scared, confused. Those women are dead because your father killed them—'

'But if I'd called the police sooner?'

'Maybe,' Adam replies. 'But you were in a terrible situation. Your mother was dead, you had nobody else. You loved your father.'

Romilly starts to cry again. 'I did,' she says through her tears. 'But maybe—'

'DCI Bishop is right,' Detective Shepherd says. 'We knew you were lying to us. And we wanted you to tell the truth. But not so we could arrest you, or anything like that. We wanted to get you help. We didn't want you to spend the rest of your life with this hanging over you. Because this sort of thing . . .' He pauses. Shakes his head. 'It can screw you up. It's a miracle you've turned out the way you have, frankly.'

'I've had a lot of therapy,' Romilly says, laughing through her tears.

But the detective's face is serious. 'You would have needed it.' He leans forward, taking her hands in his. 'Thank you for coming here today, Romilly,' he says. 'Thank you for telling me.'

'I still think about her,' Romilly says. 'That woman I saw. It was Grace, wasn't it? Grace Summers?'

Shepherd nods.

She almost doesn't dare to ask. But it's out there now, she might as well hear it all. 'Do you know when she died?'

Shepherd sighs. 'That night. The PM estimated TOD as between eleven and two a.m. Blunt force trauma to the head.'

Romilly frowns. 'But that's not . . . It can't be.' She stops. It was a long time ago, maybe her memory has faded, maybe she's wrong. She remembers sitting, waiting in the dark. To hear the noise she dreaded: the squeak of the back door, the soft tread of her father's footsteps heading down the garden. But he'd stayed in the house, all night.

Maybe she'd fallen asleep. Maybe he'd gone out another way. The fact remained: Grace Summers died. Because Romilly hadn't called the police soon enough.

The detective sits forward again. 'Please try and move on, Romilly. Have a life of your own. That's one happy ending I'd love to see.'

'And that's it?' Romilly says. 'You're not going to arrest me? It's over.'

He nods. 'It's over.'

She feels a wave of relief, as if a weight has been lifted from her shoulders. And that's when she realises. She isn't like her father. She isn't like her half-sister. She loves; she cares; she has empathy for the people in her life. Sure, she's a bit confused, a bit fucked up, but who wouldn't be, given the circumstances? The thought of what Maggie was doing disgusts her. She was horrified when she found out about Elijah. These are the natural reactions of a normal human being.

She is not a killer.

She looks over to Adam. And for the first time in days, he's smiling.

DAY 10

MONDAY

Chapter 75

The case is closed, their suspect is in prison, but there is still work to be done. Jamie knows he shouldn't be here. The usual reasons: it's too personal, conflict of interest, accusations of evidence tampering too easy to throw around. But they're down on senior officers. Especially now Marsh has gone.

The death of their detective chief superintendent has blindsided the whole team. Everyone is in, but the atmosphere is hushed, dampened down. Jamie keeps expecting him to walk in the door, demand coffee, bark at a DC he didn't think was working hard enough. But despite his blunt manner, John Marsh was a cop's cop.

The funeral is scheduled for a week's time. Jamie will go, along with most of the station, he's sure. They'll have to put someone on duty, but everyone will want to pay their respects. Jamie saw Marsh's husband arrive the day before, and stood in the corridor, watching him. He was tall, lean like Marsh, with a receding hairline and a full greying beard. His head was tilted to the floor, his hands gripped each other one way, then another, as if he wasn't sure what to do with them. Jamie remembered those early hours only too well – the desolation, the confusion, the loneliness, feelings that still haunt him – and he stepped forward to greet him.

'DS Jamie Hoxton,' he said, holding out his hand. 'I worked for your husband.'

The man shook it warmly. 'Anthony Marsh-Beckett. John talked about you. I'm sorry about your wife.'

Jamie mumbled a thank you. He's still not sure how to respond when people say that.

'Were you there? When John died?'

'Yes.' Jamie didn't mention the fact he'd barely thought about Marsh at all, so blinded by the rage of having Pippa's killer in front of him. All he'd been able to think about was making this woman suffer. Inflicting pain. Making her pay.

'He was a great man. A brilliant copper.'

Marsh-Beckett nodded. 'He lived for this job.'

'He talked about you, and your kids. That night.' The man's head went up quickly; he looked at Jamie with eager eyes. 'He said he was going to retire, to spend more time with you all.'

Anthony laughed, bittersweet. 'And I'm sure he meant it too. But he was a policeman, through and through. It would have driven him mad, being sat at home.'

There was a slamming of doors behind them, a hurrying of footsteps, and the chief constable appeared next to them. He stopped dead as he saw Jamie.

'I'm sorry to keep you waiting, Mr Beckett.'

'It's fine.' He smiled at Jamie. 'DS Hoxton was keeping me company.'

The CC directed a warning look at Jamie, then ushered him away. To talk politics, no doubt. To smooth away possible lawsuits, bad feeling from the fact that a senior detective had been murdered at his own nick, by the very killer they were searching for.

Jamie sighs and turns his thoughts back to his paperwork. There's a lot that needs to be done before Maggie Clarke can go to trial. The evidence needs to be catalogued; every scrap recorded precisely so she can be convicted without a shadow of a doubt from the jury. And there's such a lot of it. The fingerprint found at Wayne Oxford's house is gone, smudged out of all recognition in Maggie's own lab. But others have been found: at Ellie's, in Jamie's own hallway. Blood is present on clothes at Maggie's house, blood Jamie knows will match the woman killed at the park, the victims found on the wasteland. Not to mention the horrific samples in the fridge.

They are combing through the VW Transporter now and will no doubt find hair, skin, DNA. She hadn't even tried to be careful. Jamie assumes she only needed to bide her time long enough to complete her mission. Answer Cole's whims. She hadn't cared about her own future.

He knows any defence lawyer worth his salt will claim insanity. That she didn't have the *mens rea* to know the nature and quality of the act she was committing. And it's not so hard to believe. Her mind is certainly diseased, even before you consider the corruption from Cole. But while this was all going on, she'd carried on going to work, and none of them had noticed a thing.

He turns his attention to the list of names in front of him. The visitor logs from HMP Belmarsh, and Maggie's name crops up, again and again. She'd gone to see him at least once a month for five years. Obsessed, reverent, a disciple. Why had nobody flagged it?

But she hadn't been the only one. He scans the list: a few coppers from the case, Cole's lawyers – visits getting less frequent as time passes. Then a collection of other names, ones he doesn't recognise. He types the first into the PNC. No record, so he enters it into Google. A few random matches, then a link to a true crime website. So that's it. Sick fans, wanting to meet their idol. He frowns and picks up a pen, making a note for someone to follow up, ensure there are no red flags. They don't need more acolytes right now.

He runs his highlighter across the line, marking the name that needs a background check, then is aware of someone standing by his side. He looks up and blinks in surprise at DCI Cara Elliott, a person of infamy and gossip, from the other nick, whom he's never met before today.

'I'm sorry to disturb you,' she says. Her voice is soft. Sad. 'But they said you were in charge.'

'I . . . I guess,' he replies. 'In the absence of anyone better.'

She smiles, no more than a flicker. 'I wanted to come in and help. To . . . you know. Pull the investigation together.' She stops and stares resolutely at the table for a moment. 'Marsh . . . he was a good boss. He was good to me.' She looks at Jamie again and there are tears in her eyes. 'Anything I can do. Please. What do you have there?'

'Prison logs. Names that need to be checked.'

'Sure. Whatever.' She sits down at the desk next to his and holds out her hand.

'But you're a DCI,' Jamie says. 'You can't be doing paperwork.'

420

'Not today. It's my day off.' She waits, and after a moment he hands her the list.

There's no pause. No request for coffee. She just boots up the computer next to her, logs in and starts tapping away. Slow, methodical work. He glances her way. Her dark hair is tied back in a neat ponytail at the nape of her neck. She's wearing faded denim jeans and a checked shirt, a delicate silver chain resting on her collar bone. To Jamie she seems okay, not the destroyed mess he's heard about from the rumours around the station.

'DCI Elliott?' he says, and she looks up, her light brown eyes on him. 'Do you mind me asking, how did you cope? After?'

He doesn't need to give any more detail; she knows what he's referring to. Her gaze slides back to the list in front of her, but her pen pauses on the paper.

'I didn't, I guess,' she says after a moment. 'I went back to work. Didn't stop. I thought if I carried on that somehow things would be okay.'

'And they weren't?'

She laughs softly under her breath. 'No. After something like the Echo Man—' She looks up at the incident room. 'Like this,' she adds. 'It's a lot to process. That another human being could act in this way. Inflict so much violence and hatred and pain. Especially when it's so personal.'

She looks back to Jamie. 'Take some time, DS Hoxton,' she says. 'That would be my advice. To think. To grieve. To feel and work through everything that's happened. And remember the good times. The ones we love are more than the events that befell them. More than the things they did to hurt you.' Jamie knows she's not talking about Pippa now; she's gripping her pen so hard her knuckles have

421

blanched white. 'There are the good memories too,' she continues softly. 'They were loved for a reason.'

'And how are you doing now, Cara?'

She looks up suddenly, staring at him for a moment. Jamie worries he's overstepped the mark. 'I'm sorry, DCI Elliott, I shouldn't have—'

'No, it's fine.' She smiles, more warmly this time and her face is transformed. 'It's just no one ever asks me that. Everyone always assumes . . .' She sighs. 'I don't know, quite honestly. At the beginning, I was numb. And then I was angry. Fucking furious. At everyone and everything.' She makes a quiet snort. 'You can hardly blame me, but I wasn't pleasant to be around. And now? Now I have hope. Hope that my children will stay ignorant to everything that happened that day. Hope that I will get a full night's sleep. And hope that the good in people will always triumph over the bad, and that I'll be able to continue to do my job.'

'I hope that too, DCI Elliott. Maybe we'll even get to work together one day.'

She blinks hard, as if pulling herself from a trance, then looks at him and smiles. 'Maybe. And how is DCI Bishop? He's at home, or in hospital?'

'Yeah, at home. He's doing okay, thank you.'

She nods, gives a tight smile, and goes back to the list.

Jamie doesn't mention that Adam is on his way to Belmarsh. Visiting the person behind your own kidnapping and attempted murder probably isn't high on the list of advice for self-care after trauma, but he understands why Adam is going.

'What if he shares something important?' Adam said last night when Jamie voiced his concerns. 'What if he wants to speak to me for a reason?'

The two of them were sitting on Romilly's sofa, *Countryfile* on the television in the background.

Jamie shook his head. 'He wants to mess with you. Fuck with your mind.'

'Then so be it,' Adam replied. 'I'll go on the off chance he says something. Anything. It's worth it, surely?'

Jamie let it go, knowing there was no point in arguing with his stubborn boss. He's moved in to Romilly's along with Adam, and she's said he's welcome to stay as long as he wants. But Jamie knows that it won't be long before they'll need their space. And then what? He has no wish to go home. To sleep under that roof, in that room, in that bed. He'll sell it all. Start again, slowly, painfully, without Pippa.

So, for the moment, he'll stay with Adam. Look out for each other, although neither will admit that's what they're doing, male pride as it is. And Romilly is good company too. Jamie's glad they're back together; they always had a symmetry about them, a connection that can't be explained. He heard them last night, laughing, the quiet murmur of their voices. He felt it as a physical pain in his gut, knowing he had that with someone, and she's gone.

But for now, back to this. He picks up the second page of the visitor's log and starts highlighting names again for Cara to check. And he pauses on one. It feels familiar.

He types it into Google and a well-known face pops up. She's got the same name as a celebrity, that's all, he tells himself, highlighting it and moving on to the next. But something niggles. He puts his pen down again and stares at it frowning. Where does he know it from? A case file? It'll come; he'll remember. He'll return to it later.

His phone beeps; it's Adam, from the prison. Jamie

imagines him pausing outside the high brick wall, readying himself to face Elijah Cole. The serial killer. His father-in-law. Who wanted him bleeding and tortured and in pain.

I'm going in now, Adam writes.

Chapter 76

Cole is already seated at the table, his back to the door, as Adam is shown into the cold, bare room. Two guards stand in opposite corners, watching him carefully. Different guards; ones Adam hasn't seen before.

Adam sensed the difference the moment he entered the prison. All procedures were carried out exactly, no stages or processes missed. Complaints have been made; strongly worded recommendations passed down from on high. Cole won't have any privileges now: police officers have been killed, senior detectives among them. Jobs have been lost; letters written.

Cole looks up as Adam enters. He is handcuffed, his hands out in front of him, metal scratching against the Formica as he turns. He meets Adam's eyes. He smiles.

'I'm glad to see you, DCI Bishop,' he says. 'It's been quiet around here.'

Adam sits down slowly. Cole looks like he's aged ten years since Adam saw him only three days ago. How can it be that short a time? Cole looks tired, his skin sagging.

A day-old bruise sits around his eye, red and swollen, but Adam fails to conjure up any sympathy for how it got there. He's wearing prison issue uniform: oversized grey joggers, a grey sweatshirt. He looks withered and spent, hardly the ferocious killer Adam spent a sleepless night worrying about.

He hadn't known how he'd react to this moment. Face to face again with the man who masterminded this whole horrific plan. The blood and murder and manipulation. But now, he just feels calm. He wants answers, then to get the fuck out of here.

'Why did you do it, Elijah?' he says.

Cole smiles. 'Do what?'

Adam sighs theatrically, then puts his hands flat on the table, as if pushing himself up to leave.

'Okay, okay,' Cole says quickly. 'You want to talk, let's talk.'

'Why did you do it?'

'Boredom. Sadism. Because I could? You want a neat little reason tied up in a bow, DCI Bishop, but the truth is a lot more dull. I don't know. Maggie was always there, ready and waiting, so I took advantage to see what would happen.'

'How?'

Cole turns around and looks at the guard. The guard stares back, unblinking. 'Can we get some drinks? A nice coffee?' he asks. The guard looks at Adam.

'Fine, yes,' Adam replies wearily.

Elijah smiles. 'Excellent. Now we can talk properly. Civilised. And in a proper mug,' he shouts after him. 'None of this plastic crap.'

'Talk, Elijah.'

426

'Maggie. She was . . .' He looks up to the ceiling, thinking. 'She was always susceptible. Horribly abused after her own mother abandoned her – did you know about that?'

Elijah pauses for a response; Adam looks at him impassively, waiting.

'I requested her file, while I was still a GP,' Elijah continues, unabashed. 'A doctor needs to know patient history, a crap excuse but it worked. And it read like a horror story. When those foster parents were arrested she was covered in bruises. She had more than twenty healed fractures. She'd been starved, force-fed salt when she complained. That kid had been deliberately deprived of sleep, made to stand for hours facing a wall until she collapsed of exhaustion – that's the start in life Maggie had. And the people who did that to her will get out of prison before me, that's how fucked up our society is now.'

Adam doesn't reply. It seems even sadistic killers have their morals.

'Sandra brought her to the surgery for the first time when she was four. And I knew. The thought that she could hide who her father was? It was ridiculous.' He grins. 'She looked just like Romilly did at that age. And she was such a sweet kid. Confused. Starved of affection. I notice things like that, that desperation, need for love. And I gave it to her.'

'You abused her?'

'No. No, I didn't,' he says firmly. 'I'm no paedophile, Adam. But we played together. Hide and seek. Jigsaw puzzles. Silly games, that I would often play with Rom. Her attachment disorder was so pronounced a little went a long way.'

427

The guard comes in with two mugs of hot black coffee, putting them down on the table.

'Thank you,' Elijah says sweetly. He turns back to Adam. 'I'd already seen the signs. The tell-tale delusions, an early susceptibility to mental illness. She was fascinating.'

He takes a sip from his coffee, not looking away. 'She fixated onto things, people, even at that age. I'm amazed she was managing to hold down some semblance of normal life, frankly.'

Adam remembers what Jamie told him about the state of her house, the mess, the dirt. 'I'm not sure she was,' he replies. 'How did she know? That you were her father?'

'She didn't. But we'd already forged a friendship, so I wrote to her from prison, and she came to see me. Such love, such trust in her eyes. Even before I told her. After that, it was easy. She had my blood in her veins, a natural predisposition to violence. Just needed a few pointers in the right direction.'

It's hard for Adam to hide his disgust. But he needs to know the truth. 'What changed?' he asks.

'Her adoptive father died. That man was a major stabilising influence in her life. Incredible how much difference a loving parent can make.' Elijah looks up, smiling. 'But he died, six months ago, sudden heart attack, and from that moment I could see how Maggie was coming apart at the seams. I was more important than ever. I was the only man left in her life.' He laughs. 'The only man, of course, apart from you.'

Adam recoils. 'Me?' he growls. 'What the fuck did I have to do with it?'

'I convinced her that Romilly was still in love with you, despite the divorce. That including you in our little plan would be the ultimate revenge for what she had done. In Maggie's head, Romilly is the reason I'm in here. The reason we can't be together – in the outside world.'

Adam feels the disgust swell. He swallows it down. 'You told her to kill.'

'Yes. And who.' He lifts a hand, cuffs jangling, and points at Adam. 'She was always obsessed with signs. Little pieces of information the universe would throw out to guide her way. And from that I knew I could complete my plan.'

Adam shakes his head. This was fucked up, too fucked up. 'But why? Why try to get to twenty?'

Elijah ignores his question. 'Did you do what I thought you would? After you were last here?'

Adam stays silent. He knows Cole's referring to his patient files, now an investigation of their own. Detectives slowly disseminating information, cross-checking patient notes against cause of death. It was long and drawn out and boring.

'We're looking,' he replies.

Elijah nods with satisfaction. 'I knew you'd go there. To the old surgery. I knew all she'd have to do was wait.'

'For me.'

'Yes. For you, Adam.' His eyes go down to Adam's arms, now covered by his shirt. He reaches forward slowly; the guard takes a step and stops him. He smiles again, the leer of a snake, of an alligator denied his kill. 'How far did she get, Bishop?' he says slowly. 'With her needles and her scalpel? Did you scream? Cry? Before they saved you?'

Adam feels the cold again, the dread returning to his bones. The flash of metal, the steel of the blade against his skin.

'How did you know?'

'About your phobia? I didn't. Maggie told me – after those routine jabs. But how much you were affected . . . We hadn't known it would work so well.' Elijah continues with a grin. 'And I rather liked the idea. What she did. No father likes their son-in-law, do they?'

'Most fathers-in-law don't arrange for them to be tortured!' Adam shouts. Then he stops. He closes his eyes for a second. He will not give him the satisfaction of letting him see his fear. He will not.

He needs to focus on why he's there. The victims. Justice.

'How many are there, Elijah?' he says.

The doctor chuckles softly. 'Are you scared, Bishop? That it's more than three? That it's hundreds, like Shipman?' Adam stays quiet and Elijah sighs. 'Do you know how long I was a doctor? Before they arrested me?'

Adam glares; he's refusing to play his game.

'Thirteen years. Thirteen years of saving lives, Bishop. Do you know how many people that equates to? Because I don't. It must be hundreds. Maybe even thousands of people I helped.'

'So what?'

'So – that must work in my favour, surely?'

'It's not a fucking get out of jail free card,' Adam explodes. This man's logic, it's insane. 'You don't get a free pass because you diagnosed someone's cancer! You kill and rape and torture even one woman and that's it, game over.'

'Maybe so.' Elijah nonchalantly tilts his head to one side, considering. 'But I think I should get some credit. I could have killed far more.' He meets Adam's disbelieving stare. 'Oh, calm down. You can sleep easy at night.'

He lifts his hand, his fingers in a fist. Then slowly he raises one by one.

'Ethel Henshaw,' he says, the first finger pointing skywards. 'Vera Fox, and Fred Powell.' He stops. 'Three. As I said.' He shrugs. 'I soon learnt it wasn't my thing. Have you ever killed anyone, DCI Bishop?'

'No.'

'Ever wanted to?' He laughs. 'Don't answer that. I'm sure you have. But you're too weak a man to go through with it. It takes someone made of sterner stuff, to take a life.'

'Who was the first, Elijah?'

'Joanna. Romilly's mother.'

Adam takes a sharp breath in.

'Not like that,' Cole carries on quickly. 'All legal. All above board. She died from her cancer. It doesn't count. But I was there. I helped her, as her husband, her doctor. I made sure she didn't suffer. And until that point, until Joanna died, I made sure I held it together, suppressed any urges. For her. I didn't want to destroy our family, like my father had.'

'You raped Sandra Poole.'

Elijah shrugs. 'Oh, that. That's nothing. I could have done far worse. That feeling, when you're there, on the edge, as they take their last breath. It's . . . almost divine, Adam. Like you're close to God, in that brief moment. So I thought I'd give it another try.' He frowns. 'But it's not the same. These old things, wasting away. Don't know why Harold bothered. Where's the fun?'

Adam waits. What this man is saying, his flippancy, it's disgusting. But he can tell Elijah wants to talk and as much as it turns his stomach, this is their best chance of knowing the extent of Cole's crimes.

431

Elijah turns his eyes onto Adam. Black and dark. 'Those girls. Now that's what I discovered I enjoyed. But not the act of keeping them, or killing them. It was the omnipotence. It was intoxicating.' His eyes gloss over, lost in the memories. 'The edge of survival. The total control over those girls. What they would do for me . . .'

Adam cuts him off. 'So why did you leave the keys?'

'For Romilly to find?' He laughs. 'Same reason. I wanted to see how much I could push her. Like father, like daughter. Turns out the apple didn't fall so far from the tree. She kept quiet, little Romilly. I was proud of her. For keeping my secret for so long.'

'Romilly is nothing like you,' Adam hisses through clenched teeth. 'She is good, and strong. She knows what you did was wrong and has spent her entire life trying to atone for it.'

'But don't you wonder, Adam? How much like me she already is?' Cole leans forward across the desk, closer. 'Nature or nurture? Doesn't it prey on your mind when you talk about having children? Because I see that wedding band is back on your finger. You can't possibly have got married again so quickly, so it must be more symbolic. And good for you both. But when something happens – if your child ever has an accident, falls, bangs its head – wouldn't you wonder? Because I did. About myself. Did you read any of the books, Adam, when you first met Romilly? About me and my past?'

'A few.'

'A few!' Cole laughs. 'I bet you did! Take in all that information about your father-in-law, about the woman you'd married. But most of them were rubbish. Made up crap to fill in the gaps.'

'Are you saying your childhood was perfect?' Adam bites back.

'Of course not. My father was an abusive drunk. My mother, a killer. And I didn't blame her, not for one second.' Cole's voice gets almost wistful now. His eyes drift away from Adam, looking into middle distance. 'But what he did. To her. To me.'

He pauses, the clank of chains as he pulls the sleeve up on his jumper. He reveals his forearm, the skin puckered, a mess of tiny round scars. 'Payday, the twentieth of the month. Always. And he'd get drunk. He'd take that money and he'd go to the pub with his mates. Drinking until the early hours. I'd hear him come home, the shouting outside. The front door banging as he kicked it closed. And that's when the fun started, DCI Bishop. Right then.'

Adam doesn't dare move, listening to Cole talk.

'Because – the lack of money, my mother taking odd jobs, whatever she could, to keep food on the table. Mending my school clothes, over and over again. That was all fine. It was payday we dreaded. He'd go for her first. His slow heavy footsteps on the stairs, the noise as he opened their bedroom door. He'd pull her out of bed – she was never asleep, waiting for him – and I'd run to my door, open it a gap, and watch him drag her down the stairs by her hair. Sometimes he'd throw her down, give her a kick for good measure. But she always tried to keep quiet. For me. To protect me. Because the more noise she made, the more he'd punish her. "Don't wake the neighbours," he'd say.'

Elijah pauses. He takes a long swallow from his coffee mug.

'On the best days, he'd rape her. Even as a kid, I could tell what was going on. That rhythmic thud, her stifled

433

cries. But if he was too drunk, if he couldn't get it up? That's when it got really bad.' He runs his finger along his forearm, as if seeing the scars for the first time. 'He would tell me to hide. And then he'd count. Down, from twenty. Looking for me around the house. A simple child's game. Coming, ready or not. There was one rule – the longer I managed to stay hidden, the lesser the punishment. Do you know how well I did, that night, DCI Bishop?' he asks. 'Can you guess?'

Adam feels saliva flood his mouth. He swallows. 'Not long,' he replies.

Elijah nods slowly. 'Not long at all. Dad got to seventeen before he found me. Seventeen. Seventeen times he sat there, in his favourite armchair, smoking those fags down to the butt. Seventeen times he stubbed them out on my arm. Can you guess how long that takes? All night. All fucking night. Hours of darkness, of hearing my mother cry. Begging him to leave me alone.' He shakes his head. 'But that wasn't the worst. He was creative. Experimental. Fifteen hours locked in a cupboard. Until my legs and my back cramped and throbbed with pain. Another time, the first, nine lashes with his belt. And the last.' He looks to the table. 'I made it to two. Two – when he found me. And do you know what he said he would do? Take two parts of my body. An ear, an eye. A finger.' He splays his hands out on the surface, fingers spread, and for the first time Adam notices the tip of his pinkie is missing. 'I thought it would be quick. It wasn't.' He pauses, lost in the pain of the memory. Then he looks up. 'But my father made one big mistake. He told my mother to fetch a better knife. A bigger one. To take out my eye. She did, and she killed him.'

He looks up, suddenly roused from the memories. 'That's the DNA in my blood, Adam. The DNA in Maggie Clarke. The DNA in your wife. That will be the DNA in your children.'

All while Cole has been talking, Adam has felt his breathing get faster, shallower. The panic. Everything he's wondered about Romilly, for so long. But he can't let this man get into his head, he can't. Everything that Cole is, that happened to him. It's not Romilly. It's not the woman he loves.

He's got the answers he came for. The final names of his victims. He knows Elijah will never be released. He'll die in here. Rot, alone, for the rest of his life.

He pulls his shaking legs into a stand. Adam doesn't need to hear any more. He steps backwards, away from the chair, from the table, putting distance in between him and Cole. The repulsion is strong now, the desire to get away.

He hears the door being opened and walks quickly towards it. But in the doorway he stops, turning back to Cole.

'You didn't do it,' Adam says.

Cole swivels in his seat, fixing his eyes on him. 'Do what?'

'Get to twenty. Kill twenty. We stopped you, and Maggie. You weren't even close.'

Cole laughs, sudden and sharp. 'Do the maths, DCI Bishop. Time will tell. You'll see.'

Adam doesn't wait. He strides away down the corridor, barely breathing until he's out of the prison. He hears the slam of the heavy doors behind him as he collects his phone and his belongings; he takes deep lungfuls of cold clear air once he's outside.

He stands next to his car, rests his hands on the freezing metal of the bonnet, and takes slow breaths in. He'll never go back there again.

He gets in his car and pulls a scrap of paper out of the glovebox. With shaking hands, he writes down names and places, including the wasteland, ten days ago. Counting down from twenty.

20 to 17. The four women in the outhouse.

16 to 12. The victims at the wasteland.

Wayne Oxford – 11

Woman at the park – 10

He can barely manage to write the next few names. *Pippa.*

9

His three patients – down to 6

Ellie – 5

Marsh – 4

Three. There were three left. Three away from his goal of twenty. Three people he, or Maggie, would never kill.

Adam starts the engine and drives away. He puts the radio on. He swaps to music and turns it up loud. But he can still hear Elijah Cole in his head. His laugh. His mocking tone.

Time will tell, he had said.

You'll see.

Metal against metal, doors slamming shut. Voices shouting: angry, slurred swear words from the cell next door.

I've been moved to a women's jail. Out of custody at the police station – to here. A home from home. By myself. Quiet.

They say they're going to get someone to speak to me. About what? I wonder. They give me drugs, pills that dull and blur my head.

To pass the time I think about you. Your deep brown eyes, looking at me. Smiling, welcoming me into your arms. Will you smile now I have disappointed you? Now I have failed in my task?

But I tried, Elijah, I tried. You always knew what I needed. Whether it was a smile, or a tube of Smarties, or a squeeze of my shoulder. Or more, once I was older. The guards looked the other way; they gave us space in the visitation room. You knew how I liked it, as I begged for more. On my knees on the cold hard floor. Please.

I would have done anything for you. I still will.

I hear the guards in the corridor. The keys rattle at their waists, heavy from too many biscuits and cups of tea. The slot in the door opens; disembodied eyes stare. They narrow, a look of disapproval I see from everyone.

Even if I was allowed out, I know the other inmates would steer clear. They instinctively know who can be bullied, who should be respected, or left alone. For their own safety.

But I hear them whispering. Crazy. Weirdo. Cop killer. That last one with an air of respect, of trepidation.

The slow slam shut of the flap. A shout: 'All quiet in cell three.'

They will leave me. Not for long. For about ten minutes or so. But enough.

They've taken my bed sheets, my shoelaces, my belt. Anything that might be useful. But they don't know me. What I can do.

I am used to the blood. To the smell of it; the feel, claggy and warm. The way it dries on your skin, like a protective layer. It is unique to us all; it keeps us alive. Flowing in our veins.

That's why I kept some, from the victims. I had killed them, I owned them. I wanted to keep a piece as I completed my mission.

I lower my face to my forearm. I think of what I did to Adam, how I made him suffer. So he survived, but there's nothing I can do about that now. No point crying over spilt milk, as Elijah used to say.

It is only blood that is spilling now.

My arm is pale, warm. I run a cold finger down towards my wrist, tracing the soft blue lines, the fragility of my skin. I can almost smell the blood, hear it flowing in my veins. I place my lips against my arm. And then I bite.

The pain doesn't hit straight away.

At first, there's the sweet warm taste on my tongue. It flows thick and fast. It fills my mouth, running down my chin as I draw my teeth together, taking a large chunk of my own flesh. I spit it on the floor. My whole arm burns with a searing hot pain. Throbbing, pumping out blood. Tears roll down my face but I ignore them. I must do as you said. Nothing more, nothing less.

I turn my attention to my left wrist. The skin is dry, white, warm. But not for long. I tear at my own flesh with my incisors, making sure I go deep. I chew down to the network of veins and arteries, gnawing until I feel a lump of tissue in my mouth.

I know the job is done.

Even if they find me, there is no way to salvage this. My head is light, my body dizzy with pain. I lie down on the floor, smelling the ever-present disinfectant and the scent of the rage and ache and damage from the women that have come before me.

I have served my purpose. I have done what you asked.

I hear you, for one last time. Coming, you used to say.

But you have gone.

I have gone.

Ready or not.

DAY 14

FRIDAY

Epilogue

Adam rings the buzzer next to the gold name plate on the wall. Three names are listed, all followed by an impressive array of letters. People that know their shit. He hears the answering buzz and pushes the door open, walking through into the quiet lobby. There's nobody around.

It's a small room, with two blue armchairs in front of a coffee table. A typed sign is on the wall. *Please Wait,* it says. *We will be out soon.*

Adam takes a few nervous paces across the tiled floor, his hands in his pockets. He takes out his phone and sends a quick text.

I'm only doing this for you x, he writes.

The reply comes back immediately. *You're doing it for yourself. It'll be worth it. x*

Then a follow up. *But thank you. x*

He smiles. He imagines seeing Romilly later, recanting the story about how it went. This is the same place she goes to, the same counsellor. He never imagined himself at therapy, yet here he is.

To try and control his nervous pacing, he sits down on one of the chairs, crossing his legs and arms in front of him, first one way, then the other. He fidgets with his phone, clicking on social media sites he should be avoiding.

Reports of Maggie Clarke's death have been polarised. Good riddance. Saves the taxpayer money. Versus shouts of vengeance, of making her pay. His own thoughts are more complicated. He's glad she's gone, that she can't do harm to anyone anymore. But it bothers Adam that Cole got his wish – that she will be one of the twenty.

At least nobody will have to go through a trial. He worries about Jamie; he hears him pacing late at night, muffled sobs at three a.m. Adam knows it's not healthy for him to still be at work and is glad he will be back himself on Monday. There's only so long he can bear to be at home, watching daytime television and waiting for Romilly to get back from work.

The noise of a door pulls him away from his phone, and he turns to look. A woman walks out towards him, her high heels clicking. She holds her hand out and smiles.

'Adam?'

'Yes.' He shakes it.

'Come through. Sorry to keep you waiting.'

She gestures for him to go ahead, and he walks through the door into the darkened corridor, then towards the square block of light. He steps into a plain office. White walls, a bookshelf on one side and a desk on the other. There are two chairs facing each other in the middle of a brightly patterned rug.

The woman closes the door behind him. She's dressed in a grey suit, a basic white shirt underneath. Prim and proper. Simple silver jewellery on her hands, her brown hair tied tightly back in a bun. He guesses her age at mid-forties, maybe older.

'Please, take a seat,' she says, pointing towards the chair, and he does.

'It's quiet,' he says, making conversation to fill the silence.

'My colleagues are out today,' she replies. 'No other patients. We won't be disturbed.'

She picks up a clipboard from the desk and passes it to him with a biro. 'Just a simple form. Personal details for our records.'

'Sure,' he replies. He writes in his name, his address.

'You seem nervous,' she says. She's watching him as he fills in the form.

'Yes.' Telephone number, date of birth.

'I won't bite.' He looks up, she's smiling. He manages a small smile back.

Emergency contact details. *Dr Romilly Cole,* he writes, feeling the warmth grow. Relationship. He thinks for a second. What should he write? More than ex-wife. More than girlfriend. It's hard to put into words what's happening between them now. *Spouse,* he writes. Maybe they will be again.

'Is this a conflict of interest?' he asks. 'My wife is a patient of yours.'

She shrugs. 'Let's have a preliminary chat, and then we'll see. I can always refer you to one of my colleagues if we both think that's best.' She folds her hands in her lap. 'So what brings you here today?'

He hasn't finished filling in the form, but now rests it on his knees.

'I have a phobia of needles,' he replies.

She nods. 'And?'

442

'What do you mean?'

'You could have gone to see a hypnotist about that. And yet, here you are, in front of a psychotherapist. In front of me.'

He pauses. He looks away from her face, around the room. At the books on the shelf, the certificates on the wall. Can he trust this woman? She sweeps a strand of hair off her face and the gesture feels familiar.

'Have we met before?' he asks.

'I don't think so.'

'Have I interviewed you? Perhaps through my work? I'm a detective.'

'Definitely not then.' She pauses. 'Do you always deflect away from the important questions, Adam?'

He smiles. 'Yes. Yes, I do,' he replies. But it's not just that. Something about her. It's niggling. He pushes the feeling away. It's that you don't want to be here, he tells himself. Stop looking for excuses.

'My wife – my ex-wife – says I have a problem with trust. With letting people get close to me.'

'And would you agree with her assessment of you?'

Adam thinks about Jamie. How he struggled to be there for his best friend. How he pushed Romilly away – and nearly ended up dead because of it.

'Yes. That's probably true. Do you think that's something you can fix?'

She smiles gently. 'Therapy is not designed to fix what is broken. It is there to make what is cracked, beautiful again. So the light can shine through.'

The phrase resonates slightly in Adam's mind. He frowns. Then he points to the form on his lap. 'Should I finish this?'

'Sorry. Yes, do.'

One final question: *Therapist's Name*. Adam feels his mind blank and glances up to the certificate on the wall. *Dr Catherine Jones*. He writes it in capitals on the form.

Something sparks in his brain, synapses firing in recognition. He pushes his eyes shut, then looks up and stares at the woman.

'Is something the matter?' she asks evenly.

'No, it's just . . . I'm sure I've met you before.'

She shakes her head slowly. 'I would have remembered, DCI Bishop.'

It all comes back in a flash. Standing next to the bar, the smell of sweat, of beer. Her hand down his trousers, her lips against his neck. It had been dark, her hair wild, her face heavily made-up. But it was her. His head snaps up but he stays sitting. A prickle runs through his whole body. He feels her eyes on him, forcing himself to stay calm.

'You remember me,' she says. A statement.

'Yes.'

'Do you do that often? Pick up women in bars?'

'Sometimes.'

'Closeness. Intimacy. But without the fear of rejection?'

He pauses. 'Yes.'

She smiles. 'See? Ten minutes in therapy, and we're already getting somewhere.'

This is wrong. He knows that. This is Romilly's therapist. It can't be coincidence she'd met him that night in the bar. She must have gone looking for him. Sought him out. But why?

'I know something about that too, Adam,' she continues. 'I look for men. Men I shouldn't be close to. Men that

444

are bad for me. Men that take advantage. Are you one of those, Adam?'

He thinks of Ellie. 'I don't want to be,' he replies slowly.

'That's what he thought too. He said he wasn't a bad man. That he'd take me home and look after me.'

Adam freezes. His muscles tense, his mouth goes dry.

'And he did, Adam. He put a roof over my head. Gave me food. Water. So I did what he asked. Unlike those other girls.'

Shit. *Fuck.*

'I survived.'

It's her. The fifth woman. The one that walked out of that outhouse of horrors, into the outside world. Court orders banned the showing of her photograph; she changed her name and disappeared.

Except she hasn't. She's here. Not dead, after all.

There's merely six foot between them. And she's small, slender. He could easily overpower her if he needed to.

'I went to visit him,' she continues. Her voice is quiet and cool. 'I missed him. How could I not? We were so close when we were together all those years ago. Every day I've been away from him since is agony.'

Adam blinks in surprise. 'But he kidnapped you. Locked you up. Raped you.'

'At first, I was scared of him. He said he would kill me, hurt me, if I didn't do what he said. But then he realised I didn't care. I had nowhere else to go. He gave me life.' She pauses, crossing one slim leg over the other, slowly. Considering. 'Those guys on the street,' she continues. 'That was rape. I didn't want to have sex with them, but I needed the money. For the heroin I pumped into my veins. All those men, those stinking desperate beasts, wanting to hump me like animals. For me to suck their dicks. They didn't care about me, as long as I did what I was paid to. But with him, it was different. I was loved. He saved me, got me clean. Kept me safe. And then they took him away.'

'You refused to testify at his trial,' Adam says, slowly realising the truth. This woman was brainwashed. All those months, locked away in that shed, and her allegiances turned.

'We chose them together. Elijah and I.'

'Chose who?'

'The victims. Drug dealer. Hooker. A husband who pretended to be a family man while cheating on his wife with prostitutes. The worst society could offer. And the people that had let us down. Lawyers. A teacher. A social worker.' She pauses. 'Police,' she says with a smile, and Adam feels a burn of hatred. 'He told me his story. What that man had done to him. Who could blame Elijah for what he's compelled to do? Twenty victims, in his father's name. Revenge on the people who didn't save us.'

'But those people were innocent,' Adam replies. 'What had Pippa Hoxton ever done to you?'

She ignores him. 'A cop came to his door. When Elijah was a child. The neighbours finally called 999 in response to his mother's screams. And what did they do? They had a beer with his father. Sat in the front garden. That's why he hates them. Me too. They never did anything to help me. Arrested me for solicitation. Then they took me away from him. From the only man who ever loved me.'

'Elijah Cole didn't love you,' Adam says in disbelief. 'He was using you.'

'I was his first.' She smiles, as if lost in a warm memory.

446

'And then he brought those other girls along. Screwed them in front of me. But he was only trying to make me jealous.'

Adam can't speak, horrified by the words coming out of this woman's mouth.

'I told him to lock them in those cages. I decided whether they could eat that day; if they could have a blanket to keep them warm at night. Sometimes he even brought me up to the house. To sit at his kitchen table and eat with him when his daughter was in bed. Like man and wife. It was his reward, his way of thanking me.'

Adam can barely dare to ask. 'For doing what?'

'For choosing who should be next. Who should die. Those women could only serve a purpose for so long, so when they became too sick, too pathetic . . .' She shrugs. 'But Grace. Christ, that woman never lost hope. Not even when *she* closed the door on us. She lost it then. Started shouting, pulling at her chains. Thought she'd take her hands right off, she was that determined.' She looks at Adam again. 'Do you know what that's like? To see freedom and have it taken away from you? I thought it would kill her. But she started shouting about getting out, making him pay. Testifying in court. Of course, I knew then that it couldn't happen.'

Adam tries to swallow but his spit is like sand. 'You killed her.'

'Whacked her around the back of the head with a bottle.' Her voice is cold, matter-of-fact. 'She went down without a fight. And I was right to. They came barely hours after that. Set me free, so they said.' Her face hardens. 'But all they did was take him away from me. We found a way to speak, eventually. You have no idea what that was like,

447

to see him again, at the prison. We were reunited. My Elijah.'

Adam's hands go to his mouth. He glances to the door, to the mobile phone he's left in his coat pocket in the hallway.

'He protected me. He never said a word. He loves me.'

'You need help, Catherine,' Adam says gently. 'I can help you.'

'You can't help me! You can't even help yourself, you useless man. Elijah was right, you aren't worthy of his daughter. You weren't then, and you certainly aren't now. You chased around for days after Maggie. A woman so deranged she thought that she could earn her father's love by killing those people. I was her therapist, too. That made things easy. Nurturing her madness until there was barely room for reality in her crazy brain.'

'But Catherine, look at yourself. You're successful. You're a Doctor of Psychology, you're living a normal life—'

'You call this successful? You call this normal?' Her face contorts, her body tenses with anger. She rips the front of her shirt open so forcefully the buttons ping off and bounce across the room. Adam can't help but wince. Her chest is a mass of slashes and bruises, scars, scratches, some partly healed, others red and sore around her bra. 'I do this. The only way I can control what's going on in my head. I tried to get help, and then when I couldn't, I tried to cure myself. But knowing what's wrong – putting a name to the PTSD, the borderline personality disorder, the reactive attachment disorder – doesn't help me know how to fix it.' Her hand has gone up to one of the cuts; she scratches at it without flinching. The scab comes away.

Blood pools around her nails. He watches with disgust, wanting to stop her but not daring to move.

She shifts in her seat, then pulls her arm out from behind her back. Adam fixes on it. A small knife, the silver blade pointed towards him.

He needs to get away. He needs to distract her. 'But why?' he asks. 'Why track me down to that bar? Why—'

'Fuck you? Curiosity.' Idly, she runs her finger down the blade of the knife. A line of red blooms on her fingertip; his stomach turns. 'You're all Romilly talks about. Maggie was obsessed. I wanted to know who the fuss was for.' She shrugs. 'Nothing special. But Romilly?' She looks up, a smile lighting up her face. 'She is fascinating. It wasn't hard to become her therapist. I approached her. I listened to her, sympathised, basic human connection. It's easy to look good when all the other counsellors had done was treat her like a scientific study. They wanted to write papers, can you believe that? Savages.' She points the tip of the knife at Adam again. 'And I know Elijah. I understand. That love.'

'What do you want, Catherine?' he says slowly. His body is taut in readiness.

'From you? Nothing. I am here to do as Elijah asked, that's all.'

Adam can barely bring himself to speak. 'And what did Elijah ask?'

She laughs again. 'What do you think?'

Adam forces himself to take a deep breath; he can feel his heart thumping hard. His gaze flickers from the knife to Catherine's face and down again.

'I know I won't be able to see him,' she says. 'Not now. What else do I have? If he's gone.'

449

She holds the knife out further, then stands up. Adam pushes backwards quickly, grabbing the chair and holding it in front of him as a defence. She takes a few steps towards him.

He considers his options. He could go for the knife, try to wrestle it out of her hand. Or go for the door, get out and trap her inside while he calls for backup. But she's in the way, blocking his exit. And there's no one around, no one will hear him if he shouts. It's just the two of them.

'I don't want to hurt you, Catherine. Give me the knife.'

He puts the chair down slowly, holding his hands out in front of him. He hopes to calm her but it has the opposite reaction.

She lunges forward, once, twice, Adam dodging her attempts. He's against the wall now, pinned into a corner. She goes for him again, and this time he manages to grab her wrist. But she smashes the heel of her other hand into his face, and his nose explodes in agony. He backs away from her, his eyes watering, blood pouring from his nose. He frantically wipes his eyes, trying to clear his vision, to see the knife.

She's still got it in her hand. But he can see red now, it's covered in blood.

He blinks and looks down; his hands are bloody. From his nose, from his . . . There's a dull ache in his side, and his gaze shifts to his stomach. A bloom of red is seeping out across his shirt, a rip in the cloth visible around it. He feels a disconnect, between what he is seeing and what he's feeling. Then a slow realisation. This blood, it's his.

His legs wobble slightly. His body feels strange, as if everything is moving in slow motion. His strength fades, and he sags to his knees.

'I stood by,' she snarls. 'I watched as Maggie carried out those murders. That mess, barely getting the job finished. I could have done so much better, but Elijah said no. He would need me later. I was more important.'

Catherine takes a step towards him; he helplessly holds his hands out, but he can't stop her. The blade hits his fingers, slicing to the bone. Another jab. He feels the knife go into his stomach again. Once. Twice. The pain shooting, red hot and biting as it slides through his flesh. He drops to all fours, his hands on the ground. He lifts his head weakly, watches as she steps backwards.

'I am more important,' she repeats. 'I was his first.'

Adam can't hold himself up any longer. His body gives way; he sinks to the carpet. 'You weren't, Catherine,' he slurs. 'You weren't his first.'

She frowns. 'What do you mean?'

Adam lies on his back. He feels his blood ebbing and he moves his hands down, a fruitless attempt to stop the bleeding. It seems to be coming from everywhere, the warmth smooth to his touch.

'His wife. Romilly's mother.' Talking is painful. The words come in short gasps. 'He loved her. Without her, he was nothing. She was the beginning. Not you.'

He looks up at her. Her face is pale, the knife still in her hand. He reaches out, trying to grab at something, anything, but his limbs feel heavy. Every movement is instilled with pain. He puts his bloody hands on the chair next to him and tries to haul himself up, but it's no good. He looks at the pool of scarlet on the floor around him. How much? he thinks. How long before I die?

'Call an ambulance, please,' he whispers. He looks up at her. She still has the knife in her hand. 'Please.'

451

'Don't resist it, Adam. Your life, it doesn't matter. Only your death. And mine.'

And Adam watches in horror as she holds the knife against her neck, and pulls.

Her pupils dilate with shock; the shower of blood is thick and powerful. It cascades in an arc, her heart pumping furiously as she drops to the floor next to him. Her limbs are tangled beneath her. Her head is pushed back, the wound to her neck a yawning mouth of blood. There was no hesitation, no lack of commitment – she's taken it almost to the bone, a jagged V of tendons and flesh and skin.

He tries again to move. His shirt is soaked, the carpet around him saturated. He feels his vision waver. Romilly knows where I am, he tells himself. When I don't come home, she'll know where I am. But he doesn't have that long. Minutes, maybe seconds.

He tries to lift a leg, to push himself across the floor, but nothing is working. He moves weakly. But there's no point. What can he possibly do? His chest is awash with blood, he feels it bubbling anew from the holes in his chest. He's so tired.

Oh, Milly, he thinks. He looks up at the ceiling, the white lightshade blurring in and out of focus. We came so close. I came so close. I'm so sorry.

He feels movement next to him. It's her, shifting help-lessly, the wound in her neck gaping. Her eyes close slowly.

And all he can think is:

two

He sees Romilly's face. He knows the importance of things now. Clarity. He moves his thumb on his right hand to the ring on his finger, feeling the hard platinum through the slick of his blood. I'm sorry. I tried. I love you. I'm so so sorry.

He hears a noise. A thud, bashing. Voices. Is it real, or is he imagining it? He's not sure. The pain fades. Sleepy. So sleepy. The banging is closer now, he feels movement around him. Green uniforms, faces, people. Barked orders. Soft hands.

He thinks of Jamie. His friend, reviewing the prison visitor logs. Finding Catherine. Making the connection.

Maybe too late.

Panicked shouts. Paramedics. Pain.

The room disappears. He closes his eyes. Her smile. Her eyes.

A voice next to his ear. *Adam, if you can hear me, squeeze my hand.*

Adam. The first man. The last to die.

Warm fingers close around his. A slight shake to his shoulders. Those words again. *Squeeze my hand.*

But everything is grey. He's weak, so weak.

I'm sorry. I can't.

one

Images flash. He sees her. Her hair tousled, against the white pillow. Her mouth, laughing as she kisses him. Her hand in his. Warm fingers. Entwined.

I can't, he thinks. I can't let it end like this.

His fingers close around the hand in his.

And he holds on tight.

He will survive. He will live. He has to. For her.

Acknowledgements

This book is dedicated to Dr Matt Evans. It's about time. Matt has worked with me from the beginning of my writing career, patiently and diligently answering my terrible questions, red penning everything in sight. All this, around a young family and a busy job as a Consultant Anaesthetist. He is my muse – I regularly steal from his actual lived experience for inspiration, and this book is no exception. Matt, thank you. I am forever in your debt.

To everyone at HarperCollins – to Kathryn Cheshire, Julia Wisdom, Angel Belsey, Susanna Peden, Olivia French, Sophie Raoufi and the rest of the team – thank you so much. It is an honour to be a part of HarperCollins and I love every second I get to write these weird and wonderful books. Thank you for giving me the opportunity.

Thank you to Ed Wilson and the rest of the team at Johnson and Alcock. I am exceptionally lucky to have Ed as my agent, and his support and motivational speeches have kept me going more times than I can count. Thank you to Hélène Butler – queen of foreign rights.

Thank you to Dominic Nolan. The second novel is traditionally difficult and this one continuously knocked my confidence. Dom helped me work through the story, as well as reading an early draft. Dom, thank you. Your essays give me hope.

To the rest of the Criminal Minds group – to Niki, Elle, Heather, Jo, Rachael, Barry, Tim, Victoria, Fliss, Susie, Phoebe, Simon, Kate, Clare, Harriet, Liz, Rob, Adam and Polly – you absolute stars. You all make me laugh every day, keeping me company in this strange and bizarre profession. May your llamas always be woolly and your badgers chonky. Pincers up, my friends.

Thank you to Noah Ballard, my US agent, and to Matthew Martz, Madeline Rathle, Melissa Rechter, Rebecca Nelson, Dulce Botello, and the rest of the team at Crooked Lane books, my US publishers. It is a real career highlight to go stateside, and a joy to work with you all.

Thank you to Soraya Vink and the rest of the team at HarperCollins Holland.

Thank you to Janette Currie for the copy-editing and Charlotte Webb for the proofread.

A huge thank you to Dan Roberts. As I regularly tell you – as you get me out of my cop-related plot holes – you are a fucking genius.

Thank you to Steph Fox, real-life CSI, for your advice and especially your work on report MG 22 A. Thank you to Dr Sam Batstone for help on the Clinical Psychology, and to Lauren Sprengel for answering my questions around prison life. Thank you to Susan Scarr, for everything pharmaceutical (and for loan of the Bishop name), and to Charlie Roberts, Laura Stevenson and AR, thank you.

455

But the experts can only do so much. All mistakes, deliberate or otherwise, are mine and mine alone.

Thank you to my family – to Chris and Ben, to Max (who nearly made me kill that dog), to Mum and Dad, and Tom and Mel. I love you.

Finally, thank you to all the readers and bloggers out there who have been buying and reading and cheerleading my books. I am nothing without you, and I love hearing all your comments and questions. Do keep in touch on Instagram, Facebook or Twitter (@samhollandbooks.)

And, in answer to your questions, Nate Griffin will be back. Soon . . .